a novel

SWIFT JUSTICE

JOHN KENNY

INCENDIARY PUBLICATIONS

Also by John Kenny

The Spark
(book 1 in the Donny Robertson series)

SWIFT JUSTICE, Copyright © 2025 by John Kenny. All rights reserved. No part of this book may be used or reproduced in any manner whatsoever without written permission, except in the case of brief quotations embodied in critical articles or reviews. For information contact the author at books@ebbsbay.ca

ISBN 978-0-9920708-3-0 (paperback)

Cover concept by Annemarie Polis.
Cover and interior design by Jennifer Stimson.

For my sister, Eva Montville, and my brother, Richard Kenny. We are like spokes on a wheel, each pointing in a different direction, but joined together at the hub.

AUTHOR'S FOREWORD

Swift Justice is the second novel in the Donny Robertson series. Many of the core characters - Donny, Eddy, Moose and others will be familiar to those who have read The Spark, my first novel. So too will some of the locations such as the fictional Thirsty Sparrow pub. However, I believe this book stands on its own.

Once again, I have emphasized the action and drama of firefighting in order to craft a captivating narrative. *Swift Justice* is a suspense/thriller, not a documentary. And it is not an autobiography. Still having served thirty-three years as a firefighter, I hope the book gives the reader some insight into day-to-day life in the fire service.

In some cases, I have used the names of friends and colleagues for the characters in this book. (You know who you are). It in no way implies that the real people have anything in common with the fictional characters. It is simply a tribute to some of the people I cherish.

I hope you enjoy the story.
John Kenny
July, 2025

And there will sit in faithfulness, in the Tent of David, one who judges, seeks justice, and is swift to do what is right.
—Isaiah 16:5, ISV

CHAPTER 1

WHEN PUSH COMES TO SHOVE

Donny Robertson leaned forward in the captain's seat of Pumper Six and peered at the smoke coming from the house up ahead. To a firefighter, smoke was the body language of a fire, and Donny didn't like what this smoke was telling him. It should have been some shade of grey: lighter if it was mostly ordinary combustibles, darker if there were a lot of plastics and synthetics. Heavy, chocolate-brown smoke meant the possibility of a deadly backdraft explosion.

This was a curious red-brown haze, the colour of clotting blood. It had to be some kind of chemical. Pesticides? Fertilizer? People kept all kinds of crap in their garages and basements. Whatever it was, Donny's instincts—instincts that had been honed over twenty-seven years as a firefighter—told him it wasn't good.

Officially he was Captain Donald Michael Robertson. Most people knew him simply as Donny or "Wedge." He was a tall, thin man, with a narrow chin and protruding Adam's apple. Gawky in his youth, he had filled out some in middle age, thickening at the waist, but he still qualified as "wiry." His brooding blue eyes and wide brow, topped with curly copper-coloured hair (now flecked with grey at the temples), were a testament to his Celtic ancestors.

Donny reached for the truck radio's mic. "Toronto Fire, this is Pumper Six Captain. We have smoke visible on approach to Homewood Avenue."

"Roger, smoke visible," the dispatcher confirmed.

Donny snugged the shoulder straps of his SCBA, the self-contained breathing apparatus nestled in the bracket in the back of his seat. The SCBA was a comforting burden, as familiar as the "racehorse in the starting gate" rush of adrenalin he felt sharpening his senses. His fingers brushed over the medallion of St. Florian he kept in the pocket of his bunker coat—the patron saint of firefighters. The house was only a block away now. He took a deep breath. He was ready.

Beside Donny, in the driver's seat, loomed Moose—six foot six, a man of enormous strength, fierce loyalty and deep compassion. Moose scanned the street ahead for a hydrant. The two firefighters in the back of the truck craned their necks to get a look at what lay ahead. Eddy "The Ladle" Moleiro sat in the senior man's seat behind Donny. He was a tough, skilled veteran, short, dark-haired and broad-shouldered. Baby-faced Patrick "Scout" Thompson, with just under a year on the job, rode the junior man's seat behind Moose.

"You want a line off the back or the side?" Eddy asked Donny over the wail of the siren.

"Let's go off the side—straight in." Donny's SCBA pulled free of its bracket in the seat back with a metallic "pop." He swivelled to face his rookie. "Scout, I want you to ..."

"I know, I know: hook up the hydrant."

Donny's mouth tightened. In the old days an attitude like that would have earned the kid a smack upside the head.

"Hey, Cap." Moose hit the brakes and killed the siren. "We got a blue canary down." It was an old joke among firefighters—cops getting a whiff of smoke and going down like the proverbial canary in the coalmine.

Donny spun back around. The cop was on his knees, coughing and spitting, half hidden by the scraggly weeds clinging to the patch of dirt in front of the house. "Get the oxygen, Scout. Moose can get his own hydrant."

Moose nodded, shifted the truck into pump gear and jumped down from the driver's seat. He moved with surprising lightness and precision for such a big man.

"Pumper Six arrived seventy-nine Homewood Avenue," Donny radioed. "I need medics right away. We've got an injured cop." He grabbed his red captain's helmet from the dash and hopped down.

Eddy was already pulling the preconnected fire hose from the transverse bed on the side of the truck facing house. Moose dragged the larger, heavy suction hose from the back of the truck to the hydrant.

Donny hurried to the cop. Scout retrieved the first aid kit and oxygen from a compartment on the side of the truck and followed.

"My partner," the cop gasped, "inside."

The wind swirled the smoke towards them, and Donny caught the sharp smell of ammonia. "Drug lab?"

The cop nodded. Scout put down the first aid kit and fitted an oxygen mask to the cop's face.

"Where is he?" Donny asked.

"Not sure. I tried ..." The cop collapsed in a fit of coughing.

"Forget the hose, Eddy," Donny called over his shoulder. "It's a lab. There's another cop inside."

Eddy dropped the hose. They both knew a drug lab would contain reactive and toxic chemicals. Blasting them with high-pressure water was a bad idea.

Donny sized up the situation. No two fires were alike, but this was a unique challenge. Facing him was a detached, two-storey frame house, probably ninety, maybe a hundred years old. The flaking paint on the window frames and the islands of moss on the roof shingles spoke of years of neglect. Unlike most of its neighbours on this downtown street, this house had yet to experience the fairy god-mother touch of gentrification.

Fine, he'd been in hundreds of run-down houses. But now, in addition to the usual hazards of decay and bad wiring, this was a drug lab. The foul reddish haze that bled from the open side door betrayed its poisonous contents. And there was the possibility of booby traps. The gangs that ran these places had fertile and deadly imaginations when it came to protecting their operations.

Worst of all, they would have no hose line. The hose wasn't just a means to put the fire out—it was a lifeline. If things went bad, they could always follow the hose back out, the way they had come in. Or they could shove it out of an upper window like an improvised fire escape and slide down.

All they would have this time would be the thick quilted bunker suits they wore and the air in the SCBA on their backs. At least the cops had left the side door open. They wouldn't have to break in.

The size-up took only a second. Donny keyed the mic of his portable radio. "Toronto Fire, this is Pumper Six Captain. We have a working fire in a two-storey frame, detached; a drug lab with residential exposures. Requesting a second alarm and a HazMat response. We have a report of a cop down inside. I need additional medics. Pumper Six Captain is mobile command—primary search. We're going in dry."

"Roger."

"Scout, get this guy to the medics when they arrive." Donny slipped the face piece of his SCBA over his head. His voice became tinny inside the mask. "Take him back to the truck for now, then lay out a line for decontamination."

"Aren't I coming in with you? Why am I always stuck ..."

"I told you what I want. Now do it!" Donny's anger flared. Times and attitudes had changed since he was a probie, but the fireground was still not a debating society. Orders needed to be followed quickly and without question. Lives were at stake.

Scout turned back to the cop. Donny shook his head. Eddy shrugged.

Donny pulled his flame-resistant hood up over his head to the edge of his mask, then donned his heavy leather firefighting gloves. He was completely covered from head to toe. Chemical vapours and carcinogens would still seep through the fabric of his gear, but it was the best he could do. Whether you breathed it or not, all smoke was toxic—this was just especially so. He had accepted long ago that a career as a firefighter meant decades of slow poisoning.

He reached behind him and turned on his air tank, double-checked that his gauge showed that the tank was full, then clicked the regulator onto his face piece. Eddy did the same. Fresh air flowed into their masks, but the sour chemical taste of the smoke lingered in their mouths.

"What were the cops doing, trying to take down a drug lab with just two of them?" Eddy asked at the side door. "That's a major operation."

"Who knows? Cops." Donny shook his head. "You ready?"

Eddy nodded. The smoke enveloped them like a thick, rusty fog as they stepped through the door. Blinded, they dropped to their knees and crawled, working by touch, sweeping their hands in front of them.

Donny made a mental map of their progress. Three stairs up from the side door. Left turn into some kind of a hallway. One metre, two, now three ... He kept tabs on Eddy's position behind him, listening for the "Darth Vader" sound of Eddy's breathing. Donny's hands brushed along the walls on either side of them. Suddenly his left hand waved in the air. "I got a door. Going left."

"OK." Eddy waited by the door, marking the exit, while Donny circled the room.

"Never mind. It's a closet."

"Time you came out anyway," Eddy said.

"You never get tired of that one, do you?" Donny started back down the hallway. "What happened to all that sensitivity training they gave you?"

"I stopped taking the anti-rejection drugs."

No matter how grim the situation, Eddy always found a way to relieve the tension with his quirky sense of humour. It was one of the things Donny loved about his senior man.

Donny's radio crackled with the arrival messages of other crews. Perimeters were being established, hose lines laid out to protect the neighbouring houses, decontamination and entry control zones set up—all the components of a major operation. Donny filed it all away in the back of his mind. His attention was focused on searching the house as quickly and efficiently as possible. The cop's chances were fading with every second.

Another doorway, wider, and the acoustics were different this time. "Big room here, Eddy. You go left, I'll take right."

The voice of District Chief Joe "Ratzo" Razzolini cut through the radio chatter. "Chief Forty-one on scene, assuming command. Pumper Six Captain, what's your situation?"

"Primary search, ground floor, par two. It's shit soup in here, Chief."

Donny's report told Ratzo what they were doing, where they were, and that there were two of them. That was important. While it was equally informative, the colloquial part of Donny's report made Ratzo scowl. They had been classmates in the Academy and were still friends, but Donny had a knack for straining the relationship, especially when it came to rules and procedures.

Donny crawled forward, his right hand keeping contact with the wall beside him, his left sweeping in wide arcs, groping for the cop's body. He patted a large, round, heavy object in front of him. He couldn't see it, but he recognized the shape as a forty-five-gallon drum. At one time, this was probably the living room, he thought; now it was a chemical warehouse.

"My armpits are burning," Eddy said from across the room.

"It's the ammonia. It reacts with water. Try not to sweat."

"Don't sweat? I'm Portuguese. You want me to stop breathing too?"

A glowing rectangle appeared through the smoke in front of Donny—another door, with fire beyond. Maybe the kitchen? "Looks like the fire's through here. I'm gonna check it out."

Donny's hand caught on something as he swept through the door—a trip wire.

There was a flash in front of him, a deafening roar, and a shock wave that smacked him in the face. He dropped onto his stomach, momentarily stunned. A warm wetness soaked his pants. Had he been cut? There was no pain, and he could move his legs. Damn, he had pissed himself. Otherwise, he seemed unhurt.

Donny raised himself back to his knees and cautiously reached his hand out in front of him. There it was, the long, round profile of a shotgun barrel, rigged as a spring-gun trap.

A sound penetrated the ringing in his ears. Yelling. It was Eddy's voice. "Donny, I'm hit! *Jesus Cristo, filho da puta!* I'm hit!"

Eddy! How had he ...? Donny put the pieces together. The gun had been aimed to hit a standing man in the chest. Donny being on his knees, the buckshot had gone clear over him, spread out, and hit Eddy on the other side of the room.

"I'm coming! Keep talking." Donny crawled towards the voice, forcing his own fear and shock down. "Where are you hit?"

"In the hip. I can move, but aw shit, it hurts like a bastard."

"Pumper Six Captain, this is Chief Forty-one," the radio squawked. "What the hell's going on in there?"

"Booby trap, Chief. We're coming out." There were more enquiries, but Donny ignored them. He reached Eddy's side. It was impossible to tell how bad the wound was. He couldn't see anything in the smoke. "You need help? Can you make it?"

"You lead," Eddy grunted. "What about the cop?"

"We tried." There was no choice. He could feel the heat from the fire growing, pressing in on them. The shotgun must have hit one of the drums of flammable chemicals. They had only a minute or two before the whole house flashed over. Without a hose, they were defenceless.

He felt a different type of burning in his crotch—the ammonia reacting with his urine-soaked bunker pants. "Come on, let's go."

Donny crawled, trying to stay as low as he could under the heat. He retraced his path through the big room, sweeping his hands warily in front of him, feeling for the trigger of another booby trap. Eddy followed, keeping a hand on Donny's heel.

Donny's hand brushed against something. He pulled back and froze, then gingerly reached out again. It was soft, solid and heavy—the unmistakable bulk of a human body. "I got the cop here."

"Sorry, man, I can't help you."

"Can you make the door?"

"I think so."

"The hall's straight ahead. Left, past the closet, then right, down three stairs and out." Donny said, reading his mental map. "I'll be right behind you."

Eddy grunted and crawled away.

Donny felt around until he located the man's arms. The fire was building rapidly. The higher he raised himself, the more intense the heat, but he needed a better grip. It was probably too late to save the cop, but there was always that faint hope. And he couldn't leave the body behind to the flames. Not if he could help it.

"Donny? Where are you?"

He recognized the voice of Suzie Kozarovitch. Two years ago, she had been assigned to his crew as a probie, fresh out of the Academy. Now she was a member of the HazMat team. "Over here, down the hall on your right. I got the cop."

Suzie met him at the doorway to the hall. "You all right?" she asked.

"Yeah. Where's your crew?"

"We met Eddy at the side door. Captain Cooney and Bugs are taking him to decon. What the hell happened?"

"I'll tell you later. Here, take an arm." Together they dragged their limp burden the last few metres and staggered out the side door.

Behind them, a solvent container erupted with a deep "whump." Donny and Suzie flinched as broken glass tinkled to the ground and flames leapt from shattered windows. Neighbours stopped on their porches and stared, then hurried away, shepherded by police and fire crews.

The Haz crew took the cop from Donny and Suzie and carried him to the sidewalk, towards the decontamination pool. It looked like an oversized child's wading pool. They needed to wash off as much of the toxic residue as possible before the paramedics could begin their work. The pool would catch the contaminated runoff.

Eddy stepped out of the pool as the cop was brought over. The late-summer warmth of the afternoon had faded. Eddy stood naked, wet and shivering, having stripped off his contaminated gear and clothes. Rivulets of blood ran from his right buttock down his leg. A team of paramedics helped him onto a stretcher, wrapped him in blankets and wheeled him to an ambulance.

Donny watched the Haz crew lift the cop into the pool and cut away his clothes. Scout held the decon hose over the cop's body, while Moose scrubbed quickly with a long-handled brush. Then the medics took over. They laid the cop on a stretcher, attached electrodes to his chest and started CPR. An airway and intravenous line were inserted, then they hurried towards a waiting group of ambulances.

"Mind if I go next?" Donny asked Suzie. "The friggin' ammonia's burning my balls."

"Be my guest."

Donny stepped into the pool and stripped off his fire coat and bunker pants. He took the nozzle from Scout and shoved it into the waistband of his trousers.

"Are you OK, sweetie?" Moose asked Suzie.

"Yeah, fine," Suzie smiled up at him. She and Moose had been living together since shortly after she had transferred to the Haz.

Sighing contentedly as the stream of cool water washed over his crotch, Donny reflected on how the department had changed during his twenty-seven years. Not that fire-hall romances were entirely unknown in the days before there were women on the trucks.

Donny saw Ratzo making his way towards them from the ambulance staging area. "The medics say anything about Eddy?" Donny asked.

"Looks like he took two pellets in the ass. It's not too bad. The bunker suit gave him some protection." Ratzo looked at the hose Donny had jammed in his pants.

"What? It's the ammonia," Donny protested.

"Whatever. Strip down and report to the medics. You need to get checked out after being in that crap. You too, Q," Ratzo said, calling Suzie by the nickname Eddy had given her as a probie.

Donny stripped down to his briefs. Moose scrubbed. The house blazed behind them. Hose lines protected the neighbouring homes and kept the fire from spreading, but no one else was going inside to fight this fire.

Donny stepped from the pool, wrapped himself in a silver Mylar emergency blanket and walked towards a pair of ambulances.

The cop they had found in front of the house sat on the back step of an ambulance, wearing an oxygen mask. Two paramedics and another cop tried to get him to climb into the back, but the cop in the mask wasn't budging. He simply stared after the ambulance that carried his partner as it receded into the night. He looked over as Donny approached.

"Christ Almighty, what took you so long in there?" the cop asked, his voice still raw.

Donny stopped and glared at the cop. "Excuse me?" he replied slowly.

"He doesn't mean it, buddy," the other cop replied. "We know you tried. Come on, Ericson, you need to go to the hospital."

Ericson tore the oxygen mask off his face and threw it down. "Yeah, thanks for trying. Great job," he croaked. "Randy's dead. Thanks for everything."

"You can thank yourself, fuckwit."

Ericson stood up and stepped towards Donny. "What did you say?"

"You heard me. What the hell were you doing trying to take down a drug lab by yourselves? You some kind of cowboy?" Donny felt foolish, arguing with the cop while standing half naked, wrapped in silver Mylar. It only made him angrier. He clutched the cheap plastic blanket around himself with one hand and jabbed a finger at Ericson with the other. "Now I got a crew member that's been shot and that's on you, asshole. That's on you."

Ericson sprang at Donny, and the two of them fell to the ground. Everyone else was momentarily stunned as the men grappled and rolled. Moose sprinted over, grabbed Donny, and pulled him free. The other cop grabbed Ericson and yanked him to his feet. A small crowd of paramedics, cops and firefighters began to gather.

"What the hell is going on here?" Ratzo yelled as he ran towards the commotion. A police sergeant trailed close behind.

"That man's under arrest, Sarge," Ericson rasped, pointing at Donny. He swung his arm to include Moose. "Both of them—I want them both arrested. Assaulting an officer."

Staff Sergeant Daya Singh looked at the two firefighters, then turned back to Ericson. "And what about all the procedures you violated here? Shall we write those up while we're at it? Now get your ass in the ambulance. You're done here." She turned to look at Ratzo.

Ratzo nodded. "Moose, get your captain back to his truck."

Donny opened his mouth to speak, but Ratzo cut him off with a glare. "Not a word, Robertson, not a goddamned word. We got enough trouble here. We'll sort this out later."

Sergeant Singh turned back to the other cops who had gathered. "We got people wounded and two whole blocks to evacuate. Let's get to work."

Donny sat in the captain's seat of Pumper Six. The truck hummed beneath him, its engine pumping thousands of litres of water into a tangle of hoses aimed at the fire. He clutched the tattered shreds of his plastic blanket around him and shivered. He was wet and cold, but mostly he shook with the residue of adrenalin from the fight and the frustration of watching the house burn in front of him. He hated losing. This evening, he had lost on virtually every front.

"What the hell was that all about?"

Donny turned away from the fire. Ratzo was standing at the front corner of the truck, his expression a mixture of anger and concern.

"The guy was a complete dickhead." Donny climbed down from the cab of the truck and stood facing his district chief.

"Maybe so, but you seem to attract them, don't you?" Ratzo said. "You are a magnet for shitstorms, Wedge, a friggin' magnet."

"I'm sorry. It's just ... Eddy, and ..." Donny swung his arm to encompass the whole scene.

"Yeah. Well, you still need to get checked out."

Scout and Moose were standing by the pump panel. Ratzo dug a set of keys out of his pocket and tossed them to the younger man. "Take the Tahoe and drive Captain Robertson to the hospital. Find Q and take her too. She's over by the Haz."

Donny followed Scout towards the HazMat truck.

"And try not to get into a fight with the nurses," Ratzo called after him. "Most of them would beat the crap out of you anyway."

Donny let the hint of a smile cross his face. At least they were still friends.

CHAPTER 2

AN AFTERNOON AT THE SPARROW

Scout wiped beads of moisture from the pint glass in front of him with his index finger and thought of places he'd rather be. It was a long list, comprising pretty much anywhere that didn't include sitting between Moose and Eddy in the Thirsty Sparrow.

The Sparrow, as it was affectionately called, had been the unofficial downtown watering hole for Toronto's emergency services for generations. Civilians occasionally wandered in; they were served politely, but they rarely stayed for long once they realized they were outsiders. The walls were decorated with pictures and memorabilia from the fire, police and paramedic services. The pressed-tin ceiling and ornately carved wooden bar dated from when the Sparrow had first opened its doors over a hundred years ago. Naugahyde had replaced the original leather and horsehair upholstery in the booths that lined the wall opposite the bar, but little else had changed. The vintage jukebox now spun CDs instead of 45s, but it still played more oldies than hip hop.

Cops tended to drink with cops and firefighters with firefighters, but there was usually an easy interplay between the groups.

Not today.

Bill Ericson sat with three other cops in a booth across from where Scout, Eddy and Moose sat at the bar. The two groups eyed each other warily, but spoke only among themselves. The sombre mood was emphasized by the black-draped portrait of Constable Randall Copeland that hung just inside the front door.

Scout had never liked the Sparrow. What others saw as warm and cozy seemed to him, like so many of the job's traditions, simply old and oppressive.

"OK, OK," he said. "Donny doesn't hate me. But he treats me like a child. I want to be part of the action."

"You want to get shot too?" Eddy asked. He shifted his weight, leaned on the bar and winced. It had been only two days since a pair of shotgun pellets had been removed from his rear end, and it was still a little too tender for him to sit comfortably.

"No," Scout replied. "But I don't want to spend my whole career hooking up hydrants and babysitting patients."

"You won't," Moose replied casually. Even sitting, he towered over his crewmates. His voice was oddly soft for such a large man. His close-cropped hair was thick and dark; his eyes were the grey of an autumn sky, and close set, which seemed to give them a special intensity. "You'll get your time on the nozzle when Donny thinks you're ready."

"Whenever that is," Scout snorted.

"When you've earned it," Moose replied.

"Whatever."

Eddy's dark eyes flashed, his face reddened, and his hand clenched. He had grown up as a street fighter in the immigrant community around Kensington Market in downtown Toronto. Eddy was an olive-skinned bulldog, with broad shoulders, a square jaw and all the passion of his Portuguese ancestors. He grabbed Scout by the shoulder and spun him on his bar stool.

"No, not 'whatever.' This isn't some kind of video game. There's no restart," Eddy hissed, his face inches from Scout's. He nodded towards the portrait of the dead cop by the entrance. "When things go wrong, somebody pays the price."

For a moment Scout thought Eddy was going to hit him. Instead, Eddy released his grip and ordered another rum and Coke. Scout straightened his jacket and went back to mopping his beer glass with his finger.

Ratzo's summons to the bar on their day off wasn't a social invitation; it was an informal attempt to deal with the fallout from the scuffle between Donny and Constable Ericson. Outside, the investigation into Randy Copeland's death was in full swing. It was the top priority for the Toronto Police. But this needed to be dealt with too, off the record and out of the public eye if possible. Though it was a minor distraction, it had the potential to be a major embarrassment to both services.

One by one, the cops and firefighters involved had been called into a room at the back of the bar to answer questions from Fire Department Platoon Chief Tom Humphrey and Police Superintendent Bob Collins and give their version of the events.

Donny emerged from the back room, followed by Daya Singh, the police staff sergeant who had been at the call. "Marion Feinberg?" she called to the group of firefighters at the bar.

"It's Moose. Nobody uses that name." Moose flushed as a murmur of laughter spread among the cops. He glared at them as he walked towards the back room. He was the last to be called.

"Marion?" Scout asked, happy to have a change of subject. "I never knew that was Moose's real name."

"His mother was a huge John Wayne fan. The Duke's real name was Marion. But I wouldn't ask Moose about it if I were you," Eddy advised. Eddy's anger, though quick, usually passed just as quickly.

"OK," Scout nodded. "How'd you end up being called 'Wedge,' Cap?"

Donny smiled, something he hadn't done much in the two days since the fire on Homewood. It was nice to think back to happier times.

"It was Fitz. He was the senior man when I was a recruit. Anyway, he just started calling me Wedge one day. I got curious, so I asked him if it was because I was tall and thin. 'Nope,' he said. 'It's the simplest tool known to man.'"

Eddy chuckled. He'd heard the story a hundred times before, but it was still funny. "See? 'Scout' isn't so bad."

"Maybe." Though his birth certificate said Patrick Thompson was twenty-four, he looked like he was fresh out of high school. He had the awkward lankiness of a teenager, with sandy blond hair, and freckles scattered across apple cheeks. Eddy had christened him "The Boy Scout," and gradually it became simply "Scout." Patrick hated the name. It was bad enough that he looked like a kid. Why couldn't they have named him "Axe," or "Bull," or something with a little macho and respect attached to it? Even "Ratzo" seemed more grown up than "Scout."

Donny and Eddy were reminiscing about some of the famous nicknames of the past—"The Reverend," "Fluffy," "Cod Face"—when Moose emerged from the back room.

"So?" Eddy asked.

Moose reached for his beer. "They said to wait. They'll call us in when they reach a decision." Twenty minutes later, Ratzo beckoned them all to the back room.

It was a simple room, one Donny had been in many times before, usually for private functions of one sort or another. Like the rest of the bar, it was decorated with police and fire memorabilia. A pair of large, west-facing windows let in the afternoon sun through glass rippled with age. Donny led his crew to a group of chairs lined up in front of a long table by the windows; Ericson and his fellow cops sat on the other side of the room.

Daya Singh sat at one end of the table. Donny hadn't paid much attention to her when she had come running over with Ratzo at the fire, or earlier today, for that matter. Now the afternoon sun streamed in through the big windows and reflected off her shoulder-length hair, jet black with an almost iridescent blue sheen. She was in her late thirties, with Bollywood good looks and quick, dark eyes. Donny had heard she had a mind to match and that she had been tapped as one of the police force's rising young stars.

Ratzo sat at the other end of the table. The two senior officers, Platoon Chief Tom Humphrey and Police Superintendent Bob Collins, sat in the middle. Everyone was dressed in civvies, but there was no doubt that rank and authority were very much present in the room.

Donny tried to read Humphrey's expression for some hint of what was to come, but there was none to be found. Humphrey's face was deeply lined and framed by silver hair. In his younger days, he had earned a reputation as a skilled and fearless firefighter. A charismatic man with an aura of natural leadership, he could have risen higher up the chain of command, but platoon chief was as high as he could go without moving to headquarters. Even if he now spent most of his time behind a desk, Tom Humphrey preferred to work out of a fire station, surrounded by firefighters rather than bureaucrats. At least that was the version Donny had heard.

"To begin with," Humphrey said gravely, looking first at Donny and then at Ericson, "I cannot tell you how disappointed I am that this is even necessary. The two of you have brought shame to the long and distinguished relationship between our two services."

Long and distinguished indeed, Donny thought. He remembered some of the bench-clearing brawls during the old inter-service hockey games.

"Constable Copeland will be buried with full police honours in a few days," Humphrey continued. "An official hearing would only tarnish his memory, and the media attention would damage the reputation of both departments. So this is all unofficial. Regardless, if anyone here would rather go the route of a formal disciplinary hearing, you have that right. However, I assure you"—Humphrey paused for emphasis—"that would not be to anyone's advantage."

Donny knew Humphrey was tough, but ultimately fair. He and Ericson had screwed up, and he, for one, would take his lumps. If he could catch a break and avoid a formal hearing, he'd take it. Donny nodded his assent. Ericson did the same.

"Very well, then, I'll turn it over to Superintendent Collins."

Bob Collins had a fleshy face and a pale complexion, with the thinning remains of a widow's peak. To Donny's eye, he looked more like an accountant than a cop, right down to the wire-rimmed glasses. But he was the commander of Fifty-one Division, which covered the east side of the downtown core, one of the city's toughest neighbourhoods.

"Thank you," Collins said. He took off his glasses and looked hard at the two groups in front of him. The soft bureaucratic exterior melted away, revealing the iron core beneath. "Every cop in this city is busting their ass trying to find whoever murdered Randy Copeland, and here we are." Collins shook his head. "I hope you idiots realize how incredibly lucky you are that none of what happened ended up on YouTube. You're fortunate that the press and civilians had been evacuated down the street by that point. Normally, it's not so easy to make something like this go away. This really is a one-time thing.

"The stress of that day's events might be an excuse for normal people, but we are not normal people. These are the professions we have chosen, and we do not have that luxury." Collins looked over at Humphrey.

"So there will be no formal record of what occurred," said the platoon chief, taking his cue. "If anyone asks, the official version is that Captain Robertson slipped and Constable Ericson tried to catch him. They both fell down. Is that understood?"

There were nods of assent all around.

"Good," Humphrey continued. "As you are aware, a fund has been set up for Randy Copeland's wife and children. Robertson, you will donate $3,000 to that fund. Moose, Eddy and Patrick, though you were not directly involved, you will each give $500 as a gesture of goodwill. These donations are to be delivered to District Chief Razzolini by the end of next week."

Superintendent Collins took over. "Constable Ericson, you will make a donation of $3,000 to the Fire Fighters' Cancer Research Fund at the Princess Margaret Hospital." Collins looked at the cops sitting beside Erison. "The rest of you will each contribute $500. These donations are to be delivered to Staff Sergeant Singh by the end of next week. Any questions?"

The room was silent.

Collins' voice softened. "The coroner figures that Randy was probably dead before Robertson and his crew even arrived. The forensic team found another booby trap that had been triggered. That's what released the chemicals and started the fire.

"We are not enemies. The criminals who make the drugs and sell their poison on the streets are the enemy; the gangs that set up booby traps that kill cops and injure firefighters are the enemy. Now shake hands and let's go raise a toast to Randy Copeland."

CHAPTER 3

THE FUNERAL

Laurie Zhou's hand dropped into the warm void where Donny's hip had just been. Maybe she shouldn't have been so insistent.

"I'm sorry," Donny mumbled, "I'm just not in the mood."

"It's OK," Laurie said, trying to mean it.

Donny sat on the side of the bed, staring down at his feet as if to verify they had not made an unscheduled departure during the night. Laurie rolled back onto her side of the bed, clasped her hands on her stomach and peered at the morning light seeping in around the curtains. Their lovemaking had grown gradually less frequent in the months since Donny had moved in with her and the boys. It was inevitable, she told herself, as the grind of daily living replaced the thrill of stolen moments and weekend rendezvous.

Part of it, she knew, was his job. Every now and then he would come home silent and pensive after a bad shift. She tried to give him space. Sometimes he would talk about it, sometimes it just got filed away—the corrosive memory of witnessing what people did to themselves and each other.

Now this.

Laurie had seen it before. She had served fifteen years as a combat engineer with the Canadian armed forces in Bosnia, Afghanistan, and several other shitholes in between. She'd seen soldiers suffering from combat stress, post-traumatic stress and every other kind of stress. You never knew who was going to break down or when. Then one day you'd hear that the toughest guy in the unit, the one guy nobody thought would ever crack, had put a twelve-gauge in his mouth. Fade to black.

Laurie had felt the darkness trying to swallow her when they had shipped her husband, Steve, home in a shiny metal box draped with a Canadian flag—at least all the pieces of him they could find. He had been an army medic serving his second tour in Kandahar when the IED tore him apart. She had looked into the abyss, wondering if she would ever feel normal again. It was the thought of her boys, Daniel and Kevin, that had helped her hang on.

Donny stood up from the bed and walked to the bathroom.

"You're not the only one going through this," Laurie said softly.

Donny stopped but didn't turn around. "I know."

"Maybe you could talk to someone?"

"Some guy in a suit?" Donny sneered.

"How about the padre, Ron Nickle? He seems like a really decent guy. I mean, he understands the job, right?"

"Sure."

She knew he wouldn't call anyone.

Donny flicked the switch on the bathroom wall. and a narrow bridge of light spilled through the door across the hall floor. "I'll take the boys to school," he said, and shut the door behind him.

If only it were a normal day, she'd have left for work before he got back to dress for the funeral. That would have been a relief. She hated herself for the thought.

"I was an asshole," Donny said. It was a confession he knew could apply to several areas of his life, one that he should probably repeat again at home. He could see that Bill Ericson wasn't quite sure what to make of the statement.

Both men were wearing their dress uniforms: crisp white shirts, navy serge tunic and trousers, with gleaming chrome buttons, shoes polished to a black mirror finish. Donny always felt awkward in his uniform. He was a tall, thin man, and it hung loose on him like a scarecrow. He had a wiry strength and a fierce determination on the fire ground, but no one ever suggested he was a candidate for the firefighter calendar. The unmistakable scars of skin grafts snaked up from his collar across his cheek and curled under his chin.

Ericson, on the other hand, looked to Donny like he was born to wear a police uniform. With his blond-haired, square-jawed, blue-eyed good looks and athletic build, he was the epitome of Nordic manhood.

They stood among thousands of similarly dressed men and women. Randy Copeland's funeral had been held in the arena that was normally home to the Toronto Maple Leafs hockey team. The place had been packed as ordinary citizens joined with cops, fire-fighters and paramedics from across Canada and the U.S. The death of a cop in the line of duty was always a big deal, but this one had really touched a nerve.

Now, Donny stood facing Ericson in the nearby Metro Convention Centre, where the reception was being held. Folding chairs and lin-en-draped tables were scattered about, but there was no hiding the trade-show ambience of the place. The echoing buzz of the crowd surrounded the two men.

"I know what it's like," Donny continued. "I lost a partner in a fire a couple of years ago. He was my captain, actually, and my best friend. Paul Fitzgerald—we called him Fitz. It felt like I'd been sucker punched."

"Is that how you got those?" Ericson asked, pointing to Donny's wrinkled scars.

"My beauty marks?" Donny asked. "Yeah, same fire, Commissioners Street."

"I remember that one," Ericson nodded. The suspicion faded from his face. "Listen, about the fight, or, well, whatever it was ..."

"I had it coming," Donny said, shaking his head. "Shit happens."

"Shit happens," Ericson agreed. It was not a dismissal, but rather an acknowledgement of the grim reality of their jobs.

Donny held out his hand. Ericson hesitated, but it was too much work to hold on to what remained of his resentment. He let it go with a sigh and grasped Donny's hand.

A woman dressed in black approached the two men. Donny released Ericson's hand and turned to face her.

Sharon Copeland held herself with dignity, but the strain of the past week showed on her face. Superintendent Bob Collins stood beside her.

"I've been looking for you, Bill." Sharon made an effort to smile. "That was a wonderful tribute you gave to Randy. He would have been embarrassed by all this, but he loved being a cop." She threw her arms around Ericson's neck and sobbed softly into his shoulder for moment.

"I'm sorry." Sharon dabbed at her eyes as she stepped back. "Sometimes I'm OK, you know, and then sometimes it all ..." She shrugged. Her face contorted as she tried to suppress her tears.

"That's OK," Ericson said, close to tears himself.

Bob Collins stepped forward. "Sharon, may I introduce Captain Donny Robertson. Donny, this is Sharon Copeland, Randy's wife."

"Of course—Captain Robertson," she said, her face lighting with recognition at the name. She held out her hand. "You were there, weren't you? You tried to rescue Randy and you got hurt. Are you all right?"

"It was my senior man, Eddy, actually. A couple of stitches. We're both fine, ma'am," Donny said, taking her hand and smiling awkwardly. "I want to say ..." he continued, then stopped. There was an uncomfortable pause as they waited for him to speak.

"I don't know what I want to say," he blurted at last. "I'm not so good with words. And saying 'I'm sorry' just sounds stupid. But I feel it; I feel it in my guts. And I wish to God none of this had ever happened. And lame as it sounds, I *am* sorry, ma'am."

Sharon reached out and touched his arm lightly. "Thank you. That means a lot. And please call me Sharon." She looked around the huge hall. "It helps. It helps me feel a little less alone. At least for now.

"And thank you for trying to save Randy. I'm glad you weren't seriously hurt," Sharon smiled up at him. Even through the shroud of her grief, Donny could see the radiance of that smile. "I should get back to the children; they're with my sister. I just wanted to thank you again, Bill. Nice to meet you, Captain Robertson."

"Donny," he volunteered.

"Of course. I'll talk to you later, Bill."

Collins escorted her back through the crowd. Donny watched her go, awed by her strength and poise.

"That's the worst part," Ericson said softly.

"Yeah," Donny agreed. "At least Fitz's kids were grown up, but still ..."

"Listen," Ericson said. "A couple of us are going over to the house the day after tomorrow. Randy was building a deck out back, and we're going to finish it. Maybe you and some of your crew would like to lend a hand."

Donny turned back to Ericson. "Saturday? Yeah, we're off then. Sure, I'd like that." He fished a gas receipt from his pocket and scribbled his phone number on the back. "Text me the address."

Ericson glanced at the slip of paper and shoved it into his pocket. "OK, then. See you Saturday."

The two men shook hands and parted.

Ericson spotted a group of cops by the bar. He was halfway there when he heard a familiar gravelly voice calling his name.

"Bill, you got a minute?"

He turned to see Tom Humphrey moving to intercept him. "Sure, I was just going to get a beer."

"Got one right here for you, son." Humphrey held out a bottle.

Ericson took it and clinked it against the bottle the chief was holding in his other hand. "Cheers!"

"To those we remember," the older man replied, and took a drink. "I saw you talking to Wedge, uh, Donny. Everything OK between you two?"

"Yeah, that's all history now." Ericson wiped his mouth with the back of his hand. "I invited him to help us finish the deck Randy was building."

"That's good. That's the way it should be," Humphrey nodded. "You spoke very well at the service. How are you feeling now?"

How did he feel? The past week had been a blur: reports to write, interviews with the detectives investigating Randy's murder, statements for the coroner's office, even the Ministry of Labour was involved. Then there were Sharon and the kids, preparing for the funeral. He'd barely had a moment to himself. "I don't know. Sad, angry, confused."

"I've lost a few friends along the way myself. Sometimes there's a bit of comfort knowing it was for a rescue or something noble. But this, a booby-trapped drug lab?" Humphrey shook his head. "Cops and firefighters die while the criminals get a slap on the wrist."

"God, tell me about it. It makes me want to puke." There was comfort in the old man's words, but there was something else, too. Ericson's police instincts told him Humphrey was more interested in his reactions than his feelings.

Humphrey sighed and patted him on the shoulder. "I'm sure your people are doing everything they can to catch whoever is responsible."

"I guess, but I'm not part of that." Ericson scowled and took another pull on his beer. "Hell, even if they do find him, what happens? The guy goes to prison, gets free room and board, maybe even a free education. Meanwhile Randy's kids grow up without a father, scarred for life. Where's the justice in that?"

"You're right. It isn't fair." Humphrey took a card from his wallet and handed it to Ericson. "That's my personal cell number on the back. I'd like to talk some more, but perhaps this isn't the time or place. Give me a call when you're free for lunch. I'll buy."

Ericson looked at the card, slightly puzzled. "Uh, thanks, but we've got our own, like, grief counsellors and stuff on the force."

"Of course you do. I'm sure they're a great comfort. This is about something else. Give me a call. I'll explain then."

Ericson took the card. "OK, maybe next week."

"That'll be fine," Humphrey smiled.

"Thanks for the beer." Ericson walked away, still puzzled. Humphrey reminded him a bit of his own father, a male product of another era, a man's man, gruff but still caring. He liked the old fellow, Ericson decided, slipping the card into his pocket alongside Donny's number. When things calmed down a bit, he'd call Humphrey and see what was on the old guy's mind.

Tom Humphrey rubbed his chin as he watched Ericson join the group of cops at the bar. He turned and made his way through the crowd in the opposite direction.

"You're right, Bob," Humphrey said when he found Collins again. "I think he's a good choice."

"What about Robertson?" Collins raised an eyebrow.

"No." Humphrey shook his head. "Donny's a good firefighter, but he can be erratic. Maybe a little obsessive, too."

"It's your call."

"I'll talk to Ericson again, then we'll see. Any leads on the official end? Do we have a picture of this guy or anything?"

"No picture. But we have a description, and word's out on the street. You fire guys are always in such a rush. These things take time, Tom." Collins patted his friend on the shoulder.

"You got that right," Humphrey sighed.

Collins lowered his voice. "I know the lead detective pretty well. His kid was up on a cocaine charge a while back. The case got tossed—problems with the evidence, you know. Anyway, this guy Carson, he owes me. And he's a good guy. He wants to see the right thing done."

"So where does that leave us?"

"Carson said they've got a lead on the guy's girlfriend. If it pans out, he'll give me a heads up."

CHAPTER 4

RAMÓN

Ramón put his hand on the doorknob, felt the smooth, cold metal, and stopped. He should stay in the room. He knew that. It was safer. But he also needed to get supplies; the food he had brought with him—a few cans of soup and a couple of loaves of bread—was almost gone.

What if someone recognized him?

It was unlikely. He had always been careful to avoid having his picture taken and to keep a low profile—no Facebook, no Instagram, no social media of any kind. There was a police sketch of him circulating on TV and in the papers, drawn from various descriptions, but it wasn't that good.

Ramón retreated from the door and turned on the tiny, ancient TV that had come with the room. The coverage on the twenty-four-hour news stations had shifted from the manhunt to the cop's funeral.

But it wasn't just the police who were after him. His former employers, the Wo Shing Wo Triad, would be on the lookout for him too. He had lost the lab and its valuable contents, attracted unwanted attention, and worst of all, taken the Triad's money. They would have the word out on the street.

But he couldn't stay in the small, stuffy third-floor room forever. He not only needed food, he needed fresh air so he could think clearly. He needed a plan. And High Park was only a few blocks away. The thought of walking in the open filled him with a combination of dread and giddy delight.

Ramón cracked the door open and peeked through the narrow slit. The hallway was empty. He made his way down the stairs and out the side door. He pulled up the hood of his sweatshirt, kept his head down and walked west along the side streets to the park. Food could wait. The plan came first.

The Parkdale neighbourhood got its name from the four hundred acres of gardens, playgrounds and woodland that made up High Park. The land itself, bordering Lake Ontario, was a gift from John and Jemima Howard, who had deeded their sheep farm to the city in 1873 on condition it be used as a public park. At the time, several city councillors had objected that the land was too far from the city proper to be of any real use. But the city had grown, and the park had become a bright charm in Toronto's urban bracelet. Proud Victorian mansions had sprouted on the nearby streets.

But while High Park itself became an inner-city oasis, the surrounding neighbourhood fell on hard times as the twentieth century waned. The mansions were converted into rooming houses, home to those on the desperate fringes of society. It hadn't been hard for Ramón to rent a room by the week for cash. The landlord wasn't too concerned about ID or references as long as Ramón had the money. He was just another small brown man down on his luck. No one knew him on this side of town. It was unlikely anyone would recognize him, but he couldn't be too careful.

Ramón tugged the hoodie tighter around his face as he walked, his antennae on high alert for any sign of danger or recognition. Once he reached the park, he kept to the wooded trails. He tried to quell his paranoia so that he could think clearly and weigh his options rationally.

Hiding was only a temporary solution. He should leave Toronto, maybe leave Canada entirely. He needed to disappear. For that he would need fake ID and a passport. That would be expensive. Fortunately, Ramón had had the presence of mind to grab the knapsack of cash when the cops showed up at the lab. He had dashed out the side door and hopped the back fence. He had years of experience running from the police, and these big, slow Canadian cops were no match for him.

There was just over $100,000 in the knapsack, a fortune back in Mexico. Some of the money was legitimately his, but most of it belonged to Wo Shing Wo. The Triad had set up the lab and paid him to run it. Taking the Triad's money was bad enough—the Tijuana Cartel had killed and mutilated his father for skimming only a tenth as much. But killing a cop, even accidentally, was bad mojo, and the heat it brought was very bad for everyone's business. Even if he returned the money now, Ramón was sure the Triad would give him up to the cops to ease the pressure—if they didn't kill him first.

How had it come to this? He had gone from being a relatively happy teenager to a shadow drifting along the margins of society, always looking over his shoulder. The Cartel had killed his father and then claimed Ramón's two sisters as compensation for the old man's theft. Ramón had run for his life.

Across the border and north, always north. The Cartel had long arms. Canada should be far enough, Ramón had thought. He was tired of running and tired of hiding. But when his refugee claim was turned down and he was faced with a deportation order, he was forced back into the shadows once again, working under the table at dead-end jobs just to survive.

It seemed to Ramón that God had cursed him. It was his fate, not his fault, Ramón told himself, that he was back in the family business, cooking meth and ecstasy. One criminal syndicate was much like another. At least here the conditions were better than they had been in Mexico. He had a house with the lab on the main floor and a nice apartment upstairs. The lab had modern equipment and filter masks, so he didn't have to breathe the noxious fumes.

And he had Roxanne. Roxanne, who wrote poems about caterpillars and danced under the full moon. Roxanne, who made him feel that maybe life wasn't just an endless struggle simply to survive. She had promised him that she was done with the pipe, done with it forever. His own father had made Ramón swear on his mother's grave to never, ever use the drugs they made. It was one thing to work for the Devil, his father had said, and quite another to be his slave.

Ramón had been so proud when Roxanne blew out the candle on her cake to celebrate a whole year of being clean. Then, barely a month later, it all came crashing down. She denied it, of course, but the changes in her were unmistakable. Then he had caught her red-handed, and with a needle this time, not just the pipe. He beat her in a blind rage. God forgive him, but he had hit her again and again until she had run out into the street screaming. And someone had called the cops.

Ramón sat with his back against a tree and looked down the hill towards Grenadier Pond and the distant sparkle of Lake Ontario. He thought of the time his father had taken him to San Pedro Mártir National Park. As the road wound up the mountainside, they had left the scrub desert of Baja behind and entered a world of green. At the top, he had sat with his back against one of the huge pine trees and drunk in the cool, pine-scented air. It had seemed to Ramón as if the whole world were spread out below him. On one side he could look out over the expanse of desert to the turquoise shimmer of the Sea of Cortez; on the other side, the Pacific gleamed dully on the horizon.

He remembered telling Roxanne about it. He had promised to take her there one day. But Roxanne had chained herself to the pipe and needle once again. She was the only one who knew his whole story and his real name, Ramón Miguel Fernando Sánchez. To everyone else he was simply Carlos.

Ramón put his face in his hands and drew a deep breath. He needed to vanish without a trace, and Roxanne had become a liability. He had learned the hard lessons of survival at his father's knee. Sometimes to save your skin you had to break your own heart.

CHAPTER 5

DECK PARTY

The Saturday after Randy Copeland's funeral dawned cold and crisp. The first frost had brought the fall colours to their best, and the city's neighbourhoods were tinged with crimson, ochre and gold.

Donny, Eddy, Moose and Scout joined the group of cops busily sawing and hammering away on the deck Randy had never finished. The friendly rivalry between the two emergency services seemed to have returned. They worked with a sense of purpose and accomplishment.

Inside the house, a group of police wives were helping Sharon Copeland go through her husband's clothes and personal belongings. From the deck, Donny could see through the sliding glass doors as the women sorted through the collected essence of a life.

He remembered helping Anna, Fitz's widow, with the same terrible task after Fitz had been killed. There had been moments of joy, even occasional laughter, as some object sparked a pleasant memory. But mostly it had been a grim chore, reducing a full and vibrant life to a few photographs, a handful of trinkets, and boxes of clothes for donation. It had seemed to Donny that with every shirt, every pair of shoes, every toothbrush and razor donated or thrown away, they were, if not erasing Fitz, at least reducing the person he had been to little more than wisps of memory.

Donny had kept one of Fitz's pipes. A talisman perhaps, by which he could conjure the image of Fitz, wreathed in fragrant blue smoke, laughing and spinning yarns at the kitchen table of the Lombard Street fire station. But even that memento was gone now, vanished in an instant when Donny's house was destroyed by a gas explosion a few years back. He had been lucky to escape with his life. Now all he had were his memories. And the problem with memories, no matter how sweet, was that they anchored you to the past.

For now, Donny was glad to be with the group working on the deck. They were building something; not quite a monument, but something lasting, something that would connect the past to what was to come. Randy Copeland had set the posts and built the frame, touched the same planks that Donny and the others now touched. Randy would never get to sit on his deck, but there would be family barbecues and birthday parties as Randy's children grew. Maybe his family would feel a little closer to him when they gathered here in the years to come. Donny was comforted by the thought, one that he knew was shared by the rest of the work party.

By midday they had finished screwing down the deck's planks and were starting on the railing. Sharon Copeland loaded up a tray of beer from the fridge and walked out onto the newly laid surface.

"That's a big mistake, Sharon, starting these guys drinking before the work's done," Bill Ericson warned with a wink. "It's hard enough to get firemen out of bed and actually working in the first place."

"I think this is the first time I've ever seen a cop with dirty hands, eh, Moose? From honest work, I mean," Eddy responded.

"Just one for now," Sharon said. She passed around the beers, ignoring the jibes being traded back and forth between the two groups. "There's more in the fridge when you're done. It looks fantastic. Randy would be so pleased. I wish he could ... I wish ... I'll be back with some sandwiches."

She turned and hurried back into the house. The men sat and drank their beer in silence. The day had developed a real late-season warmth, but there was a sudden chill as the memory of why they were there returned with sudden force.

"That's a good woman," Donny said. He clinked his bottle with Bill Ericson. They all drank the toast.

"She won't be single for long," Scout piped up. Everyone turned and stared at him.

"Excuse me?" Ericson said, rising slowly to his feet. In a flash, the grief they all shared had turned to outrage.

"Nothing, just, you know, I mean, she's kinda hot and ..."

Donny got up and intercepted Ericson. "He doesn't mean it. He's new."

"Randy's not even cold in the ground and you want to bang his widow, punk?" demanded one of the other cops.

Scout started to back away as the cop advanced towards him. "I'm sorry, I ..."

Donny stepped between Scout and the cop. "He didn't mean it like that." Donny turned back to Ericson. "He just doesn't know any better."

"Then I guess you didn't teach him very well, did you?" Ericson glared at Donny, his voice full of menace. "I think you'd better leave. All of you."

Donny read the grim expressions of the cops on the deck. The mood on the deck had changed suddenly and irrevocably. He and his crew gathered their tools and left.

CHAPTER 6

PROFESSIONAL COURTESY

The mass of crumpled metal jammed sideways against the telephone pole was barely recognizable as a minivan. Smoke streamed from under its hood, and a cop was tugging desperately but vainly at the driver's door. Half a block away, a dump truck with barely a mark on it was parked at an awkward angle. Donny took in the scene the moment Pumper Six turned the corner onto Richmond Street. He reached for the mic.

"Pumper Six on scene, Richmond and Sherbourne. We have a minivan into a pole with smoke showing. Looks like we got people trapped. Is there a rescue squad responding?"

"Affirmative, Pumper Six, you have Rescue Two inbound, as well as Chief Forty-one," came the dispatcher's reply.

"Pumper Six, this is Rescue Two," said a new voice. "We're about two minutes out, Donny. Traffic's all backed up, it's brutal."

"Roger, we'll try to stabilize." Moose brought the fire truck to a halt. Donny put down the mic and turned to his crew. "Moose, put her in pump gear and get a hydrant. Eddy, you sure you're OK?"

Eddy was already stepping out of the truck. "As long as I don't have to hold anything with my ass."

"Try to get under the hood. I'll bring a line. Scout, we're going to need cribbing. Let's go!"

They dismounted and the crew sprang to their assignments. Eddy took a Halligan bar to pry up the van's hood. Scout grabbed a crate of cribbing—thick blocks of wood to place under the van's frame. The vehicle needed to be stabilized so it wouldn't shift or roll when they started to cut.

Donny pulled hose from the side of the truck. The cop who had been struggling with the driver's door ran over to him. "I can't get the door open, and there's a kid in the back. I think the engine's on fire."

Donny saw flames licking out from the corner of the hood that Eddy was prying up with the Halligan. People were crowding in, unable to resist the horrifying appeal of impending catastrophe. Many held up cell phones to record the unfolding drama.

"Get those people out of here," Donny told the cop. "Now!"

"You got it."

Donny finished pulling the hose from its bed. A man ran over, seized Donny's arm, and pointed at Scout with his phone. "Why is he piling kindling under the car?" the man asked.

"It's cribbing, not kindling. Now get the hell out of here." Donny wrenched his arm free and swatted the phone out of the man's hand. It skittered into the gutter across the street, and the man scrambled after it.

Donny grabbed the nozzle and ran to Eddy, dragging the hose behind him. "Charge it," he called over his shoulder to Moose. The hose surged and jumped as high-pressure water filled the line.

Donny opened the nozzle and jammed it under the corner of the hood Eddy had pried up. The flames stubbornly refused to go out, and smoke was beginning to fill the passenger compartment.

"My baby! Get my baby out! Please!" the woman in the driver's seat screamed at Donny. The airbag hung limply in her lap. The talc it had been packaged with covered her face with fine white powder, making the scarlet drops of blood even more vivid. Shards of glass from the van's shattered windows stuck to the blood. They sparkled like diamonds in the bright sunlight, giving her a weirdly festive appearance.

"We're going to get you and your baby out as soon as we can," Donny said reassuringly. "But first we've got to put this fire out. You got to be strong, OK?"

"Oh my God," the woman moaned.

"It's got to be propane. Here, take it." Donny handed the nozzle to Eddy. "I'll get the shutoff."

Donny saw District Chief Razzolini duck under the police barrier tape. "What do you need?" he yelled to Donny.

"Room for the squad," Donny replied.

"I'm on it!" Ratzo and the police began to force people and cars back, clearing a lane for the rescue squad.

Donny tossed his helmet aside and dived under the van's back end. He reached up and felt for the handle of the shutoff valve on the propane tank's rounded end. The force of Eddy's hose stream pushed the flames and heat back under the van towards him. The smell of burnt hair from his knuckles mixed with the smoke. *Too late to put my gloves on now*, Donny thought. He tried turning the handle, but his fingers slipped on the oily grime coating it. He tightened his grip and tried again. His hand slipped again on the slick metal. The burning in his fingers was excruciating. He reached up with his other hand, clasped one over the other, squeezed with all his might, and turned.

The handle moved.

It was loose now, and turned more easily. Donny closed the valve with a few more twists of his wrist, and uttered a silent word of thanks to the God he didn't believe in. The flames began to die down.

The bang was unbelievably loud under the car. Donny felt the vehicle lurch and instinctively closed his eyes. The report echoed off the buildings that surrounded the intersection, and several bystanders screamed.

Donny was surprised he was able to open his eyes again. The frame was only a fraction of an inch from his face, but the car had settled on the cribbing before it could crush his head.

"You all right, Cap?" Scout asked, peering anxiously under the van.

"Yeah. Yeah, I think so." Donny pulled himself out. He felt the edgy rush of adrenalin, a curious mix of elation at having narrowly avoided a gruesome death and the terrifying reminder of how thin the line can be between living and dying. "Good job on the cribbing."

Eddy reached down to help him up. "The front tire blew! Guess the fire got to it just as you shut off the tank."

There was no time for personal drama. Donny picked up his helmet and walked to the driver's window. The woman turned her glazed eyes to him. She was still clinging to the wheel, as if she could, even now, somehow steer away from the immutable past.

"The fire's out now. You're going to be OK," Donny told her, still catching his breath. "We'll get you out as soon as we can."

"My baby, her name is Louise. Please help her."

There was a steady wail coming from the baby seat in the back. That was a good sound. Donny knew the worst calls were those where the children were too weak or too far gone to make any noise. Silence was the sound of real horror. Louise's tiny pink face was scrunched up in a mass of wrinkles that would be the envy of any bulldog, and she was thrashing vigorously with both arms and both legs.

"Your daughter's fine. She's got a healthy set of lungs and she's getting plenty of air. That's a good car seat you've got her in. We'll get her out first, OK?" Donny reached in through the broken window and shifted the transmission into park. The engine was dead but he turned the ignition off to kill the electrical power, and removed the keys. "What's your name?"

"Nadia." The woman grabbed Donny's arm with surprising strength. "I ... I can't move my legs."

Donny looked over his shoulder. A team of paramedics was approaching. "Everything's going to be fine, Nadia. My name's Donny, and these guys are Mingzhu and Greg. They're two of the best paramedics in the city."

Donny turned to the paramedics. "Sorry, we haven't had time to do a preliminary or get a collar on her. We had to get the fire out and stabilize. The baby seems to be fine. Nadia here says she can't move her legs."

"No problem, we got it from here," Mingzhu replied. She turned to Nadia. "Try to keep your head still. I'm going to put a collar around your neck, OK?" Mingzhu took a stiff plastic collar from the medical kit she carried and secured it around Nadia's neck, while Greg fitted a heart and oxygen monitor onto Louise. Donny turned to go, but Nadia seized his hand.

"Don't leave me," she cried.

"We have to get you and Louise out of the car," Donny said, freeing his hand as gently as possible.

"I need you to focus on me, Nadia," Mingzhu said. "Do you have any pain in your neck or back?"

The rescue squad had arrived, and Donny made his way towards them. Moose and Scout were helping them lay out the extrication tools, while Eddy stayed on the hose line in case of a flareup. The tools, what civilians called "the jaws of life," were a set of powerful hydraulic cutters, spreaders and rams that could be used to dismantle any vehicle. It wasn't so much a process of getting the person out of the car, as it was removing pieces of the vehicle from around the person. It was like carefully unwrapping a precious gift.

"Hey, Blacker," Donny greeted the squad captain. "Blacker" Dixon had earned the nickname with a tendency to one-upmanship. He was the sort of person, it was said, that if you had a black cat, his was blacker.

"Wedge," Blacker replied, "what've we got?"

"Woman in the front, baby in the back. The doors are all jammed. Truck did in the driver's side. Passenger side is against the telephone pole at the B pillar. Cribbing is all set."

"OK," Blacker nodded, and turned to his crew. "Rosie, strip the trim, driver's side. Eight-ball, start on the back door."

Donny watched the squad crew set to work. This was their meat and potatoes. They worked quickly and efficiently. Rosie reached in with a flat tool, a bit like an oversized screwdriver. She pried away the plastic trim around the front and rear doors, checking for airbags and seat belt tensioners that hadn't fired. Cutting into one of those could seriously injure or kill the passengers they were trying to rescue or the firefighters themselves.

Eight-ball cut the rear door from its hinges first, then snipped the Nader bolt in the latch. With a little prying, the rear door came away from the wreck. Greg, the paramedic, cut the seat belt holding little Louise's car seat. She was still wailing at top volume as he carried her to the waiting ambulance.

A few minutes later, the vehicle's front door and the B pillar between the front and rear doors were removed, leaving the whole driver's side wide open. A hydraulic ram pushed the dashboard up, freeing Nadia's legs. With two final cuts, Eight-ball removed the back of the driver's seat. Nadia was laid on a backboard and lifted from the minivan, and Donny, Moose and Scout helped Mingzhu carry her to the ambulance.

As the ambulance drove away, the fire crews began packing up their gear. Once the cops had finished measuring skid marks and mapping the vehicles' positions, the tow trucks would take away what remained of the wreck, and the evening rush hour would pour over these streets as if nothing had ever happened.

Donny wondered how the story would end—whether Nadia would walk again, or whether she would carry Louise on her lap in a wheelchair. Officially, he wasn't even supposed to ask; there were issues of medical and personal privacy. Unofficially, there were back-door channels he could use to find out, but usually it was better not to know. Donny had found that out the hard way.

The Prince Edward Viaduct over the Don River Valley was a magnet for suicides—the second most popular spot in North America after the Golden Gate Bridge. Velma had landed in the soft mud on the river's edge. That's where young Firefighter Second Class

Donny Robertson had found her, as broken as a person could be and still be alive. She was his first jumper. She gripped his hand as he knelt beside her. Her voice was weak, but clear: "I want to live!"

Donny cajoled emergency-room doctors and charmed nurses until he found himself standing at the foot of Velma's hospital bed. He returned week after week, getting to know Velma and her family. Even after she was released from hospital, Donny kept up the contact.

Then one day Velma's sister answered the phone. Donny knew instantly from the woman's voice that Velma's demons had returned to claim her. The rest of that night was a blur. He found himself shivering in the grey light of dawn, standing in the soft mud on the riverbank, wrestling with a truth he couldn't un-know.

Never, never again, he swore. Better to leave Schrödinger's cat at least half alive; leave the hope of a fairy-tale ending intact.

Donny pushed the memory away, pulled out his notebook and began writing down the details of the call—names, licence plate numbers ... The incident report demanded information, not feelings or philosophical musings. His job was simply to do what he could and leave the rest up to whichever capricious gods sent dump trucks careening into minivans and left a jaded fire captain alive, cursing the fate that spared him.

Ratzo congratulated them on a job well done and cleared the scene. Donny was taking down the dump truck driver's details when a cop approached him. Donny recognized him as one of the officers who had helped with building the deck at Randy Copeland's house the weekend before—the one who had wanted to rip Scout's head off.

"Nice to see you again. How are you doing?" Donny asked in a friendly tone, trying to take the high road.

The cop was having none of it. "I noticed none of you were wearing your seat belts when you rolled up. I need to see some ID from each of you."

"You're shitting me, right?"

"Nope." The cop pulled out his ticket book, pen poised.

"We just saved that woman and her kid from burning to death, I almost got my head crushed trying to shut off the propane tank, and you're going to write us up for seat belts?" Donny asked in disbelief.

"I'm so impressed. You're regular goddamned heroes," the cop sneered. "But you know what? Even heroes are subject to traffic laws. Now I need the licence from your driver and ID from the rest of you."

"And you're a regular goddamned asshole!" Scout challenged. He put down the crate of cribbing he was carrying and walked over to the cop. "Is that something you're born with, or is that a special course they have for cops?"

Donny whirled on Scout. "Shut up and get in the truck." Scout stood his ground. "Right now, rookie!"

Seeing the anger burning in Donny's eyes, Scout turned and slunk away. Eddy and Moose paused and looked up, then went back to rolling up the hose.

The squad crew walked over to see what all the commotion was about, but Donny waved them away.

"I'm sorry," Donny said to the cop, trying a conciliatory tone. "He's a kid, he's young and he doesn't think."

"Young and stupid is more like it. Your boy needs to learn to shut his mouth or someone's going to shut it for him."

"Listen, if this is about what happened last Saturday on the deck ..."

"Save it. You're getting four tickets. Be grateful it's not more," the cop said, and began writing.

Donny stood silently fuming until the cop had finished. He took the tickets, climbed into the truck and threw the tickets onto the dash with his helmet.

"Home?" Moose asked, as they pulled away from the scene of the minivan accident.

"No." Donny stared at the four tickets on the truck's dash. "Fifty-one Division."

Fifty-one Division was housed in an old industrial building in Corktown, one of the city's oldest neighbourhoods. Many of the area's historic buildings had been demolished to make way for expressways, car dealerships and offices. But not all of them. The interior of the old gas filtration plant had been gutted and retrofitted to serve as a modern police station, but the building's Victorian brick exterior had been sandblasted and preserved. The large arched windows gave the place a light, airy look, as opposed to the concrete-bunker style of many of the city's modern police stations.

Donny told Moose to park the truck right in front of the main doors to the police station, right under the "No Parking, No Stopping, No Nothing, Don't Even Think About It" sign. He grabbed the tickets off the dash, strode through the front door and demanded to see the duty officer. The officers at the front desk were taken aback, but a minute later a door buzzed open and Staff Sergeant Daya Singh appeared. She ushered him into the station's interior.

Her office was a plain, functional space. Aside from Daya's desk and two visitor chairs, the only other furnishings were a long filing cabinet and a pair of notice boards. The office had none of the wood-panelled, hand-crafted Victorian charm of the Lombard Street fire hall, Donny noted.

"Have a seat." Daya indicated one of the visitor chairs.

Donny looked down at his bunker pants. He was filthy.

"Never mind," she said, taking her seat behind the desk. "What's up?"

He had come ready to raise absolute bloody hell, but her calm, courteous manner had disarmed him. He placed the four tickets he had scrunched up in his hand on her desk and tried to smooth them out.

She picked up the tickets and looked at them. "Tell me what happened."

Donny began by telling her what had transpired on the deck.

"I heard about that," Daya said. Donny looked surprised. "Bad news travels fast, and gossip even faster. What about today?" Daya asked.

Donny gave her a rundown on what had happed at the collision. He left nothing out, including Scout's remarks.

Daya steepled her fingers and thought for moment. "There's nothing that exempts firefighters from the seat belt law."

"OK, but ..." Donny began.

"Beyond the fact that everyone is equal under the law," Daya interrupted, "it's a matter of health and safety. I could name several cops I know who have been seriously hurt in collisions because, in the heat of the moment, they didn't put on their seat belt before responding to a call. I'm sure it's the same on your job."

Donny felt like he was back in public school, getting a talking-to in the principal's office. He couldn't, however, remember any of his principals looking quite like Staff Sergeant Singh. Her fine features and high cheekbones were framed by shiny black hair done up tightly at the back of her head. Normally he found the uniforms worn by police and firefighters quite asexual, but in this case, the uniform somehow accentuated Daya's beauty. Well, as Eddy liked to say, even if you're on a diet, you can still look at the menu. Donny noticed she wasn't wearing a wedding ring.

"You're right," Donny said, bringing himself back to the moment. "But this isn't about health and safety and we both know it. I can't be looking over my shoulder every time I run a call with one of your officers."

"You had a talk with, uh, Patrick, is that his name?"

"Yeah, we call him Scout. He understands now. Widows are off limits. And he needs to keep his mouth shut—period."

"You men. So much foolishness," Daya frowned. "In India, a Hindu widow was expected to throw herself on her husband's funeral pyre."

"Somehow I don't think that's something you would do," Donny smiled.

"No. I am a Sikh." Daya spread her hands as if the statement explained everything. When Donny didn't respond, she continued, "Guru Nanak, our founder, banned the practice, along with the killing of female children. He proclaimed the equality of men and women as two sides of the same human coin. That was more than 500 years ago, but sometimes I wonder how much has really changed."

She shook her head. "I'll cancel the tickets, but not Patrick's. Not because of the widow thing, it's for the asshole remark. That insults all of my officers, men and women alike."

"Sorry, that's not good enough."

"You're not in a position to make demands, Captain Robertson," Daya said, raising an eyebrow.

Donny found himself keenly aware of the fullness of her breasts as she leaned across the desk towards him. "I'm not making demands," Donny said, riveting his eyes on her face. "It's just, well, I can't have you singling out one of my people. We're a crew. It's gotta be all or nothing. Trust me, I'll look after Scout, but it needs to come from me."

Her looks had always been both a blessing and a curse. Daya was used to the way men looked at her. Sometimes she even enjoyed it, provided they respected her as well. At least Robertson had the decency to try to hide it.

"Trust you, eh? Do you have any idea how many times a day a cop hears that sort of crap?" Daya already knew what she was going to do, but she let Donny twist in the wind a few moments longer, tapping her pen against the edge of the desk. "I'll do it. I'll do it because this needs to end, and because you look like a man of your word. Don't make me regret it."

"Thank you. That's very kind of you." Donny rose to go.

"That's my name," she observed.

Donny cocked his head quizzically.

"Daya means 'kindness' in Punjabi," she explained, coming around the desk to see him off. "We'll put this all behind us now.

I'll let my officers know it's over. Period. You won't have to look over your shoulder."

"I'll make sure you won't regret it."

They walked out of the office, past the reception desk, towards the station's front door. "How's the investigation going?" Donny asked.

"Which investigation?"

"The drug lab. The search for the guy who set the booby traps and killed Copeland."

"Ah," Daya nodded. "I think half the department's working on that. Something will turn up, I'm sure. And how is your other fellow doing? The one who was shot. Eddy?"

"You have a good memory. He's fine," Donny said. "He has to put up with a lot of 'pain in the ass' jokes, but that's the worst of it."

"And you?" They paused at the station's front door, and she looked at him. "It was a close call for you too. Are you OK?"

Her question made Donny oddly uncomfortable. He tried to think of some clever quip, but simply shrugged the question off.

"I'm sorry, I didn't mean to pry. I'm glad you're all right," Daya said. She shook his hand and smiled at him warmly. "Let us hope the next time we meet will be under better circumstances."

"Let's hope so," Donny replied, holding the handshake just a moment too long.

He walked back to the truck wondering which made him more uncomfortable: her question or the guilty pleasure of her touch.

CHAPTER 7

CONVERSATIONS

"I don't have time to take the girls to dance class!" Bill Ericson glared at his wife across the breakfast table. "I told you yesterday, I have a meeting. Do you ever listen to what I tell you?"

"I'm sorry, Bill," his wife said. She focused on gathering up the Cheerios the toddler seated beside her was scattering around the highchair. "It's just that Cindy and I were supposed to ..."

"Then you'll just have to cancel, won't you?" Ericson could feel his face flushing, the tension building in his shoulders. Breathe: that's what they had told him in the anger management course. Breathe. Relax the neck. Relax the shoulders. Breathe and relax.

"Yes, of course. I'll call her after I clean up here."

She didn't meet his gaze, but Ericson could see the fear on her face. Spineless, that's what she was. For a moment he almost felt sorry for her.

"Do you think maybe you should go back to ..." his wife began. "I mean, I know it hasn't been easy since Randy ..."

"What the hell do you know about it?!" Ericson roared. He slammed his hand on the table as he stood. "You have no goddamned idea ..." Ericson caught himself in mid-stride. The toddler in the highchair started to wail. His wife had retreated, her back against the fridge. Breathe, just breathe. He puffed out his cheeks and exhaled a long breath. Breathe, relax, and step away from the situation. That's what he needed—just to get the hell out of there.

"I'll take the dog with me." He turned and headed to the door.

"Let's just say I kind of had my fill of the Fire Department in the last little while." Ericson bent down, picked up a stick and tossed it. The bouncing bundle of canine energy at his side charged off in pursuit.

"I thought that might be it. That's why I took the liberty of calling you. I appreciate your coming to meet me." Tom Humphrey stepped to the side of the path to let a bicycle past. It was a drab autumn day with a damp wind that seemed to cut deeper and colder than the winter storms it foretold. Aside from the odd jogger or cyclist, there were few other people wandering the ravine paths in the river valleys that wound through the city.

"The dog needed walking anyway," Ericson said noncommittally.

"I heard about what happened with Scout, and for what it's worth, I'm sorry." Humphrey stepped back onto the path, glancing sideways at Ericson. "In the old days, that never would have happened. People understood. There was respect. And if it did happen, someone would have tuned up the kid pretty quick. These days ... well, I don't have to tell you, do I?"

The dog brought the stick back and dropped it at Ericson's feet. "Good boy, Charlie. That's enough stick for now. Go play."

The dog cocked his head questioningly at Ericson, looked down at the stick and then trotted off, immersing himself in the bouquet of damp decay that rose from the autumn ground.

"Charlie," Humphrey mused. "That's your father's name, isn't it?"

"It was the kids' idea, not mine. They love their Grandpa. Anyway, how'd you know that?"

"I met your dad a few times when I was still pretty new on the job. I didn't know him that well, but we had a few runs with him. He seemed like a stand-up guy," Humphrey explained. "Bob Collins knew him a lot better, of course. He said your old man was a good cop."

"You friends with the superintendent?" Ericson asked.

"You could say that," Humphrey replied.

Ericson looked at the man walking beside him. The thin, short hair that peeked out from beneath his cap was completely white. He looked like some ancient sea captain. It was almost as if you could read time itself, like geological strata, on the deep creases of his face. But the eyes that looked back at Ericson were bright, inquiring and totally focused on the present. Not like those of his father, a man now lost in the decaying prison of his own mind.

"My dad used to tell me stories about the old days. Stuff like how they used to take perps out on the Cherry Beach Express."

"Hmm, you know about that, eh?"

"Dad said they saved the courts and taxpayers a lot of time and money. Got results, too."

"That they did," Humphrey chuckled. "I took a ride on that old Cherry Beach Express myself, you know."

"Really?" Ericson's surprise was obvious.

"I had a bit of an attitude problem," Humphrey shrugged. "I was sixteen, running with a pretty rough crowd, wouldn't listen to anyone. Anyway, I got caught with stolen property. I was lying and mouthing off to the cops, so they figured they'd teach me a lesson. They let me sweat it out in the station for awhile. Then, about two o'clock in the morning, they took me out to Cherry Beach. It was even more deserted back in those days. They worked me over a little first; didn't break anything—they knew how to do it right without leaving marks. Then they took my shoes and jacket and left me there. It took me all night to limp home barefoot, shivering in that cold November rain.

"My mother was frantic by the time I got home, wondering what had happened to me. When I told them, my dad didn't say a word. He was a butcher, though, and the next day he sent a dozen T-bones to the police station as a thank you."

"A thank you? Really!" Ericson shook his head. He whistled and the dog came bounding back towards them. "You'd never get away with that now. These days, you'd lose your badge."

"I understand." Humphrey patted him on the shoulder. "You know, I damn near froze to death walking home that night, but I had a lot of time to think. I decided that maybe a life of crime wasn't really for me. In a way, you could say those cops saved my life."

"Yeah? Well, now it's cops who pay the price and the punks who walk away laughing." Ericson's blue eyes narrowed. "I tell you, if I got my hands on the bastard who killed Randy, he'd get a lot more than a ride to Cherry Beach. I don't care what they'd do to me."

"Do you mind if we sit for a moment?" Humphrey pointed to a picnic table a few metres away. "My arthritis bothers me a bit when the weather's damp like this."

They sat facing each other across the table. The dog lay at Ericson's feet chewing a new stick. They were quite alone, but Humphrey spoke more softly now. "A lot of people feel the same way, Bill. A few of us have decided to do something about it."

"Firefighters?"

"And others. People who are sick and tired of the way things are. That's why I wanted to talk to you."

"What, you starting some kind of community group? Send around another petition that the politicians can ignore?" Ericson said dismissively.

"No," Humphrey said firmly. "No petitions. I'm sorry, but I can't tell you much more at this point. I'm not trying to be evasive; it's just that we need to be careful. But let me assure you, Bill, we are people of action. Does that interest you?"

"I don't know." Ericson shifted in his seat. The old man didn't seem like a kook. He squinted at Humphrey and pursed his lips.

"Trying to figure out if I'm some sort of Timothy McVeigh crackpot?" Humphrey shook his head. "It's nothing like that. No blowing up buildings, no innocent victims, no collateral damage. But we are serious, Bill, deadly serious. Now, you can walk away, and this conversation never happened. But if you're willing to make a commitment, there's an opportunity for you to help us right a few wrongs, maybe even a chance to get some justice for your partner."

Ericson stopped patting the dog and looked Humphrey straight in the eye. There was no hesitation.

"Why didn't you say so? I'm in."

Eddy and Scout stood in front of Station Six. They pulled their bunker jackets tight around them against the chill wind. Eddy pointed up at the carved sandstone phoenix that perched under the peak of the slate roof.

"And that more than anything says who we are," Eddy explained. "That image of the phoenix has been painted on every truck that's run out of this station, right back to the old steamers. Every guy whose plaque hangs on that memorial wall inside was buried with the phoenix on his right sleeve. Now, if you look at that and all you see is a stone carving, I don't know what more to tell you."

They had been walking around the Lombard Street station, inside and out, for half an hour, as Eddy pointed out the hoisting post where hay had once been lifted into the old hayloft that was now the exercise room. He explained how what was now the locker room for their bunker gear used to be the horse stalls. He drew Scout's attention to the names and dates scratched into the bricks beside the stairs that spiralled up the inside of the hose tower. Many of the inscriptions were more than a hundred years old. Lombard was a tiny downtown island of Victoriana surrounded by a sea of twenty-first-century glass and steel.

"I get it, I get it," Scout exclaimed. "The hall was built right after Noah landed the ark, and every brick is overflowing with tradition. Can we go inside now? I'm freezing my ass off."

They went in and hung their jackets back in their assigned positions on the truck. Eddy beckoned and Scout followed him into the floor watch room.

The floor watch was a small, sparse room. A large window looked out onto the apparatus floor where the truck sat like some gleaming, slumbering beast. The department phone, radio equipment and dispatch printer sat on the counter that ran the length of the wall beneath the window. A panel of buttons was wired to the electric motors that had replaced the system of weights and pulleys that opened the heavy wooden apparatus bay doors. A battered recliner and a second, smaller chair faced the second-hand TV sitting on the end of the counter beside the door.

The floor watch was seldom occupied during the day, but someone always spent the night there. There were the phone and radio to monitor, and once in a blue moon someone would come banging on the station door in the middle of the night to report some neighbourhood emergency.

Eddy flopped down into the recliner and muted the local cable news on the TV. "So, you still want to go through with this harassment thing?" he asked.

Scout leaned back against the floor watch door and folded his arms. "Do you think Donny will change the floor watch schedule?"

"I haven't asked him, but I doubt it." Eddy chewed his bottom lip for a moment. "You know, you can be right and still be wrong."

Normally floor watch duty rotated weekly. Donny had assigned Scout to floor watch for what was left of this month and all of the next.

"You know why he's doing that, eh?" Eddy asked.

"Yeah, yeah, yeah." Scout dismissed the question with a wave. "We had the big father-son talk. But you know what? Someone needs to tell Donny that the serfs have been freed, they've banned public hangings and there are no more floggings in the town square."

"Hmm, more's the pity," Eddy mused. "Listen, I could give you the big speech about how rookies got treated when I came on the job, but that's not the point. The point is you were out of line. Way out of line—twice."

"OK, but I said I was sorry," Scout protested. "What am I supposed to do?"

"How about growing up?"

Scout's face flushed as he gestured inarticulately, first at Eddy and then at the office upstairs.

"You got a real short fuse, Scout. That's a big problem." Eddy kicked the empty chair towards him. "Now sit down and just listen for a minute."

Scout hesitated for a moment, then sat, leaned the chair back on two legs and folded his arms across his chest.

"Remember when you wanted that weekend off to go to your buddy's wedding, back in September, and there was no holiday time available? But Donny made it happen. You ever stop to wonder how many favours he had to call in for that?"

"I never asked him to," Scout objected.

"No, you didn't have to ask, because Donny was taught 'back when Noah landed the ark' that a captain looks after his crew," Eddy replied evenly. "You know, the cops were going to cancel all the seat belt tickets except for yours. Donny said no, either all of them or none."

"Bullshit!"

"On my mother's grave," Eddy said, looking Scout straight in the eye as he crossed himself.

"Why would he do that?"

"You really need to ask? It's not about the fine, it's not about the points off your licence or anything like that. We don't leave a man behind on this crew, not ever. Even on a stupid little thing like a seat belt ticket. Donny told them it would be settled here, in the station. This is where we look after things." Eddy paused and looked through the window at the phoenix painted on the side of the truck. "And now you want to hang him out on a harassment beef. Well, you got him dead to rights. By the book, it is clearly discriminatory treatment. The pencil pushers will back you one hundred percent. They'll reprimand Donny, maybe dock him a week's pay, even transfer him out to some shit hall in the suburbs. Meanwhile, any kind of respect or reputation you had on this job? You can kiss that goodbye. All because you won't man up and take your medicine."

Eddy looked back at Scout, but the younger man would no longer meet his gaze. "Guys like you and me, we're here for a few years and then we're gone. But all that stuff I was showing you and telling you about, that stuff goes on. It was here before I was born and I pray to God it will be here long after I'm dead. Maybe that doesn't mean much to you right now, but trust me, it will.

"See, you're like a glass of water sitting beside a river. The river begins far away and long ago and flows on clear out of sight. Sometimes the flow is turbulent and muddy, but the current is deep and strong. You can stay in that glass all by yourself, or you can pour yourself into the river and be part of something truly great and powerful. You know what I think, but it's your choice."

They sat looking at each other in silence.

"Well, we got company coming and I got supper to make. Shepherd's pie and carrot cake tonight." Eddy rose out of the recliner and headed to the stairs. He stopped just beyond the door and turned back. "You got thirty days to file a complaint, right? All I'm asking is just think about it, OK?"

Eddy climbed the stairs to the second floor where the station's living quarters were located. He passed Moose in the hallway, returning from a workout in the gym.

"So?" Moose enquired, wiping the sweat from his face with a towel.

Eddy shrugged. "I told him the glass of water and the river story."

"I like that one," Moose nodded. "Did he buy it?"

"We'll see. He's thinking about it, at least. It'd be a shame if we had to kill the kid," Eddy laughed, and walked into the kitchen.

"Hello, Roxanne."

"Who are you?" She turned to face the smartly dressed older man in the doorway.

Superintendent Collins closed the door behind him and studied the young woman who sat fidgeting on the bed. She was probably in her mid-twenties, though she looked much older. She had doubtless once been quite beautiful, but her sallow skin was scabby and drawn tight over her face like some grotesque mask. She ran a bony hand through her stringy blonde hair.

Collins quickly took in the shabby motel room. Faded floral drapes covered the window that looked out across a potholed parking lot towards one of the empty auto parts factories that dotted Windsor. A small round Formica table and two chairs with cracked vinyl seats and rusted chrome legs sat in front of the window.

A large man with a shaved head, dressed in a sweatshirt and jeans, sat in one of the chairs watching a football game on television. The two men nodded to each other, but said nothing.

"I don't like this," Roxanne protested, rising from the bed. "I don't do doubles."

"Sit down," Collins instructed. She yielded to the authority in his voice, drawing her knees to her chest. Collins turned to the man with the shaved head. "I've got it from here."

"You sure?"

"Yeah, thanks."

"No problem. The room's paid for—cash. She came easily enough." The bald man turned off the TV and stood. "Guess I'll watch the rest of the game at home."

The two men shook hands. The man in the sweatshirt left and Collins took his chair. He looked at the pathetic figure huddled on the bed across from him.

"I don't do anything kinky, OK? Just the regular." Her hands twisted and fussed with the covers like small nesting rodents.

"That's not why I'm here." Collins stood, pulled a photograph from the inside pocket of his jacket and handed it to Roxanne. It showed a man from the chest up, lying on an autopsy table. "Do you know who this is?"

Roxanne wrinkled her brow, stared at the picture and shook her head. "I never seen him. He looks ... he looks dead. Are you a cop?"

Collins nodded. Roxanne looked rapidly back and forth between the photograph and the man standing over her. Fear and comprehension crowded in through her high. "No, I don't know him. I didn't kill anybody. I just do a little business so I can buy my medicine, but I never killed nobody, see ..."

"Shut up!" An edge crept into Collins' carefully controlled voice. His hands clenched and unclenched. Roxanne dropped the picture and scrambled across the bed away from him. He forced himself to take several deep breaths before resuming. "That's Randy Copeland. He was one of my officers. You were living in the house he was killed in. That makes you an accessory."

"I don't know what you're talking about. I don't know anything about killing cops." Roxanne's eyes widened as Collins took a pair of black leather gloves from his pocket and slowly pulled them on. "This isn't proper. You're supposed to read me my rights. I want outta here."

Roxanne's eyes fastened on the door. She sprang in one motion. Collins caught her with one arm and flung her, like one of the hay bales he had slung in his youth, back onto the bed. He stood over her, glaring menacingly.

"You're a stupid little tweaker, Roxanne. You don't have rights. And you don't really want me to arrest you, either, because if I do, I will make it my personal mission to make sure you spend the rest of your worthless life locked up in some shithole with the meanest, most badass bitches you ever met." Collins leaned over her on the bed, placing his hands on either side of her. Roxanne crossed her arms protectively across her chest. "What you want to do instead is help me find your boyfriend. It's him we really want."

"Yeah, it was him, it was Ramón," Roxanne blurted before she knew what she was saying. Ramón had told her never to say anything to anyone about him. But Collins' angry face leering down at her filled her with terror.

"Ramón, that's his name?" Collins asked.

"He goes by Carlos a lot. On the street, you know."

Collins stood back up. "You see? Now we're getting somewhere. This Ramón, does he have a last name? You got a picture of him?"

Roxanne shook her head. "I took his picture once. He got real angry and smashed my new phone. He said he'd kill me if I ever did it again. He's got a bunch of names, you know? All, like, Mexican names. I can't think right now."

"But you're going to help me find him, aren't you?"

Knowing there was only one answer, Roxanne nodded mutely. Collins walked to the bathroom and looked through the door. There was no window through which she could escape. "Have a shower and clean yourself up. We're heading back to Toronto and you're not riding in my car smelling like that."

CHAPTER 8

HIGH-RISE

The kitchen of the Lombard Street fire station was the one place Donny felt truly comfortable; a place where he and his fellow fire-fighters shared food, stories and camaraderie, a place of sanctuary. He watched Eddy lift slabs of carrot cake from the pan and pass them around the table. Eddy the Ladle—laughing, joking and slinging out the grub. Guys like Eddy always knew what to say and do without even thinking about it. That was the key, of course.

Donny trusted his instincts on the fire ground, but in social situations he often felt like he was trying just a little too hard. He felt awkward, as if his skin didn't fit right. Even as a kid, he'd had the strange feeling he'd been left behind as a baby by an alien spaceship.

But not here. From the first day he walked into Lombard, he'd felt at home, like this was what and where he was meant to be.

The kitchen faced south, with three large sash windows set deep in the stonework. Donny had read in the old logbooks that when the station was built, you could look out those windows and see the masts of barques and schooners tied up along the Toronto water-front. Now it was barely possible to catch a glimpse of the sky above the downtown canyons of glass and steel.

Donny particularly loved the pictures that lined the kitchen walls. Many were from that early era, showing teams of finely groomed horses and proud, stern men with long, flowing beards. The station was already forty years old when the first motorized fire truck arrived at the end of World War One.

The kitchen was where Donny had learned not just how to fight fires, but what it meant to be a firefighter. It was where tough love and sacred lore were handed down. Here, in this kitchen, generation after generation of men, and now women too, who shared the same vocation had also broken bread together. Donny leaned back in his chair, cradled his coffee cup in his hands and smiled contentedly. This was his happy place.

"Another piece of cake, Chief?" Donny offered.

"You guys are going to be the death of me." Ratzo dabbed at the crumbs on his plate, put down his fork and patted his ample waist. "I have ended more diets at this table than I care to think."

Donny and Joe Razzolini had come on together as recruits. Ratzo's intelligence and determination, not to mention a certain amount of calculated charm, had led to a rapid rise through the ranks. He had been a district chief for five years, while Donny had made captain only two years earlier. Though age and indulgence had softened him, Ratzo still had the barrel chest and brawny arms he had acquired as a bricklayer's apprentice. His wreath of dark, wavy hair gave him a monk-like appearance, and his small, bright eyes were set deep in his fleshy face.

Donny knew that little escaped the notice of those eyes. He saw Ratzo raise an eyebrow when Scout came into the kitchen. Scout complimented Eddy on the shepherd's pie, helped himself to a piece of carrot cake and returned to the floor watch.

"Something I need to know about?" Ratzo had refrained from asking about Scout's conspicuous absence at dinner. Normally, floor watch wasn't expected to begin until after the meal.

"Not really," Donny shrugged.

"The kid earned himself a couple of extra floor watch shifts," Eddy explained. "He's sulking."

"Hmmph," Moose commented through a mouthful of carrot cake. He was tucking into his second slab with gusto. "I was driving the aerial out of Runnymede, just after I started, and I left a compartment door open after the morning check. We got a call, and when I turned onto Bloor Street, the CO_2 extinguisher went sailing right across the intersection into the side of a Caddy. 'The Ripper' was my captain and he was some pissed. For the rest of that winter I shovelled the front and back of the station by myself every time it snowed. And it snowed a lot that year. But I didn't dare complain."

"Times are different now." Ratzo turned to Donny. "You sure it's OK?"

Donny decided the best defence was a good offence. "Did you guys ever hear about the time our esteemed chief here took out a brand new Mercedes with Pumper Twelve?"

"It was three years old, not brand new," Ratzo protested. Moose and Eddy looked at him with renewed interest. "Besides, the guy ran a red, and we had lights and siren going. But the Benz was a writeoff. Then the cops charged him with running the red and failing to yield to an emergency vehicle. I mean, we T-boned the guy. He was lucky to live, but man, he was screaming at us and the cops the whole time they were loading him into the ambulance. I don't think he bought any tickets to the Firefighters' Ball that year."

The conversation became an animated debate over who were the worst drivers on the job, past and present. The discussion was interrupted by the bee-bop tones of a dispatch message.

"Fire call: Pumper Three, Pumper Six, Pumper Seven, Aerial Seven, High-Rise One, Chief Forty-one. Respond at four zero Gerrard Street East, report of heavy smoke on the twenty-seventh floor. Tactical channel two. Acknowledge."

Residents spilled out onto the grass and sidewalk in front of the apartment building. Some gathered in little groups and began talking excitedly, some tried to reassure small children, some even laughed nervously.

Donny wasn't laughing. He climbed down from the truck and frowned at the black smear wiping itself across the upper floors of the building. The wind was from the south, pushing the smoke back onto the building as it belched from the windows high overhead.

Donny forced his way through the growing crowd, past the trucks from Stations Three and Seven that had already arrived. He had listened to their arrival messages and updates on the radio, noting items on his mental checklist. So far everything was going as per standard procedure. The pumper crews were heading to the twenty-seventh floor to fight the fire. The drivers were running hoses from Pumper Three to the building's standpipe system and hooking the pumper up to a hydrant. The aerial crew had taken command of the elevators and were ferrying smoke ejectors, spare air cylinders, tools and other equipment to establish a forward staging position on the twenty-fifth floor. A second alarm had been declared and those trucks were on their way.

Ratzo caught up with Donny at the front of the building. "I'm setting up the command post there." He pointed to a section of the lobby that was out of the main flow of people leaving the building, midway between the elevators and the alarm panel with its PA system. "I need you and your guys on ventilation, OK?"

"Got it," Donny replied. He'd rather join the crews attacking the fire on the twenty-seventh floor, but clearing the smoke out of the building was just as important. Smoke was the most dangerous part of a fire. Few people ever actually burned to death.

High-rise fires were always complicated. There were hundreds, sometimes thousands of people to deal with. Some of the residents—the very old, the very young and the ill—would need help. There were access and evacuation bottlenecks in stairways and elevators. Getting civilians out and enough fire crews and equipment in was always a challenge. Tracking crews and assignments was essential, both for efficiency and, God forbid, in case anything went wrong.

The building's standpipe system was another limitation. It should supply enough water, but it had only so much capacity. The wind was pushing the fire and smoke back into the building. As long as they could keep the fire from spreading from the original apartment out into the hallway, the situation would remain a routine disaster.

Donny turned to his crew. "We'll use the west stairwell for smoke. Scout, get the bolt cutters and the attic ladder. You and I will head to the top." They would open the roof hatch at the top of the stairwell, effectively creating a giant chimney through which they could evacuate the smoke.

Scout headed off to get the equipment Donny had requested. Donny spoke to his two veterans. "You're walking up from the bottom. That stairwell needs to be clear before we start pushing smoke into it. Check the conditions on each floor as you go."

"That'll work off the carrot cake," Moose said. He tightened the straps on his SCBA. He and Eddy would make the long climb wearing forty kilograms of gear.

"Don't worry, there's still some in the pan," Eddy replied. He and Moose moved off to begin their ascent.

Scout returned with the tools, and he and Donny boarded the elevator when it arrived back in the lobby.

"Where can I take you gentlemen this evening?" asked the firefighter operating the elevator.

"All the way to the top, Spike. We're popping the hatch," Donny replied.

Spike pushed the buttons to close the door and start the elevator moving. In emergency mode, the elevator could be controlled only manually, from the inside. It ensured the fire department retained control. "The penthouse, eh? I always knew you Lombard guys were high rollers."

"Hmmph, ventilation," Scout grunted. "I'd rather be doing some actual fire fighting."

"Yeah, everybody wants to be a hero. I'll trade you, if you'd rather be an elevator chauffeur," Spike offered, but Scout only scowled.

"Chief Forty-one, this is Pumper Three Captain," their radios squawked. "This fire in apartment 2710—it appears to be a grow op. We're knocking it down pretty good with two lines, but we're going to need the cops up here once it's under control." Cannabis was legal now, but just like bootleg alcohol and cigarettes there was still a lot of money to be made with black market marijuana. Grow-ops were still a thriving, if illegal business.

Ratzo acknowledged the message. There were a couple of anonymous offers to bring up pizza and nachos before Ratzo imposed radio discipline.

"Hey, ventilation might not be so bad on this job," Spike grinned. "Take a couple of deep breaths before you get rid of all the smoke."

Donny didn't answer; he simply watched the floor numbers progress.

"Thirty-third floor, housewares, ladies' fashions and stairwell hatches," Spike announced as he opened the elevator doors. Donny and Scout stepped out. Spike acknowledged a radio message to return to the lobby and closed the doors as Donny and Scout moved down the hallway to the west stairwell.

Folded up, the attic ladder looked like a three-metre-long hinged and riveted aluminum bar. Unfolded, it became a narrow ladder of about the same length. It was designed to fit into tight spaces like elevators, or go around corners on stairs. It could be set up in a closet to gain access to an attic, or, as in this case, to get to the hatch on the ceiling at the top of a stairwell.

Scout climbed the ladder, used the bolt cutters to snip the padlock holding the hatch closed, and opened it. Air whooshed upward through the opening recessed into the ceiling. A square metre of low grey sky hung above, and the clouds glowed with the reflected light of the downtown core.

Smoke ejectors, high-powered fans, could now be set up at the west end of each affected floor to blow the smoky, contaminated air into the stairwell that had now become, in effect, a thirty-three-storey chimney.

There had been only a light haze of smoke on the top floor. Donny and Scout began walking down the stairs, checking the smoke conditions in the hallways, floor by floor. The fire was declared under control by the time they reached the twenty-ninth floor.

The twenty-ninth floor was identical to all the others. Fluorescent lights shone with an annoying flicker onto worn blue and red, faux Oriental carpeting. The walls were covered with beige floral wallpaper that looked like a sepia-tone photo of peonies. It was one of an endless series of variations Donny had seen in the aging downtown apartment towers.

The smoke was heavier here on twenty-nine. They began knocking on apartment doors, checking that any residents who hadn't evacuated were OK. Donny was particularly concerned about the south side of the apartment block, where the wind had been pushing the smoke back into the building.

They had checked only the first few units when a man emerged from an apartment farther down the hallway. He moved towards the elevators, keeping his back to Donny and Scout.

"I'm sorry, sir, the elevators are in emergency operation. You'll have to use the stairs," Scout called to him. "We're checking smoke conditions. Is everything OK in your apartment?"

"Yeah, everything's fine, thanks," the man said over his shoulder, moving away from them towards the end of the hallway.

"Sir! Excuse me, but you'll have to use the stairs at this end," Donny said, approaching the man. "We're blowing the smoke out through the west stairwell."

The man stopped but didn't turn around. All Donny could see was the back of the man's bald head and the faded leather Harley-Davidson jacket he was wearing. A single drop of syrupy red liquid slid from the man's fingertips and dropped thickly onto the carpet, glistening like a cabochon ruby. A few strides brought Donny even with him. The man's right hand was splattered red, and the front of his T-shirt was soaked and pasted to his chest. The warm, earthy scent of fresh blood penetrated the smell of smoke in the hallway.

"Jesus! Are you all right?" Donny exclaimed. He had seen his share of gruesome scenes over the years. It was the surprise of it that took him aback.

"Yeah, yeah, I'm fine. I cut myself. The, uh, fire alarm startled me and I cut myself in the kitchen. I'm going to get stitches." The man's expression seemed more annoyed than anything. His gaze darted up and down the hallway before he turned and moved the other way, towards the east stairs, back past the apartment he had just left.

"Hang on, we'll get you an ambulance," Scout offered.

Donny glanced at the apartment door the man had come out of. It looked like it had been kicked in. The whole situation felt wrong. Donny turned his radio to an empty channel and keyed the mic. "Pumper Six Captain, twenty-ninth floor, Code One."

There would be no confirmation or reply from the dispatchers in the communications centre. From what he had just radioed through to them, they knew where he was, they knew he needed help, and they knew he couldn't talk. There would be radio silence on that channel from here on.

The man stopped in front of Scout and turned back to Donny. "Code One? That was a mistake," he said menacingly. "That was a real stupid mistake."

"Oh, that just means there's only light smoke on this floor," Scout improvised. "Code Zero is no smoke, and Code Five is like, real bad, right, Cap?"

"Why don't we go back in your apartment, buddy, and we'll see if we can patch up that cut for you," Donny said, reaching towards the battered door.

The latch had been broken, and the door opened with a light push. A body lay sprawled in a large pool of blood on the living room floor. The eyes gazed blindly towards the entrance. The throat had been cut and the head, half severed, was cocked at an unusual angle, as if asking, "What are you staring at?"

"I used to be a cop, asshole. I know what Code One means." There was a flash of silver, and in an instant the man had his arm around

Scout's neck and a straight razor pressed to his throat. "Now you get back on that radio and tell them it was a mistake. Tell them everything is just fine, or your boy here is going to have a new smile, from ear to ear."

There was panic in the man's voice, and that more than anything made Donny nervous. There was no way to cancel the emergency he had set in motion. He needed an alternative.

"Cap ...?" Scout's voice quavered.

"Shut up!" The bald man jerked Scout's head farther back.

"If you know Code One, then you know I can't call it off. Listen, you want to get out of here? Tell you what." Donny unzipped his fire coat and took it off. "You put on my gear, you walk right out. Nobody will even think twice about a fireman leaving the building."

The man narrowed his eyes, considering the proposal. Donny kept talking as he rolled down his bunker pants and stepped out of his boots.

"Just let him go. I'll even go with you down the stairs with you if you want. I'm the captain—I'm worth more as a hostage, right?" Donny started walking slowly towards the man, holding his gear out to him. "Just let him go."

Donny heard the elevator door open behind him. He turned to see a small hand mirror barely protruding from the elevator doorway. Then he heard a familiar voice.

"Hey, Darrel, it's been awhile. How you doing?"

The man with the razor turned towards the elevator, pulling Scout tighter to him as a shield. "Ericson?? Jesus fucking Christ, is that you, Ericson?"

"Just like old times, eh, buddy?" Ericson shifted the mirror to scan the entire hallway. "What's this, now? You give up cutting on whores and switch to firemen? Not much of a step up, if you ask me. Looks like you've already been busy."

Darrel looked down at the blood on his chest and hands. "He had it coming. The asshole set fire to my grow op. Fucker tried to burn me to death along with it."

"OK, so maybe this goes down as self-defence. I can work with that."

"Quit stalling. I know the game. I'm getting out of here, or this asshole will bleed out before you get off the first shot. I'm not going back inside. Do you have any idea what it's like for a cop in prison?"

"If you want to cut that one, that's fine with me," Ericson said, poking his head out the elevator door. "He wanted to throw a length into Randy's widow, anyway."

"I ... I ... please ..." Scout whimpered.

"It's going to be OK, Scout. Stay cool." Donny took a cautious step forward.

"Stay the fuck back!" Darrel screamed.

"I don't like the other one much either, Darrel," Ericson continued. "You can slice 'em both as far as I'm concerned. But it's not going to make it any easier for you."

Eddy and Moose burst through the stairwell door behind Darrel. "What the hell ...?"

Darrel turned towards the new sound. Scout no longer shielded him, and Ericson had a clean profile shot. The 9mm slug smashed through Darrel's ribs and shredded his lungs; the razor fell away from the tender skin of Scout's neck, leaving a short, thin red line, little more than a scratch. Darrel slumped to the floor with a gurgling sound.

Scout spun away and put his hand to his throat as Eddy and Moose ran towards him. Donny stood in his socks, staring, still holding out his fire gear in mute offering.

Darrel's head lolled towards Donny. Their eyes locked. Darrel's lips worked soundlessly, a stream of bloody foam bubbling from the corners of his mouth. His hand grasped at the air just above him.

Ericson stepped out of the elevator, took three steps towards the fallen man and fired again. This shot added a good portion of Darrel's brains to the faded pattern of the carpet.

"I wasn't going to let him kill you," Ericson said without looking up. "I just had to keep him off balance 'til I could get a clean shot."

Scout nodded, leaning against the wall.

Ericson kicked the razor away towards the elevator. He laid a boot into Darrel's side, then holstered his gun and looked up at Scout. "Now listen. He was trying to cut you as he went down, right? That's why I had to fire again. We all got that?"

"Sure thing, absolutely," Scout replied. He took a kick at the lifeless body himself. Donny pulled him away. Moose and Eddy looked at each other and nodded.

To Donny, time seemed to move in staccato jumps after the shooting. The five of them were standing there, staring at the body on the hallway floor. Then, suddenly, the hallway was full of cops. A moment later, it seemed, he, Eddy and Moose were standing outside, watching Scout climb into an ambulance. Ericson had disappeared. Then they were back at Lombard, cleaning themselves up.

It was shock, this fragmented perception. Donny tried to shake himself out of it. After all, he was no stranger to life-and-death emergencies. Crisis was the bread and butter of the job. He had always known what to do before—grab a hose, set up a ladder, start CPR. What had he done this time, as Scout, a razor to his throat, had pleaded for his life?

Nothing.

He hadn't been able to save Fitz either, or keep Eddy from being shot. It was his most sacred duty, beyond anything else: to keep his crew safe. And once again, when it came to the crunch, he had failed.

Someone else had taken charge. Ericson had saved Scout's life. Donny would always be grateful for that. Gratitude warred with his sense of personal failure, but something else gnawed away at him, too.

The image played over and over in Donny's mind: Darrel Simpson lying on the floor, gasping his last, as Ericson calmly walked up to him and fired a bullet into his head.

Bang. Pause. Step, step, step. Bang.

Two officers from the Special Investigations Unit arrived at the station later that evening. The SIU was responsible for investigating all police shootings in Toronto and the rest of the province. They interviewed the firefighters one at a time in the kitchen.

The captain's office was just down the hall from the kitchen. Donny listened from behind the closed door as first Eddy, then Moose gave his version of the events. Their accounts were substantially the same: there were two shots in quick succession, immediately after they came through the stairwell door. All they saw was a body falling to the floor, and Scout with a cut on his neck.

"Was the second shot fired before or after the body fell?" the officers asked.

"It all happened so fast," Eddy answered.

"It was a blur," was Moose's reply.

Donny was seated behind his desk when the knock came on his door and the officers asked him to come into the kitchen.

The two men introduced themselves. Donny didn't bother trying to remember their names. The older one was sitting in Donny's chair at the head of the table, and Donny wondered if it was a ploy, assuming the position of power to put him at a disadvantage. No, that was crazy; these guys were just doing their job.

The SIU investigators walked Donny through the beginning of the call: the crew's arrival, opening the hatch at the top of the stairwell, checking the upper floors for smoke. Then they got into the meat of the matter.

"Tell me what happened when you and Patrick arrived on the twenty-ninth floor," the older officer said.

Bang. Pause. Step, step, step. Bang.

Donny looked up at the pictures ringing the room. Stern-faced Victorian men stared back implacably, as if reserving their judgement of his worthiness. He shifted in his seat. For the first time, Donny felt awkwardly out of place in the kitchen.

"I know how upsetting it must have been to have one of your crew threatened like that," the younger investigator said. "Would you like a drink of water?"

"It's my goddamned kitchen. If I want a glass of water, I'll get it myself." Donny hated himself for yelling at the two men. They were just doing their job, but he was lost and floundering. Here in his safe place.

The older man got up from his chair, walked over to the middle window, and looked out at the lights of the offices and condos that surrounded them. He spoke with his back to Donny. "We just need you to tell us what happened."

Bang. Pause. Step, step, step. Bang.

Donny stood up too. "I don't have to tell you anything, do I?" It wasn't really a question.

The older officer turned to face him. He spoke steadily, looking Donny straight in the eye. "No. Legally, only cops are required to talk to us. You don't have to say a word, but I *do* expect you to act like a professional."

Donny returned the man's gaze. "Then professionally speaking, you can get a copy of my report when it's filed."

"We'll talk later, when you've had a chance to calm down."

Donny retreated to his office and tried to ignore the murmur of voices in the hall as Eddy showed the SIU officers out. Donny sat at his desk and tried to fill out his section of the department's Fire Report. He wrote down the date, time, and address of the call, and the events up to their arrival on the twenty-ninth floor. The empty part of the page stared accusingly back at him.

It was a quiet night, a rare thing at Lombard. Donny knew the dispatchers were trying to give them a break. He'd rather be busy. He lay on his bunk staring at the ceiling while the scene played over and over in his head.

Bang. Pause. Step, step, step. Bang.

BANG. PAUSE. STEP, STEP, STEP. BANG.

CHAPTER 9

A WALK IN THE PARK

Laurie drained the last of her coffee, set down her cup, and looked at Donny across the breakfast table. It was a scene they had enacted many times: she getting ready for work, he bone weary after a twenty-four-hour shift in the fire hall. It always reminded her a bit of the old Looney Tunes cartoon of the sheepdog and the coyote at the time clock. But there was no humour this morning.

"I'm the captain. I'm supposed to protect my crew. That's my job."

Laurie cocked her head as the sound of squabbling boys and virtual explosions drifted in from the living room. She didn't like them playing Xbox before school, but Donny had wanted to talk. She turned back to him: "It wasn't a normal situation, Donny. It wasn't your fault. You're not God."

"He was lying on the ground, dying, looking at me, trying to speak. And Ericson just walked up to him ..." Donny ran his fingers across the stubble on his chin.

"It must have been horrible. I get that, but I still don't see what your problem is. He saved Scout's life. Maybe yours too." She could see the exhaustion in him, mental and physical. He just wasn't thinking clearly. Laurie counted the points off on her fingers as she listed them. "You said the guy was a scumbag. He was a dirty ex-cop. He was a pimp and a drug dealer. He'd just killed someone else. And you want to quibble about a couple of seconds one way or another when he dropped the razor?"

"But ..."

"There is no 'but.' Donny, I love you and I am so glad you're OK. But you need to get on the right side of this. You've never fired a weapon. I have, in Bosnia and Afghanistan." Laurie stood. She was dressed in her overalls, ready for her job as a supervisor with the city's works department, but she was speaking now as Sergeant Zhou, combat veteran. "Let me tell you, it's not like the movies. It's terrifying and horrible. The screaming, the smell of gunpowder and blood. The adrenalin is flowing, and it's life or death. It's not something you can just turn off instantly, like throwing a switch."

"Which is why there are rules, right?" Donny asserted.

"Rules written by people who sit behind desks. You complain about that all the time yourself." He made no reply. Laurie shook her head and sat back down. "I'll phone in sick if you want me to stay with you."

"No."

"Then how about talking to Eddy or Ratzo or someone?"

"They'll say the same as you."

"Lordy, Lordy, well, maybe that's a clue, eh? I'm going to be late." She walked around the table and kissed him on the cheek. "Tell the boys to get dressed. You need to leave to take them to school in fifteen minutes. Then you need to get some sleep."

Laurie walked around the kitchen, picking up her shoulder bag, lunch pail and car keys. Donny got up and stood by the side door that led to the driveway. "It's partly the way he said it. Like he assumed we would all go along with the coverup."

"It's not a coverup!" Laurie squeezed by him to get out the door. On the threshold, she turned and faced him. "Honest to God, Donny, you can be such a self-righteous prima donna sometimes. You need to get your personal feelings and your history with this guy out of the

way. You're not thinking clearly. Get some sleep—you'll feel better."
She yelled over Donny's shoulder, "Time to get dressed, boys! Love
you. See you tonight."

"Bye, Mom," came the distant reply, followed by the sound of
more bickering and virtual explosions.

Donny's phone rang. It was the SIU calling again. He sent the call
to voicemail and made another call.

Daya looked at the number displayed on the car's screen
and sighed.

Work. Damn.

She tapped the answer button on the steering wheel. "Singh."

"Hi, Sarge, it's Maxine. Sorry to bother you on your day off."

"No problem. What's up?"

"I'm on the desk today and there's this guy who's been calling for
you. Says he's a fire captain. Donny Robertson."

Daya puffed out her cheeks and blew out her breath in a long
stream. Had she imagined it? A spark? Something they had both
felt. Something they had both been mature and professional enough
to dismiss.

"You there?" the voice on the phone asked.

"Yeah, sorry, Max." Daya collected herself. "I think we got disconnected there for a moment. What did he want?"

"Your number. Of course, I didn't give it to him, but I said I'd pass
his along. I hope that's OK. He said it was important. I think he's one
of the firemen who was at the Ericson–Simpson thing last night."

Daya had been off duty last night, but she'd heard about the incident through police channels, both official and unofficial, and on the
news. One of her officers, Bill Ericson, was being hailed as a hero,
and for once the media weren't dumping on the police about a shooting. "Give me the number."

Maxine read it to her, and Daya repeated it to herself twice. "OK,
thanks, Max."

"How should I log this? Is it business or personal? I mean, it's none of my business, but ..."

Daya looked at the highway traffic whizzing around her—six lanes in each direction, thousands of people, all racing along with their own agenda. "I don't know." Daya did her best to adopt a friendly, conspiratorial tone. "Put it down as business, but unless someone specifically asks, let's keep it between you and me, OK?"

"You got it. He sounded like a nice guy."

"Don't they all at the beginning?"

"True," Maxine chuckled. "Well, have a nice day."

"I'm on my way to pick up my mother."

"Then have a nice day after that."

Daya pulled off the highway and found a spot in a Tim Hortons parking lot. She drew a deep breath, then dialled the number Maxine had given her.

Donny said he needed to talk to her in person. Daya suggested they meet at the Thirsty Sparrow later that afternoon. Donny pointed out that the place would be full of off-duty cops and firefighters. He was right, of course, and Daya knew the truth was never a barrier to a savoury rumour in either organization. Donny suggested they meet someplace less conspicuous.

"I have to drive my mother to the temple on Pape. Why don't we meet by the baseball diamond in Greenwood Park?" she suggested.

Guneet Singh had lived just long enough to see his daughter Daya graduate from police college. It was, he had said, the proudest day of his all-too-short life.

Before bringing his young family to Canada, Guneet had been a police officer in Punjab. It was a far less tolerant and inclusive time. Despite his experience, Guneet hadn't been accepted into the Toronto Police. He was too old, they said, too short. His English wasn't good enough. But he knew the real reason: he was a Sikh and wore his turban proudly.

Guneet Singh hadn't complained. Instead, he'd got a job driving a truck, then bought his own truck, which turned into a cartage business with several more trucks. All so his children could have better opportunities. It was a quietly extraordinary story, one repeated over and over in immigrant communities across the country. Miraculous but unnoticed.

Some in the Sikh community disapproved of a woman doing a "man's job." Daya's father did not. When Daya had come to him, seeking his advice about becoming a police officer, Guneet had given her his blessing and full support.

Daya's mother, Mita, on the other hand, always more traditional than her husband, had been less than enthusiastic about Daya's career choice.

Daya glanced across the car at her mother in the passenger seat. Mita had been less than enthusiastic about most of her choices, Daya reflected, from her refusal to accept an arranged marriage to her adoption of a secular life. Daya still treasured her Sikh heritage, but her faith in God had died with her father's sudden death from a brain aneurysm at only fifty-three. It was a theft she would never forgive.

They were driving along Gerrard Street East, through Little India, the neighbourhood where her parents had first settled when they arrived in Toronto. Though Mita now lived in a condo in Scarborough, she insisted on coming to the old temple on Pape Avenue to serve Langar, the traditional Sikh communal meal. At least it was only a couple of blocks from the park where Daya had arranged to meet Donny.

"Tell me again why you need to see this man?" Mita asked, as if reading Daya's mind.

"It's business, Mama. I told you, he's a fire captain. One of his crew was hurt at that call yesterday, the one I told you about," Daya explained. "I'm not sure exactly what it's about, but he's upset."

"Hmm, business!" The older woman dismissed the explanation with a wave of her hand. "So, you meet in a park instead of the police station?"

"It's not like we're sneaking around in some back alley, Mama. He's upset about something and asked if we could meet privately, that's all. I'm thirty-eight, Mama. I'm a woman, not a child. Anyway, I think he's married."

"Yes, you are a woman. That is why I worry. And I am not so old that I am a fool." Mita shook her head. "And you are still married, too ..."

"We have a separation agreement, Mama. It's over."

"A piece of paper. In the eyes of God these things are not so easily undone."

"We're here." Daya pulled the car to the curb across from a flat-fronted two-storey building. The temple, decorated with Sikh motifs in yellow and blue paint, was set among neat Edwardian row houses. The neighbourhood had always been working class, and over the past hundred years it had hosted wave after wave of immigrants. This temple and the mosque across the street were simply manifestations of its latest incarnation—symbols of the cosmopolitan, multicultural soup that Toronto had become.

Mita opened the car door but hesitated before she got out. "I understand, Daya. You think I don't, but I do. I have been alone these twelve years since your father died. And I am not made of stone. I know loneliness and desire. That's why you should come to temple with me."

Daya smiled weakly at her mother. "Mama ..."

"All right. You say this man is upset. Remember, men have great physical strength but inside they are weak. They cannot accept pain or suffering as we do. Or disappointment. Be careful."

The suffering of women was one of her mother's favourite themes. Daya knew she should be grateful. She had been raised to be a strong and independent woman; she had had opportunities her mother had never dared to dream of. And she knew her mother would never fully understand the world Daya lived in.

"Yes, Mama," Daya replied wearily. "Call me when you want me to pick you up."

She drove to the park, muttering to herself, more disturbed than she would like to admit because there was more than a grain of truth to what her mother had said. She parked the car and walked down the hill to the bleachers beside the baseball diamond.

Donny was waiting.

"It was like something out of *Dirty Harry*," Donny said when he had finished telling her his version of events.

"You're sure the guy had dropped the razor and was on the floor when Ericson shot him the second time?" At first Daya had been relieved to think about something other than her relationship with her mother, but this was just as unsettling.

"Yes, it wasn't like 'bang-bang.' He walked over and just blew the guy's brains out."

"Is that what you told the SIU?"

"No, I haven't talked to them. At least not yet." Donny hung his head. "But I didn't say anything about it in the Fire Report either. I just ... I just left it out."

He had thought talking with Daya would help clarify things, but now he just felt stupid and awkward. What did he expect from this schoolboy confession? Absolution? Praise? Motherly comfort?

"Do you mind if we get up and walk around?" Daya asked. "These metal bleachers are freezing."

They strolled past a group of Asian seniors doing tai chi. Horse-tail clouds flattened the November sky, and the wind fretted at the few leaves clinging stubbornly to the trees.

Daya took a deep breath and sighed. "You can sometimes tell which way an investigation is going to go. This one feels like it's going to wrap up clean. Everything I've heard sounds good. Well, for Ericson, that is. All the papers have his picture on the front page, with a headline that says 'hero.'"

"So you think I'm full of shit? Just being a troublemaker because of my beef with him?"

"No," Daya said, laying her hand lightly on his arm. "But it would be your word against everyone else's, trying to make a case that no one really wants to look at. And you've already made a statement in the Fire Report. That's a legal document, right? Trying to change your story now would put you in a very weak position."

Donny wasn't sure if he was more disappointed in himself for painting himself into a corner, or annoyed by Daya's rational pragmatism. The fact that she had logic on her side didn't make what she was saying any easier to take.

She continued gently but firmly, as if the time had finally come to explain to a child that Santa Claus was only a myth. "Aside from making you the odd man out, it's also a question of optics. Darrel Simpson was a dirty ex-cop who liked to cut women; he was also a convicted felon and a drug dealer. He was a murderer who had just brutally killed the guy who'd torched his grow op. Then he tried to kill a firefighter. And even if Ericson crossed the line, everyone is going to feel that Simpson got exactly what he deserved."

"Did he? Is that how the system works now? Optics and public opinion?" Donny didn't regret the question, but he did regret the edge of self-righteousness that crept into his voice. They stopped at the off-leash area, leaned on the fence and watched a pack of mutts merrily chasing each other.

"You don't think he got what he deserved?" Daya cocked an eyebrow. "I'm talking about justice, not procedure. I'm not so sure I'd want to be the one standing up for a piece of crap like Simpson on a point of order."

"So you think I should drop it."

She turned to face him. "Have you ever heard of Robert Peel?"

"Is he a cop?"

"Peel founded Scotland Yard in 1829. He's regarded as the father of modern policing. He's the reason British police officers are known as bobbies; Robert—Bobby, you know. Anyway, his principles are still taught today—among them, that the police are there to uphold the law, not to judge or punish anyone, and that violence is always a last resort. I don't like the idea of vigilante cops either, OK? It goes against everything I've ever been taught or believed. But you've got to look at this realistically. At best you might throw a wrench into the works, but they'll make it go away. If it ever came to a hearing, a good lawyer would have a field day with this. It would be you against the world, they'd bring up your history with Ericson, and you'd wind up looking like a fool."

Donny bit his lip and started back towards the baseball diamond. Daya watched him go. Her mother was right: men had great physical strength, but inside ... She ran to catch up with him and took his arm. "I'm sorry, Donny."

"It's OK." He stopped, and for a moment lost himself in her deep brown eyes. "I asked for the truth. It's not always pleasant. Thanks for your time—you've been very kind." He tried to smile.

Daya continued to hold onto his arm, some part of her wanting to comfort him. "Like I said before, that's what Daya means, 'kindness.'"

Donny placed his hands on her shoulders and kissed her lightly on the lips. She didn't respond, but neither did she pull away.

"Why did you do that?" she asked, keeping her voice carefully neutral.

"I ..." Donny swallowed hard and tried to read her expression. "I don't know. I didn't think you'd mind."

"Whether I mind or not is none of your business," she said, more angrily than she intended. She turned and walked back to her car, her mother's voice echoing in her head.

CHAPTER 10

THE TRANS PERSPECTIVE

"Stupid, stupid, stupid," Donny repeated to himself. "What were you thinking, you idiot?" He wasn't sure what bothered him more, his potential infidelity or the fact that he was talking to himself out loud.

He shook his head, started the Honda, and paused. He should probably just go home.

Home. Was it really?

He had moved in a few belongings and hung some tools in the garage, but it was really Laurie's house and probably always would be. The places he felt most comfortable were at the Lombard Street station and at the helm of his boat. The fire hall was a place of refuge and camaraderie, but it could never really be home. It wasn't his, any more than it was anyone else's. And as for the boat, *Red Bird* now lay in eternal darkness, six hundred feet down, at the bottom of Lake Huron.

At least the sense of rootlessness was familiar. Instinctively, he turned towards downtown, across the broad valley of the Don River, which had once formed Toronto's natural eastern boundary, and drove towards the city's gritty roots—the streets and back alleys that were, if not home, at least familiar turf.

The east side of Toronto's downtown had never fully surrendered to gentrification. The area south of Bloor Street between Yonge Street and the Don River still harboured students, the down and out, hipsters, addicts, artists and others who had spurned or been spurned by the monochromatic compromise of the suburbs.

It had always been home to immigrant communities: Scottish and Irish peasants two hundred years ago, and more recently, an eclectic mix of Somalis, Southeast Asians, and Sri Lankans, among others. The Gay Village was still centred at Church and Wellesley streets, but in recent years the Village had grown, both geographically and spiritually, from a refuge to a community that proudly proclaimed its queerness.

The area was also home to the Tenderloin. Though the active streets and blocks changed over the years as policing and neighbourhoods morphed, most of Toronto's sex workers who chose to ply their trade on the streets still worked within a fairly small area.

Donny began scanning as he turned onto Sherbourne. The street was a microcosm of the city: old Victorian homes, some converted into swank offices, others split into rooming houses. There were bland high-rises, public housing, trendy condos, and homeless shelters, all shoulder to shoulder. The people Donny saw reflected the mix: huddling on street corners, riding courier bikes, slumped on park benches, carrying purse dogs, or staring vacantly from porches.

She was several blocks further north than usual. Donny honked the horn and pulled the Honda to the curb. A tall woman wearing stilettos, tight turquoise slacks, and a short, white faux fur jacket turned and waved to him.

Donny had first met Terry shortly after he had joined the department, when Terry was still a young man desperately struggling with his sexuality. Donny still remembered trying to staunch the blood that flowed from those pale, delicate wrists. And then, two and a half years later, responding to another call when Terry, now she/her, had been found savagely beaten by a gang of skinheads. Donny and Terry's paths kept intersecting over the years and they had gradually become, if not best friends, at least companions in some shared destiny. She had become Donny's window on a world that, as a boy from a mining town in northern Ontario, Donny had never known. He in turn liked to think he had played some small part in the caterpillar-to-butterfly metamorphosis that had produced the happy, exuberant woman now walking towards him.

Donny rolled down the passenger window and leaned over. "Hey, Terry, how are you doing? Got a minute? I need a favour."

"For you, Donny, always." Terry leaned in the window, taking advantage of the opportunity to display her cleavage. "But actually, I'm not working right now. I'm on my way to meet a friend for lunch."

"It's not that kind of favour. But I'll make it worth your while." Donny fished in his wallet and pulled out a fifty.

"Oh, Donny, I thought we were friends," Terry pouted.

"We are, but time is money. And a girl's got to eat, right?"

"True." Terry took the bill. "You sure there's nothing else I can do for you? You wouldn't be the first fireman to come for a walk on the wild side."

"You know me, I'm kind of a meat and potatoes guy." Donny reached over and opened the passenger door. "Where are you headed? I'll give you a lift."

"Bloor Street." Terry slid into the passenger seat. "You can't blame me for asking. You never know until you try."

"If I ever decide to switch teams, you will be the first to know. That I promise."

"We're all on the same team, darling. Some of us just have better uniforms." Terry winked and gave Donny's leg a squeeze. "You recruiting for a trans fire crew?"

Donny put the car in gear and pulled away from the curb. "I never thought about it, but that's not a bad idea. You'd have to trim your nails, though." Donny looked down at the hand that still rested on his thigh. It was tipped with inch-long blue nails, each inset with a sparkling gold lightning bolt. Donny continued, "Actually, I'm more interested in cops right now than firefighters."

"Cops?" Terry pulled her hand back.

"Yeah. You know anything about a cop by the name of Bill Ericson?"

"Ericson? Isn't he the one who shot Darrel Simpson? I saw his picture on the news. He saved a firefighter too, or something like that. Quite the hero."

"Yup, that's the guy." Donny tried to relax his grimace.

"Well, I can tell you that none of the girls are going to shed a tear over Darrel Simpson. You know about him?" Terry asked.

"I heard he was a real creep. He liked to cut people."

"And burn, and beat. 'Creep' is putting it mildly. Like I said, no one's going to miss Simpson."

They stopped at a red light, and Donny turned to face Terry. "What about Ericson? You ever hear anything on the street about him?"

"You're being very serious, Donny, even for you, and that's saying something."

"I need to make a decision. And it's not going to win me any popularity contests."

"A decision. About Ericson?"

Donny nodded. The light turned green and he accelerated through the intersection.

Terry thought for a moment. "There's not much to tell—at least, not that I've heard. I guess he's as honest as most of them. Word gets around pretty fast if a cop takes advantage or rips someone off."

"No intimidation? No *Dirty Harry* shit?"

Terry shook her head. "Nothing that comes to mind."

"Really? Nothing?"

"I don't keep detailed personnel files on every cop in the district." Terry frowned. "Jeez, Donny, you know what it's like—any day you don't get beat up by a john or ripped off by some punk or hassled by the cops is a good day."

Donny raised a hand in surrender. "I know, it's rough out there. I'm just asking, that's all."

"You've always been good to me, Donny, even when I wasn't being very good to myself." Terry's finger traced the scars on her wrist below the cuff of her jacket.

Donny ran his hand over the burn scars and skin grafts that showed above his own collar. "I think of them as badges of survival."

"Yes." Terry looked out the window. "I can ask around, if you want."

"Thank you. I'd appreciate that." They drove the rest of the way in silence.

Donny pulled over just south of Bloor Street. "I don't want it getting back to Ericson. Try to be discreet."

"Donny, darling, I'm nothing if not discreet. Call me in a couple of days. You have my number, right? I'll see what I can find." Terry opened the door and stepped out. She blew Donny a kiss as he pulled away.

Donny was halfway home when his phone rang. The SIU again. There was no sense putting it off any longer.

"So Darrel Simpson was holding a razor to Patrick's throat when the elevator doors opened. Is that right?" the older officer asked, the one who had introduced himself as Bud Sallipo. He was sorting through a stack of folders on the table in front of him.

"Yes," Donny mumbled, leaning back in the ergonomic chair.

"Can you please sit a little closer? And speak up." Crawford, the younger officer, pointed to the recorder in front of Donny.

Donny sat up and folded his hands in his lap. The three men were seated in a small conference room at SIU headquarters, a squat office building fronted with textured concrete and dark glass, across the highway from Toronto's Pearson Airport. The regular rumble of planes taking off and landing was far from the top of Donny's list of irritations.

"Did Constable Ericson say anything?" asked Crawford. Donny looked out the window at a plane on final approach. "Captain Robertson? What did he say?"

"I don't remember exactly, but he and Simpson obviously knew each other."

"Did Ericson tell him to surrender or drop the razor?" It was Sallipo again.

"I think so."

"You think so? It's a simple thing. Did Ericson tell Simpson to surrender or not?"

Donny picked at a loose thread on the cuff of his shirt. "He said a lot of shit—smack-talk mostly. I guess he was stalling for time."

Crawford leaned forward in his chair. "So Ericson was trying to de-escalate the situation."

"I don't know." Donny threw his hands in the air. "It was pretty clear they didn't like each other. I wasn't taking notes, OK?"

Sallipo poured water from a carafe into a plastic glass and slid the glass across the table to Donny. "How long was the verbal exchange between Ericson and Simpson?"

"I wasn't looking at my watch. I was trying to keep my guy from getting killed."

"Just an estimate. Short? Long?" Sallipo asked.

"It seemed like forever." Donny shook his head. "I don't know, maybe thirty or forty seconds."

Crawford nodded. "So there was time for Simpson to surrender, but he kept holding the razor to Patrick's throat."

"Yes." Donny closed his eyes briefly and saw again the steel blade glinting against the tender freckled skin of Scout's neck. He shook his head and opened his eyes. "Ericson said killing Scout, uh, Patrick, would only make things worse. Simpson made it clear he wasn't going back to prison."

Sallipo opened a folder and scanned the contents. "Did Ericson have his gun drawn while he was talking to Simpson?"

"I think so. Yes, he was behind the elevator door, but he had his pistol like this." Donny mimed holding a gun up, in front of his chest.

"Then what happened?"

"Eddy and Moose came in through the other stairwell door. That surprised Simpson, and he turned to look. That's when Ericson shot him."

"The first shot," said Sallipo.

"Yes. It was really loud."

"And ...?" Sallipo urged Donny to continue.

"He shot him again."

Crawford narrowed his eyes. A warning, Donny wondered?

"Where was Ericson when he fired the second shot?" Sallipo asked.

"Scout was bleeding." Donny clung to the simple truth like a drowning man.

Sallipo closed the file he was holding. "Was Ericson still in the elevator when he fired the second shot?"

Donny shifted his gaze between the two investigators and took a sip of water from the plastic glass. "I don't know," he said in a barely audible voice.

"Look," Sallipo said. "Darrel Simpson was a violent, dirty ex-cop. That's in the public record. Nobody's going to miss him. But if there's something you need to tell us ..."

They knew. And they knew he knew. Did they really want the truth, or were they just trying to see how far out on the limb he would go before they cut it off?

"One of my men almost died. Do you know what that's like?" Donny stammered.

"Yes. Yes, I do," Crawford answered coolly. He took a file from the stack of folders in front of Sallipo and opened it. "Have you had any other recent interactions with Constable Ericson?"

There it was. Daya had told him which way the wind was blowing; Donny just hadn't wanted to believe her. "I was at the call when

Ericson's partner, Randy Copeland, was killed. You've probably got the details right there in front of you."

Crawford closed the file. "Yes, a real tragedy, that one. You've had a string of tough calls. Very stressful. Is there anything you want to add?"

Donny shook his head.

CHAPTER 11

AUDITION

"And the second shot?" Humphrey asked, keeping his eyes on the road ahead.

"Like I told the SIU, as he fell, he was trying to cut Scout, or whatever his name is. I had to fire again. I think all the statements back that up."

Humphrey gave Ericson a tired look. "Lie to me one more time, and you're out."

Ericson sat tight-lipped in the passenger seat, his arms folded across his chest.

"The rest of the Committee wanted to dump you like a hot potato," Humphrey continued. "I convinced them to give you another chance. Now, what really happened?"

Ericson looked out the window at the puddles of pale yellow street light bleeding onto the wet pavement. A jogger pounded the sidewalk towards them, hair slicked down, her face set in ecstatic determination. A solitary dog walker bundled against the drizzle stepped aside to let her pass.

"You know Simpson's record?" Ericson asked after a minute. Humphrey nodded. "He set me up, tried to make it look like I was the one on the take, running girls and shit. Fortunately, Internal Affairs had been tapping his phone. But it still took months for me to get cleared.

"But beyond that, Darrel Simpson was a piece of shit. What do you do with a rabid dog?" Ericson turned to face Humphrey. "You want me to say it? OK, I stepped up and put a bullet in his head. And I'm not going to apologize. The world is a better place without him. Isn't that what you were talking about last week?"

"In a way, yes, but that's not how we operate. For one thing, we cannot afford to bring that kind of attention to ourselves. You need to understand that." Humphrey turned the car onto a residential side street. In summer it would be canopied with green; now the bare branches formed a tangled black web silhouetted against the grey mist of the city's glow.

"Sure, I understand," Ericson nodded. He tried to keep track of where they were as Humphrey wove the car through the side streets.

"We're not a gang of cowboy vigilantes," Humphrey continued. "We follow set procedures, and we look at all the facts. Nothing is done without due deliberation. We select only the most egregious cases, and we act only when we are absolutely certain. We operate outside the law, but our aim is justice. We are trying to correct a broken system that has become soft and corrupted because of loopholes that give the criminals all the breaks.

"The legal system is based on deterrence. Hell, even the criminals use fear and deterrence. We don't. The Committee is beyond deterrence. There is only one sentence, and it is used not to punish, but to remove the cancers in our society. However, our goal is always justice—real justice. Not revenge. Personal feelings have to be kept out of it. You got that?"

"OK, OK, I get it," Ericson agreed earnestly. He was getting tired of the lecture. "How did you know?"

"About Simpson? I'm a platoon chief. I got firefighters lying to me every day. Believe me, they're some of the best liars in the world. If I didn't have a nose for it, I'd drown in bullshit," Humphrey chuckled.

"Besides, Superintendent Collins told me the ballistics angles were a little peculiar."

Humphrey turned to check the intersection at a stop sign. He saw Ericson tense. "Don't worry. Like you said, the statements all line up. Donny's a bit of an issue, but it's not a big deal."

"Robertson?" Ericson spat the name out. "What the hell is his problem?"

"Donny's a bit of a Boy Scout," Humphrey replied. "He's a good firefighter, but he can also be a pain in the ass on matters of principle. Don't worry about it. He'll come around."

"Whatever," Ericson sneered dismissively. "So besides you and Collins, who else is on this Committee? Do I get to meet them?"

"There are two sides of the Committee: planning and operations. We keep them separate for everyone's protection. Bob Collins and I run the operations side of things. You'll meet some of the others in that group once you've got some skin in the game." Humphrey pulled the car to the curb. They came to a stop amidst the broken shards of a Hallowe'en pumpkin rotting in the gutter.

"Well then, how do I get some skin in the game?"

"What do you think we're doing out here tonight?" Humphrey opened the car door. "Get the bag out of the trunk."

Dundas and Sherbourne, the corner of crack and pipe. It was an area Roxanne knew all too well. She recognized some of the faces peering out of the shadows, the bodies huddled in the doorways, trying to stay out of the rain, trying to make it through one more night. It was all so pointless.

Depression was part of withdrawal—she knew that from the time she had gone to treatment. But she had been back on the stuff for only a few weeks, so it wasn't as bad this time. They had kept her in a nice room for several days while she detoxed. How many days she wasn't sure. She had slept a lot.

When she wasn't sleeping, there were the endless questions. "Tell us about Ramón. Describe him to us. Where does he go? Who does he hang out with?" Over and over and over, the same questions.

They hadn't hurt her, had barely even touched her. Still, she was afraid of them. They had made it very clear that trying to run would be a serious mistake. "Tell us about Ramón."

They'd pumped her full of vitamins and fed her fresh, healthy food. "Tell us about Ramón."

Physically, she was feeling better. She'd even put on a little weight. They bought her a couple of nice outfits and promised her a fresh start and a new life if she did what they wanted. "Tell us about Ramón."

This wasn't regular police procedure. This was something else entirely. That much she knew. "Tell us about Ramón."

This evening Collins had picked her up and they had gone for a drive. It was good to be out of that claustrophobic little room and away from the endless questions. But now here she was back in the old 'hood, back in the same rat-shit, dead-end world. Ramón had paid off her pimp and got her off the street, but here she was again. And it looked exactly the same. It was all so pointless.

Collins pulled over. He was asking her something. "That's your old corner, right?"

Roxanne looked around. There was the church behind them, the variety store on the north side. "Yeah, that's it, but I think somebody else works it now."

"Not anymore. Let's go." They got out of the car and crossed the street. It was a cold, wet night and business was slow; most of the other girls who worked the area had quit early. The few who remained, farther down the street, looked at Roxanne and Collins briefly with idle curiosity, then turned their attention back to the passing cars.

"The word is out. No one is going to bother you." When they reached the corner, Collins handed her a cell phone. "If anyone does hassle you, call the first number on the list—Allan. OK?"

"Who's Allan?"

"It doesn't matter. Just leave a message. I want you out here every afternoon and every evening, no matter what, OK? Business as usual," Collins stated.

"That's it?" Roxanne asked.

"No. You talk to people. You find out anything you can about Ramón, or Carlos, or whatever his street name is. But you do it real casual, like. You don't just ask, 'Where's Carlos?' You chit chat for a while first. Or maybe they bring it up and ask you about him. And you say, 'No, he disappeared. Have you heard anything?'

"Anything you find out, even the smallest, most insignificant thing; if you hear he caught a cold or bought a pair of shoes, you call Allan and leave a message. You're to call in once a day whether you hear anything or not."

"OK." Roxanne turned her collar up and turned her back to the wind.

"Anyone you talk to, you get them to face across the street. Like this." Collins stood facing the variety store on the opposite corner.

"You got a camera over there or something?"

"Something," Collins replied. "If they're looking another way, you move around so that they're facing the store. It's for your protection too, OK?"

"Sure," Roxanne agreed. She liked the idea of protection, but Collins and his friends didn't make her feel a whole lot safer.

"And you don't do cars, either. We got you a place. Come with me." They walked a few doors up the street to a three-storey red brick building. Collins opened the front door, then handed her a set of keys.

"Number six, on the ground floor." The hallway smelled of stale cooking, stale tobacco and stale lives.

It was a sparsely furnished bachelor apartment. There was a bed. A box of condoms rested on the night stand, and two faded posters were tacked to the wall on either side of the bed.

"That's nice." Roxanne smiled and pointed to the poster on the left. "I like kittens."

Collins found the remark strangely disconcerting.

"There's milk and cheese, a loaf of bread and some apples in the fridge." Collins pointed to the kitchenette in the corner. There was a small counter with a sink, microwave and coffee maker. "There's some soup and stuff in the cupboard."

"Great, thanks." It wasn't fancy, but she had lived in far worse places.

"The main thing is, everything happens in here. Got it?"

"You got cameras in here too?" Roxanne looked around the room, trying to spot where they might be hidden. "You guys making porn or something?" She mimed jerking off.

Collins ignored the taunt. "We just want you to be safe. Cars aren't safe."

"I'm so touched by your concern," she snarled. The depression morphed into anger and boiled to the surface. "That's why you kidnapped me and grilled me, and now you're putting me back out on the street. 'Cause you're so goddamned concerned about my safety and well-being."

"You can go to jail if you'd rather. Killing a cop is a minimum of twenty-five years," Collins replied evenly. "And don't even think about trying to skip town."

She didn't doubt they were tracking her. Maybe they'd planted some kind of chip in her while she slept. She'd seen stuff like that in the movies. Roxanne sat on the bed. It was all so pointless.

"Any questions?" Collins moved to the door.

"What about the money?"

"It's yours. You can keep it all. In a week or two, if this works out, you'll never have to turn another trick again. It's up to you."

That was one bright point. At least she wouldn't be spreading her legs so some pimp could drive around in a fancy car and play the big shot.

"You want to try it out?" She managed to say it almost shyly, patting the bed beside her. She had no illusions of tenderness; she just wanted a little human contact, to feel like something more than just a pawn in some gambit.

Collins turned away and opened the door to leave. "I had a daughter about your age. She was a nice girl."

And you're a dirty little whore. He hadn't said it aloud. He didn't have to.

CHAPTER 12

PIZZA DELIVERY

"Should I ask how you got keys to this building?" Ericson asked as he and Humphrey stepped into the empty lobby. They had walked several blocks from where they had left the car to a group of high-rise apartment buildings.

"The superintendent had a little problem with his parole. He decided he'd rather not go back to prison. Wait here." Humphrey disappeared down the hall to the garbage room and came back a moment later with an empty pizza box from the recycle bin.

"Everyone likes pizza," he said, pressing the button for the elevator. They waited in silence.

They stepped into the elevator. Humphrey pressed the button for the eighth floor. The hallway was empty when they got off. They moved to the stairwell and let the door close behind them.

"Are you going to tell me what we're doing?" Ericson had been feeding off the older man's quiet confidence, but he was beginning to feel uneasy.

"Give me that." Humphrey took the gym bag Ericson had been carrying and handed Ericson the pizza box. Opening the bag, he took out two pairs of leather gloves and handed one to Ericson.

"There are security cameras in the lobby and one in each elevator," he said as he pulled on his gloves. "There are none in the hallways or in the stairways between floors. As far as the cameras are concerned, we went to the eighth floor. We'll walk up two from here. Just a precaution."

"Yeah, but ..." Ericson wasn't sure how to phrase his question.

Humphrey listened to the echoing silence for a moment to make sure they were alone in the stairwell. "You remember a few months back, a guy ran over a woman pushing a stroller on the sidewalk? Killed the kid and dragged the woman for three hundred feet before he smashed into a telephone pole."

"Yeah, I remember that," Ericson replied as they started up the stairs.

"It wasn't his first DUI. Right now, he's out on bail. He might get ten years, out in five. We're going to make sure it doesn't happen again. You're going to be the strong, silent type. Just follow my lead."

Humphrey cracked the door to the tenth floor hallway and peered out. The hallway was empty. They stepped out of the stairwell and walked to apartment 1012. Humphrey motioned for Ericson to stand aside, then knocked on the door.

"Who is it?" Light flickered behind the peephole.

"Pizza!" Humphrey held the box in front of him and smiled.

"I didn't order a pizza," replied the voice behind the door.

Humphrey examined the slip taped to the lid of the box. "Apartment ten twelve? Well, someone ordered a pizza and it's paid for. You want a pizza or not?"

There was the sound of a latch turning. The door opened a few inches, revealing a man's face. "Listen, I didn't ..." the man began.

Humphrey pushed the door the rest of the way open.

"Hey!" the man protested as Humphrey stepped inside.

"Hay is for horses, Jason."

Jason retreated when he saw Ericson's bulk filling the doorway behind Humphrey. The two of them stepped into the apartment and closed the door behind them.

"I'm going to call the cops!" Jason said. A slight man in his mid-thirties, he was dressed for an evening at home in a plaid flannel shirt over sweat pants. His fine features were emphasized by a ponytail and a narrow, closely cropped beard.

"Don't you think you've already got enough trouble with the police, Jason? I mean, killing that woman and her kid? Such a tragedy." Humphrey watched the colour drain from Jason's face.

"It was ... I ... You better go," Jason stammered. "My brother, he'll be home any minute now."

"He should be here, shouldn't he?" Humphrey agreed. "I mean, that was one of the conditions for your bail—that you live with your brother. But your brother actually moved in with his girlfriend, didn't he?"

Humphrey strode past Jason and took a seat at the table next to the kitchen. "Judges take a very dim view of people who violate their bail conditions. Come, have a seat."

Jason looked like he'd been struck by lightning. He sagged against the wall. "Who are you? What do you want?"

"I'm Tom, and this is Bill. You can think of this as a sort of intervention. Sit down." Humphrey indicated the chair across from him. Jason made his way uneasily to the table, glancing back over his shoulder at Ericson standing in front of the closed door. Humphrey beckoned to Ericson and held out his hand; Ericson handed him the bag he had been carrying.

"Don't worry about Bill," Humphrey said. "He won't hurt you as long as you do as we say." Humphrey nodded towards an armchair by the hall that led to the apartment door. Ericson sat, guarding the only exit.

The place had a sort of IKEA look of impermanence about it. A worn angular couch sat across from Ericson beside the sliding door to the balcony. The brass plating was peeling from the glass-topped coffee table in front of the couch. A few empty takeout containers lay scattered about. A couple of nondescript framed pictures were the only decorations. The wall next to Ericson was dominated by a large TV.

"What do I have to do?" Jason asked warily.

"What you do best," Humphrey smiled. He reached into the bag and brought out a bottle of rye, a glass and a bottle of Coke. "Have a drink."

Jason's eyes widened and he pushed his chair back. "I quit. I'm in recovery now, going to meetings and everything." His voice trembled; his eyes fixed on the liquor bottle. Jason fished in his pocket and brought out a yellow plastic disc with black lettering. He held it up to show Humphrey and Ericson. "See, my two-month chip. I've been sober for two months now."

"Yes, but you've done that before, haven't you, Jason?" Humphrey said, filling the glass half full of rye and topping it up with Coke. "Every time you get arrested you sober up for a few months. But you always end up going back, don't you? You smash another car and send someone else to the hospital—or in this case, a mother and her baby to the morgue."

"It's only twice before," Jason said defensively. He stared intently at the glass. He watched tiny bubbles form, cling for a moment to the side of the glass, then surrender to the inevitable.

"It's only twice you've been convicted, but this is the fifth time you've been charged for drunk driving. Isn't that right, Jason? It's nice to have a family that can afford the best lawyers money can buy, isn't it? No matter how many people you cripple or kill." Humphrey slid the glass across the table to Jason. He watched Jason's nose twitch as the whiskey fumes rose to him.

"I didn't mean to. I didn't want to hurt anybody!" Jason protested.

"But you go back to drinking and driving anyway, don't you? And now you've killed two innocent people, one of them just a year old."

"I need to go." Jason stood up to leave. Ericson rose immediately and moved to block the door.

"Sit down!" Humphrey commanded. Jason looked at the two men, desperation in his eyes, then down at the glass of rye and Coke on the table. He sat slowly.

"Good," Humphrey said more gently. "Now, if you do as we say, this will be the last drink you'll ever have. That's what you want, isn't it?"

"Really?"

"Absolutely," Humphrey nodded. "But we're going to talk truth, Jason. We're going to talk about the things you've done, and it isn't going to be fun. But I promise you'll never drink again. So go ahead and have that drink. Bill here will have one with you." Humphrey pulled another glass from the bag and poured. "I'd drink with you myself, but I'm driving. And drinking and driving is something I just don't do."

Ericson walked to the table and took the glass from Humphrey. It was mostly Coke. He raised the glass to Jason. "Cheers," he said, and took a sip.

"Go ahead," Humphrey smiled encouragingly at Jason. "I know you want to. We have some tough work to do and it will help you relax."

Ericson returned to the armchair. It was fascinating to watch the old man work.

Jason closed his eyes for a moment, then seized the glass and drained half of it in one gulp. He slammed the glass back on the table, scattering a constellation of glistening brown drops. The whiskey coursed through every fibre in his body like a bomb exploding in slow motion. It was soothing. It was terrifying. It was everything he had always wanted. And he wanted more.

Humphrey topped up the glass. "That's good. Drink up!"

"Two months," Jason murmured, taking another swig. He set the glass down more gently this time. "I had two months."

"Don't worry about it," Humphrey waved away his concern. "So tell me, Jason, why do you do it?"

"I don't know." Jason turned the glass around and around in his hand, then drank deeply again. "It's the only thing that stops the noise inside my head."

Humphrey filled the glass once more, then pulled a prescription container from his pocket. He shook out two tablets and passed them to Jason. "Take these."

"What are they?"

"It's part of the program, Jason. Just take them. Now tell me about growing up."

Humphrey kept pouring as Jason rattled on about expectations he could never satisfy, about a home that was an emotional wasteland, about never fitting in, and about how the booze filled that big empty space inside.

"Yes, but none of that explains why you would get in a car and run down an innocent young woman and her child." Humphrey confronted him when a third of the whiskey in the bottle was gone.

Jason put his head in his hands. "I didn't mean to. I never wanted to hurt anyone," he protested. "I don't even remember it. All I remember is sitting in the back of the police car."

"No? Why don't you take a look at these?" Humphrey pulled some photos out of the gym bag and passed them across the table. Jason looked at the first two and dropped them as if his hands had been burned. The outline of the body was vaguely human, but it looked more like someone had dumped the contents of a butcher's counter.

"I don't wanna ..." He was beginning to slur his words. "Why are you doing this?"

"Time to take responsibility, Jason. What do you think it felt like, eh? Being dragged underneath the car, screaming?"

"Why are you doing this to me?" Jason cried. He staggered to his feet, but Ericson was behind him in an instant and forced him back down into the chair. "Let me go. I don't want to do this anymore!"

"Emma's husband—that was her name, Jason: Emma. Her husband couldn't even identify the body. Only what was left of her clothes.

They had to use dental records to be sure. He has to live with that every day, Jason," Humphrey said emphatically. "Why shouldn't you?"

"Not to mention the paramedics and cops and firefighters who had to clean it all up," Ericson added, still standing behind Jason's chair.

"Good point," Humphrey nodded.

"I'm going to jail," Jason moaned. "They said I'm going to jail for sure this time. OK? Does that make you happy?" he added peevishly.

"Not really," Humphrey shrugged. "You want to make it right? Then you've got to take responsibility. That's how it works, right? You make amends for the things you've done."

"How?"

Humphrey poured him another drink, then produced a note pad and pen from the bag. "How about writing an apology to Emma's husband? That would be a good start."

"I can't!"

"Sure you can. It will make you feel much better. I'll help you. Take a drink to steady yourself and write exactly what I tell you." Humphrey hoped he hadn't overdone it—that Jason wasn't too drunk to write legibly.

Jason took another swig and took hold of the pen and paper. "OK, I'll try. What's his name?"

"Don't worry about that. I'll address it. Just write what I tell you." Humphrey moved beside Jason and began to dictate slowly. "I'm so sorry. I've hurt so many people ..."

"I didn't mean to hurt anyone. I want to write that." Jason said, looking up from the paper.

"That's good. Yes, add that in." Humphrey waited for Jason to finish writing. "We're going to keep it short and sweet, OK? It sounds more sincere if you don't ramble on, so just end with this: 'Please forgive me. The pain is more than I can live with.'" Again, Humphrey waited for Jason to finish writing. "Good. Now sign it."

Humphrey took the pad and looked at it. The writing was sloppy but legible. "Good. That was very good. How do you feel now?"

Jason gave him a rubbery, drunken grin. "Better. I don't know. I feel kinda funny. What was in those pills?"

"How about some fresh air? That will perk you up. Help him, will you, Bill?" Humphrey opened the sliding door to the balcony, and Ericson half supported, half carried Jason out.

They stood on either side of him as Jason leaned on the railing, marvelling at the panorama of city lights spread out before him. Humphrey motioned with his head and Ericson nodded. They grabbed Jason by the pant legs and heaved.

Jason didn't make a sound on the way down. He was suddenly, wonderfully weightless as the lights of the city cartwheeled around him. He was light, so very light …

There was a dull, soggy thud as Jason landed on the wet grass at the back of the building. He lay face up, the misty rain beading on his forehead as his vacant eyes stared up into the night.

Humphrey left the glass, the whiskey, the bottle of pills and the notepad on the table; everything else went back into the gym bag. They set the door to lock behind them and headed back down the stairs to the eighth floor.

"What were those pills?" Ericson asked when they were alone in the elevator.

"Oxys," Humphrey said. "It's a nice combo for a suicide autopsy."

They didn't speak again until they were back at the car.

"I wonder," Ericson began as they threaded their way back home. "I wonder if he really was going to get sober this time."

Humphrey glanced over at him. "And what if he didn't? What if he got out in a few years and killed someone else? Even if he did stay sober, that doesn't change a thing. That doesn't bring that woman or her kid back."

"I was just wondering, that's all."

Humphrey pulled the car to the curb again and put it in park. He turned to face Ericson, looking him straight in the eye. "You know what the two most important jobs in the city are?"

"I got a feeling you're not going to say cops and firefighters."

"You're right. Things would be a little more chaotic without us, but life would go on. The same with lawyers, bankers, stockbrokers, even doctors. None of them are indispensable. But sewage workers and garbage men? They do what most people aren't willing to do. It's dirty work and they don't get a lot of respect, but without them we'd drown in our own filth.

"That's who we are, Bill. You want to be a social worker, go join the John Howard Society."

Ericson didn't reply. Humphrey put the car back in gear and drove on.

"I guess," Ericson said, a few minutes later, "I guess that means I've got some skin in the game now."

CHAPTER 13

THE ATTIC

"Wow! Did you see this?" Moose asked. They were parked at the far end of the grocery store parking lot. Eddy and Scout had gone in to buy supplies for supper. Moose sat in the driver's seat, scrolling through his phone. Donny sat next to him in the captain's seat, watching in the side mirror as a trucker backed his rig into the grocery store's loading dock.

"See what?" Donny asked.

"Remember that drunk driver who killed a woman and her kid?" Moose asked. He held up his phone to show Donny the news feed. "Dragged them, like, a block and a half down the street? Looks like he got drunk one more time and fell off his apartment balcony."

"And the world's a better place without him, right? Just like Darrel Simpson."

"The guy was going to kill Scout." Moose put his phone down and looked across at Donny. "I think you did the right thing."

"Ya? Then why doesn't it feel like it?" Donny scowled. He had made his statement to the SIU. He hadn't outright lied, it was more a sin of omission, but that didn't really make him feel any better.

"Doesn't feel right, or doesn't feel comfortable?" Moose asked. "They're not always the same thing."

"When did you become such a philosopher?"

Moose shifted his bulk sideways so he could look directly at Donny. "Remember that call we had a couple of weeks ago? The one where Grandma went face down in the mashed potatoes?"

"What about it?"

"By the book we should have gone full court press, right?"

Donny shrugged. "It wasn't a legally valid DNR, it was just the old lady's wishes not to be revived. I mean, the family all backed it up, but there was no doctor's signature, so legally, it wasn't valid."

"But you accepted it anyway. Were you comfortable with that?" Moose asked.

Donny pursed his lips and tapped his fingers on the truck's mobile data terminal beside him. "It's tricky. Those things can come back to haunt you if someone changes their mind. There's liability and lawsuits ... if it went to court, I'd be screwed."

"But it was the right decision," Moose nodded. "The old lady was, what, ninety-three or ninety-four? She'd already had a couple of strokes. If we'd started doing CPR on her we would have broken every rib, driven broken ribs through her lungs, the whole family would have freaked out and been traumatized. It just would have made a bad situation worse. The same thing with this. In the end, what do you accomplish? It's not like Ericson's some rogue cop shooting people in the street."

"Well, it's over with now, anyway." Donny waved the matter away. "Remember the daughter-in-law at that call?"

"Lord thunderin'," Moose said, affecting an East Coast accent, "how are we going to get the gravy stains out of her good dress for the funeral?"

They both laughed, then lapsed into silence.

"So how are things with you and Q?" Donny asked, as they sat staring out through the windshield.

"Fine," Moose replied. "How's Laurie?"

"Good, yeah, great." Donny cracked his window open for some fresh air. "It's kinda funny, isn't it? A couple of old bachelors like us ending up with instant families. Is it what you expected?"

"I had no idea what to expect. It's certainly different, I'll tell you that much." Moose wondered where Donny was going with this, but his speculation was cut short by the dispatch tones from the radio. Donny wrote down the details and verified they matched the information on the data terminal. Moose started the engine.

Scout and Eddy ran to the truck, threw their grocery bags into the back, and wriggled into their fire gear as Moose pulled the truck out into traffic.

It was a row house: five attached dwellings with a common attic. The first alarm crews were in the southernmost house, fighting the fire where it had originated. Most of the open flames had been extinguished, but the walls inside the house still radiated heat like an oven. The fire had been well established. Having lost its battle in the open, it had retreated into the walls and ceilings, inside the old lath and plaster, playing cat and mouse with the crews.

Donny stepped down from the truck and eyed the smoke that was starting to chuff from the eaves above the other houses. Modern building codes required fire separations between attached dwellings, even in the roof spaces, but those codes hadn't existed when these houses were built. Ratzo was looking in the same direction and scowling as Donny approached. If the fire took hold in the common attic they could lose all five houses.

"Want us up there, Chief?" Donny asked.

"Yeah," Ratzo replied, glancing sideways at Donny. "Seven Aerial's setting up for ventilation on the roof. I want you to try get a line to the attic in the middle house. We should be able to stop it."

Donny threaded his way through the growing mass of curious onlookers that inevitably gathered at such events, and headed back to his truck to gather his crew and the equipment they would need. Bill Ericson was a few metres beyond the truck. If he had seen Donny, he made no move to acknowledge him. Donny decided to do the same. Ericson and several other police officers were trying to control the crowd, shepherding them to the end of the block and setting up barrier tape. Donny wondered briefly if Ericson would shoot those who didn't readily comply, then dismissed the thought. It was childish. And it was a distraction. The task at hand required his full attention. The past was done. With any luck he would never have to deal directly with Ericson again.

Donny and Eddy stacked several folded, preconnected lengths of 45mm hose on their shoulders and made their way into the middle house. The hose would become stiff and unwieldy once it was charged, but empty, it unfolded and trailed away easily behind them as they wound their way up the stairs. Scout followed with the attic ladder.

They located the attic hatch in an upstairs closet. Scout set the ladder in position, and Donny climbed up and pushed aside the painted plywood board that covered the opening. Dark smoke puffed down through the black hole over his head. Donny and Eddy sniffed cautiously. It was mostly wood smoke, only faintly tinged with tar. The fire had not yet eaten too deeply into the roof structure.

They donned their SCBA face pieces, turned on their tanks and listened for the familiar sequence of electronic chirps that indicated everything was functioning properly.

Donny turned to his junior man. "You're with me. We got one way in and one way out. Stay on the hose line and keep your weight on the joists—the ceiling won't hold you. OK?"

"OK," Scout answered impatiently. "Let's go!"

Donny took two steps up the ladder, then glanced back down. "Eddy ..."

"I'm your anchor," Eddy confirmed. He would stay on the ladder. Someone needed to feed the hose up from below and mark the location of the hatch. Even in such a confined space, it was easy to get turned around, especially when you couldn't see. Until the aerial crew opened up the roof, that tiny opening would be their only escape route if things went bad.

Donny climbed up into the darkness of the attic. It was hot and there was no room to stand. He bent over double in the cramped space and reached out into the void, running his hand along the roof boards over his head. Between the smoke and the darkness, he couldn't see a thing. The attic hatch was a faint square of light at his feet, and the beam of his flashlight penetrated only a few centimetres into the murk in front of him.

Donny took the hose when it was passed up to him, then moved to make room for Scout to climb up. He reached out, feeling for the joist that had to be there, twenty-four inches on centre. He could hear the whine of a chainsaw overhead, two houses over, where the aerial crew was cutting a ventilation hole in the roof over the fire. That would get rid of most of the smoke and heat, and help limit the fire's advance.

Scout climbed up behind Donny.

"Come on up here beside me and take the nozzle," Donny said, giving the young firefighter the position of pride. Scout took the nozzle and cautiously moved forward into the dark void in front of him. There was fire up ahead. They could feel the heat flooding back at them, though the smoke obscured everything.

"Brace yourself, I'm gonna tell Moose to charge the line." Donny radioed down to Moose. The line bucked and stiffened as the water rushed towards them. "OK, now open it slowly and let the air out."

"I know what I'm doing," Scout said irritably. There was the sound of hissing air as Scout opened the bail on the nozzle. He rocked backwards in reaction to the force of the water when it reached them, but Donny was there backing him up. Scout shut the nozzle and steadied himself.

"Spread your legs," Donny instructed. "One foot on the joist in front, the other behind. Brace your shoulders against the roof and give it a shot." This time there was no protest from Scout.

The water hit the fire and turned instantly into steam. The heat pressed back hard on them. Even through their bunker suits, the effect was like someone had just dumped a pail of water on the rocks in a sauna.

"Holy shit!" Scout exclaimed, shutting off the nozzle again.

"You're OK. There's a little more fire there than I thought. Sit down on one of the joists, and just give it short bursts," Donny told him. "The aerial guys will have the roof open in a minute."

"You could have told me that before," Scout grumbled, settling himself on the narrow lumber with his legs spread in front of him. Being even a little lower made a huge difference in the heat.

"Don't they teach you at the Academy what happens when you put water on a fire in a confined space?" Donny asked casually. Reading and theory were one thing, but Donny knew there was no teacher like experience. It was a lesson he knew Scout would never forget. "Anyway, that wasn't so bad. I've been in lots hotter."

Scout sent brief spurts of water in a wide arc in front of him and scowled at the darkness. They were always doing it to him, setting him up like this and letting him embarrass himself. It had been his childhood dream to see himself in the heroic role of a firefighter. The day he had been accepted as a recruit had been the happiest day of his life, but things had gone downhill from there.

In the academy, he had worked and studied hard. As a probie, he been assigned to one of the plum downtown stations, but he got no respect. They treated him like he was second class. Well, technically his pay grade *was* third class, but they treated him like a flunky. And even when they gave him an opportunity like this one, letting him take the nozzle, it was only to see if he would screw up.

The sound of the chainsaw died away, and the ghostly beam of a flashlight stabbed down into the smoke and steam a few metres in front of them. Scout looked towards the opening that had winked into existence in this claustrophobic world and unconsciously swung the hose towards it. Gruff voices above them spluttered and cursed.

"Sorry," he said, quickly shutting off the nozzle.

"That you, Billy?" Donny called towards the opening. The attic began to cool almost immediately as the smoke and heat streamed out through the ventilation hole and into the night.

"Wedge?" came the reply. It was hard to distinguish voices muffled by breathing apparatus. Everyone sounded a bit like Darth Vader. "I *thought* I heard rats in the attic. You guys OK in there?"

"Yeah, we're good," Donny said. He crouched and made his way along the joists towards the opening. He poked his head out of the hole in the roof, like a magician's rabbit peering out of a top hat. Smoke and steam swirled around him.

"Aren't you a little old to be climbing around up here?" Donny asked the grizzled man perched on the roof ladder beside him. The ladder had curved metal prongs that hooked over the peak of the roof, allowing the firefighters to work on pitches that were too steep to provide solid footing.

"I was working on roofs while you were still hanging off your mamma's tit." Billy was the sort of guy who could say something like that without it sounding dirty. And it wasn't far from the truth. With forty-two years of service, he was *the* senior man on the job. He'd turned down many a chance for promotion to district chief and beyond, preferring to remain at the pointy end. Billy liked to claim that he had forgotten more about firefighting than most of the pencil-pushing senior officers had ever known. And that wasn't far from the truth, either.

"As long as they keep making spare parts, I may never retire," Billy smiled. He had already had one hip replacement.

"I'm going to have to kill him, Donny." Spike stood on the tip of the extended aerial ladder, holding the chainsaw. "It's the only way I'm ever going to get promoted. Nothin' personal, Cap, it's just business."

"Just make it a clean shot, Spike. I'd rather die up here than die of boredom in some old folks' home."

Donny smiled. He knew exactly what Billy meant; he wondered if Scout ever would. "How's your air, Patrick?" Donny asked, ducking down into the hole again.

"Just under three-quarters."

"OK. Hey, Eddy, come on up and back up Scout. I'm heading down the aerial to give the chief a report. Look for hot spots and come on down when you need to change your bottles." The attic was now clear enough that Donny could see Eddy climbing up through the hatch and following the hose towards Scout.

Donny stood back up through the hole in the roof and braced his arms on either side. Billy and Spike reached over and helped to pull him up. Donny stood on the steep roof, holding onto the rail of the aerial ladder to steady himself. He shut off his air tank, removed his face piece and looked around him. He loved this eagle's-eye view of the fire ground.

No firefighter ever wanted to see someone hurt or killed or to see a person's treasured belongings and a lifetime of work reduced to sodden ashes. Yet that was what fed the firefighters' addiction: their need to face and conquer man's earliest tool and oldest enemy. Maybe it was a need to confront themselves, too. When a crew began to squabble and bicker among themselves, it was a sure sign that things in the fire hall had been too quiet for too long. It was one of the mysterious contradictions of the job: death and destruction gave them purpose.

From up here there was a sort of terrible beauty to it. Fire trucks ranged up and down the street, their red and white lights spinning and flashing as if illuminating some strange carnival. A tangled web of hoses wound from hydrants to trucks and snaked their way into the row of houses. Firefighters bustled, carrying tools into the buildings and debris out. Bystanders looked on, fascinated by the disaster and relieved it hadn't happened to them.

There was the steady throb of the trucks' diesel engines, the drone of generators powering lights, and the whine of smoke ejectors. From inside the building came the crunch and snap of overhaul as firefighters opened walls and pulled down ceilings to find the fire's secret hiding spots.

Even the aerial ladder that reached up to Donny was a marvel to him. The aerial truck was a behemoth. It was no easy feat to position it on the narrow streets of the city's older neighbourhoods, and then thread the ladder between tree branches and power lines to the right spot on the roof. That in itself was an art that often went unappreciated, even by other firefighters.

A sudden cry from inside the attic snapped Donny out of his reverie. It was followed immediately by Eddy's voice, "Holy shit!"

Donny whirled, dropped to his knees and peered down through the opening in the roof. Eddy was beneath him, prostrate and peering down through a hole between the joists.

"Are you OK?" Eddy called down through the hole.

"Yeah, yeah, I think so," came the faint reply.

"What the hell happened?" Donny demanded.

Eddy rolled over to look up at Donny. "I was pulling hose and told him to move up. The kid must have stepped between the joists. He just disappeared." Drywall had little strength to support a person's weight; wet drywall had even less.

"Do you need medics?" Donny called down.

"I'm OK." Scout looked up through the two holes at the firefighters stacked above him. "I'm fine. I landed on a bed."

The group on the roof broke out laughing, as much with relief as anything. Falling was a constant worry. You never knew when a weakened floor, roof or ceiling would give way, plunging you into a raging inferno below. Fortunately, Scout had been over the second of the row houses, the one beside the end unit where the fire had originated.

"He fell onto a bed," Eddy smirked. "The boy was born to be an aerial man, Billy."

"Aerial men don't fall, Eddy. We leave that to you pumper clowns," Billy retorted.

"You sure you're OK?" Donny asked again. Bed or not, it was still a bit of a drop.

"Yes, I can walk." Scout's face burned at the older men's laughter.

Donny saw him moving around. "Make your way down the stairs," he instructed. "I'll see you outside."

By the time Donny climbed down from the aerial turntable, Scout was waiting for him. "How are you feeling?" Donny asked.

"Fine. My knee's a little sore," Scout admitted, rubbing his right leg. "Other than that, it just scared the shit out of me."

"That's a terrible feeling, falling like that. Believe me, I know. Come on, let's get you checked out," Donny said, moving towards the paramedic crew stationed down the street.

Scout didn't budge. "I told you, I'm OK. I don't need them laughing at me too."

"Eddy and Big Billy? They're just relieved you're OK."

"Really? They got a funny way of showing it."

"Come on, you gotta admit, it's kind of funny landing on a bed like that," Donny smiled. Scout remained grim, arms folded across his chest. Donny's smile faded. "Listen, this is not optional, OK? Go get yourself checked out by the medics. This thing's winding down anyway. You did good up there."

Scout scowled and limped off towards the ambulance. Donny turned the other way. He found Ratzo talking to Platoon Chief Humphrey, inside Command Ten. Command Ten, casually known as Winnebago One, was one of the department's mobile command centres. It didn't look like a fire truck; it looked more like an RV with flashing lights, which was essentially what it was. But instead of the comforts of home, it was crammed full of radios, computer terminals and everything else needed to manage a multiple alarm or other major emergency.

Donny stepped into the command centre and gave the two chiefs his report on the extent of the fire in the attic and Scout's fall through the ceiling.

"Is the kid OK?" Humphrey asked.

"His knee's a little sore, but I don't think it's too bad. He's with the medics right now," Donny replied. "I'll do the injury report when we get back to the station."

"There's going to be lots of paperwork from this one," Ratzo observed, looking down at the incident command sheets on his clipboard. "They found a body in the basement of the first house. The whole place was set up as a hydroponic grow op."

"Really?" Donny slipped the SCBA off his back and set it down. "Seems like there's a lot of that going around."

"What do you mean?" Humphrey gave Donny a curious look.

"A lot of drug labs and grow ops going up. First Homewood Avenue, then the high-rise on Gerrard, now this place." Donny raised his eyebrows. "That's three in under a month. Sure feels like something's going on."

Ratzo chuckled. "Always looking for the conspiracy, aren't you, Donny? Homewood started because that cop, Copeland, God rest him, tripped a booby trap. Gerrard was torched because that Simpson guy had a beef with one of his competitors. And this place? They bypassed the circuit breakers and the electric meter—what do you expect? The wiring in these old places can't handle that kind of load. Things go in streaks, you know that."

"Could be a streak," Humphrey stroked his chin. "Could be a gang turf war. Who knows? I'll mention it to the fire marshal's investigator when he shows up."

"You want me to put it down as a suspicious fire?" Ratzo asked, scribbling a note on his clipboard.

"No, but let's keep our eyes open."

"OK." Donny bent to pick up his SCBA. "Well, I gotta go check on Scout and change my bottle."

Humphrey put his hand on Donny's shoulder. "Listen, speaking of Gerrard, I heard you had some concerns about what went down. I'm glad you did the right thing in the end."

"Did I?"

"Of course. Everything happens so fast in those situations. The adrenalin's pumping. Things get confused."

"I know what I saw, Chief." Donny put the SCBA back down.

"What you *thought* you saw. Four other people saw it differently. So be it. The fact is, the SIU cleared Ericson. If there was any doubt, he'd still be behind a desk on admin duty instead of out here, doing his job." Humphrey pointed out the command centre's window. Ericson could just be made out standing behind the barrier tape at the end of the street.

"And he saved Scout's life. That's the bottom line," Ratzo added.

Donny glanced down the street at Ericson. "They're two different things."

"Not in my book, they're not. Anyway, it's over. Let's move on," Humphrey said definitively. It was not a suggestion. Humphrey turned his attention to the chatter on the radio as Donny stepped down from the command centre.

Ratzo climbed down with Donny. "What is it with you?" he asked, closing the door behind him. "Do you get some kind of perverse pleasure out of stirring up shit and pissing off the brass?"

"Just trying to be honest, Chief."

"There's a time for honesty and a time to say, 'No, those pants don't make your ass look fat.'" Ratzo pursed his lips. "We go back a long way, Wedge. I'm in your corner—you know that, right?"

"Sure, we're twins—just like Arnold Schwarzenegger and Danny DeVito." Ratzo barely came to Donny's shoulder. Donny put his arm around the smaller man for emphasis.

Ratzo shrugged himself free. "Well, let me tell you this, bro. You don't exactly make it easy to be your friend. You got crappy people skills, and you need to learn to pick your fights. Eddy and Moose, and anyone else who for some unfathomable reason still likes you, will tell you the exact same thing."

"They already have. I'm gonna check on Scout." Donny slung the strap of his SCBA over his shoulder and let the mask dangle by the air hose. He walked over to the ambulance staging area.

"You should probably get it X-rayed," one of the paramedics was saying as Donny approached. Scout was sitting on the stretcher in his underwear and bunker coat, his legs hanging over the side. He was wearing his trademark look of defiance, which Donny knew all too well. Donny wondered briefly if Scout had been carrying that big chip on his shoulder his whole life, and what had put it there. He quickly decided he didn't like Scout well enough to care that much.

"You said it was just strained, right? I'm not going to the hospital." Scout eased himself off the stretcher and pulled up his bunker pants. The dislike of hospitals was almost universal among firefighters. It was one thing Donny could agree with the kid about.

"Probably. I said *probably* just a strain, but I'm not a doctor." The paramedic looked towards Donny for help.

"You should get it looked at. Just to be sure," Donny agreed.

"It's *my* leg." Scout limped away to the pumper truck and sat on the back step. He watched as crews rolled hoses, stowed ladders and collected their equipment. Bill Ericson walked past, taking down the yellow barrier tape that had kept the bystanders out of the way and out of danger.

"Taking a break?" Ericson asked with more than a tinge of sarcasm.

"Strained my knee," Scout replied. "I fell through the ceiling from the attic."

"Oh, you OK?"

"Yeah, I'm fine. I landed on something soft." Scout decided to leave out the detail about the bed.

"How's the neck?" Ericson asked, leaning against the truck.

Scout reached up and touched the small pink mark beneath his ear. "It's good. I've cut myself worse shaving." Ericson doubted that, looking at the sparse stubble on the young man's chin.

"Listen," Scout continued, "I never really thanked you. I mean, you saved my life." He looked up at the big blond cop with respect.

Ericson shrugged. "It all worked out, right? In spite of your boss. The rest is just paperwork."

"I don't know what's up with Donny." Scout shook his head. "He's such a prick sometimes. I'm thinking about putting in for a transfer."

"Whatever." Ericson moved off, balling up the yellow plastic tape.

Scout watched him for a moment, then limped after him. "About what happened on the deck that day—you know, me mouthing off about Copeland's widow. I'm sorry about that. It was, you know ... Sometimes I just say stuff without thinking. I am really sorry."

Ericson studied the young firefighter for a moment. Humphrey and Collins had told him to leave the whole matter of Donny and his crew behind. Ericson's first instinct was to dismiss Scout's apology, no matter how sincere it might be. But his gut told him something else. It might be good to have an ally on Donny's crew.

"You're right," Ericson said, taking a step towards Scout and dropping his voice. "She is hot. I've thought that ever since I met her, and you're not supposed to think that about your partner's wife. But I have enough sense not to say it. You made a real bonehead move there."

"I know. I was way offside."

"Fair enough." Ericson extended his hand, and they shook firmly. "You should get that knee looked at."

"I did," Scout frowned. "They want to take me to the hospital for X-rays. I said no."

"Don't be foolish." Ericson saw Scout bristle and softened his tone. "Listen, these things can come back to haunt you later, even the little injuries. Believe me, I know: I got an elbow I can't fully straighten." Ericson held up his left arm and demonstrated. "Thankfully it's not my shooting hand, but I'll never be able to make a claim, because I ignored it at the time. I thought it was just sprained, but it was a bone chip. Now I'm looking at surgery."

Ericson saw Eddy approaching and moved off to continue taking down the barrier tape. "See a doctor," he advised. "Get the X-rays. That's the smart play, but it's your choice. See you around."

"What was that about?" Eddy asked, dropping two rolls of wet, dirty hose on the back step of the truck.

"Nothing," Scout said, walking back towards the ambulance. "Tell Donny I'm going with the medics."

CHAPTER 14

TINY DANCER

"Tiny Dancer"—Elton John's voice flowed from her earbuds into her soul. Roxanne ignored the cars passing her corner. She closed her eyes and swayed slowly, as the song played the bittersweet ballad of her life. It was her song. She remembered her father hoisting her in his arms and whirling her around the living room to it. That had been her, the tiny dancer, moving to the music that seemed to well up within her.

The lessons began when she was four. At age eight she had ballet classes five days a week. At ten, she auditioned for the National Ballet School and was accepted. The training became even more intense, but Roxanne applied herself with determination. She was going to be a prima ballerina, she knew it. At twelve, she was chosen to dance the role of Clara in the following year's production of *The Nutcracker* with the National Ballet of Canada. The teachers and dance masters spoke quietly among themselves, with approving nods. As hard as they drove her, she drove herself harder.

And then her body betrayed her. Height was good in a ballerina up to a point, but she kept growing: five foot eight, five foot nine, five foot ten the last time she had measured herself. Her hips widened, and though she still had an excellent turnout, the teachers now shook their heads when they looked at her. Worst of all were her breasts, which grew well beyond the polite suggestions of womanhood seen in great ballerinas. The boys didn't seem to mind, but the teasing from her female classmates was relentless. Physical balance was one thing, but more than anything it was her mental balance that was crippled. Her confidence crumbled and her dream vanished like a wisp of morning fog in the harsh glare of day.

At fourteen, Roxanne transferred to a public high school. She felt like she had landed on an alien planet. Demanding as it had been, ballet school was a familiar, structured, intimate world of a couple of hundred students and teachers devoted to dance. Now she was just one of over a thousand students. She was no longer special; she was anonymous, a lost soul in the adolescent jungle. The cliques were impenetrable and the teachers aloof. For most of that first year, she felt like killing herself.

Roxanne met Tina at the end of that desperate year, and the two outsiders clicked immediately. Mostly it was the music. Tina was seriously into techno-trance. She was Roxanne's doorway into a mysterious musical world that had always seemed forbidden. They spent most of that summer in Tina's basement. Roxanne danced as Tina spun the tracks. Sometimes it was Moby, Tiësto or Deadmau5, but often it was Tina's own creations. Roxanne leapt, spun and swayed as Tina wove her pulsing musical tapestry. Tina moved from keyboard to drum machine to computer as Roxanne dived into the music, moving to the rhythms in a way Tina had never seen before. They spoke to each other in a language beyond words.

Neither of them had any interest in drugs when they started attending raves. Tina naturally gravitated towards the DJs, while Roxanne lived for the dance floor. Both of them gained some minor notoriety: Tina when the DJs began to play some of her mixes, and Roxanne for dance moves that merged fluid grace, sensuality and visceral intensity.

Some of Roxanne's new friends took ecstasy, some didn't. For several months she was happy simply to share the music and the friendship. For the first time in her life she felt relaxed and accepted. There was no real pressure, and looking back, Roxanne wasn't really sure why she took that first little pink pill with the butterfly on it. Maybe it was the promise of an energy boost that would allow her to dance all night long; maybe it was the stories of feeling the music come alive; maybe it was just curiosity. The reasons may have been ambiguous, but the effects were not. Roxanne felt herself melting even deeper into the music. The bass was a pulsing purple volcano, the synthesizer tasted of cinnamon honey, the cymbals and snare cut through the air like lasers. Melody and harmony flowed from her fingers, and joy surged through every fibre of her body. She felt a hyperdimensional bond merging her with the other dancers. Did the music create the dance, or did the dance create the music? It all became one seamless, beautiful, organic whole.

Then it was over. The void left behind when the magic faded was almost more than Roxanne could bear. She remembered crying as Tina led her home through the grey dawn light.

Roxanne tried to recapture the feeling, but it was never as good as that first time. She danced harder, took more and different drugs. Sometimes she came close, but gradually the magic melted away until all that was left was a hollow emptiness and the need for something to take the edge off.

Tina saw what was happening and tried to talk to her. Tina was no Puritan, but she wasn't going to let anything get in the way of her music. Roxanne wasn't interested in cleaning up or cutting down. School and home were sacrificed to her pursuit of the elusive magic or whatever faint echo of it was left. The two friends parted angrily, each saying things they later regretted but couldn't bring themselves to apologize for. The last Roxanne heard, Tina had found some success as a DJ in the club scene in Berlin.

Roxanne was working a different circuit. Sometimes the little voice in her head would ask how it had come to this. How had she moved from dancing the lead in *The Nutcracker* to dancing naked in front of drunken, leering men? But it was easy money, and a pipe or a line would quiet the little voice, at least for awhile. And unlike most of the other girls, Roxanne told herself, she could actually dance.

When it got so bad that even the strip clubs wouldn't put up with her behaviour anymore, Roxanne hit the street. She tried to get clean; sometimes she even managed a week or two. Darrel Simpson, her pimp, didn't like that. A high hooker was a compliant hooker. That made Darrel happy. When Darrel wasn't happy, bad things happened. Whether it was fear of Darrel or just the hopelessness of it all, in the end it was always the same: back on the street, turning tricks so she could get enough medicine to quiet the ghosts of what might have been.

She learned to distance herself, to treat her body as an object. A few of her tricks were looking for some sort of comfort beyond just a physical interaction. She sensed in them the same lost desperation she tried to numb in herself, but she had learned she couldn't really afford to care. There was room for only one person in her lifeboat, and it was already taking on water.

It was during one of her brief clean intervals that she first met Ramón, or Carlos, as he called himself on the street. There was something different about this small brown man. He didn't treat her as a temptress or a whore; he treated her simply as a person. It was business, but it was business conducted with courtesy.

He became one of her regulars, and in spite of herself, she found herself liking him. Some of her tricks liked to talk; they talked of their broken dreams and secret fantasies, and Roxanne pretended to listen from across the gulf of detachment between her mind and her body.

Ramón told her about Baja. He described the desolate beauty of the desert; how the infrequent rain would bring forth a sudden blush of flowers, startling and ephemeral as a rainbow; how the evening sun would set the Pacific ablaze as it sank beneath the waves. She found herself not only listening, but talking to him in return. She told him of a family vacation to Florida: how the warm, soft sand caressed her feet; the miracle of holding a starfish, glistening, alien and alive, in her hand. He seemed to glimpse the faint flicker of the tiny dancer inside her fragile soul.

One day Ramón asked her if she wanted to get out, if she wanted to get clean and straight for good. But it had to be forever, he said, looking her straight in the eye, because he would kill her before he'd let her fall back into this life.

That was before she knew his real name was Ramón, or anything at all about him, really. But she knew that she liked him, that she wanted to see the desert bloom, and that this was probably her last chance at a real life. Ramón paid Darrel off the next day and got her into treatment. Roxanne worked at her recovery harder than she had worked at anything in her life.

When Roxanne left the treatment centre and learned that Ramón ran one of the largest drug labs in the city, she felt her world crumble away. Like her dream of being a prima ballerina, it had been just another of life's cruel jokes. Ramón held her firmly but gently while she railed and beat her fists against him. When fear and rage had exhausted her, he explained. He told her it was simply business; if he didn't make the stuff, someone else would. He told her he was saving money. He had used most of his savings to pay off Darrel and send her to the treatment centre. But soon, in a year or two at most, he would have enough to buy a new life for both of them. They would leave it—all of it—behind and start over again.

Roxanne worked the twelve steps and stayed clean for a whole year. Her recovery group held a celebration and gave her a medallion. She was careful to tell them nothing of Ramón or his business. A world of opportunity lay spread out before her.

She was never sure exactly why it had happened. She was visiting an old friend, someone who had not been as successful in recovery. When the pipe was passed to her, Roxanne simply took it. Just one hit to take the edge off, she told herself. It would be different this time, now that she knew so much more about herself and addiction.

But it wasn't any different. And now she was back on the same corner, trying to tell herself that it was only her body doing these things. It was hopeless anyway, so what was the use in even trying?

CHAPTER 15

ST. JAMES

Ramón sat on the step of a doorway across the street, half a block away. He watched Roxanne sway gently to the music from her earbuds. Intuition had told him she would be here; something even more primal told him it was foolish to come back here to see for himself. She was out in the open. She could be bait, either for the cops or for the Wo Shing Wo Triad. Both groups, he knew, were eager to get their hands on him.

He slumped motionless in the shadow of the doorway. From all appearances, Ramón was just another burned-out loser on the scrap heap of life, but he was acutely aware of every sound and movement around him. He had gained a lifetime of experience on the streets of Ensenada, and the years since had only sharpened his senses.

He slouched there, unmoving, for over an hour, watching her. She leaned into a car window and shook her head, gave a cigarette to a homeless man, chatted briefly and shared a laugh with one of the other working girls passing by. At one point she disappeared up the street with a man, but she was back fifteen minutes later. Nothing seemed out of place. Nothing disrupted the grinding futility that passed for normal in this neighbourhood.

Ramón stood, stiff and aching after sitting so long on the cold concrete. He leaned against the wall, pulled his hoodie a little closer around his face, and took one final slow look up and down the street. He couldn't be sure. The undercurrent of misery and menace produced a sort of static that made it difficult to identify possible threats.

He crossed to Roxanne's side of the street and shuffled towards her. He kept his head down as he passed her, but for a moment he seemed to lose his balance and stumbled against her.

"Hey," she said, startled, stepping back from him.

"Sorry," he mumbled, and shuffled on. He didn't dare face her or look back. It was only an instant, but it was enough.

Ramón had learned something of the art of the pickpocket when he was a boy. He had never become as expert as some of his friends, and often as not he had been the decoy as they darted among the rich, fat, drunken gringos. This time, though, his intention was not to take something. Instead, he had left a slip of paper in her jacket pocket, the one he had seen her put her cigarettes into. "St. James – 3," it said. The rest was up to her.

Keeping to side streets and back alleys as much as possible, Ramón made his way to St. James Park. Once there he found a bench in the shadows, away from the lamps that lit the walking paths.

St. James Park, beside the Anglican cathedral of the same name, was a leafy three-acre oasis on the downtown east side. Roxanne loved the place and had introduced Ramón to it. She taught him the English names of the flowers as they strolled through the formal Victorian garden that surrounded the fountain on the south side. She would bend a rose to her nose, close her eyes, and inhale its perfume with a smile that surely came from the angels themselves.

Ramón sat on the bench considering his options. He had already dismissed the best option, which was to forget about her and just take care of himself. The heart is a funny thing, he told himself. But sometimes—his father's words came back to him—sometimes to save your skin you have to break your heart.

The worst option was the one he wanted the most. It was foolish, worse than foolish, he told himself; it was practically suicidal. Everything would cost twice as much. She would slow him down. And would he ever be able to fully trust her? Even if she really did love him, an addict answers to only one master.

More than anything, it was peace he wanted. For those few months with Roxanne he had tasted it once again, for the first time since his father had been killed. He would never know it again as long as she haunted his thoughts. He was prepared for the worst, prepared to do what needed to be done, but he needed to know for sure.

Ramón looked up through the trees at the clock on the cathedral's soaring steeple. Ten to three. He would know soon enough. If she didn't show, that would be it. And if she did ... That was the tough part.

He had sworn that he would kill her if she went back to the street. But what did he expect? It was who she was, or at least what she had become. Once the shit got ahold of you, it rarely let go. But maybe he was partly to blame, cooking right under her nose. There was more to her than just the addict: she was also the poet, the singer, the tiny dancer. Maybe if he had been more supportive ... He was prepared to give her one more chance, but he needed to be sure. If she lied, if she wavered even one bit, Ramón would leave her and this city behind for good. He fingered the hot dose in his pocket, enough to kill a couple of big men, let alone a woman like Roxanne. She would be just another overdose and he would disappear like water running down the drain.

Ramón looked over his shoulder again at the Gothic bulk of the cathedral. Perhaps this wasn't such a good place to decide Roxanne's fate. He dismissed the pang of guilt. He had looked inside the cathedral. There were no Stations of the Cross, no shrine to the Blessed Virgin where he could light a candle for his mother. This church and its austere gringo God had nothing to do with him.

He had chosen the park not out of nostalgia, but because it was secluded from the streets while offering clear views and escape routes

on all four sides. A few homeless men slept under the open gazebo
in the centre of the park, preferring to take their chances in the cold
open air rather than endure the crowding and violence of the shelters. Aside from the sleeping men, he was the only one in the park.

Five after three, the clock on the steeple read. Maybe she hadn't
found the note. Maybe she was afraid of him. Whatever, it was for
the best, he told himself. As he rose to go, a silhouette appeared on
the stone path leading into the park from the northwest. She would
always walk like a dancer. It made her unmistakable. No one followed
her. No one had parked. The sparse traffic kept moving. He advanced
through the trees towards her.

"*Mi corazón,*" he called softly.

"*Tigre,*" she answered, and ran to him.

The tears that streaked her face were genuine, of that there was
no doubt. "Shhh," Ramón soothed, as much to quiet as to comfort
her. Roxanne wanted to sit in the gardens, but Ramón insisted on
a more secluded spot. He led her back to the bench in the shadows.
His eyes scanned the park as they spoke in lowered voices.

"I'm sorry, Ramón. I really messed up. Oh, God, this is all my
fault." She started sobbing again.

"Shhh, no more tears," Ramón said quietly but firmly. "It's over.
The past is done." What he needed was a plan for the future. For that
he needed information. He needed to know what he was up against.
He asked her how she had come to be working the street again. She
told him the whole story, how she had left the city and been brought
back, questioned and put back out on the street.

"These men, they are cops, you said? But they didn't arrest you?"

"I'm not sure. Some of them are cops. One of them is a fireman,
I think." Roxanne wiped her eyes on the sleeve of her jacket. "I mean,
they never told me, but I overheard stuff, you know? That's what it
sounded like."

That was odd. "They never took you to a police station, never
took pictures or fingerprints?"

Roxanne shook her head.

This was bad. Back home in Mexico, the cops routinely worked outside the law. But they could also be bought. And the cartels had weapons as good as or better than the police's. He had nothing.

"They are watching you, no?"

Roxanne told him about how she was supposed to stand so that whoever she was talking to faced the variety store. She told him about her suspicion that there was a camera in the little apartment. She told him about her nightly phone call to "Allan."

He could still walk away, his survival instincts told him. Leave her behind. His chances were slim enough without trying to cross this minefield.

"You need to act like nothing has changed—that's very important. Can you do that?" She was a performer, but could she be convincing in real life? Ramón wondered.

"Yes, but we can't stay here. I mean, we're going away, right?" It was a plea more than a question.

"Yes, we're leaving and we're never coming back. But it takes time. We need to do this right. And you need to tell me: are you done with *los drogas*?" He reached out, took Roxanne's hand and looked into her eyes.

"I'm done." Roxanne shook her head. "I'm clean now. They got me clean, at least, those cops. It's only been a couple of weeks, but it feels different this time."

"There can be no more mistakes, no more slips." He gripped her hand tighter. With his other hand he fingered the hot dose in his pocket. He searched her face for the slightest hesitation.

There was none. She looked deeply into his eyes. "I swear, Ramón," Roxanne said, crossing herself. "I want to start over and leave it all behind. When can we go?"

"Soon, but first we need to get ready." Ramón looked around the park once more. Everything looked the same. He told Roxanne exactly what he wanted. "Can you do that?"

"Yes. Can I call you?" Roxanne took out the phone they had given her.

Ramón looked at the phone suspiciously. "No, no calls. Don't say anything to anyone. And next time, leave the phone behind. If they ask where you went tonight, just tell them you came here for a walk."

He stood and pulled her to her feet. "We'll start a new life. But for now, you must be strong and brave. Everything must appear the same." He held her to him, savouring the sensation of her breasts pressed against him, her hair on his shoulder, his hand on the small of her back. He pulled away and walked back through the trees, following the deeper shadows.

It wasn't a complete plan, but at least now he had a course of action. The first step would be new identities. He had a lead on that. Good documents would be expensive, twice as expensive for two, but he couldn't afford to go cheap. Bad forgeries were dangerous. Leaving Roxanne behind now, dead or alive, was also dangerous. Every choice was fraught with risk, but he had no stomach for killing.

He dropped the hot shot in a garbage bin, rounded the corner of the cathedral and was gone.

CHAPTER 16

THE COMMITTEE

The members of the Committee sat around a large, polished oak table: Tom Humphrey, Bob Collins, two women and another man.

"And the Copeland matter?" asked the woman at the head of the table. "You said you had something to report, Bob." Cheryl Newlands, heir to the Newlands Distillery fortune, leaned back in the plush leather chair. Authority fit her as comfortably as her tailored slacks and Burberry shirt. She was in her late-forties, moon-faced and greying at the temples. She twiddled her pen, something she often did when posing questions to the junior executives who stood nervously before her at the office.

They were gathered in the library of Newlands' home, a sprawling century-old Tudor-style house in Rosedale, a neighbourhood that, despite the city's changing demographics, still spoke of private clubs and old money. A few of the library's shelves at one end of the room still held books; the rest held tennis and golf trophies, plaques honouring various accomplishments, and other mementoes charting the milestones of a privileged life. Varnished bamboo fly rods nestled among a selection of pictures showing Newlands and her late husband holding or standing beside an impressive variety of very large fish. Between the framed fish, French doors led out to a flagstone patio that glowed softly in the light of discreetly situated solar lamps. The grounds were as tastefully landscaped as the interior of the house had been decorated.

"Yes, thank you," Collins told Newlands. "The police investigation into Randy Copeland's murder is, of course, being pursued vigorously. I have sources inside that investigation keeping me informed of any new developments—unofficially, of course, since I'm Copeland's former commanding officer. I won't bore you with the details. Suffice it to say, I think we're still a couple of steps ahead. We have the girl, for one thing. But even if the police do catch this Ramón first, we have ways to deal with that scenario. However, I think we've finally caught a break."

Bob Collins nodded to Humphrey sitting beside him. Humphrey touched his tablet and brought a map up on the large screen hanging on the wall opposite the French doors.

"The yellow line is the GPS tracker from the girl's phone," Collins explained. "As you can see, it's pretty much the same day after day. Everything's within a couple of blocks: stores, fast food places, a couple of trips to the Eaton Centre, all pretty normal."

"This is the last twenty-four hours." Collins nodded to Humphrey again and a new overlay appeared on the map. Collins pointed to the red line running south. "This morning at 2:54, she suddenly decides to go for a walk down to Jarvis and King—St. James Park, to be precise. She stays there for ten minutes, then goes back to the apartment.

"Then, just after noon today," Collins pointed to another extension of the red line running north, "she breaks the usual pattern again and goes to a place on Yonge Street, just north of Wellesley."

Humphrey showed the Google street view of the location.

"A camera store?" one of the women asked.

"Yup. This is from inside the apartment a few minutes after she got back from the camera store." The image changed again. This time it showed Roxanne holding a small white rectangle.

"Unfortunately, this is the best view we have, but we think what she's holding is a passport picture. The dimensions are right," Tom Humphrey said, taking up the story.

"You think she's planning a runner? Should we bring her in again?" asked the younger woman across the table from Collins. Laticia Raincourt was a tall, slim Black woman with close-cropped hair and high cheekbones. By day she was a Crown attorney—a prosecutor, one of the best by all reports. It was her responsibility to select the cases to be brought before the Committee.

"I'd rather not," Collins replied.

"You don't yank in the bait just because you get a nibble," Newlands stated. Humphrey wasn't the only one who looked over at the pictures of the trophy fish. "We'll leave her out there until we get the big one. He may have been in touch. How did we miss that?"

Humphrey shook his head. "I'm not sure. This Ramón is no dummy; he got away from the Cartel, after all. I'll go over the previous day's video footage again and see if I can find anything."

"This case has already eaten up an enormous amount of our resources." Raincourt leaned forward. "Too much, in my opinion."

It was true: the search for Ramón had already consumed almost half their annual budget. Humphrey had been wondering when the whining would begin. "This isn't just any case, Laticia. Ramón was running one of the largest meth labs in the city. On top of that, he's a cop killer who damn near killed two of my men. We made a decision. We need to follow through."

"I understand the importance of this case, but you've become obsessed with it to the exclusion of several other important matters that I've brought forward." Raincourt rested her hands on the table and looked around the room for support. "Leo Rothberg, for example, a serial pedophile. Is anything being done about him?"

There were nods from the other members of the Committee. The colour started to rise from Humphrey's collar. "We're working on it."

"I know it's easy for those of us who aren't in Operations to forget that these things take time," began the man sitting on Humphrey's other side. His voice was soothing, softly shaded with a Latino accent. Albert Fernandez was a top defence attorney. He was a handsome, well-groomed man in his late thirties, with a thin mustache. The Committee didn't consider cases where there was much doubt about where responsibility lay. Still, given the finality of their sanctions, it was important to weigh all the details. It was Fernandez's job to act as a sort of devil's advocate and bring up any mitigating factors that might sway the Committee's decisions.

"However," Fernandez continued, "Laticia is right: we can't allow one case, or one type of case, to dominate us. We are not going to solve the city's drug problem by eliminating one lab or the person who ran it."

"And what about the murder of a police officer?" Collins asked, his voice barely controlled.

"I'm just saying," Fernandez replied, giving Collins his best courtroom smile, "we need to keep this Ramón thing in perspective."

If looks could kill, the one Collins gave Fernandez would have dropped the lawyer in his tracks and buried him in a shallow grave. Collins rose to his feet. "Perspective? Tell me, Albert, how many lawyers were killed in the line of duty last year? Maybe you'd care to explain your 'perspective'"—he spat the word at Fernandez—"to Randy Copeland's widow and his kids."

"Sit down, Bob," Cheryl Newlands said firmly. Fernandez was about to reply, but she silenced him with a look. Newlands looked around the table at each of the Committee members. "This is exactly why we keep our personal feelings out of things. This is why we have the procedures we do. The murder of Constable Copeland is still open, and we can't make a final decision on the matter until we have more information. We need to know who this Ramón is, and how to find him."

Newlands turned to Laticia Raincourt. "As for budget, that's my issue and I don't have a problem. The murder of Constable Copeland is our top priority. But we can walk and chew gum at the same time, right, Tom?"

"Yes, absolutely." Humphrey shut down his tablet and the screen on the wall went dark. "And we're not ignoring the other cases. We'll wrap up the Rothberg matter in a couple of days. I'm meeting with Ericson about it after this meeting. You're welcome to come along on the job, Albert, if you don't mind getting your hands dirty."

Fernandez stiffened. "That's not my ..." he trailed off.

Humphrey and Collins exchanged a satisfied look.

"I was going to bring up the matter of Bill Ericson," Newlands said, stepping into the vacuum. "How's he working out?"

"All right," Humphrey reported. "He's a bit impulsive, but I've given him the lead on the Rothberg matter. It's fairly straightforward."

"I don't doubt his operational skills. It's his judgement I worry about," Newlands replied. "I hope he understands that there can be no repetition of anything like the Simpson shooting at the apartment building. He must understand that we are not vigilantes—that we have a process."

"He understands."

CHAPTER 17

LOOSE ENDS

The body hung by a thin yellow rope from an eye bolt in the ceiling, like some grotesque mobile. Donny touched one dangling arm, and the body spun through the dust motes that danced in the rays of the late-afternoon sun slanting in through the dirty window.

"He's still warm; cut him down," Donny said. If the man had been obviously dead they would have left the scene to the police. But still warm—there was a chance. Slim, but still a chance.

Donny grabbed the man around the hips and tried to take most of the weight. Moose pulled the table over and climbed onto it warily. The table's spindly legs wobbled, threatening to give way under him. The hanged man's purple face and bulging eyes stared back at Moose. He reached up with his knife. The thin yellow rope parted easily.

Donny staggered as the full weight of the man's torso flopped down over his shoulder. He and Eddy laid the man on the floor near where Eddy had placed the defibrillator and oxygen kit. The quarter-inch rope had bitten deep into the flesh of the man's neck. The medics arrived as Moose pried away the noose and tossed it aside.

The medics attached the defibrillator pads to the man's chest. Eddy started compressions, and Donny squeezed the plastic chamber of the bag valve mask every few seconds, forcing oxygen into the man's lungs through the tube the medics had inserted into the man's airway. Scout held the IV bag as one of the medics searched for a vein in the man's arm. Eddy counted the steady rhythm of his compressions; the medics noted the time and amount of each drug that was injected. Other than that, there was little in the way of conversation. It was a scene that was all too familiar to them. Familiar and futile, as they all struggled to loosen death's iron grip on the man.

Constable Ericson and his partner arrived and watched quietly from just inside the doorway. Donny didn't notice them until he and the team were lifting the man onto the stretcher. The cops walked into the room as Moose and Eddy helped the medics rush their patient out to the ambulance. Scout followed, carrying their equipment. It was a mission they all knew would end in failure, but it wouldn't be official until confirmed by the doctors at the hospital.

Ericson again. Donny wondered why the Fates were punishing him like this. Maybe it was their capricious nature, or maybe he just needed to grow up and accept that the world didn't always make sense. He decided to go with the latter, and nodded at Ericson with professional courtesy.

"Well, this is a hell of a way to begin a shift," Ericson said, looking around. His gaze settled on the cut end of the rope dangling from the eye bolt screwed into the ceiling.

Though the apartment was only one room, it was a large room with a high ceiling. It was one of twelve apartments that had been carved out of a big brick house built in the mid-1800s, back when Sherbourne Street was lined with the mansions of the city's well-to-do. Now, those mansions that remained had been split up into rooming houses for the desperate and the down and out.

A mattress lay on the floor, surrounded by discarded clothes. The only decorations were a Chinese calendar tacked to a cupboard and a faded print of Renoir's "Girl with a Watering Can" that hung crookedly beside the window.

"You just start?" Donny asked.

"Yeah, we just got in the car when this came in," Ericson replied, writing in his notebook. It reminded Donny that he needed to make notes too. He removed the blue nitrile gloves he was wearing and pulled out his own notebook.

Eddy returned, rubbing sanitizer on his hands and sniffing at them. He held the bottle out to Donny. "This stuff always reminds me of my grandfather's grappa."

"In that case, you probably shouldn't drink either one," said the other cop as she looked around the perimeter of the room. "You guys touch anything besides Leo?"

"Leo? You knew him?" Donny asked, looking up from his notebook.

"Leo Rothberg," the female cop answered. "He was on the register. Sex offender. He liked them young. Not too picky other than that."

"My new partner, Natasha Pratt," Ericson said by way of introduction.

"Call me Tasha."

"Donny Robertson." Donny held out a freshly sanitized hand. "Nice to meet you."

"I'm Eddy. How come the cops get all the pretty ones, eh, Cap?"

"Oh, good, just what the world needs: another smart-mouthed, bullshitting fireman." Tasha rolled her eyes.

"Hey, just ... Never mind." Eddy went back to packing up their first aid gear.

"Well, I'd never hang myself. That's all I'm saying," Scout's voice sounded from the hallway. He was returning with Moose to retrieve their tools and equipment. "I'd blow my brains out."

"Too messy. You ever been to one of those?" Moose asked him as they stepped into the room. Scout stopped and looked over at Ericson. The memory of blood and brains splattered on the carpet of an apartment hallway returned to them all.

"Yeah, well, me ..." Moose searched for a way out of the awkward moment. "I'd go for an overdose, eh, Donny? I mean, if you had some terminal disease or something."

Donny shrugged and continued making notes.

"Well, nobody's going to miss that piece of shit," Ericson declared.

"Perv," Eddy explained to Moose and Scout. "Kiddie diddler."

"You gotta wonder what went wrong with a guy like that," Donny mused, staring at the loop of yellow rope at his feet.

"Who cares?" Ericson shook his head. "He had multiple convictions, but some smart-ass lawyer found a technicality and he got released with time served under 'community supervision.' But guys like that? They never change."

"Anyway, like I asked before, you guys touch anything?" Tasha asked Donny.

"Moose pulled the table over to cut him down. Other than that, no."

"I moved the chair out of the way," Eddy said, pointing to the chair beside the fridge. "It was on its side underneath him. That's probably what he used, eh?"

"The door was locked?" Ericson asked, looking towards the splintered door frame.

"Yeah, we used the irons—an axe and a Halligan," Donny nodded, closing his notebook.

"Well, you guys can take off, if you've got all your stuff. We'll hold the scene for the coroner," Ericson said.

Donny reviewed the statement he had written for the incident report, then checked his notes one last time. It was all there, what they had found on arrival: the locked door, the body hanging by a length of quarter-inch yellow polypropylene rope. He listed who had done what. It was a simple statement of facts detailing the circumstances of the end of a person's life. An abhorrent person in this case, but still a person. Donny sighed and sent the report on its way with a click of his mouse.

How many suicides had he written up? He had no idea. A few had seared themselves into his memory, but most had faded into the background noise of human misery.

He recorded facts. Every statement was true. Names, times, locations—every quantifiable detail was noted precisely. And yet the reports were woefully incomplete. Who were these people, these lumps of flesh they loaded onto stretchers and into body bags, to lay beneath the coroner's knife? Had they too "felt dawn, seen sunset glow, loved and been loved"?

Suicides always made him maudlin. Donny's own father had done it on the instalment plan, drinking himself to death. His mother had simply given up on living. And run as far and as fast as he might, he always feared that someday the past would catch up with him too and condemn him to the same fate.

He turned away from the computer, got up from the desk and walked to the kitchen, where Eddy was putting the finishing touches on a pie, crimping the edges of the pastry together. Donny poured himself a coffee. Too many of those, too, he thought; I need to cut back. He sat at the big, heavy maple table that dominated the centre of the kitchen and looked out the windows at the last embers of what must have been a lovely sunset. When the station was built, a hundred and fifty years ago, he would have had an unobstructed view of the horizon. Now he had to crane his neck to see a few patches of sky between the office and condo towers.

"Meat loaf and cherry pie," Eddy stated.

"What?"

"I know you, Wedge. You're in one of your 'What's the meaning of life?' moods. Well, today the answer is meat loaf and cherry pie." Eddy slid the pie into the oven and stood up. "If that isn't reason enough to live, then I'm sorry for you. You think too much."

"I know."

"If you're going to sit here moping, then grab a peeler and make yourself useful." Eddy handed him a bag of potatoes, and Donny spread a layer of newspaper on the table and got to work. Eddy retrieved a bag of green beans from the fridge and sat across the table.

"How's your ass?" Donny asked.

"As cute and fuzzy as ever, according to Linda."

They worked in silence for a while. Donny worried at a potato with the peeler while Eddy snapped the ends off the beans and tossed them into a pot.

"Just take the skin off, OK? Leave some of the potato." Eddy frowned. "Listen, the guy was a scumbag. You got kids too, now. You want a guy like that walking around? The world's better off without him."

"You're right." Donny tossed what was left of the potato he'd been peeling into a large pot and reached into the bag for another. "It's not that. I'm just tired."

"Of what?"

"It's ... It's a bunch of stuff." Donny dragged the peeler in long deliberate strokes along the hapless tuber. "Too many dead guys. Too many close calls for us. First you, then Scout. I don't think I could live with myself if something ... you know."

"Well, you know what pilots say: any landing you walk away from is a good one, right?"

"Fitz didn't walk away."

"I miss him too, but that's ancient history. And I don't think that's what's eating you." Eddy tossed the end of a bean at Donny.

The bean bounced off Donny's forehead. He held the peeler up to Eddy. "I'm not afraid to use this, you know. Zip-zip and you'd be Eddy the Earless."

Eddy laughed and went back to his beans. "Is it Laurie?" he asked after a moment.

"It's not her. It's like ..." Donny put down the peeler and shook his head. "It's just not what I thought it was going to be. I mean, I love the boys, but it's either soccer practice or swimming lessons or parent-teacher meetings. It's always something."

Eddy looked at him like Donny had just pointed out that the sky was blue and fire was hot. "And? You knew from the start that she had two boys. What were you expecting?"

Donny picked up the peeler again, grabbed another potato and scraped the peeler across it as if he were carving into granite. "I knew

I'd have to give up some free time. It's just ... I'm used to ... I don't know, maybe it's too late to suddenly become a family man. I thought Laurie was the one—you know, 'The One.' To be honest, I'm not sure anymore."

"The One? There is no such thing as The One. There's only the one you're willing to work with, and the one who's willing to put up with your crap, too. 'Cause that's what it takes, Donny—work, lots of it. Did you think it was going to be champagne and wild sex all the time?"

"No."

"Then grow up and quit feeling sorry for yourself. Everybody gets their own bag of shit. Deal with it."

"I'm not some teenage kid, Eddy."

Eddy shrugged. "Then quit acting like one."

Donny picked up another potato and scowled at it. He and Eddy worked in silence for a minute. "Is it what you expected? The kids, family, everything?"

"It's what happened. Nobody knows what to expect."

"But ... I mean, is it worth it?"

"Most of the time. For me, anyway." Eddy paused and looked at the ceiling. "You know, Linda and I started dating in high school, then one day we're getting married, the next we're changing diapers, and then suddenly the kids are in high school. One day they put their arms around you, hug you and tell you they love you, and you wouldn't trade it for anything. And the next day they push every single one of your buttons and you wonder if there's some tropical island where you could just disappear."

"But you didn't."

"No. When we got engaged, Linda told me that she thought being a widow was better than being a divorcee and that bullets were cheaper than lawyers. You don't ever want to piss off a Portuguese woman. They make pit bulls seem compassionate."

"How many more potatoes?"

Eddy looked in the pot. "Well, there's the Moose factor. Might as well finish the bag."

Eddy took the pot of beans to the sink, covered them with water and set the pot on the counter beside the stove. He spoke with his back to Donny. "You stepping out?"

"What? No!"

"A man feels the thrill slipping away, sometimes he looks for it somewhere else."

"Jesus, Eddy, I said no, OK? Not that it's any of your business."

"No, it's not." Eddy turned around and leaned back against the counter. "Except I like you, Donny, and you're one of those guys who's book smart and life stupid. Just remember, no one ever solved a relationship problem by starting another relationship."

"Thank you, Doctor Phil."

"You're welcome. You should also remember that the police do carry guns." Donny started to object but Eddy cut him off. "Yeah, yeah, yeah. The captain doth protest too much, methinks. I don't think I'm the only one who's noticed the way you look at Sergeant Singh. Can't say I blame you, but it's a bad idea."

Donny whittled at the remaining potatoes while Eddy mixed a salad. At last the bag was empty. Donny held the final peeled potato up to the light, turned it suspiciously, and tossed it in with the others. "I asked her to drop by after supper."

"Who? Singh? Are you completely nuts? You can't do that here!"

"I just want to ask her about the suicide." Donny put down the peeler and held the pot of potatoes out to Eddy. "You ever see that before—an eye bolt?"

"Could you be a little more vague about that?" Eddy took the pot to the sink and began rinsing the potatoes. "Honest to God, Wedge, sometimes I wonder what it sounds like inside your head. And yes, I've seen an eye bolt before; so what?"

"At the suicide. That guy Rothberg went to all the trouble to find a ceiling joist, drill a hole and screw in a heavy-duty eye bolt. Never seen that before. Usually they just tie off to a pipe or a light fixture or something."

"Yeah, and half the time they rip the light fixture out of the ceiling or something else breaks." Eddy started cutting the potatoes into quarters and dropping the pieces into another pot.

Donny tipped his chair back on two legs and tapped his fingertips together. Eddy recognized the posture. How many years had he watched Donny talk himself into or out of something, sitting just like that? Sixteen? Seventeen? Christ, it was just like being married, without the sex. For better or worse ...

"It was new rope, too, I'm pretty sure of that. Sure looked new, anyway," Donny said to the empty chair across the table. "The place was a mess, clothes and garbage everywhere; the guy was a complete loser. So why did he go to all that trouble in planning to kill himself?"

"Who knows? The guy's gonna kill himself—by definition he's fucked in the head to begin with. Anyway, who cares? Nobody's gonna miss him." Eddy finished cutting the potatoes, covered them with water and set the pot on the stove beside the beans. "Moose and Scout still working out?"

Donny nodded.

"Tell them to finish up and hit the shower. Supper's in half an hour."

CHAPTER 18

CHERRY PIE

Daya Singh parked the cruiser in front of the pedestrian entrance to Station Six, to the side of the large wooden doors at the front of the apparatus bays. She rang the bell and stood back to admire the station's Victorian architecture as she waited: the gargoyle that stared menacingly down at her from the lintel above the door, the graceful hose tower that once offered a commanding view of the city and its harbour.

And there under the peak of the slate roof, carved from fiery red sandstone, a phoenix, wings outstretched, launching itself from a nest of flame. How had she never noticed that before? During her years in the district, Daya had driven past the station countless times. She marvelled at the stonemason's skill that could capture living flame and make it solid.

Scout answered the door and held it open for Daya. "Hi. Over there, to the right, just before the floor watch room." It wasn't unusual for cops to stop in to use the washroom.

"Actually, I'm here to see Captain Robertson. He asked me to drop by."

"Oh, sure. Come on up." Scout led the way up the stairs that spiralled around the interior of the hose tower, and held open the door that led to the second floor. The savoury aromas of roasted meat and fresh baking greeted Daya as she and Scout headed for the kitchen.

Donny and Moose were seated at the table. Eddy stood at the counter beside the stove, cutting a pie and handing out the pieces.

Donny rose from his chair as Daya appeared in the doorway. "Come on in, you're just in time. Eddy made a cherry pie."

Eddy glanced from her to Donny, then turned to the cupboard to fetch another plate and fork.

"I can't stay long. I need to ... Cherry pie?" Daya said, reconsidering. She sat in the chair beside Moose. "I obviously joined the wrong department."

"We've been trying to tell you guys that for years," Moose grinned as he shoved another forkful of pie into his mouth.

Daya accepted the plate from Eddy. Plump globes of fruit nestled in crimson syrup beneath a flaky golden blanket. She closed her eyes and inhaled the rich, tart aroma. "Now I know why they call you Eddy the Ladle."

"It's partially self-preservation," Eddy explained as he returned to his seat and picked up his own fork. "If I don't feed Moose, someone's liable to end up missing an arm or a leg."

They talked about impending cuts to the City's budget, what effects they might have on their departments, and various other petty grievances they had with their respective administrations. Daya pushed her plate away, leaving the edge of the pie crust, which Moose unceremoniously picked off her plate and popped into his mouth whole.

"Moose!" Donny shook his head and turned to Daya. "The finer points of etiquette have never been our strong point in the fire service."

"Sorry, I forgot you were company," Moose mumbled, pastry crumbs drifting from his lips.

Daya laughed. "Don't worry, food never went to waste in our house when I was growing up. So what's on your mind? Like I said, I need to get back soon."

"Do you mind if we talk in the office? We'll let the guys clean up."
Donny stood and ushered her out of the kitchen and down the hall.

Daya stepped through the open door of the office and stopped.
"You could at least have reserved a nice hotel room and some champagne," she said dryly. Donny came up beside her and stared at the neatly made bed that occupied most of the middle of the room.

"Oh, shit!" He rushed into the office and folded the Murphy bed back into the wall. "I'm sorry," he muttered, arranging the chairs into their normal daytime positions in front of the desk. "It's just a habit ... something I normally do before we sit down for supper."

"Hmm, there are times I've wished I had one of those in my office." She sat in one of the chairs and admired the Victorian craftsmanship of the cabinetry. "Nice room. Guess I really did join the wrong department. So what's up?"

Donny leaned back against the panel that hid the Murphy bed. "You hear about the suicide this afternoon? The guy who hanged himself?"

"The sex offender? Yeah, I heard. The homicide guys just finished there. Why?"

"Homicide?" Donny straightened up. "They think it was a murder?"

"Not that I've heard. It's just routine for any unnatural death: photographs, scene analysis, that sort of thing."

Donny sat in the chair opposite her. "Do you know if there were any tools found there? Like a drill and a stud finder, specifically? I don't remember seeing any tools."

"I don't know. It's not my case." Daya fixed him with a curious look. "And it's not yours either. Anyway, you can borrow tools or rent them."

Donny continued, undeterred. "You ever been to a suicide like that? Where a guy goes to all the trouble to buy new rope, find a stud and sink an eye bolt?"

Daya waved the questions away and shook her head. "I've been to suicides where people have done all sorts of crazy and bizarrely creative things. Their last grand gesture to the world, I guess. Why are you digging into this? And why are you bringing it to me, anyway? Like I said, I'm not even on the case. I'm a staff sergeant, not an investigator."

Donny started to reach out to her, but stopped and slowly lowered his hand. "Because I trust you."

The way he looked at her was flattering and made her uncomfortable at the same time. She turned towards the window and looked out at the city, at all the glowing windows that looked back, where a thousand other stories were unfolding. That was where she needed to be.

She stood and stepped towards the door without looking at him. "If you have concerns, then file a report. Or talk to someone who was there, like ..." She stopped and turned to face him. "This isn't about the suicide. It's about Ericson, isn't it?"

"No! Well, sort of. But you've got to admit it's a little strange—a 'suicide,'" Donny made air quotes with his fingers, "another person everyone's glad to be rid of, and Ericson just happens to be there."

"Whatever unfinished business you two have, you need to settle it." Daya shook her head and opened the office door.

Donny followed her into the hall. "OK, OK. Jeez, I just thought I could talk to you."

"And whatever you think there is between us, you need to sort that out too. I'm not your personal police therapist, OK?"

The sound of raised voices drifted into the kitchen. Moose and Eddy paused at the kitchen sink and looked at each other, a freshly washed pan dripping between them. Scout leaned on his mop and looked towards the door, smirking. "I guess they're having either a really good time or a really bad time."

"Just finish cleaning the floor," Moose said, drying the pan vigorously. There was the sound of a door opening.

"Thanks for the pie, Eddy," Daya said as she passed the kitchen door. She didn't stop as she strode down the hall to the stairs.

"You're welcome," Eddy called after her. He shook his head and plunged another pot into the soapy water.

Donny was waiting for her when she reached the bottom of the stairs. Daya stopped, confused. How could he …? Then she saw the brass pole that disappeared into the ceiling behind him.

"This conversation is over, Donny."

"Listen, if this is because of what happened in the park, I'm sorry. I shouldn't have done that. It's just, I feel like I can talk to you. But you're right: I'll take the other stuff through channels. I mean, I don't want it to affect us."

"There is no 'us,' Donny!" Her voice echoed up the hose tower.

"Yeah. No. I mean, as friends … colleagues."

"Sure, that's why you kissed me, because we're buddies." She walked past him and put her hand on the door. "I have two basic rules: First, don't get your honey where you get your money. Second, no married men."

His gut told him it was a bad idea to try to argue details with her, but like most men, he couldn't help himself. "I'm not married."

"You have kids living with you and you share your bed with a woman. In my book, that's married. We have responsibilities, Donny; we're adults. Time you started living like one." And with that she walked out to her cruiser.

Donny stared as the door closed in front of him. He heard the squeal of tires as Daya pulled away, then slowly made his way upstairs.

Eddy was waiting for him as he stepped into the office. "You're putting out fires with gasoline."

"I don't recall asking for your opinion." Donny walked by him, kicked the chairs out of the way and lowered the Murphy bed.

"Either way, it doesn't change the situation."

Donny turned and glared at him. "And this is your business because …?"

"Because friends, real friends, don't stand by and watch people mess up their lives."

"Screw you, Eddy. I've had enough of your amateur psychology for one night."

"I'll give you that one for free, 'cause you know I'm right." Eddy closed the door behind him and headed back to the kitchen.

Donny lay back on the bed and counted the dots in the ceiling tiles.

CHAPTER 19

HARDWARE

There were only three stores on his list and this was the last one. Neighbourhood hardware stores were becoming a thing of the past, but a few still survived in the inner-city areas where the rents were too high for the big box stores. Good Luck Hardware was across the Don River from Station Six, on Gerrard Street, in what was commonly known as Chinatown East. It was one of a number of Asian communities that had sprung up across the city as the old downtown Chinatown became too crowded and too expensive.

Donny wove his way through the gauntlet of stalls and people that crowded the sidewalk. A bouquet of aromas swirled around him: barbecued pork, ripe fruit and dried shrimp. Whole fish stared dully up at him from their beds of crushed ice.

Good Luck Hardware's windows were crowded with small appliances, kitchen gadgets and garden tools. Behind the jumbled display was a faded poster from a paint company; the poster dated back to the '80s, judging by the model's Farrah Fawcett hairstyle.

"Ní hǎo," Donny nodded to the man behind the counter as he walked in.

"Xin chào," the man replied. "I'm Vietnamese, not Chinese."

"Sorry."

"No problem. You guys all look same to me, too," the man said with a twinkle in his eye. He was about a foot shorter than Donny, with wispy grey hair atop a thin, triangular face. The man looked both ancient and timeless, Donny thought. He suspected the store owner had lived through more than Donny could possibly imagine. He would have been a kid during the war. Donny wondered about the incredible journey that had brought him to a hardware store half-way around the world. He was probably driven by the same factors that had motivated Donny's own Irish/Scottish ancestors a hundred and fifty years earlier: hunger, desperation, and the dream of something better.

"What you need?" the owner asked, bringing Donny back from his reverie.

"Do you have rope?"

"Sure," the man said, stretching the word out as he led the way down a narrow aisle lined with boxes of nails and screws, plastic packages of wall anchors, cup hooks and the like.

"Got rope, chain, wire—whatever you need." The owner pointed to a rack of large spools mounted on the wall at the end of the aisle. Donny fingered the leading edge of a yellow polypropylene rope that dangled from its spool.

The owner nodded. "That good stuff, strong. Float, too, good for boat. How much you want?"

"Do you have a security camera in the store?" Donny asked, turning to face the man. He saw the man's friendly expression harden.

"You police?"

"No. Fire department. I think someone may have done a bad thing with rope like this."

"Hmm." The man relaxed slightly. "Yeah, I got camera. Old ones, not so good, but new one too expensive."

Donny followed the old man's pointing finger to a spot on the ceiling at the far wall, where two large, clunky cameras were suspended. One covered the back half of the store, the other surveyed the front.

"Do you remember a man buying rope like this recently? A tall guy, about my height but with big shoulders and blond hair. He probably bought an eye bolt too."

"Me old. Memory not so good." The man shook his head.

"Please, it's important."

The owner rubbed the thin stubble on his chin. Donny suspected he was wrestling with his choices more than struggling to remember. "You not police, not immigration?"

"No, like I said, fire department," Donny replied, holding up his hand as if he were taking an oath. "I swear."

The man paused for a moment. "A guy buy this rope two days ago, maybe three? I remember, he definitely look like police."

"Did he buy anything else?"

"Couple of things, maybe," the owner shrugged. "Lots of people in store every day."

"The cameras are recording, right?"

"Computer. My grandson look after that." The owner retreated behind his cash register. Donny followed him. "Screwdriver I understand; computer, no."

"Can you ask your grandson to make me a copy from that day?" Donny pulled a fifty-dollar bill from his wallet and laid it on the counter. "Please, I'll pay you for it."

The two men locked eyes. Donny felt like he was having his soul weighed. This must be what Judgement Day feels like, he thought.

The man slid the money back towards Donny. "My uncle was fireman in Nha Trang. He was good man." There was obviously more to the story that Donny would never hear. "Come back tomorrow."

"Thank you," Donny said, bowing his head with gratitude.

"You're welcome." The man nodded grimly.

Donny mentally patted himself on the back as he closed the car door. Now to keep the momentum going. He pulled out his phone and scrolled to Terry's number.

"Donny, darling, how are you?" purred the voice on the phone.

"It's turning out to be a pretty good day." Donny started the car and pulled away from the curb. "I'm hoping you're going to make it even better."

"Oooh, I'm all aquiver. What's on your mind?"

"How about coffee? I'm in the neighbourhood."

Terry gave him the name of a Cabbagetown café. Donny turned the car around and headed back across the river, towards downtown.

Donny arrived first. The coffee shop was a pleasant place: lilac walls hung with tropical pictures of coffee plantations, half a dozen small tables, and a glass-fronted counter displaying a selection of decadent pastries. The air was filled with the aroma of cinnamon and roasting coffee, the sound of subdued conversations, and the periodic hiss of the espresso machine. Donny ordered a black Americano and a chocolate pecan brownie and took a seat at a table in the front window. Terry arrived a few minutes later, ordered a cappuccino and joined Donny at the table.

Donny got down to business immediately. "Bill Ericson. Did you find out anything about him?"

"Nice to see you too," Terry sighed. "Well, I asked around, discreetly, like you said."

"And?"

"He's not shaking anyone down for money or blowjobs or anything like that." Terry stirred sugar into her cappuccino. "At least not among the people I know. It doesn't sound like he's running dope or any scams either."

"That's it?"

"He's a cop, Donny. It's not like he's BFFs with anyone I know. And he's got a bit of a temper."

"Oh, really?"

"He knocked out one of Brenda's teeth. You know Brenda? Big red 'fro, works the corner of Seaton and Dundas? She's a friend of mine," Terry explained. "Anyway, Brenda spit at him once and he punched her in the mouth."

"And that was Ericson? So he's got a history of violence," Donny nodded.

"I don't know," Terry said. "Cops really don't like it when you spit on them. Especially a working girl. Brenda should have known better."

"Did she file a complaint?"

"What planet are you living on?" Terry scolded. "A Black trans hooker spits on a cop—how you do think that's going to go down?"

"Sorry, just asking," Donny said.

"On the other hand," Terry continued, "seems like he's friends with one of the regular working girls, Roxanne. She was gone for a while, but she's back now. Anyway, some of the other girls said Ericson likes to stop and talk with her now and then. But that seems to be all, just talk."

"Really, just her?" Donny mopped up brownie crumbs with his finger. "I wonder what that's about?"

Terry shrugged. "Roxanne used to work for that piece of shit Simpson, the guy Ericson shot. Might have something to do with that. Maybe they're just friends."

"Like you and me," Donny smiled.

"Just friends?" Terry winked. "I heard you don't need a smoke detector if you sleep with a firefighter."

Terry turned the conversation to local gossip, the increasing gentrification of the neighbourhood, and fashion commentary on the pedestrians passing the café's window. They finished their coffees and went their separate ways.

The streetlights popped on as Donny started his car. It was barely five o'clock, but the November days were getting progressively shorter. Donny merged with the exodus of traffic spilling from the forest of downtown office towers. He had meant to be home by now and prayed the traffic wouldn't make him late for supper. Life was so much simpler when it didn't matter what time he was home. He could come and go as he pleased … Would it be any different with Daya?

He forced the thought away and turned to a review of the day's findings. He had made some progress. The question was, where to go from here? Maybe when he actually had the video footage from the hardware store, Daya might ... No, that was perilous ground.

CHAPTER 20

THE SHIT LIST

"Two right lanes closed ahead," the overhead sign read. Tom Humphrey looked at his navigation screen and sighed. One long red line. His meeting with the deputy chief had run late and now here he was, stuck in rush-hour traffic on the 401. The highway sliced east–west through the middle of Toronto. Traffic was bad at the best of times; now it was six lanes of cars and trucks crawling in each direction, as people tried to squeeze past the accident ahead and rubberneckers going the other way slowed down to get a good look. He was going nowhere fast. He was already in a bad mood, and what needed to be done wouldn't make it any worse. Might as well use the time. He pressed the call button on the steering wheel. "Call Robertson."

"Calling Donald Robertson," the car replied.

The phone rang twice before it was picked up. "Chief, how are you doing?"

"I'm fine. The question is, what the hell are you up to?"

"I'm not sure what you mean."

Humphrey scanned the traffic on either side of him. None of it was moving. "I'm not in the mood for any bullshit. I'll tell you that right from the start."

"Of course." Donny's voice sounded less than certain despite the assurance.

"I just got out of a meeting at headquarters. Among other things, the deputy wanted to know why our switchboard got calls from not one, but two hardware store owners wondering why a fireman was going around asking about rope, and was the guy on the level or was he some imposter?"

"Oh."

"Yeah, big 'Oh!'" Humphrey scowled at the car's speaker. "Those stores are in your district and the man they described fits you, right down to your curly red hair."

"You see, it's like this. We had this call for a ..." Donny began.

"You know what I really hate, Donny?" Humphrey cut him off. "I really hate the deputy asking me questions I don't have an answer for." Humphrey's concerns extended well beyond any questions from the fire department's deputy chief. The Committee would be none too happy about this development either. "So I need to know everything you've been up to. And I mean *everything*."

Donny gave him the details of his inquiries, including his visit to Good Luck Hardware. "The guy said he'd had a customer who looked a lot like Ericson. He's making me a copy of the footage from his security cameras."

"Security cameras?" Humphrey's grip tightened on the steering wheel. How could Ericson have been so careless—buying the rope in the same neighbourhood as the job, let alone being caught on camera? He took a deep breath and forced himself to keep his voice level. "Now look, Donny, you are way out of line. If there is anything to this, which I strongly doubt, then you may have contaminated the line of evidence. Did you ever consider that? We are not cops! You need to get that through your thick head."

"I'm sorry, Chief. It's just that there were some odd things about that suicide."

"And you know what you do when you have concerns like that?"

"Put them in my report."

"That's right. And then they get passed along through proper channels to the right people." Humphrey's soothing tone changed abruptly. "TO PEOPLE WHOSE JOB IT IS TO ACTUALLY INVESTIGATE THINGS!"

"Sorry, sir."

Humphrey hated losing his cool, but on occasion it served a purpose. "Sorry doesn't cut it. I will go to the wall for you, Donny, if you're straight and level with me. I can't control what you do in your time off, but this needs to stop. Do you read me?"

"Yes, sir."

"Don't you think you've strained relations between us and the cops enough lately? I don't want to have to deal with this again. God help me, but I actually like you, Donny. You're a good firefighter. But you are also a pain in the ass, and I will not hesitate to clip your wings for the good of the department. Is that understood?"

"Yes, sir."

"It better be." Humphrey punched the "end call" button and stared at the long line of stationary traffic in front of him. It was the least of his problems.

The call from Humphrey ended abruptly as Donny turned onto his street. The day had been going so well until now, but once again he had somehow ended up back on the shit list. He pulled into the driveway, turned off the car, and took a moment to collect his thoughts before entering the house.

Laurie stood in the kitchen doorway with her arms crossed. It wasn't a good sign. Donny's mind raced as he took off his shoes and hung his jacket on the hook by the side door. How had he screwed up this time?

"How was your day?" Donny asked, looking up at her. Did his tone smack a little too much of feigned innocence?

"My day? My day was fine." Her tone told him it had been anything but. Donny followed her as she headed back to the kitchen. When she heard Donny open the fridge, Laurie turned and leaned on the counter. "You were supposed to be home this afternoon. You want to tell me what's going on?"

"I was checking out hardware stores. It's a long story." Donny twisted the cap off a beer and sat at the kitchen table. "It's that cop Ericson; he's ..."

"Hardware stores, eh?" Laurie cut him off. "I guess that was more important than picking up Daniel and Kevin after swim team practice."

"Oh, crap! I forgot. Where are they?"

"In their rooms doing their homework, wonder of wonders. I was at the hairdresser's when the boys called me. I phoned Jennifer, and she picked them up and brought them home."

"Jesus! I completely forgot. I am so sorry." He reached across the table to take her hand, but she pulled it away.

"Sorry? That's all you've got to say—'sorry?' You left two little boys stranded."

"Damn it, why didn't they call me?"

Laurie leaned on the table, glaring down at him. "Probably because they don't know if they can trust you. You're a nice guy, Donny, but parenting takes way more than just being a nice guy. You're self-centred and unreliable. You think Daniel and Kevin don't pick up on that? And what about me? When was the last time we made love?"

"Don't, please." Donny flushed. He had begun to wonder what had happened to the passion that used to flare in him when he even thought of Laurie. Now it was the thought of Daya that made his pulse race.

Laurie closed her eyes, took a slow, deep breath, and opened her eyes again. "This." Laurie swept her arm, taking in the rest of the house. "This whole thing. This takes commitment—mentally, emotionally, everything. You need to be all in. I see it in other parts of your life. You're totally committed to your job. You're obsessed with this Ericson thing. And the boys and me? We get the scraps, whatever's left over." She sat across from Donny. Her anger had drained away, leaving a tired sadness. "I don't know, maybe we're just not exciting enough for you. Maybe you've found someone else."

Donny's s throat tightened "It's not that. I swear." He pushed the thought of Daya's soft brown skin away. He wanted this to work, he really did. He wanted it all to mesh seamlessly. Maybe that was the problem—trying to have it all. "I screwed up. And I know it's not the first time, either. I truly am sorry, if that still means anything. I'm trying to change, but it's hard, you know, after all these years. And I've got this situation at work with Scout that's a bit of a mess. And Ericson, jeez, I don't even know where to start with that. He's like this one-man ... "

"Stop. Just stop."

Donny's mouth hung open. The storm winds were blowing and he had no clue if there was safe anchorage anywhere.

"Do you hear yourself? Not once did you mention Daniel or Kevin or me. It's all about you. It's always all about you." Laurie shook her head. She got up and walked across the kitchen. She stopped and spoke to the window over the sink. "I'm not going to do it, Donny. I don't want to become the nagging spouse, and I'm not going to play second fiddle to your job—or to anything or anyone else, for that matter."

She turned to face him, her features drawn with weariness and disappointment. "I want a partner, not just someone else to take care of. I want someone who wants to be part of my life too."

Donny started to speak, but Laurie silenced him with a wave. She opened the fridge. "I need to get to work. There's salad in here and a lasagna in the oven. Make sure the boys finish their homework." She reached into the fridge and removed her lunch pail. "You've got a decision to make, Donny. Make it soon."

She moved down the hall, kissed the boys goodbye, and left without looking back.

Screw it! That was his first thought. He didn't need this. How had he ended up in this situation, anyway? He'd been single and happy most of his life. Well, he hadn't been unhappy. At least most of the time. He'd certainly never planned on having kids, and now suddenly here he was with a nine-year-old and an eleven-year-old.

Cut and run. That was his gut instinct. It was what his own father had done. The realization made him pause. Following in his father's footsteps was the last thing Donny wanted to do.

He could throw himself at Daya's feet. The way she looked at him—there had been some interest there. It couldn't be all his imagination. Surely he could make her understand that this whole "instant family" thing had been a mistake on his part.

It was a cheap variation on his first thought, and he knew it.

Donny looked at the timer on the oven. Ready in fifteen minutes. If only the rest of life were that convenient.

CHAPTER 21

PASSPORTS

"I need passports, not pieces of paper!" Ramón hissed. He shoved the documents back at the man and glanced around nervously to see if anyone had overheard him.

"These are not just 'pieces of paper,'" the man replied, in a low voice tinged with a soft German accent. He replaced the documents in the manila envelope Ramón had tossed aside and leaned back in his chair.

They sat across from each other in one of a dozen or so circular Plexiglas study pods on the third floor of the Toronto Central Reference Library. Being out in the open like this made Ramón nervous, but the German had insisted on meeting in a public place. Ramón had suggested the reference library. At least the plastic walls of the study pod gave some privacy for their conversation.

The Central Reference Library was a building Ramón had grown to love. During his first few weeks in Toronto, in the depths of his first Canadian winter, it had simply been a place for him to try to keep from freezing to death. At the time, he had been living by his wits and mostly on the street. At first, he took books off the shelves simply to look like he belonged. Gradually his choices became more focused. There had never been much time for books during his hard-scrabble youth in Ensenada. Ironically, it was here in this frigid gringo city that he discovered the voices of his own people: Juan Rulfo, Guadalupe Nettel, and his favourite, Gabriel García Márquez, a Colombian who had lived much of his life in Mexico.

The library building itself was a beautiful home for beautiful words and ideas. Each floor wrapped around the soaring central atrium in soft curves. Ivy and philodendron trailed from the half walls that bordered each floor. It was everything a public building should be: bright, open, inviting and alive.

Ramón had come to think of the library as something of a sanctuary, but now he felt exposed. Still, the German had what he needed: new identities for him and Roxanne. He tried to size up the man sitting across from him. The German tourists Ramón had known in Mexico were loud and brash. This man was different.

Stephan, if that was the German's real name, was a balding, near-sighted, self-indulgent-looking man in his sixties. His fleshy cheeks and ample waistline spoke of a taste for rich food. He was unobtrusively dressed, but Ramón noticed the Tag Heuer watch and tailored camel hair coat. The man clearly had a taste for the finer things, but without ostentation. Ramón caught a whiff of a slightly feminine odour—cologne or fine soap. Stephan probably drove a Lexus ... no, he was German, it would be a BMW or an Audi, high-end but unassumingly discreet. No Porsche, that would be too flashy.

Ramón knew Stephan was studying him as well. What did he see aside from need and desperation?

Stephan felt some kinship with the Mexican. Both of them had come to this country with skills learned in a past life. Stephan had learned his during his years with the Stasi, the East German secret police. The KGB, their sister agency in the Soviet Union, were thugs, a legacy of the more brutish aspects of Russian history. While the Stasi could be ruthless when that was required, it was their skills in intimidation, seduction and all manner of manipulation that made the East Germans the most effective, feared and repressive intelligence agency in the world. With typical German efficiency and precision, they had surpassed their former Soviet masters.

It had all come tumbling down; the Stasi were no more, but the skills Stephan had learned continued to serve him well. In his hands, greed, lust, dreams and delusions all became the tools of a master craftsman. They had allowed him, among other things, to build his network within the Citizenship Court.

Stephan smiled reassuringly. "These are certificates of citizenship," he explained, patting the manila envelope. "They are the key that opens the whole vault: passports, driver's licence, social security, whatever you want."

"But I need the passports now," Ramón insisted.

"Modern passports have holograms, invisible print, embedded chips and encryption. Forging such a thing is no longer possible for the individual. Mossad, the CIA, maybe a few others can do it, but no one else. You can probably find someone who will promise to make you a quick passport, but it won't be worth the paper it's printed on. I guarantee you'll be caught the first time you try to use it."

"And those?" Ramón pointed to the envelope containing the certificates of citizenship.

"The real thing." Stephan explained that he had people within the Citizenship Court who could insert documents into the files, enter the data, and approve changes to the computer records. And *voilà*, whole new people were created. It was a chink in the armour, the unguarded back door. It seemed like genius, but Ramón was still skeptical.

Stephan tucked the envelope with the sample certificates back in his coat. "The important thing is not the piece of paper. You will actually be in the system. You could even collect welfare if you wanted, but I recommend against that. Use the certificate to get whatever other ID you need, create a new life, and keep a low profile. It's foolproof, but it takes a little time."

Time was one luxury Ramón didn't have. On the other hand, he couldn't afford to be careless. "How much time?"

"Normally, a couple of weeks. It can be done in a few days, but that costs more," Stephan shrugged. "Certain records need to be created and back dated. It needs to be done step by step, properly and carefully."

"Twenty thousand?"

"Thirty for a rush job. Each. Half now, half on delivery. This is non-negotiable."

It would consume more than half of the money Ramón had taken from the Triad. Just arranging this meet had cost him five thousand dollars, paid to contacts Ramón barely trusted. It wouldn't leave much for starting a new life, but he had few other options.

He could leave Roxanne behind. He needed money to make a fresh start. *Ser inteligente, ser seguro*, said a voice in his head that sounded remarkably like his father. "Ah, *mi corazón*," Ramón muttered to himself, "you'll be the death of me." Careful to make sure no one could see what he was doing, Ramón lifted the backpack he had brought onto his lap, reached into the inside pocket of the puffy jacket he was wearing, and transferred six bundles of bills into the pack. He put the pack back on the floor and slid it towards the German with his foot.

Stephan reached for the pack, but didn't open it. "The pictures and signatures?" he asked.

Ramón pointed.

Stephan removed an envelope from the side pocket of the pack, opened it and examined the contents: three copies each of standard passport-style photographs of Ramón and a young woman; two sheets of plain white paper, each sheet with a signature repeated three times. Donna Elizabeth McNall was the name on the first sheet. Stephan frowned at the name signed on the second page—Gustavo Daniel Sandoval. "Gustavo? Really?"

Ramón shrugged. "I'm a fan, and it was my grandfather's name."

"All the more reason to use something else. Whatever." Stephan folded the sheets of paper, put them back in the envelope along with the photographs, and tucked the envelope into the inside pocket of his coat. The signatures and pictures would be used to complete the appropriate forms, Stephan explained, which would then be filed, digitized and archived. "I'll contact you when everything is ready. Nice meeting you ... Gus."

Stephan picked up the backpack and opened the door of the study pod. Ramón watched him as he made his way towards the atrium and the escalators that led to the main floor. He thought of following Stephan, but to what end? Germans were thorough, Ramón told himself. He hoped that somehow translated into trustworthy, though he wasn't sure of his own logic.

Stephan put the pack in the trunk of the BMW and looked around. There was no one else on this level of the garage, and there were no visible cameras. He leaned in, unzipped the bag and counted the bundles of hundred-dollar bills as he stacked them neatly in his own briefcase. It was all there. He folded the empty backpack, placed it in a small plastic garbage bag and tied the top. There was a trash barrel at the end of the row of parked cars. Stephan buried the garbage bag under a layer of takeout coffee cups, sandwich wrappers and other detritus that accumulated in people's cars. It was overkill, perhaps, but he was trained to be methodical. Covering his tracks was an old habit.

Stephan pulled out of the parking garage and turned north onto Yonge Street. At a red light, he took the envelope from his coat pocket and laid Ramón's photograph on the passenger seat. He stared at it until the light turned green. Yes, he felt a certain kinship with the Mexican, but it would not for a moment cloud his judgement.

He could simply give Ramón his documents, collect the other thirty thousand dollars and be done with it. It was straightforward and profitable enough.

He could also turn the lad over to the authorities. That would also net him some money, but there were far too many strings attached to the reward. There were others, however, who were also seeking the cop killer. Stephan had heard the whispers on the street.

Ramón's former employers in the Triad would pay handsomely for news of his whereabouts, and it would strengthen Stephan's existing business relationship with them. That had been his initial plan.

More recently, Stephan had heard that someone else was interested in finding someone who fit the Mexican's description. It was a secretive group, one that seemed to be particularly well connected. The reward here would be something more valuable than just money: leverage at the highest levels. That could be worth looking into.

It was good to have options.

CHAPTER 22

BEER CAN CHICKEN

Nancy Humphrey slid the patio door open and held a glass of white wine out to her husband. Tom Humphrey stared at the chicken perched on a beer can on his barbecue, absorbed in his own thoughts.

"Work?" Nancy asked.

"Hmm? Oh, thanks." Humphrey accepted the wine and took a sip. "It's nothing."

"Yes, it's always nothing, and then you can't sleep." *Retire, already—* that was Nancy's unspoken insinuation.

Perhaps she was right. Forty-two years was enough. But first ... He took another sip from the glass. "That's nice. Chardonnay?"

"Gewürz," she corrected. "Notice the spicy hints. Chardonnay is more buttery and smooth."

"Of course," Humphrey nodded. Nancy was taking a wine appreciation course at the local college. He did his best to share her enthusiasm. Humphrey made a show of swirling the glass and inhaling the wine's bouquet, but in truth he rather envied the chicken for the can it was sitting on.

"You'd rather have a beer, wouldn't you?" It was a statement more than a question.

"Thanks, I'll have this with dinner." He handed her the wine glass and followed her inside.

"Everything OK?" Nancy asked, reaching into the fridge for a beer. She turned back to him, one eyebrow raised, and handed him the can.

He popped it open and took a big swig. "It's fine. It's just ..."

"Stuff."

"Yeah, stuff," he nodded. She knew when to ask and when to stop asking. It was one of the many things he loved about her. "The joys of management. Sometimes I wish I'd stayed on the trucks. I need to make a call. The chicken will be ready in about ten minutes."

Humphrey slid the patio door closed behind him and reached into his jacket for his phone. He scrolled through the contacts and selected Bob Collins.

"We have a problem."

Humphrey and Collins had known each other for most of their working lives. It had started as a nodding acquaintance at calls, when they were both fresh-faced and eager to save the world for their respective departments. As both men rose through the ranks, their paths would sometimes cross at major incidents. They had even shared the occasional pint at the Sparrow. They were friendly, if not exactly friends.

It was their children who had brought them closer together. Humphrey's daughter Cassy and Collins' Melissa had met on the college hockey team. The two young women had become good friends and eventually lovers.

It had been an adjustment for both families. Tom Humphrey had wrestled with his feelings the most, but when Cassy and Melissa announced that they were going to be married, he had given his blessing. When the day came, all four parents had proudly escorted their daughters down the aisle.

And then came the day that Cassy and Melissa announced that they had found a donor. Cassy was pregnant; Tom was going to be a grandfather. Somehow, opening the door onto that phase of his life, a door he thought had been nailed shut, allowed him to cross the bridge from tepid approval to wholehearted acceptance.

And then the unthinkable happened.

Shots rang out as the two women stepped onto the sidewalk from a popular downtown restaurant. Glass shattered, people screamed, and two bodies fell to the ground—a drive-by shooting gone horribly wrong, and once again the only casualties were unintended victims. A stray bullet had passed through Cassy's neck, severing her carotid artery, and entered the top of Melissa's head, which she had just laid on her partner's shoulder.

Cassy bled out before the paramedics arrived. Machines kept Melissa breathing until Bob Collins and his wife, Grace, could accept that the person their daughter had been was gone forever. The four parents who had walked down that aisle side by side now wept together. Eight people would be given a new chance at life thanks to Melissa's donated organs, but it was hollow comfort.

Murder charges were laid against Elijah Jennings, a known gang banger. Jennings had gunpowder residue on his hands, and the bullet that lodged in Melissa's brain matched the gun found in his possession.

But there were problems, the prosecutor told the Humphrey and Collins families. The police had conducted the investigation into the murder of their colleague's daughter and daughter-in-law with zeal—too much zeal. There were credible allegations that Jennings had been beaten while in custody. Worse, there were issues with the search warrant and chain of custody for the gun, technicalities that could render it inadmissible as evidence. And the few witnesses who were willing to testify could give only a general description. Most had been intoxicated, and a few had other credibility issues.

Flimsy as Jennings' alibi was, the prosecutor explained, there was a chance that he might walk. Better he serve at least some time rather than go scot-free. Elijah Jennings agreed to plead guilty to manslaughter rather than face the possibility of twenty-five years for murder.

As a cop, Collins knew that these deals were made; he'd even been party to some of them. But this was his daughter. The numbness had turned first to grief, then to anger. Now it became rage. Jennings was given two-for-one credit for the time he had spent in jail awaiting trial. In four years, he would be eligible for parole, while Cassy and Melissa lay side by side in the cold ground, haunting their parents' memories.

It was a year after the plea deal that Tom Humphrey and Bob Collins each received a phone call. "I know how you feel. I know *exactly* how you feel," the caller said.

And Cheryl Newlands did. The brutal murder of her husband during a violent home invasion had made headlines across the country. She and her husband had been well known in the city's top social and philanthropic circles. The mourners at the funeral had constituted a veritable Who's Who of Canada's political and financial elite.

"Now tell me, do you just want revenge? Or do you want justice?" the voice asked Humphrey and Collins.

And so it was that Cheryl Newlands recruited the first members of her "Committee." Together they set the terms. Each case would be evaluated fairly and dispassionately, but there would be no loopholes and no technicalities. They would consider only the most heinous matters and there would be only one sentence.

Two more members with expertise in legal and judicial areas were recruited: Laticia Raincourt and Albert Fernandez. Each of them had paid the price of membership, a price no parent or spouse would willingly pay.

No charges were ever laid in the murder of Newlands' husband, but money has a way of ferreting out information where normal investigative procedures fail. Word got back to the Committee that a certain less-than-scrupulous art dealer had been approached to fence a pair of Tom Thomson paintings stolen during the home invasion. A month later, the bodies of two small-time hoods with big ambitions were found floating in the icy water of the St. Lawrence River just north of Montreal.

The Elijah Jennings case was next. He was tried again, in absentia this time, by the Committee. The conclusion, while not inevitable, was unanimous. The procedural issues relating to the search warrant and custody of the gun notwithstanding, Jennings had undoubtedly been the shooter. The day after his release to a halfway house, on parole, Jennings was found in a parking lot, shot twice in the back of the head by two different guns. When they heard the news, both Nancy Humphrey and Grace Collins simply nodded. Neither asked any questions.

"How much does he actually know?" Bob Collins held his hands out to the wood stove that warmed his family room. Humphrey sat across from him in a chair that had been fashioned out of an old barrel, sipping a mug of tea. Humphrey had explained part of the situation to Collins over the phone, but some things were best discussed face to face. He had driven to Collins' house after supper.

"Know? He knows nothing, but he's stumbling around uncomfortably close. And he's still got a hard-on for Ericson." Humphrey relayed the gist of what he had learned about Donny's activities: his doubts about Rothberg's "suicide" and his visit to the hardware store.

"Shit!" Collins looked through the glass doors to his patio and the rolling Caledon Hills beyond, outlined in silver by an almost full moon. This was horse country, the land neatly parcelled out with white fences and dotted with barns that cost more than some people's houses. Collins' house sat on a one-acre lot next to a conservation area. Compared to the mansions that had sprouted up and down this side road in the last couple of decades, Collins' split-level 1970s ranch house was modest, but it had been more than adequate for raising a family. On a good day it was only forty-five minutes into the city, but it was light years away otherwise. Here his daughter had been able to catch frogs in the stream that ran beside his property. Each year she collected autumn leaves for a centrepiece to adorn the Thanksgiving table. They were safe here, removed from the city's contagion.

Or so he had thought.

"Did you check with Ericson?" Collins asked.

"Of course. That's the store where he bought the rope, barely a kilometre from Rothberg's apartment." Humphrey shook his head. How could a cop be so careless? "Robertson says the owner promised to make a copy of the security video. We need to do something about that."

"Crap! OK, leave that with me. I'm sure we can find some kind of leverage." Collins grimaced. "What are you going to do about Robertson? He needs to be contained."

"I'll handle Robertson." Humphrey shifted uncomfortably in his seat and stretched his hands to the warmth of the wood stove. "He's offside and he knows it. He'll listen to reason if his job's on the line."

"And if he doesn't?"

"We do what needs to be done."

"Jesus, Tom!" Collins crossed the room to stand between Humphrey and the fire. "You're going to sanction one of your own?"

"No, of course not. I mean, we'll think of something." Humphrey picked up the mug on the side table and drained it. He peered at the cup's bottom, but there were no tea leaves and no omens to be read.

Collins took off his glasses and rubbed the bridge of his nose. "Good, 'cause I didn't sign up to take out our own people."

"There are other ways." Humphrey put down his mug.

They heard footsteps coming down the hall. Grace Collins poked her head in the door of the family room. "Would you like to stay, Tom? It's getting late, and the weather channel said there's a chance of freezing rain later."

"Really?" Humphrey looked out the patio door. The ragged edge of a bank of clouds glowed in the moonlight. A front was moving in.

"I can make up the guest room. It's no trouble," Grace smiled at the two men. "And I'll make French toast in the morning."

"I'll have to take a rain check. Nancy's expecting me. I'll be leaving soon." Humphrey glanced out at the advancing clouds once again.

"All right. Well, give my love to Nancy and tell her to call me. We need to start making plans for our trip to Mexico. That's still on, isn't it?"

"Of course." The two men looked at each other and nodded.

"All right. Good night, then." Grace padded back down the hall. They heard the bedroom door close.

"All right, I'll handle Donny. You look after the hardware store." Humphrey stood to leave. "What about Ericson?"

"I'm beginning to regret we brought him in," Collins admitted. "He's sloppy and too hot-headed. And he's drawing too much attention. Perhaps we should think about easing him out."

"I'm glad you think so too. He's not going to like it, though, not with Ramón still out on the street."

"You think he'll cause trouble?"

"He's your cop. You know him as well as I do," Humphrey shrugged, "But he's just as much at risk as we are."

"He might take it better if he could finish this one," Collins said quietly, as they made their way down the hall.

Humphrey lifted his jacket off the hook beside the door and sat on the nearby bench to slip on his shoes. "Sort of a going-away present?"

"Something like that. I'll talk to him."

Collins stood in the doorway and watched as Humphrey backed down the driveway and drove away. He locked the door and turned out the lights behind him as he made his way to the bedroom.

Grace was reading, propped up on a stack of pillows, his included, he noted. He sat on the foot of the bed and pulled off his socks. "What are you reading?"

"Vicki Delany's latest. Another in the Constable Molly Smith series," she replied, putting down the book.

"You'd think being married to a cop would be enough," he harrumphed.

How many times had he used that line? Grace smiled at him anyway, eyes twinkling over the rim of her glasses.

Melissa's murder had wounded them both in a way that only a parent who has lost a child can understand, inflicting a wrenching, gnawing pain, beyond reason and reconciliation. And yet his wife had been able to find a way to go on. Some days she did better than others. She had alternately prayed to and cursed God. In the end, it seemed to boil down to some type of acceptance, something he had never been able to reach.

Or maybe it was just that men were different—constitutionally unable to find peace through surrender.

"Is everything OK?" She rolled onto her side and propped herself up on her elbow to look at him.

"Yes, fine." He reached behind her to slide his pillow back onto his side and slipped into bed.

"You both seemed very serious."

"We're serious men," he said, running his hand over her buttocks and down between her thighs.

"You always do that when you don't want to talk about something. Not that that's a bad thing," she said, reaching out to embrace him.

CHAPTER 23

DO YOU LIKE YOUR JOB?

Ratzo heard the truck pull up on the front platform. He looked out his office window as Donny climbed down from Pumper Six.

Station Five, the district headquarters, had none of the charm of the Lombard Street station. A squat, two-storey concrete building, it was high tech, high security, functional and quite soulless. The fire crews had nicknamed it "the bunker" soon after they moved in.

Humphrey's instructions had been crystal clear: get Robertson back in line. It was chain of command and Ratzo was Donny's CO. "You're his friend, too," Humphrey had said. "Hopefully he'll listen to you. But if he continues to cause problems between the departments there will be consequences."

Ratzo collected his thoughts while Donny made his way up to the office.

"You wanted to see me?" Donny began.

"Shut the door," Ratzo instructed. "Do you get a lot of headaches, Donny?"

"No, not often," Donny replied, somewhat puzzled.

"'Cause you're certainly a carrier! I had a very unpleasant conversation with Platoon Chief Humphrey this morning. And evidently the smell of your shit carries all the way to the Deputy."

"Oh."

"Yeah—'oh.'" Ratzo leaned back in his chair. "Do you like your job?"

"Of course." Donny drew a chair towards himself.

"I did not invite you to sit!" Ratzo declared. "You are on thin ice, my friend, very thin ice. And that is coming straight down the pipe from the very top."

Donny shifted uncomfortably from foot to foot.

"All right, sit down. What is it with you and Ericson? You just decide to make him the focus of Donny's Obsession of the Month Club?"

Ratzo listened as Donny explained the eye bolt and new rope they had found at the hanging suicide, and his visit to the hardware store and the owner's promise to make a copy of the surveillance video.

"So we drive over there this morning to pick up the video ..." Donny continued.

"Wait. You took the truck?" Ratzo leaned forward. "Are you deliberately trying to give them an excuse to fire you? Using department resources for your personal business?"

"We were out anyway, picking up stuff for lunch." Donny dismissed Ratzo's concern. "But the guy in the hardware store acts like he's never seen me before. When I press him, he says there's no video, that the cameras weren't working."

"So," Ratzo said wearily. "You said yourself the cameras were old. The guy probably hadn't checked them in months."

"Yeah, but one day he says he remembers someone like Ericson buying rope, and the next day he knows nothing. I tell you, he was scared, like somebody had got to him. He couldn't get rid of me fast enough."

"That's something you just bring out in people, Donny." Ratzo drummed his fingers on his desk. "Who did you tell about the security cameras?"

"Just Laurie." Donny thought for a moment. "Oh, and Humphrey, when he was chewing me out on the phone."

"You think one of them is plotting against you? Say yes, and I'm putting you on stress leave." Ratzo shook his head. "Any other conspiracies you want to tell me about? Who really shot Kennedy? How they faked the moon landing?"

Donny opened his mouth to speak, then closed it.

"OK then, you need to get over this. That is *not* a suggestion."

"But Joe, Ericson is dirty. Not taking money dirty, but ..."

"No!" Ratzo stood up and pointed across the desk at Donny. "That guy Simpson who held a razor to Scout's throat, who sold dope and beat up hookers—*that* guy was a dirty cop. He was going to kill one of your crew, and Ericson did the world a favour when he flushed that piece of crap."

"But ..."

"There is no 'but.' And this guy who hanged himself—what's his name?"

"Umm ..." Donny tried to recall the name. He could picture the man's bulging eyes, his swollen, discoloured face, the yellow rope biting into his fleshy neck. "I, uh, I forget."

"Great!" Ratzo snorted triumphantly. "You're on this holy crusade and you can't even remember the guy's name."

"Rothberg, Leo Rothberg," Donny blurted as it came back to him.

"A kiddie diddler, right? Someone who preyed on the weakest, most precious, most vulnerable members of society. I'm surprised the guy could live with himself as long as he did. But you want to start a federal inquiry because of some wild hunch you have?"

"It's not just a hunch," Donny protested.

"Give your head a shake, Donny, you're way offside. Trying to win sympathy for a guy that everyone this side of hell would say 'good riddance' to is insane. And your notion that Ericson is some kind of one-man Terminator is ludicrous. So he's a little unconventional—so what?" Ratzo pointed to a shelf lined with binders containing the Fire Department's rules, regulations and standard operating procedures. "Show me one of those that you haven't broken or at least bent."

Donny pursed his lips and said nothing.

"Let me tell you another thing. The brass are fed up with this and so am I. And from what I hear, Staff Sergeant Singh is about one phone call away from filing a harassment complaint." Ratzo held up his hand when Donny started to protest. "Don't even start."

Ratzo stood and walked around the desk to stand in front of Donny. "You either let this go, or the shit is going to start raining down. Hard! And I can't give you shelter. Not when you bring this stuff on yourself." Ratzo held out his hand, his thumb and forefinger a hair's breadth apart. "You're about this far from me recommending you for a psych evaluation."

Ratzo watched the shock register on Donny's face. "Now get out of here. I have work to do and so do you."

Donny climbed into the captain's seat and slammed the door of the truck harder than he meant to. Moose glanced over at him and started the truck.

"Making friends in high places again, eh, Wedge?" Eddy chuckled.

Donny stared straight ahead through the windshield. He grabbed the mic as Moose eased the truck into traffic.

"Pumper Six is clear of Station Five, heading back to Lombard. Put us back in service."

CHAPTER 24

QUESTIONS

Daya Singh straightened her keyboard and mouse pad, as if keeping things neat and tidy would somehow diminish the drudgery. Duty rosters, overtime submissions, change of vacation requests, on and on—a seemingly endless stream of minutiae that fuelled the police bureaucracy. It all needed to be entered, approved, and kicked up or down the ladder to the next unfortunate cog in the machine. And the higher up the ladder she moved, the worse it seemed to get.

She knew when she signed on that it wasn't all car chases and shootouts, like the TV shows—and thank God for that! Still, would she have become a cop, she wondered, if she had known then what she knew now?

Was she still a cop, or was she a glorified file clerk? It was work she could almost do in her sleep. The upside was that it allowed part of her mind to detach and wander on its own. The downside was that it allowed part of her mind to wander on its own. And now, for some reason, her mind had attached itself to the idea of one Donny Robertson. And despite her biting on the inside of her cheek, humming half-forgotten tunes and staring ever more intently at the computer screen, it seemed quite uninclined to detach itself.

There was a chemistry between them, she had to admit to herself. The way he looked at her … Obviously, Robertson had felt it, or he wouldn't have kissed her that time they had met in the park. Yet even that had been a rather chaste kiss. A polite knock on the door. He was respectful. That somehow made him more attractive.

She caught herself running her tongue over her lips at the memory, and clamped her jaw shut. No married men, she reminded herself. She had learned that lesson the hard way. Even if Robertson wasn't officially married, it just wasn't worth it.

Then why was she thinking about him? He wasn't all that good-looking, not particularly witty or charming. But he was sincere. There was an air of trustworthiness about him. He had never tried to lie to her about his relationship, whatever trouble it might be in. Most of the things she had heard about him through the grapevine had been positive. Words like honest, reliable and dedicated kept coming up. Even the negative things she had heard—that Donny was too serious, focused, even obsessive—were not exactly damning. She knew people said the same things about her behind her back.

No. No married men. Absolutely not. But could she dismiss his suspicions about Ericson just because of that? She had meant every word she had said to Robertson about Peel's Principles: the police must never usurp the powers of the judiciary. A rogue cop on her watch was her problem. That was the reason Robertson was on her mind, she told herself.

She found her hands stalled above the keyboard, her eyes staring at words on the screen without taking in their meaning. She shook her head and pushed herself back from her desk. She grabbed the civilian trench coat she kept on the rack by her office door for just such occasions, when she didn't want to flash the uniform.

"I need a little fresh air," Daya said to the desk officer as she passed by. "I'll be back in ten minutes. Call me if anything important pops up."

"Sure thing."

She walked out of the station's front door onto Parliament Street and turned the corner down Derby Street, a quiet street that ran along the station's north side. The street backed onto Little Trinity Church, a squat Gothic structure of red and tan bricks, Toronto's oldest surviving church. It was surrounded by a small, pleasant green space.

It was a deceptively cool day. The sky was unbelievably clear, the blue of Dutch porcelain. But it was also the end of November, and the sun hung low over the horizon. An icy wind darted between the long shadows of the downtown office towers. Daya sat on a bench with her back to the wind and did up the top button on her coat to ward off the chill.

Honest and reliable. The words repeated in her head.

Robertson claimed that Ericson had basically walked up and executed the dirty ex-cop, Simpson. Lots of people had good reason to go along with Ericson's version of the story. What did Robertson have to gain from standing alone against the crowd? Not much, other than nursing a minor grudge.

Now he was suggesting that Ericson was somehow complicit in arranging the death of a convicted child molester so that it looked like a suicide. Had Ericson truly turned into some kind of vigilante?

Honest and reliable. How much faith should she put in Robertson's Boy Scout reputation? Not much, her police instincts told her. Not unless there was some independent proof.

The Special Investigations Unit had handled Ericson's shooting of Simpson. They'd have the lid clamped down tight on that file, and Daya didn't have the kind of pull it would take to get a peek inside. Even if she did, it would raise too many questions.

Rothberg's case, on the other hand, was being treated as an open-and-shut suicide.

It's said that dead men tell no tales. Daya knew how wrong that was. Dead bodies, in fact, told many tales, if you knew how to listen. Did she know anyone in the coroner's office? Not really, not beyond a nodding acquaintance. She did, however, have a few friends in the police Forensic Identification Unit.

Daya looked around the small park. Aside from the occasional dog walker, she was the only one there. She reached inside her trench coat, took out her phone and scrolled through her contacts.

"Forensics, Officer Proctor speaking," said the voice on the phone.

"Hey, Cindy, it's Daya. How are you doing?"

"I'm good. Nice to hear from you. We are way overdue for a night on the town."

"That is true," Daya said with a smile. Maybe it was the gruesome work of forensics, or the stress of being a single mom, but if there was one of her friends that knew how to let loose, it was Cindy Proctor. "How are the kids?"

"Things are getting a little more settled now. Greg decided he'd rather go live with his dad, but Grace and Theo are still with me. How about you?"

Daya reached over and picked up an empty coffee cup someone had discarded on the end of the bench. "Good, yeah. The separation agreement is all signed, sealed and delivered. You know. The formalities will take a few months, but there's no kids or support, so it's pretty straightforward."

"So now we're both data points on the divorced cops statistics curve. It would almost be funny, if it weren't so friggin' pathetic. You seeing anyone?"

"No, not really." Daya crushed the cup in her hand and looked around for a garbage bin. "A woman without a man is like a fish without a bicycle, right?"

"True, but every now and then I need something between my legs that's not made out of plastic."

No, Daya said to herself as she wondered what it would be like to feel Donny's body pressed warm and hard against her. Time to change the subject. "Listen, I need a favour."

Cindy snorted. "I kind of figured, since you're calling me at the office from your personal phone."

"Your office line's not recorded, is it?" Daya spotted the garbage bin and started towards it.

"Nooo," Cindy drew the word out, "but it makes me a little nervous that you ask. What's up?"

"There was this guy, Leo Rothberg." Daya described the circumstances of Rothberg's death. "They're calling it a suicide, but there are some odd pieces."

"So talk to the detectives working the case. I'm just a forensics tech."

"I can't go through channels. It's complicated."

"Complicated? Like Internal Affairs complicated?"

"Maybe. I don't know. I need more information." Daya tossed the crumpled cup in the trash and walked back to the bench. "I just want to know if Forensics found anything unusual. And you know people at the coroner's office, right? I know you guys talk about gross stuff all the time. Start a conversation on interesting suicides or something like that. Or whatever works for you. Just let me know if anything odd comes up about Rothberg."

There was a long silence on the other end of the phone. She hated doing this to a friend, but ... "Cindy, you owe me. Remember Montreal, that *Gangs and Guns* seminar? The hotel room we shared?"

"Ah, come on," Cindy pleaded. "That was three years ago. I was drunk and my marriage was falling apart. I was just letting off some steam."

"Is that what they call it? No problem, I'm sure Zorro or Batman or whoever he was dressed as was a really nice guy once you got to know him."

"Jeez, I can't even remember his name. Actually, he was a little too freaky." Cindy paused for a moment. "You don't have pictures or anything, do you?"

"No," Daya said firmly. "I just closed the door and got myself another room. Which, I remind you, I paid for out of my own pocket. Anyway, that would be blackmail, which as we both know is against the law."

"As opposed to what you're asking me to do, which is simply a gross violation of department policy."

"True, there is that." A squad car turned onto Derby Street, heading to the back entrance of the police station's parking lot. Daya looked at her watch. It was time to head back. "I wouldn't ask if it weren't important."

"I don't mind helping a friend, but if this turns into a shit show, I could end up in serious trouble."

Dry leaves crunched under Daya's feet as she walked back towards the station. "I promise I will leave your name out of it."

"Sure, like forensic information just falls out of the sky. A simple subpoena and they've got this phone call, recording or not."

"It's just a call to a friend. Nothing wrong with that. Look, I'm not asking you to launch some kind of covert investigation. Just look around. Talk to people. I know you guys talk to each other. Please."

There was silence again. Daya was out of the park, almost back at the station, when she heard the reply. "OK, I'll see what I can do. No promises."

Daya made a silent vow to herself to go to temple with her mother and say a prayer of thanks. "You're an angel."

"Funny, I think that's what Batman called me."

CHAPTER 25

APOLOGIES

Moose swayed back and forth on his knees, his arms weaving some arcane pattern in the air, as the hypnotic rhythm of Creedence Clearwater's "Suzie Q" pounded from the Thirsty Sparrow's jukebox. He looked, Donny thought, like a primordial shaman performing an incantation.

"Get up, you big goof," Susan Kozarovitch laughed, as the last keening notes of John Fogerty's guitar faded. She reached down to pull Moose up. Instead he pulled her on top of himself and planted a sloppy kiss, despite her unconvincing resistance.

"To Moose and Q! May they have many happy years together," Donny declared to the bar at large, and held his drink aloft. The early-evening crowd in the Sparrow was sparse, but they gave an enthusiastic cheer before returning to their own conversations.

"Well, if Moose's brother is going to be best man, do I at least get to be flower girl?" Eddy asked as he helped Suzie up from the floor.

"No," Suzie said firmly, brushing herself off. "Not even if you shave your back."

"See?" Eddy complained to Donny. "This is the thanks I get for setting them up."

"Setting us up? I don't remember that." Moose said.

Donny handed Moose the pint he had been guarding for him while the song played. Watching the big man rise from the floor was like watching a time-lapse movie of an oak soaring to the forest canopy.

"The sign of a true master," Eddy waved away Moose's objection. "They don't even realize you're doing it."

"Like, 'These are not the droids you're looking for?'" Scout asked skeptically.

"Something like that," Eddy nodded, undeterred.

"Anyway, that's why I asked you to come." Moose draped an arm around Suzie's waist. "I wanted you guys to be the first to know. And I figured, what better place to announce it?"

"Well, it's the best news I've heard in a long time." Donny clinked his glass against Moose's. "May you have a houseful of little probies."

"I don't know about a houseful." Suzie squeezed Moose's hand and smiled up at him. "Maybe one or two. We couldn't afford to feed any more if they eat like their father." She turned her smile to Donny. "How about you and Laurie?"

"Yeah, well, we'll see." Donny sat back down at the table they had been at before Moose had made his announcement and started the jukebox. "Laurie's boys—well, I mean, I guess they're ours now. Anyway, they're a handful."

"Hey, Stu!" Donny caught the bartender's eye and circled his index finger in the air. The bartender nodded and began pouring.

"Not for me, Stu," Scout said. "Fascinating as this discussion of family planning is, I have to go. Suzie, congratulations. Moose, you're a lucky guy." Scout held out his hand. Moose grabbed it and pulled the younger man into a hug. Scout all but disappeared.

When Scout emerged from the embrace, Donny pulled out the chair beside him. "Can you stay for just a minute? Since we're all together, there's something I'd like to say." Donny pointed to the chair. "Well, maybe two minutes. Please?"

"Do I have a choice?"

"Yes. Yes, you do, but I'd really appreciate it." There was an element of pleading in Donny's voice that surprised even him. Scout sat.

Suzie put her hands on the table to get up. "Well, I'm not really part of the crew anymore, so ..."

Donny waved her back down. "You're part of the family."

Stu brought a tray of glasses to the table and passed them around. Donny folded his hands in front of him, unsure where to begin. "It's nice to get some good news, and congratulations again." Donny raised his glass and took a sip. "It's been a tough month or so. First Randy Copeland got killed, Eddy got shot, and all the fallout from that. Then that psycho tried to cut your throat, Scout. And there's all the other shit—car wrecks and hangings. But that's what we deal with, right? Other people's misery. Only there's been a lot of it lately. And the problem is I got hung up on some of it—what I thought was right and wrong. I lost sight of the most important part of a captain's job: the well-being of the crew."

Donny looked at Scout, but the younger man said nothing.

"It's all good," Moose said, and squeezed Suzie's hand. "We're turning a corner."

"Just let me get this out, OK?" Donny looked at the carved wooden bar and the memorabilia on the walls. He turned back to face Scout. "When I started it was 'Yes, sir! No, sir!' and all that 'iron men and wooden ladders' stuff. It built strength and respect, but not much else. The world has changed. What the old ways didn't teach was empathy, openness—you know, modern leadership. I know I've been kind of a dick lately, and I want to apologize."

"Who are you and what have you done with Donny?"

"Eddy, for once, just shut up."

"So much for modern leadership," Eddy quipped. No one laughed. Eddy shrank in his seat. "OK, listening now. This is me listening, listening very attentively."

Donny took a deep breath and let it out slowly. "The guys who were in charge when I started, Aldritch and Fitz and those guys, I thought they were gods. I've been measuring myself against them ever since, always trying to do the right thing, make the right call, never make a mistake. But I always come up short. And all I seem to do is piss people off—you guys, the cops, the chiefs, pretty much everyone.

"Well, I'm done. I'm tired. Tired of trying to hang onto the past, tired of trying to save the world. I've been particularly hard on you, Scout. I thought I was doing the right thing, but maybe I was wrong. So floor watch is back to the normal rotation. I'm done playing Don Quixote."

"That it?" Scout asked, rising from his chair.

"Unless you have something to add," Donny replied.

"Just one thing. It's Pat, OK? Not Scout." He gripped the back of his chair with both hands and looked around the table. "I hate that name."

Eddy opened his mouth like a gasping fish, and quickly closed it again.

"Fair enough," Donny said.

"Sure," Moose agreed.

Eddy nodded.

The newly re-christened Pat Thompson pulled out his wallet. Moose put a hand on his arm. "It's OK, dude. The drinks are on me and Suzie today."

Pat slipped his wallet back into his pocket and zipped his jacket. "OK, see ya." The group at the table watched him open the front door and disappear. There was an awkward silence.

Donny felt sadly deflated. He'd been thinking a lot about his priorities. That in itself was uncomfortable for a man who was used to relying on his instincts. When Moose had called to get them together, Donny had seized the occasion as a chance to reset things. He wasn't sure what he had hoped for. Catharsis? Resolution? At least some sort of recognition. "I'm sorry. I kind of ruined the party. I should have done this at work."

"It's OK," Moose declared. "Anyway, the wedding will be the real party. We just wanted to share the good news. Right, sweetie?"

Suzie got up and moved to the empty chair beside Donny. She took his hand in both of hers. "Donny, we love you. Your timing and your people skills, yeah, they could use a little work, but your heart's in the right place. So don't worry about it, OK?"

"Thanks, Q." The weight in Donny's chest lifted a bit.

"But you do this at the wedding, Donny ..." Suzie released his hand, stood and looked down at him for emphasis. "And I will kill you."

"Honeymoon Homicide," Eddy mused. "That's a great title. 'It was a dark and stormy Bride ...'"

"No drama." Donny crossed his heart and held up his right hand. "I promise."

"OK, then," Suzie smiled brightly. "We should go too."

"But ..." Moose held up the pint glass in his hand. It was still more than half full.

"You're done. We have two months to pull this together and a lot of work to do. I love this place, but I'm not having my reception in the Sparrow."

Moose took a swig and put the glass down. He and Suzie thanked everyone for their good wishes and left.

"Another one bites the dust," Eddy said. He picked up Moose's beer glass and split the remains between his own glass and Donny's. "No sense wasting it, right?"

"I guess." Donny picked up his glass. The table seemed too large and empty. He and Eddy moved to a pair of stools at the bar. They watched the sports highlights on the TV in the corner across from the front door and talked about the things men talk about when they don't really want to talk.

A burst of laughter filled the bar. Donny looked over to see a group of off-duty cops spilling in from the street. The faces were all familiar; half of them he knew by name. Last to enter was Daya Singh. Their eyes locked. It was only for a moment, as fleeting and unmistakable as a flash of lightning. What it meant, Donny had no idea.

The cops kept talking and laughing among themselves as Daya and her companions moved to a table at the far end of the bar. As she walked past Donny, she gave him a brief Mona Lisa smile. Amusement? Condescension? Disdain?

"So, you said something about pissing everyone off. That include at home?" Eddy spoke quietly and kept his eyes on the TV.

"Huh? What are you talking about?" Donny tried to decide whether to order another drink or leave as soon as possible.

"I saw that look, when she came in. I may be a clown, but I'm not an idiot."

"Yeah, well, maybe you should mind your own business."

"You're my best friend, Donny. That makes it my business."

Donny glanced quickly at the table of cops, then back at the TV. "It's complicated."

"Isn't it always? Remember that call we had on Sackville Street?"

"Which one?"

"The guy who burned his face off." Eddy turned from the TV and looked Donny in the eyes. "Remember? His gas gauge didn't work, so he was trying to check his gas tank, but he didn't have a flashlight, so he used a lighter."

"I remember. What about it?" Donny said impatiently.

"Nothing. It was just the wrong solution to the problem. People do stupid shit even when they know better. You want to fix something? Fix it, don't blow it up."

"What makes you such a relationship expert?"

"Twenty-three years in the trenches, baby, married to a woman with a fuse even shorter than your dick." Eddy laughed and slapped Donny on the back. "Come on, let's get out of here."

CHAPTER 26

FIBRES

The Senator was a retro diner just off Dundas Square, one of downtown Toronto's busiest hubs. The interior was narrow and noisy, with cramped booths lining both sides of a central aisle; the sort of place that subconsciously made you think of Dashiell Hammett as soon as you walked in. By night, the Senator's upstairs lounge was one of the last places you could go to hear good live jazz in the city. By day, the diner downstairs was a favourite of those who wanted a real breakfast. The streetlights were still on outside, but the place was already crammed with business types getting a jump on the day, interspersed with a sprinkling of hipsters winding down from the previous night.

Daya Singh was greeted at the door by the scent of cured ham, and coffee that was dark, rich and pungent enough to raise the dead. A waitress ushered Daya to the last empty booth, at the back beside the swinging doors that led to the kitchen.

"Coffee," the waitress said. It was more of a statement than a question.

"No, tea, please." The waitress looked at Daya as if she'd just confessed to not having bathed in a week, handed her a menu, and dived back into the frothy bustle of the diner.

Cindy Proctor had called Daya back two days after Daya had called her, and had suggested they meet here. The Senator was midway between their respective workplaces, but far enough away that they were unlikely to run into anyone from either the forensic division at police headquarters or Daya's colleagues at 51 Division. Cindy was late, as usual. Daya sat facing the front door, perusing the menu while she waited.

Daya's tea arrived. She had almost finished the cup when Cindy appeared. Cindy Proctor was a short, heavyset woman with a taste for bright colours. She seemed to float down the aisle in a cloud of scarves and wraps, like a small mobile Tibetan shrine.

"Sorry I'm late," Cindy apologized as she shed the outermost layers of fabric. She started on a list of excuses, mostly denunciations of her kids and the subway system, but Daya waved her off.

"It's good to see you," Daya smiled. They exchanged pleasantries while the waitress brought coffee for Cindy and fresh tea for Daya, and took their orders.

"So?" Daya inquired.

"Yeah," Cindy paused. Her normally cherubic face lost its softness. "Leo Rothberg was a real scumbag. You know that, right? No one's going to miss this guy. Any particular reason you're so interested?"

Daya looked around. The restaurant was humming, and no one was paying any attention to the two women. "It's not personal, if that's what you're thinking. Like I said, it's complicated. I know I'm asking a lot, but you just have to trust me—it's important."

Cindy fished in her handbag and brought out a tablet computer. She swiped several times until she found what she was looking for. "I didn't want to take the chance of photocopying anything, so I took pictures."

"Great."

Cindy scrolled through the images. "Pretty much a run-of-the-mill hanging. Death by asphyxiation, blah, blah, blah. No signs of forcible entry, aside from the firefighters. No signs of a struggle." Cindy shrugged, offering the tablet to Daya. "You want to see?"

Daya took the tablet. The images were blurry and difficult to make out. Daya squinted and tried to enlarge the picture.

"Yeah, sorry, not the best pictures. I didn't have a lot of time." Cindy reached for the tablet.

Daya handed it back. "Was there anything out of the ordinary?"

"It's not so much what's in the report, more like what's not in it."

Daya took a sip of her tea and gave Cindy an encouraging nod.

Cindy set the tablet down in front of her. "Suicide is usually an impulse thing. People use whatever's available—a lamp cord tied to a light fixture, something like that. The rope Rothberg used was brand new; so was the eye bolt in the ceiling. There was some planning here, a shopping trip and so on. It took time, and given time, most people change their minds. Also, there was fresh plaster dust on the floor from drilling a hole for the eye bolt, but there were no tools, no drill, nothing. And there was only the one hole. The odds of hitting a ceiling joist dead centre, first time, without a stud finder are pretty low."

Before Daya could respond, the waitress arrived. She set down a dish of yoghurt and fruit in front of Daya, and a smoked salmon omelette for Cindy. "Enjoy your meal."

"Thank you. More coffee when you have a moment," Cindy called after the retreating server. Cindy took a mouthful of her omelette and swiped a couple of times on the tablet. "There is one thing: they found blue polyester fibres on his wrists, but only in a five-centimetre band."

"So he was tied up?"

Cindy shook her head. "Not tied up—that would leave deeper marks. But the fibres are consistent with what you'd get from padded, fleece-lined wrist restraints. We see that sometimes when a bondage/domination scene goes bad."

"Wow. Nobody followed up on that?"

"The fibres could have come from something else—a fleece hoodie with tight cuffs, anything. Anyway, it's all circumstantial. And no one is going to go the extra mile for this creep."

"No," Daya said, spearing a chunk of cantaloupe with her fork. "That's probably what they're counting on."

"Who is 'they?'"

"It doesn't matter." Daya waved away the question.

"It does matter," Cindy exclaimed. "I'm going out on a limb for you here."

"And I appreciate it." Daya reached across the table and took Cindy's hand. "Was there a blue hoodie, a jacket, anything like that in the apartment?"

Cindy scrolled through a couple more images. "No, but it's not like they wrote down everything in the closet. I mean, it's a suicide, right? Not a wardrobe inventory." Cindy looked away in silence. She was clearly holding something back.

The waitress returned with a coffee pot and filled Cindy's cup. "What else?" Daya asked when the server had left.

"There's a guy at the coroner's office who sometimes, you know ... we hook up."

"That's great. What's he like?" Daya was genuinely glad. Some people were good at being single. Cindy, she knew, was not one of them.

"He's OK. It's really more of a ... Anyway, I managed to get a look at the autopsy report. It was mostly routine."

"Except ..."

"Except there was some bruising on both upper arms. It could be from a number of things. It could also be from someone holding onto him, like, really tight."

"Oh my God, he was right."

"Who was right?" Cindy asked. Her patience was wearing thin. "You keep saying 'he,' 'they,' like there's some kind of conspiracy. You think there's some gang of vigilantes running around the city hanging child molesters?"

"I don't know."

"Seriously?" Cindy spread a thick layer of strawberry jam on a piece of toast. "Well, if this is the kind of work they do, they've got my vote."

Daya put down her fork. "You don't mean that."

"You don't have kids." Cindy took a bite of her toast. "That's every parent's nightmare. If some guy like Rothberg touched one of my kids, I'd rip his balls off with my bare hands and choke him with them."

Cindy's lively, high-spirited side was one of the things Daya liked about her friend, but the savagery of the remark was surprising. "Remember Peel's Principles?" Daya asked.

"Uh, no." Cindy shrugged and looked at her blankly.

"From basic training in the Academy. Sir Robert Peel, the guy who founded Scotland Yard. Remember?"

"Vaguely."

"The police must always be impartial servants of the law. They can never assume the power of the judiciary or take it upon themselves to become avenging angels. It's the basis of a free society—innocent until proven guilty."

Cindy put her knife and fork down on the empty plate. "Until it's your kid, or your brother, or your friend. Then philosophy doesn't seem so important."

"You'd rather have the law of the jungle?"

"Of course not. Up here you're right," Cindy pointed to her head. "But down here ..." She pointed to her heart. "Be careful, OK?"

Maybe he wasn't crazy after all. The thought refused to go away. All the way to work from the Senator she kept going over what Cindy had told her. And her warning. But what if Donny was right about Ericson?

One thing was certain: Daya could no longer simply dismiss Donny's suspicions. All morning the thought kept resurfacing. Finally, she gave in and picked up her phone. Not at the station, she thought. Better to try his personal number.

Donny's phone rang. Laurie looked at it, buzzing and playing its merry tune on the counter where he had left it when he went to the garage to put the snow tires on her car. She looked at the name displayed: Daya Singh, a name she didn't recognize.

She should ignore it, let it go to voicemail. Two sides of her nature warred within her, but she gave in, picked up the phone and answered it.

Laurie sagged against the counter, her worst fears confirmed. A woman's voice.

CHAPTER 27

SOMEWHERE TO CRASH

"'Someone's been sleeping in my bed,' said the papa bear."

Donny was instantly awake. It was a reflex honed over years of responding to alarms in the middle of the night. There was, however, a difference between being instantly awake and being instantly aware. He sorted through the clues to help orient himself. There were no alarm tones, that was the first thing; his sense of urgency immediately ratcheted down a couple of notches. But he was in the station—the smell, the feel of the place, and Eddy's voice. Yes, he was in the station, but not in his usual room. He could make out the dim outline of lockers. He was in the dorm, and Eddy was shining the light on his phone down at him. The curse of memory returned.

Donny sat up, shielded his eyes from the light and swung his legs over the side of the bunk. "Crap, I thought I'd set my alarm."

"No problem, it's twenty to six. I'm a little early this morning," Eddy set the phone down on the shelf in his locker and hung up his jacket. "Just a little surprised to find you here."

"I needed somewhere to crash."

The two men spoke in hushed voices. The sound of soft snoring came from other parts of the dorm. It was a large room that spanned most of the back half of the fire hall's second floor. The dorm had been built large enough to accommodate two crews, but the aerial truck had been removed in the 1930s and the station had been a single pumper hall since. There were still a few extra bunks spread around the dorm.

"You tie one on last night?" Eddy asked. Occasionally an off-duty firefighter would grab one of the extra bunks after a night on the town. The practice wasn't encouraged, but it was tolerated within limits. It was better than driving drunk.

"Not really. I just didn't feel like sleeping in my car. It's ... I'll explain later." Donny scooped his pillow and blanket off the bed and headed towards the door, silhouetted in the light of the hallway beyond. He stepped into the sudden brilliance and blinked. The door to the captain's office was closed, but Donny turned in that direction anyway. It offered at least a temporary reprieve from Eddy's questions.

And his own.

Donny opened the office door, stepped inside and closed it softly behind him. He paused a moment. The captain's office was at the front of the station, beside the kitchen. Enough streetlight filtered through the blinds to see, once his eyes adjusted. He tiptoed to his locker and pulled it open. The door's squeak seemed abnormally loud in the dark, quiet room.

"Bad dream, honey?" The man in the Murphy bed yawned loudly.

"Sorry, man. I keep meaning to oil these hinges," Donny apologized.

"Juice" Michaels, the C shift captain, reached for the reading light and turned it on. A soft glow filled the room. "No problem. Guess it's about that time anyway. Hope the calls didn't disturb you too much."

"Not really." Donny put his bedding away in the locker and stripped out of the T-shirt and underwear he had slept in. Laundry, that was another detail he'd need to ... No, he wasn't going to think about that. "It's just weird rolling over instead of heading to the truck when the alarm goes, you know?"

"Yeah."

"Anything interesting?"

Juice stretched and stood. "Bells and smells, mostly. One overdose."

"The usual."

"Pretty much. Other than that, the truck's red and the wheels are round. You should be good to go."

"Thanks." Donny wrapped a towel around his waist and reached into his locker for his shaving kit. "Just give me a couple of minutes."

"Sure. I'll grab a coffee," Juice said. He was putting his own things away. "So, you going to be staying here for a while?"

"No, I just needed ..." Donny had turned towards the door but stopped and turned back. "I don't know. I need to figure some stuff out."

"Listen, it's not a problem. Gloria pitched a wobbly a few years back. I spent about a week living here myself."

"I remember."

"Anyway, we patched it up. I cut down on my drinking. She sees a shrink twice a month, so she's got someone else to bitch at. It's all good."

"Sounds like heaven."

"Go have your shower. You'll feel like a new man."

Donny didn't feel like a new man, but he did feel a little more like his old self. Eddy and Moose were sitting in their usual seats in the kitchen. Eddy was working on the crossword in the morning paper; as usual, Moose was knitting. The TV in the corner mutely paraded the previous night's highlights on Sportsnet. The only sound was the soft, steady click-click of Moose's knitting needles.

The metronome of my life, Donny thought: Moose catching each passing moment with his needles—knit, purl, cast—like a burly embodiment of the ancient Greek Fates who spun, measured and cut the thread of destiny. Donny imagined Moose, a hulking bear of a man, sitting with the Fates, taking their thread and wrapping it around his knitting needles to turn it into sweaters, mittens and other useful items, while the implacable goddesses looked on with consternation.

He chuckled softly to himself, grabbed a mug out of the cupboard beside the sink, and poured himself a cup of coffee.

Eddy looked up from his crossword. "Glad to see you're in a good mood."

"Why not? Another day in paradise." Donny opened the fridge and looked inside. "Anything worth shit-hawking in here?"

"B shift left some chili," Eddy answered. "It's a couple of days old. Smells like they made it with roadkill."

Donny pulled a large Tupperware tub from the fridge, lifted the edge and sniffed cautiously. He filled a bowl from the tub and shoved it in the microwave. "Any port in a storm."

"Eddy told me you're camping out." Moose tried to keep his voice neutral, but Donny thought he detected a note of concern. Or was it something else?

"It's just for a couple of days." Donny grabbed a couple of slices from the half loaf of bread on top of the fridge and dropped them in the toaster. "Listen, I don't want to make a big deal out of it, OK?"

"Don't want to make a big deal out of what?" Scout asked. He took off the pack he had slung over one shoulder and set it down just inside the kitchen door.

"If you got here on time, you'd know," Eddy replied.

"The contract says the shift starts at seven o'clock. Technically I'm thirty minutes early." Scout poured himself a coffee and turned to Donny. "So what's up?"

"I'm staying at the hall for a couple of days."

"That sucks." Scout picked up the remote from the table and unmuted the TV. The coach of the Toronto Maple Leafs leapt from one sports cliché to the next, earnestly committing the team to giving a hundred and ten per cent.

"Do you mind? We're talking here." Eddy glared at Scout.

"Sorry!" Scout scowled back, turned the volume down several notches and tossed the remote to Eddy, who turned it down several more.

"You're welcome to stay with Suzie and me," Moose offered. "The couch in the TV room folds out. It's pretty comfortable."

"Stella won't be home from college 'til Christmas. Her room's empty," Eddy added.

"Thanks. I think I'll just hang here until I figure things out." The microwave chimed. Donny retrieved his bowl and popped the toaster. He sat back at the table and started eating.

Scout sniffed at Donny's bowl and grimaced. "What is that?"

"B-shift chili." Donny took another bite. "I think."

"It must be hard on the boys," Moose said. "Daniel and Kevin really look up to you."

"I guess." Up until now, Donny hadn't really thought much about how the boys would react. He'd been focused on sorting out his own feelings. His attraction to Daya Singh—was it just infatuation? The growing unease at home—had he been single too long to change? Was he simply afraid of being trapped?

He liked the boys, liked teaching them how to sail, playing ball hockey with them in the driveway, helping with homework. But beyond the activities, there was a lingering sense of failure. He knew he should love them, absolutely and unconditionally. That's what real parents did, wasn't it? He tried, tried really hard, but it always felt like a bit of an act. There was a gap he couldn't quite bridge. When he dropped the boys off at school or swim lessons, he was afraid the other parents would see his inadequacy and call him out as an imposter.

Had he missed some critical imprinting event when the boys were born? They were, in some ways, still strangers to each other. He could see it in the questioning way Daniel and Kevin looked at him sometimes. And if they had placed any trust in him, now he had betrayed it.

The trouble had started long before, Donny realized, but it had been catalyzed by a phone call from Daya Singh. He had been out in the garage, putting snow tires on Laurie's car, and had left his phone inside. Laurie's questions started as soon as he came back inside, and his evasive answers were quickly met by angry accusations.

Donny asserted his faithfulness, but his attraction to Daya made it feel like a lie, even to him. Fear and insecurity conquered love and reason. The confrontation spiralled out of control and ended with both of them screaming at each other, and Donny slamming the door behind him.

Half of him had wanted to call Daya and fall sobbing into the imagined refuge of her arms. The other half had wanted to take a vow of celibacy and retreat to a monastery on an isolated mountaintop.

Childish fantasies—some vestige of his reason recognized that. So Donny had done neither. Instead, he had driven aimlessly around the city until instinct had brought him to the one place where he felt secure: the squat sandstone anachronism that was Lombard. And now here he was, sitting in the kitchen with his crew, and the rest of his life a yawning abyss in front of him.

"They're not really your kids anyway, right?" Scout asked.

"Well, not legally."

"So get yourself a condo downtown and enjoy being single again." Scout leaned back in his chair and smiled at the elegance of his solution.

"It's not that simple," Donny said. The station was beginning to feel less like a sanctuary.

"Maybe not. All I'm saying is there's a ton of tail around." Scout pointed out the window at the forest of glass and steel condo towers that had taken over the Toronto skyline. "Each one of those is full of young, horny singles. I mean, if I wear a Fire Department T-shirt in my building, I have to try *not* to get laid."

"It's different when you've made a commitment," Moose said.

"Yeah? Well, you know one of the biggest beefs I hear around the job?" Scout asked. "Guys paying child support and giving away half their pension. That's what commitment gets you."

"When did you become such an expert?" Eddy scowled at the younger man over the top of his coffee cup and took a sip. "You moved out of your parents' basement, what, six months ago?"

"Almost a year."

"Great," Eddy scoffed. "Why don't you run along, then. The grownups are talking here."

"Fuck you, Eddy." Pat stood and leaned across the table.

"Sounds like you're doing enough fucking around for both of us," said Eddy in a soft, menacing voice. He smiled at Scout and cracked the knuckles on his right hand.

"Enough! Stand down, both of you." Donny pushed away the half-eaten bowl of chili. Eddy had grown up as a street fighter, in a tough immigrant community downtown. Donny had no doubt Eddy would mop the floor with Scout despite the twenty-five-year difference in their ages. He also had no doubt about the amount of shit such a thing would bring down from on high.

Scout straightened up. "You know what? Fuck all three of you. I'm sick and tired of this place. I'm putting in for a transfer." He stormed out of the kitchen.

Donny pushed his chair back and followed Scout down the hall.

Moose put down his knitting and shook his head. "Nice move."

"What?" Eddy protested.

"You ever hear of a thing called de-escalation? Donny has enough on his plate."

Eddy waved the criticism away. "That kid needs an attitude adjustment. Believe me, someone's going to give it to him. Anyway, we'll be better off without him."

Donny caught up to Scout at the doorway to the captain's office. "Pat, slow down. Please, take a breath," Donny told him.

"I want a transfer form and I want to talk to Ratzo. This place is toxic."

"A lot of guys would give their eye teeth for a spot downtown like this."

"They can have it."

"Come on in and have a seat," Donny invited, indicating the two chairs in front of the old oak desk.

"I don't want any 'coaching' and I don't want any 'fatherly advice.'" Scout didn't try to hide the contempt in his voice or in his expression. "The only thing I want is to never see you or this place again."

He stormed out of the office, stalked down the hall to the pole hole and disappeared.

Donny's phone jingled with a text notification. He pulled the phone out and looked at it. A message from Daya Singh, something about forensic evidence. His first instinct was to call her back right away, but something stopped him. Eddy was right. If there were any hope of getting his personal life straightened out, he needed to leave Daya out of it. At least for now.

CHAPTER 28

FRIENDLY ADVICE

Daya Singh set down her mug of tea and logged into the computer on her desk. The morning had just started and there were already more than twenty emails waiting for her. Only a couple of them were important and none of them appeared to be from Donny Robertson. There had been no return call from him, no text, nothing.

She wanted to talk to him, but she was hesitant to call again. Daya had been surprised when Donny's wife, partner or whatever she was had answered her call yesterday. Daya had identified herself, but the woman had been distinctly cool, if not outright hostile.

Daya had waited for some kind of response.

This morning she had sent him a text, asking for a chance to discuss forensic evidence. She couldn't be too explicit about the fibres or other details. She needed to be discreet, for both professional and personal reasons.

Still no reply.

Donny or no Donny, if Ericson was an issue, she needed to do something about it. But what?

The picture of her father stared back at her from its place atop the filing cabinet beside her desk. Her father in his Punjab Police Force dress uniform—blue and red turban with its plume of feathers and matching striped ascot and sash.

"What should I do, Papa?" she silently asked the stern, proud man in the photograph. She knew the answer even before she finished the question.

"Do the next right thing." It had been her father's unwavering North Star, even though it had cost Guneet Singh his career when he spoke out against corruption in the senior ranks of the Punjab police. "There is no shame in fear, only in cowardice. Do the next right thing."

Whatever that was.

The memory of her father could give her guidance, but not solid advice. But there was someone whose advice she valued almost as much.

"Come in."

Daya opened the door to Bob Collins' office and poked her head in. "Do you have a minute, sir?"

"For you, always." Collins closed his laptop and stood. He motioned towards three armchairs grouped around a small coffee table in a corner of the office, in front of a large window. "What's on your mind?" he asked, once they were comfortably settled.

Daya gazed around the room as she tried to think of the best way to approach the issue. By police station standards, it was a luxurious space. As commander, Collins had a large corner office on the second floor of the restored building that housed 51 Division. Light streamed in through seven-foot-high windows set into the two exposed brick walls. Parts of the rest of the station looked like they had been furnished from a Salvation Army store, but here things were a step up. There were leather chairs, a glass-topped table, and the other perks that came with rank.

The direct approach was best, Daya decided. Collins was a straight shooter and had always treated her fairly. "There was a case a few days ago. It was a hanging; a suicide was the finding."

"The pedophile?" Collins straightened in his chair.

"Yes, sir. How much do you know about it?"

Collins leaned back and crossed his arms. "The basics. Part of my job is reviewing major cases in the division—homicides, suicides, sexual assaults, that sort of thing. But it's a little outside your scope."

"I know. That's one reason I've come to see you. There are some unusual aspects to the case." Daya cleared her throat and forged ahead. Collins steepled his fingers, watching Daya intently as she told him what she had learned about the death of Leo Rothberg. She concluded with what she thought was the most significant finding. "There were fibres in a five-centimetre band around Rothberg's wrists. They're consistent with what you'd get from soft restraints, the kind you'd use if you didn't want to leave marks."

"I see," Collins nodded. "What I don't understand is why you're so concerned about the suicide of a scumbag like Rothberg. It's not your case, Daya."

"Someone brought it to my attention. When I looked into it, like I said, it seemed a little unusual."

Collins was silent for a moment, thinking. "And who exactly might that someone be?"

It was a reasonable question, one that Daya had anticipated and dreaded. "I'd rather not say, sir. At least at this time."

"Have you spoken to the investigating officers?"

"No."

"Who were they again? Sorry, I've forgotten."

As a detective, Collins had had a reputation for a photographic memory and unerring instincts. Daya doubted that her commanding officer had forgotten anything. She played along anyway. "Detective Tremblay was the investigator assigned. Bill Ericson and his new partner Tasha Pratt were the first constables on scene."

"Ericson—yes, I seem to recall that." Collins ran a hand thoughtfully over his bald head. "Fire responded too, I suppose?"

Daya nodded.

"And would that involve Captain Robertson?"

He had zeroed in on the weak link in the case. There was no use denying it. "Yes."

Collins made a sour face. "I suppose he's the one who's raising all these red flags?"

"Some of them. Not the fibres."

"No, that must have come from someone in Forensics, but I'll let that go for now." Collins stood and walked to the big window that looked out over the busy traffic on Front Street. "Did you know that Tom Humphrey, Robertson's platoon chief, is a personal friend of mine? I know for a fact that Robertson is something of a loose cannon in the fire department. Tom thinks Robertson is, well, not all there. You want to be careful hitching your wagon to his."

"Of course. That's why I've come to you, sir. I'd like your advice on how to proceed." Daya tried a smile but it felt forced.

"Proceed, Staff Sergeant?" Collins turned back to her. He spoke in a voice of quiet authority. "There is no 'proceed.' Not for you. Do I need to remind you that the top priority of this department is to find the man responsible for the death of Constable Copeland? I'll ask Detective Tremblay to review his notes and the forensics. But we are not going to launch a major investigation into the suicide of a pedophile just because of the fantasies of some lunatic fireman and some blue polyester fibres. Not while there's still a cop killer on the loose. Is that understood?"

"Of course. Thank you, sir." Daya stood to leave.

Collins waved her back to her seat and sat across from her. "Listen, I know being staff sergeant sucks. It's mostly administrative bullshit—death by a thousand paper cuts. I've been there. You're longing to sink your teeth into some real police work. But this is not the way to go about it."

Collins took off his glasses and set them on the coffee table between them. His face and voice softened, and once again he became the kindly mentor she had grown to love and respect. "You are one of the smartest, most capable officers I've known. And you're a woman of colour."

Daya squirmed.

"I'm not saying that to be tokenistic. I hope you know me better than that. The reality is that you can be a role model. You're what the job is looking for and what it truly needs. I'm a dinosaur; you are the face of modern policing—smart, talented, and reflecting the diversity of this city. There is a path in front of you and you can follow it as far as you want. But there is one sure way to derail your career, and that is to stick your nose in where it doesn't belong. That, and if I may be blunt, hanging out with losers like Robertson. That man is dead weight, and he will drag you down. I've seen it happen before and I wouldn't want to see it happen to you."

Collins picked up his glasses. The moment was over.

Daya stood. "Thank you, sir. I've always appreciated your honesty and guidance."

"Any time."

They shook hands at the door, and Collins watched her walk down the hall and head down the stairs. Damn, she was a fine-looking woman on top of everything else, he thought. Thirty years ago, he might have ... but that was another era and he had other things to think about.

He closed the door, returned to his desk and picked up the phone. "Tom? You were right. We've got trouble."

Stay in your lane—that was Collins' unmistakable message. Daya knew it was good advice. That was the way up the career ladder. Collins was right about her career potential. She was smart, capable and motivated; there was virtually no limit on how high she could rise, as long as she kept her nose clean.

Blue.

Daya paused in mid-step on the stairs. She didn't remember specifying the colour of the fibres found on Rothberg's wrists, nor that they were polyester. She was almost certain she hadn't mentioned those details. How had Collins known the fibres were blue polyester? Could he and Ericson ...?

No, that was crazy. Paranoia and conspiracies were a slippery slope. And the superintendent was right: Donny was ... well, at best he was a complication she didn't need in her life.

CHAPTER 29

SNATCH

"**Y**ou sure he'll come?" Ericson asked.

Tom Humphrey glanced across at Ericson, squirming in the passenger seat of the cargo van. The fidgeting was getting on Humphrey's nerves. They were parked in the small lot at the northwest corner of St. James Park, behind the cathedral from which the park drew its name. Their position was hidden by the cathedral itself on one side and the diocesan headquarters building on the other. They still, however, had an excellent view of the park's north and west sides in front of them. The two men talked softly.

"He'll come." Humphrey turned back and resumed watching through the windshield.

"How do you know? We've been here for two hours already. Maybe he's not coming."

"You're a cop and you're complaining about two hours on a stakeout?"

"I'm a beat cop. I've never done surveillance work."

"Two hours is nothing. We need to be here so we don't spook him by rushing in at the last moment. Your lack of patience is what makes you sloppy." Ericson started to object, but Humphrey cut him off. "Anyway, the guy who sent us that photo said he was coming tonight." Humphrey tapped the picture lying on Ericson's lap. It was an enlargement of a passport photo and showed a young Latino man with brooding dark eyes and neatly combed hair. "He gave our friend Ramón there his papers this afternoon. Said the guy was real anxious to bug out A.S.A.P."

Ericson drained the last of the coffee from his cup. "You trust a guy who forges passports?"

"I'm not sure they were passports. Anyway, I didn't talk to him; the chair of the Committee did. She trusts him—that's good enough for me."

"When do I get to meet her?"

"Probably never, since you keep asking." Humphrey didn't try to hide the irritation in his voice. "That's for your protection and hers. But I am willing to convey your thanks. Who do you think pays for all this? Electronics, facilities, this van—you think all this comes cheap? You think we get some kind of government grant? Without her, none of this happens. And if she chooses to keep a low profile, that's 'cause she's smarter than you. Now shut up and watch."

The two men watched in silence for several minutes. Ericson shifted again in his seat. "I gotta piss."

Humphrey sighed, "I told you not to drink so much coffee. There's a ten-litre jerry can in back. Put the cap back on tight when you're done."

Ericson squeezed between the two front seats. Humphrey heard him rustling in the back of the van and the hollow drumming sound of Ericson relieving himself in the plastic can. Humphrey wrinkled his nose at the smell of urine. Ericson wriggled back into his seat.

The city settled into the limbo of the small hours. It wasn't exactly peaceful; it was more like an act of wilful forgetting, the frenzy of the day temporarily banished. The background murmur of the city persisted: the sound of a distant siren, drunken curses seeping from an open apartment window. Cabs cruised the streets like sharks, hoping to snag the last of the club crowd or other revellers, while the all-night streetcar rattled along King Street, empty but for immigrants working the graveyard shift and others condemned to the margins of society.

"She's moving." Humphrey stared at the image on the tablet on his lap.

Ericson craned his neck to get a look. The image was dark and grainy, but it clearly showed Roxanne walking across the street towards the empty storefront where the camera had been installed. She turned to her right. "She's not coming this way. She's heading back to the apartment."

"Be patient." Humphrey switched cameras. The view on the tablet now showed the empty interior of Roxanne's bachelor apartment. The door opened. Roxanne walked in and shut the door behind her. The image was jerky, like bad animation. She seemed to teleport a few feet at a time.

She didn't take off her coat. Instead, she went to the fridge, poured herself a glass of orange juice and drank it in one gulp. She opened a cupboard and shoved a handful of granola bars into her coat pocket. The two men watched as Roxanne moved around the room. She opened the closet, partially blocking the camera's view.

"What's she doing?" Ericson asked.

"A little packing, I'd say," Humphrey replied without looking up. The closet door closed, giving them back their view. "That-a-girl."

Roxanne picked up a shoulder bag, opened the door and left. A moment later she was back. She reached into her bag, took something out, put it on the kitchen counter and left again.

"Phone?"

"Probably." Humphrey toggled screens on the tablet. The outside view of Roxanne's street corner returned. She entered the camera's field of view, walking south, and turned onto Dundas Street. Humphrey toggled the screen again. Now a map of the area appeared, showing a stationary flashing dot. "Yup, she's left the phone behind. This is it." He picked up a small radio and pressed the transmit button. "Juliet's on the move."

Ericson fidgeted in his seat. "You're sure she's headed here?"

"People are creatures of habit." Humphrey checked his watch. "Almost three o'clock, same as the last time she came here. Anyway, Lowry will tail her when she crosses Jarvis Street. If there's any change, we'll know."

A streetcar rumbled along King Street, on the south side of the park. It came to a stop, despite the green light in front of it. No one was waiting at the stop—it had to be someone getting off. Humphrey grabbed his binoculars. The streetcar pulled away and a solitary figure crossed against the light, towards the park.

"Is it him?" Ericson reached for the binoculars.

Humphrey pushed Ericson's hand away. "I think so. If it is, Kurilko will let us know."

A second later Humphrey's radio crackled to life. "Romeo's at the party."

The lone figure entered the shadows of the park. It was a man, slight of stature, wearing a backpack and carrying a gym bag, but it was hard for Humphrey to make out any other details. The man had his hood up and his head down. He glanced from side to side, carefully checking out the intersecting paths and benches as he slowly made his way across the park.

"That's it. Come to papa," Ericson chuckled.

"Shut the fuck up," Humphrey hissed.

Humphrey felt the younger man's angry glare, but ignored it. He watched the hooded man slowly approach their position in the darkened van. Eighty metres, now seventy, sixty ... The hooded man stopped and raised his head, like an animal scenting the wind. He turned slowly, looking over both shoulders. For a moment Humphrey worried that they'd been spotted. Then the man moved towards a bench under a tree, away from the faux gas lamps that lit the park's walkways.

The man took off his pack and placed it beside him on the bench, with the gym bag. He was barely fifty metres away, half a football field, from Humphrey and Ericson in the van.

A minute later the radio came to life again. "Juliet's on the balcony," announced a soft voice.

"Let's dance," Humphrey replied.

Roxanne entered the park from the northeast corner. She was easy to recognize, her head uncovered and carrying the shoulder bag they had seen her take from the apartment. She walked steadily towards where the man in the hoodie was waiting.

Thirty metres behind her, a man on a four-wheeled electric scooter followed the same path. He was a large man, but his body was bent at an awkward angle, his right shoulder forward. He drove the scooter with one arm; the other was twisted across his body and rested on the shawl that covered his legs.

A woman in a wheelchair moved on an intersecting course along the path the man in the hoodie had taken just a few minutes before. Several shopping bags stuffed with odds and ends hung from the back of the wheelchair. She muttered to herself, her long, unkempt hair swishing from side to side as she wheeled herself along the path.

Roxanne looked around as she walked, then saw the hooded man sitting on the bench and ran the last few metres.

Take your time, please, Humphrey prayed silently. Just a moment longer. He watched with satisfaction as the hooded man stood and took Roxanne into his arms. They hugged, then kissed long and deeply. Then the man broke the embrace and picked up his bags.

The man on the scooter and the woman in the wheelchair arrived at the intersection of the paths just north of the bench where the lovers had met. Roxanne smiled at the pair of disabled night owls. The hooded man put his arm around her waist and urged her away from the path, deeper into the shadows. They had taken only a few steps when there were two pops followed by something that sounded like bacon frying.

Roxanne and her companion collapsed to the ground. By contrast, the man on the scooter and the woman in the wheelchair straightened and stood up. It was as if the thin wires that led from the small square pistols the disabled pair held had miraculously conveyed the ability to stand and walk. In reality, the wires had delivered fifty thousand volts of taser power to Roxanne and Ramón.

"Open the back," Humphrey directed Ericson.

"What about the confetti?" Ericson asked. He was referring to the burst of tiny, rice-grain-sized plastic ID tags that was automatically released when a taser was fired.

"They'll disappear into the grass. Even if someone does find one, they'll trace back to a batch of tasers that disappeared off the docks in Singapore." Humphrey opened the door of the van, stepped out, and trotted over to where Lowry, the man who had been on the scooter, and Kurilko, the woman in the wheelchair, now knelt over their victims. Kurilko had pulled back the man's hood. Humphrey nodded with satisfaction. He produced two syringes from his coat pocket and quickly injected Roxanne and Ramón in the neck.

Ericson joined the group. They loaded Ramón onto the scooter, put Roxanne in the wheelchair and whisked them to the van. The two unconscious bodies were loaded into the back. In all, the operation took less than a minute.

Humphrey looked around. There was no commotion. As far as the few homeless people who called the park home were concerned, it had been a small and completely unremarkable disturbance. Humphrey climbed into the driver's seat and started the engine.

"Give us a sec," Lowry asked from the back. He and Kurilko were securing Roxanne and Ramón's arms and legs with zip ties and placing strips of duct tape over their mouths.

Ericson finished securing the scooter and wheelchair to the cargo rails on the side of the van's interior. He stepped across the van, between Lowry and Kurilko, and laid his foot heavily into Ramón's ribs.

"Hey," Kurilko protested, and shoved Ericson away.

Humphrey spun in his seat. "What the ..."

"Just let me do him now. No more screwing around," Ericson growled.

Humphrey could see the rage in Ericson's eyes. What was more, he understood it. He had felt it himself when he'd finally confronted the man who had killed his daughter. It was primordial, the need to exorcise your own pain by inflicting it on someone else. And now the man who had killed Randy Copeland lay there on the floor of the van. Humphrey knew that every fibre of Ericson's being demanded revenge. But for several reasons, it could not be permitted. Not here. Not now.

"That's not how we do things," Humphrey said softly.

"Yeah, well, fuck your procedures. I'm sick of them." Ericson made another lunge at Ramón. Lowry grabbed him by the shoulder and spun him around. Ericson caught his foot on one of the straps securing the wheelchair and went down hard.

Humphrey held a taser firmly pointed at Ericson, as the cop raised himself to his hands and knees. A thin stream of blood ran down Ericson's forehead where he had collided with the scooter. Good, Humphrey thought, maybe it would knock some sense into the man.

Ericson glared at Lowry, but froze when he saw Humphrey holding the taser. "You're kidding me."

"No," Humphrey said. "This is about justice. We're not here for your personal revenge; we're a solution to a system that's broken. But you are becoming part of the problem."

"You're protecting him. You're just as bad as the courts."

"That's not true, and you know it," Lowry said. He sat on the floor of the van between Ericson and the prisoners.

Kurilko sat beside Lowry. "We've all been there. My mother, Tom's daughter, his brother," she nodded towards Lowry. "Justice will be done. But it will be done properly and carefully, so that we can carry on with the mission."

Ericson wiped the blood off his forehead and looked at the red stain on his hand. "Put it away," he muttered, and squeezed by Humphrey into the passenger seat in the front of the van.

Humphrey put the taser away, backed the van out of their parking spot and pulled out onto Adelaide. The street was empty for two blocks in both directions.

"How's the location?" Humphrey called back over his shoulder.

"Everything's secure," Lowry answered.

"Now that we have them, we can get the rest of what we need, and start setting up," Kurilko added.

"You'll have plenty of time. The Committee wants to wait a few days anyway." Humphrey took a sideways glance at Ericson.

"A few days?" Ericson exclaimed. "For what?"

"To ask some questions and to let things cool down, among other things," Humphrey informed him. "You've been careless and drawing far too much attention. We can't afford that."

"It's that asshole Robertson," Ericson replied, "sticking his nose in where it doesn't belong. Something needs to be done about him."

"Robertson is my problem. Got that?" Humphrey's tone left no doubt. "You need to shut up and do what you're told."

"Yeah, well, it's not your ass he's after, is it?"

"No, because I don't give him a reason to go after it. So for the last time, leave Robertson to me. Besides, the Committee has a few more questions for these two before anything is done. And we still haven't decided what's to be done with the woman. We did promise her clemency if she cooperated."

"What? She was going to help him escape, for Christ sake!" Ericson exclaimed.

"That will be taken into consideration. Now shut the hell up."

Ericson looked out the passenger window. The shifting light from streetlights they passed showed his anger, but he said nothing more.

They merged onto Eastern Avenue and climbed the ramp to the short bridge that took them across the Don River. On the other side, they turned onto a small side street lined with buildings advertising transmission shops and auto body repairs. They stopped in front of a locked gate in a chain link fence surrounding a four-storey brick building, one of dozens of factories, large and small, that had once dotted this part of Toronto. Most had been converted into overpriced, upscale lofts, or bulldozed and replaced with townhouse complexes. But a few, like this one, sitting on contaminated soil, remained empty and all but abandoned, waiting until the housing prices justified the cost of cleaning them up.

Lowry got out of the van, pulled a key from his pocket and walked towards the gate.

Humphrey turned to Ericson. He could see the expression on the younger man's face by the headlights reflecting off the fence. It was hard and grim. "You need to remember that I was the one who invited you to be part of this in the first place. Don't make me regret that."

Ericson didn't reply. He stared straight ahead, stone-faced. That, as much as anything, had Humphrey already regretting it.

CHAPTER 30

BREAKFAST OF CHAMPIONS

Ericson pressed Pat's ID badge against the scanner beside the back door of Station Six. It hadn't taken much to convince the junior firefighter to loan him the ID. All Ericson had said was that he was going to teach Donny a lesson, and the kid had been only too happy to comply.

There was a soft click and a faint beep as the door unlocked. Ericson opened it enough to peek in with one eye.

The interior of the station was bathed in the soft glow of night-lights. The truck gleamed dully in the half light, like a thoroughbred frozen in mid-stride. Pants were folded down over boots, ready to be stepped into. Coats hung carefully in position. The station hovered in a special sort of stillness somewhere between poised and asleep.

It was an hour before Donny and his crew would return to duty, and Ericson needed only a minute. Cautiously opening the door, he stepped inside, stopped and listened. All was quiet, except for the sound of snoring coming from the man who was supposedly on duty in the floor watch. Ericson scanned the racks of bunker gear that lined the back of the station, behind the truck. "A shift"—there it was. He walked to Donny's stall. The SCBA face piece was in a cloth bag on the top shelf, beside the red captain's helmet. Ericson took a small vial from his pocket. It contained only a pinch of chalky dust, but it would be enough. He sprinkled the dust into Donny's face piece, then slipped it back into its protective bag and put it back on the shelf.

Ericson closed the station's back door softly behind him. He felt a brief pang of guilt as he got into his car and drove away. Robertson was a prick, but he wasn't a bad guy. Still, he was a threat. Something had to be done. He couldn't wait for Humphrey and his precious Committee to finish their dithering and start taking action.

Donny walked quietly down the stairs from the dorm. He loved the station, but it was starting to wear thin. He retrieved his gear from his stall and carried it to the truck. Today, he resolved, today he would start looking for a place of his own and get his life back on some kind of regular footing. He waved to Gus Maples, who yawned and stretched in the floor watch room. Gus straightened the recliner and got up to greet Donny.

"Not a bad night, eh?" Gus asked. "Hope we didn't disturb you too much."

"Barely even heard you go out." Donny dropped his gear by the truck's right front door and began taking the B shift captain's gear off the truck. He removed the portable radio and clipped it to his own bunker coat, took a flashlight from the charger and clipped it on, then connected his face piece to the regulator of the SCBA mounted into the back of his seat.

"Oh," Gus called to Donny, as Donny carried the B shift captain's gear to the stalls at the back of the hall, "we used four lengths of 45 at a restaurant fire. We loaded dry stuff, but we're getting a little low."

Gus pointed to the rolls of spare hose on the rack at the side of the truck bay. The rack was half empty. Hose that was used at a fire was replaced with dry hose from the rack. The used hose was washed to remove dirt, soot and contaminants, and hung to dry in the hose tower so it wouldn't mildew.

Donny returned to the truck. "We'll check what's hanging. If there's anything dry enough to come down we'll roll it."

"OK. Mind if I head upstairs to grab a coffee?" Gus asked.

"Go ahead."

Donny took a quick look around the cab of the truck to see if there was anything obviously missing or out of place. As driver, Moose would do a more thorough inspection later. Satisfied, Donny pulled his SCBA from its seatback bracket, turned on the air tank and checked the pressure gauge—just over 4,300 psi. Nominally, it was a forty-five-minute cylinder, but in practice the bottle held enough air for about twenty minutes at maximum exertion, with a little to spare, just in case.

Donny checked the SCBA's straps, hoses and connections. Everything depended on being able to breathe. Without a reliable air supply there wasn't much you could do at a fire except stand outside and piss on it. He checked the built-in alarm system, the motion detector that would sound if he were trapped or unconscious and couldn't move. There were also a thermal alarm that would alert him before the heat could penetrate all the way through his bunker suit, and a manual alarm, a sort of panic button to be used if everything went to ratshit.

Finally, he slipped on his face piece. Air wouldn't start flowing into it until he took his first breath, a safety measure to prevent wasting precious air. He shut off the tank to breathe down the residual air in the system. This would test the low-air alarm that would alert him if, in the heat of battle, he wasn't monitoring his pressure gauge.

Donny inhaled to start the flow of air. There was a puff of something. Dust? Dirt? Not much, but whatever it was, it didn't belong in his mask. He'd need to clean the face piece when he was done testing.

Yellow, then red warning lights flashed in the heads-up display in the mask as the pressure in the system dropped. The low-air warning rang as it was supposed to. Donny pulled off his face piece.

Whew, dizzy.

Donny let go of the mask and grabbed onto the truck's door handle to steady himself. A strange warmth flooded over him. How curious. He looked towards the floor watch. Yes, he would sit there for a moment in the recliner and collect himself.

As he took a step towards the watch room, the concrete floor turned to sponge and his legs to rubber. He became weightless and free as the floor floated up to meet him.

"BP is 92 over 59. Pulse 58. Respiration shallow. He's satting at 92%." Moose was kneeling over Donny, cradling his head with one hand and reading the display.

An ambulance was parked in front of the open apparatus bay doors. The paramedics unpacked their gear beside where Donny lay on the apparatus floor beside the truck.

"I found him like this," Eddy explained to Mingzhu, one of the paramedics. "I was carrying my gear to the truck and he was just lying there, unresponsive. I don't know how long he's been down."

Gus stood in the floor watch doorway, wearing the same stunned expression as everyone else. "I'd only been upstairs a couple of minutes when I heard you yell, Eddy. Couldn't have been that long."

"Maybe he had a stroke," Scout suggested.

"When did you become a doctor?" Eddy asked, annoyed at Scout as much for naming the fear as for anything. "He's too young for a stroke."

"No such thing as too young for a stroke," Greg, the other paramedic, said sadly. He held an IV bag out to Mingzhu. "You want to start a line?"

Mingzhu shone a light into Donny's eyes. "Pupils are equal and pinpoint, respiration depressed. I don't think it's a stroke. I think he's OD'd."

Scout whistled. "Holy shit. Cap's a junkie?"

"Give me naloxone," Mingzhu instructed Greg urgently.

"Shut your fucking mouth!" Eddy rounded on Scout. "Donny's no junkie."

"Whatever," Scout shrugged.

Greg handed Mingzhu a small, white plastic applicator. She inserted the rounded end of the nozzle into Donny's nostril and squeezed the plunger.

A few seconds later Donny blinked and turned his head to look around.

"I got you, Wedge," Moose said, still cradling Donny's head.

"Huh? Whaa ..."

"OK, let's get him loaded up. He needs to go to hospital to get checked out," Mingzhu stated flatly. It wasn't up to her to make a definitive diagnosis.

"Chief, it's Joe Razzolini. Donny Robertson collapsed in the station this morning."

The early morning sun flooded Tom Humphrey's office, but he felt a sudden chill. "Good God! What happened?"

"Not sure. Eddy found him passed out beside the truck at shift change. Looks like he was testing his mask. The low-air alarm was still sounding when they found him. The medics took him to St. Mike's. I just got back from there. I'll write up the report as soon as possible, but I wanted to give you a heads up first."

"I appreciate that." Humphrey's mind whirled. He'd been thinking about the final details to deal with Ramón. Those would have to go on hold now. "Is he going to be OK?"

"That's what it sounds like. They'll run tests and stuff in the hospital." There was a long pause.

"What is it, Joe?" Humphrey asked.

"There are indications it might be an opiate overdose."

"Opiates? Holy shit."

"Yeah. I'm trying to wrap my head around it." The tension in Ratzo's voice was obvious.

"He's been under a lot of strain lately. Frankly, I've been worried about him," Humphrey said sympathetically. "We'll get him whatever he needs—rehab, PTSD counselling, whatever. It's not like the old days, Joe. If he wants help, I'll make sure he gets it." Having

Robertson out of the way could be a good thing, but something still troubled him.

"It has to be contamination," Ratzo objected. "Donny's a lot of things, and he's certainly a pain in the ass, but he's no junkie. You know the kind of places we run. He could have picked it up anywhere. Anyway, I want to have his gear tested."

"Sure," Humphrey agreed. He knew his crews routinely crawled through rooming houses and shooting galleries, even middle-class homes where there were drugs. And fentanyl was so powerful that it took only a speck the size of a grain of salt to cause an overdose. There were cases where firefighters had died from accidental overdoses. Contamination was a real possibility. The question was, where had it come from? The timing was just a little too convenient. Ericson ...

"That son of a bitch," Humphrey mumbled to himself.

"What?"

"Sorry, it's just the shock. I meant Donny, that poor son of a bitch," Humphrey corrected himself. "Have the crew bag his gear. I'll have it picked up for testing. In fact, I'll do it myself. It will give me a chance to check on his crew." Another idea was also forming in his head.

Humphrey ended the call and slammed his fist on the desk. It was a rare outburst for a man who had a reputation for keeping his cool. He seldom raised his voice, even at the worst incidents. He had always believed that screaming orders and yelling at people only caused confusion and panic.

He closed his eyes, breathed deeply, and rolled his neck from side to side to relieve the tension. Spilled milk. It needed to be cleaned up.

By the time Humphrey arrived at Lombard, Donny's gear had been sealed in a heavy-duty clear plastic bag and was waiting for him. He exchanged a few words of comfort and sympathy with Eddy, Moose and Patrick, then put the bag in the back of his department-issued Tahoe and drove away.

Pulling into an empty parking lot a few blocks away, he got out, walked around the car, opened the rear hatch and looked at the plastic bag of bunker gear. He could take Donny's face piece, clean it thoroughly and put it back in the bag for testing. If the mask was clean, the only logical conclusion would be that Robertson had a drug problem. That wouldn't be a bad thing.

No. That wasn't fair to Donny. Besides, it was just treating the symptom. And he was done fixing mistakes made by people who couldn't follow orders.

Humphrey slammed the rear hatch shut. There was a café across the street. He walked over, smiled at the barista and ordered a latte. While the espresso machine hissed, he considered his options. There was really only one. Back in the driver's seat with his latte, he picked up his phone and selected Bob Collins' private number. It rang twice and went to voice mail. He tried twice more before Collins picked up.

"Tom, this isn't a good time. I'm in a meeting with the Community Relations ..."

"I think he's gone rogue."

"Who?"

"Our wonder boy."

Humphrey could hear a number of other voices in the background while Collins paused to think. "I'll call you back."

Humphrey drummed his fingers on the steering wheel. Two minutes later Collins called back. Humphrey told him about the overdose. "What do you think?" Humphrey asked.

"I think you're right. And either way, Ericson's becoming a distraction. I just don't think we can get rid of him before we deal with Ramón. He'd go apeshit."

"Agreed," Humphrey said. "We have a little time. In fact, the more the better. It would be good to get some distance between dealing with Ramón and this thing with Ericson and Robertson."

"OK. I'll let the others know."

It was settled. Contamination it was. The truth, or at least a version of it, was simpler than trying to juggle too many lies.

Humphrey hung up, started the car and headed towards the department's technical services division. They would arrange for testing of Donny's gear.

There was one more call to make. Time to grab the bull by the horns.

"Hey, Tom," Ericson answered. "How are the plans for our Mexican friend going?"

"Where are you?" Humphrey could hear the sound of children's voices and cartoon sound effects in the background.

"At home. I'm off today."

"Meet me at Cherry Beach," Humphrey looked at his watch, "in two hours."

"Sorry, I can't," Ericson said. "The kids are off school—it's another PD day."

"Call your mother, a neighbour, I don't care. Make whatever arrangements you need. This is not a request."

"OK, I'll see what I can do ..."

"Two hours. Be there."

CHAPTER 31

ON THE CARPET

It was almost noon by the time Donny removed the skimpy hospital gown and put his fire department fatigues back on. Blood tests had confirmed it: he'd inhaled heroin laced with fentanyl. For the life of him, he couldn't see what the attraction was—and it almost had cost him his life. But now there was nothing more the doctors and nurses could do for him. When enough time had passed for the stuff to clear his system, they gave him a handful of pamphlets on recovery meetings and harm reduction, and turned him loose.

Donny didn't argue with them. He was hungry, tired and a little bleary. Mostly he just wanted to leave. He dumped the pamphlets in the garbage bin of a cleaner's trolley as he passed the nursing station, and pushed open the swinging doors that led from the treatment area to the waiting room.

"Drugs? Really?"

Donny felt the eyes of everyone in the Emergency waiting room turn towards him. Laurie, the last person he had expected to see, was standing open-mouthed, shaking her head. It was bad enough being conspicuous in uniform. Now this.

"Can we just leave, please?" he said, tearing at the paper bracelet on his wrist as he walked. "What are you doing here?"

"What am I doing here?!" Laurie stopped in front of the beefy, crewcut security guard who stood by the exit. "Eddy called me. Said you'd collapsed. That you'd OD'd, stopped breathing and stuff. My God, I just grabbed my keys. What the hell was I supposed to do?"

"I don't know." Donny looked around the waiting room. Everyone had gone back to watching the muted TV on the wall, swiping through their phones, or staring blankly into space—whatever they had been doing before to fill the glacial pace of hospital time. "And they told me I never stopped breathing. It just, you know, slowed down."

"I knew you weren't happy, but heroin?" Laurie seemed on the verge of tears.

"No! It wasn't me. I mean, it was an accident. I swear, I'm not doing heroin. My mask got contaminated somehow."

Donny caught the security guard's eye. The guard gave a slight shake of his head. Was it disapproval, or just his way of indicating that Donny's domestic problems were way outside his job description?

Donny took Laurie's elbow and steered her to the exit. The doors hissed open, then closed behind them. They emerged from St. Mike's onto the corner of Victoria and Shuter. The elegant lunchtime crowd bustled around them, clutching their coats against the wind that whipped between the buildings, while panhandlers huddled in doorways, hopefully holding out their empty cups and tattered cardboard signs. He had treated overdoses from both groups—the empty, cynical rich and the hopeless dispossessed—but he felt no kinship with any of them.

Across the street was the newly renovated Massey Hall, Toronto's oldest and now also its newest and glitziest concert venue. It was a metaphor for the city. At one time this had been one of its most desirable neighbourhoods. It was still home to the Catholic cathedral, also named for St. Michael.

As the gentry left for the suburbs, the slow decay set in. Mansions became rooming houses; storefronts became pawn shops. Now the wheel was turning again. Office towers and elegant condos sprouted between the discount stores and shooting galleries.

Donny looked around. He'd worked in this area most of his career, witnessed its transformation. He felt disoriented: the buildings, this woman beside him, his life. So many changes, and he had never been comfortable with change. Nor satisfied when things stayed the same. Maybe he was just feeling the aftereffects of the drugs.

"The car's this way." Laurie turned north, up Victoria Street. "Where are you staying?"

Donny hesitated, then followed a couple of steps behind. "At the station." He looked back over his shoulder. "I could just walk. It's only a few blocks."

Laurie turned and stared at him as pedestrians flowed around them. "At the station? You're living at the station? I thought you'd at least be staying with Moose or Eddy."

"Well, Moose and Q are busy planning the wedding, and Eddy's got enough going on with the family. So the station ... I mean, it's just for now. Until I figure it out, you know. Hey, it's conveniently close to work."

The joke fell flat.

"It *is* work. That's the whole problem. It has always been the problem. Everything revolves around your job. 'Donny Robertson saves the world.'" There was a weariness in Laurie's voice. "The sad part is, you can't even save yourself."

"That's not fair."

"No? What else do you have in your life?"

"Uh, well, there's the boat." He had been working on refitting another boat from the keel up, since he had lost *Red Bird* a few years ago. That project was on hold now, though, for the winter.

"Wrong answer. What about people? Relationships? When it's three o'clock in the morning and your whole world is falling apart, who are you going to call?"

Having his world fall apart was nothing new for Donny, whether it was three o'clock or any other time. Call someone? He hadn't considered that. The notion made him uneasy.

"You?" he finally responded.

"That took way too long. And it shouldn't be a question." Laurie turned and walked away.

He knew he wasn't supposed to follow, but he did anyway. "Wait. Please, just give me a sec."

Laurie kept walking. "I've waited as long as I can. And you know, it'll be the same with that policewoman, too."

"Sergeant Singh? No, we're just friends. Colleagues."

"Lying just makes it more insulting."

Donny ran to get ahead of her and stopped. "It's not like that, Laurie. I swear I haven't slept with anyone else since we've been together."

"I don't care whether you're screwing her or not. That's not even the point. I finally realized that for you it's all about the quest, the Holy Grail, whether it's her or catching this dirty cop you're after or the next big fire. It's all the same. You're hoping you're finally going to find *it*. But *it* isn't something you find. Not out there. It's something deeper. Inside." Laurie brushed past him. She stopped at the entrance to the parking garage and pointed down the street. "The station's back that way."

"He's in the hospital. There was an accident. Here in the station."

"Oh my God, Eddy. Is he OK?" Daya struggled to fit this unexpected news into what she had already anticipated would be a difficult conversation. She had been wondering for a couple of days what to do with the forensic information Cindy had given her. After her disastrous conversation with Donny's partner, Daya wasn't sure if she should do anything about it. Everything relating to Donny seemed messy and complicated She had finally resolved to call him at the station. Now this.

"Yeah, it looks like he's going to be fine," Eddy's voice said from the phone. "I don't think they'll keep him."

"What happened?"

"I can't really ... I mean, it's not up to me ... "

"Of course, I understand," Daya said. "I'll try him later on his cell. Is this the right number?" She read off the contact she had for Donny.

"Yeah, that's right."

"OK. I tried that one before and his wife answered. But anyway ..."

"Listen," Eddy interrupted. There was an unmistakable note of tension in his voice. "You guys are adults, and it's none of my business, except it kind of is, because I care about that big Irish idiot. I care a lot. He's got a lot on his plate right now. So it might be best if, you know, you gave him some space."

Daya frowned at the phone. "Listen, Eddy, I don't know what you think is going on, or what Donny told you, but this is purely professional."

"OK." Eddy sounded unconvinced.

"Donny asked me for some information—forensic stuff—and I've got some answers for him. Just give him the message when you see him, OK?"

"The hospital released him an hour ago." Ratzo's cheerful voice spilled from the phone.

"Well, that's certainly good news." Tom Humphrey did not look like a man who had received good news. He looked at his watch—a quarter after one and still no sign of Ericson.

"He wants to report back to duty."

"What?"

"Donny. He's at the station," Ratzo explained. "He wants to get back on the truck."

"No, absolutely not. He just got out of the hospital, for Christ's sake. Tell him to go home."

Ratzo explained Donny's domestic situation, at least as much as Eddy had shared with him. Humphrey sighed. Robertson wasn't the first firefighter to hole up in a fire station, and he wouldn't be the last. "OK," Humphrey conceded, "but he's off duty until further notice."

Humphrey hung up and looked around. Cherry Beach wasn't as deserted as he had though it would be. A few hardy dog walkers trailed their charges in the off-leash area, their heads tucked against the damp, biting wind that whipped off Lake Ontario. Out on the water, a quartet of kite surfers launched themselves from foam-tipped waves. Wet-suited or not, Humphrey couldn't imagine braving the lake's grey-green waters at this time of year. Or any other time, for that matter.

But then, most people couldn't imagine running into a burning building. Like most things in life, it all depended on your priorities, your experience, and what you were willing to endure.

A silver Camry turned into the parking lot, interrupting Humphrey's reverie. Humphrey briefly flicked on the Tahoe's red flashing lights, and Ericson turned and pulled in beside him. Humphrey got out and walked to the driver's side of the Camry.

Ericson rolled down the window. "Sorry I'm late."

Humphrey did his best to keep his voice neutral. "Let's take a walk."

"I'd rather not wake her." Ericson pointed his thumb over his shoulder to the toddler dozing in her car seat in the back.

Humphrey scowled, "I thought I told you to get a babysitter."

"The other two are at a friend's house. What was I supposed to do on short notice?" Ericson unlocked the doors. "Have a seat."

Humphrey walked to the passenger side and got in. He said nothing for a moment, just looked at the tall, rangy cop, searching for some sign of remorse. "What the hell were you thinking?"

Ericson tried to match the older man's gaze. "What are you talking about?"

"Really? That's how you want to play it? Cut the bullshit," Humphrey snapped. "Donny was released from hospital a couple of hours ago."

"Lucky him." Ericson drummed his fingers on the steering wheel. "This your version of the old Cherry Beach Express? You want to beat a confession out of me in front of my daughter?"

Humphrey glanced at the sleeping child, then back at Ericson. "How about you grow a pair?"

"You said you were going to take care of him," Ericson scoffed. "Then I hear through the grapevine that someone has been making a fuss about the Rothberg thing. Your boy Donny again, I'm sure of it."

"This is not how ..." Humphrey began.

"So I took care of it," Ericson cut him off. "Now Robertson's a junkie—neutralized. His credibility is shot."

"Do you honestly think it's that simple?" Humphrey shook his head. "Donny's equipment is going in for testing. It's going to reveal that his gear was somehow accidentally contaminated with fentanyl."

Ericson's mouth moved silently.

"Because that draws the least attention," Humphrey said, his voice rising. "Because it's the closest to the truth. Because no one, and I mean no one, is going to believe that Donny Robertson is a junkie. The only thing you've done is make everything more complicated."

Ericson's daughter began to squirm and fuss in the back seat. He turned and pulled a sippy cup from the diaper bag in the back, removed the cap and handed her the cup. She quieted, and Ericson turned back without speaking.

"We're going to delay things with Ramón for a while," Humphrey said, more quietly. "We need to avoid any connection between that and what happened to Donny."

"You're overreacting."

"You could have killed him," Humphrey said.

"Collateral damage."

"No, it's not. It was deliberate. And it's unacceptable. This whole thing is about doing what's right. We don't take out our own. We do not betray our principles for simple expedience."

"Screw your principles," Ericson declared. "You can dress this up with procedures and ethics to soothe your conscience, but it's still killing people who need to be killed. Your principles are what's wrong with this screwed-up system we have in the first place."

"It's not all or nothing," Humphrey tried to explain, one last time. "Principles are all that separate us from the jungle. And right at the top is we don't kill our own for simple convenience."

Ericson slammed his hand on the dash, and his daughter began to wail in the back seat. "Robertson is a threat. I will not spend my life in prison while my children grow up."

"That's a risk we all accepted when we started this group—that if we needed to, we would accept the consequences to protect each other and what we do."

The wailing in the back seat grew louder. "I don't remember signing that waiver," Ericson said over the noise.

"Well, you don't have to worry about it anymore. You're finished with the Committee." Humphrey had hoped to wait until after Ramón had been dealt with to give Ericson the bad news, but the situation was untenable. In or out, Ericson was a liability.

Ericson's eyes widened. "But what about Ramón?"

"We'll look after him, but you're done."

"You can't do that."

"You've had multiple chances to redeem yourself. This last episode? That was too much."

"No, the problem is it wasn't enough." Ericson laughed, but there was no mirth in it. "You can't shut me out. I know things!"

There was an edge of hysteria in Ericson's voice that troubled Humphrey. "Really? You want to start making threats now? Believe me, this is not a fight you want to start. If you make waves, you will be neutralized—not physically harmed, but the problem will be dealt with."

Ericson shifted in his seat to look squarely at Humphrey. "You know what your problem is? You and the rest of your precious Committee? Lack of commitment. You hide behind your principles and your procedures because you're not prepared to go all the way. But I am. Remember that. This isn't over."

"Yes, it is," Humphrey said with finality. "And you did it to yourself. You remember that."

It was useless arguing the point further. Ericson was beyond reason, consumed by his own anger. Humphrey opened the car door and climbed out. He resisted the urge to slam the door, closing it gently and firmly. The sound of Ericson's daughter's muffled crying followed him back to his own car.

Ericson's threat was not an empty one, Humphrey reflected as he drove away. A sensible man would minimize the risk to himself, but there was little about Ericson that was sensible. He should have seen that in the beginning, but it was too late now. They would have to make contingency plans in case Ericson became completely unhinged.

In the meantime, there were other matters that needed his attention. Donny was out of the hospital now. It was time to nail that door shut once and for all. Humphrey took out his phone and scrolled to Albert Fernandez's number.

"Albert, hi. Sorry to bother you. How's your schedule tomorrow? I need a favour."

CHAPTER 32

LEGAL COUNSEL

Donny swung his legs over the edge of the daybed and looked around the unfamiliar room. His left hand rested on a large reddish-brown stain on the comforter. It matched several similar spots on the carpet. Hopefully they were coffee stains, but Donny made a mental note to buy new bedding.

It had been only a day since he had been released from hospital, but it seemed like his whole world had turned upside down. Technically he was off "injured on duty"—not for the first time. But this time it felt like he had been banished. The news of his overdose had spread like wildfire among his fellow firefighters. No one who really knew him believed he was using, and he had a reputation as something of an oddball anyway, but the humiliation of it all still stung him deeply.

He had used the time to find a place and pick up a few meagre belongings from Laurie's. Thirty square metres, a little over three hundred square feet: that's what eighteen hundred dollars a month got you in Toronto these days—basically a run-down room with a kitchenette in the corner, equipped with a half-size fridge and an ancient three-burner cooktop. The toilet handle stuck, and anyone over five foot six had to bend over to take a shower. Water had obviously leaked from the apartment above at some point in the past. Someone had tried to paint over the stain that started in the ceiling over the cooktop and ran halfway down the adjoining wall, but it had bled through, like some ghostly, mouldering, abstract work of art.

There was a window, and most of the slats in the vinyl vertical blinds worked. It gave a view of telephone wires, garbage bins and the brick wall across the alley.

It was only for a while, Donny told himself. If he couldn't work things out with Laurie, then maybe it was time for a new beginning.

Not for the first time, he thought about *Red Bird*. How he had loved that boat! Now she lay in darkness at the bottom of Lake Huron. And that, too, had been the result of his obsessive search for answers. That quest, too, had almost cost him his job and his life.

That was all in the past. It was time to look ahead. In a couple of years, he would be eligible for early retirement. By then he'd have finished refitting *Red Bird II*, another Island Packet 35—small enough to sail alone, tough enough to cruise the world.

But there were a few hurdles to be cleared first, like getting the OK to return to duty. He showered and shaved quickly, put on his dress uniform, and headed out the door.

Donny knocked.

"Come in." Platoon Chief Tom Humphrey opened the office door. It was a large, airy room, simply but elegantly furnished. A bookshelf ran along the wall beside the door, lined with copies of the Fire Code, HazMat, Emergency Management and Operational manuals—battle plans, written by bureaucrats. Like most battle plans, they rarely survived the first shot of a real emergency. A large desk sat in front of a bank of windows that gave a splendid view of the city's skyline. The desk was empty except for a phone, a framed picture of Humphrey's wife, and a large folder, which Donny assumed was his personnel file.

He felt like he'd been sent to the principal's office. He'd known Tom Humphrey his entire career—tough as nails, a good firefighter in his day. As a senior officer, he had little tolerance for slackers but treated you fairly if you gave him your best.

Another man was already seated in one of the black leather chairs across from Humphrey's desk. That was a surprise, and surprises were rarely a good thing in these situations. Donny had expected the meeting to be just him and the platoon chief. The other man was slim, with dark hair combed back; his face was framed by a pair of designer glasses. A gold watch hung on his wrist, just below the sleeve of an expensive-looking suit.

Humphrey closed the office door behind Donny and held out his hand. He smiled as they shook. "How are you feeling?"

"Fine." Donny tried to keep his voice relaxed.

"Good. You can hang up your hat and jacket if you like. We'll keep this informal."

Donny placed his uniform hat on the rack in the corner and hung his tunic beside Humphrey's—Donny's sleeves trimmed with the silver captain's band, Humphrey's with the three gold bands of a platoon chief.

"Have a seat." Humphrey pointed to the empty chair facing the desk, then indicated the man in the other chair. "This is Albert Fernandez. He's a defence attorney."

Defence attorney?! Donny wasn't sure he liked the sound of that. Or the man in the expensive suit himself, for that matter. He looked back and forth between the two men. "Do I need a ..."

"Not yet." Humphrey gave a grim smile. "Albert's a friend of mine. He's here as a personal favour."

Faint recognition swam to the surface of Donny's mind. He'd seen Fernandez's face before, on the news—a high-profile criminal lawyer.

"Pleased to meet you." Fernandez rose to his feet and held out his hand. They shook and sat.

Humphrey opened the thick file folder in front of him, scanned the contents for a moment, then looked up and took off his glasses. "The only two issues of concern here are your well-being and the good of the Department as a whole. I've always liked you, Donny.

I'm glad you're OK. You're a pain in the ass sometimes, but I'm always glad to see you on the fireground."

Coming from Tom Humphrey, that was high praise. He was not one to waste words or make empty gestures. Donny tried to read his expression, but he had never been good at interpreting other people's emotions. He allowed himself to relax a bit and smile. "Thank you, Chief."

"There are a bunch of commendations in here," Humphrey tapped the file with his finger. "Some of them I've signed myself. There are also a few reprimands. I've signed some of those too. Now, I don't think for a second that you're an addict, Donny, and neither does anyone who knows you."

Donny looked over at Fernandez, then back at Humphrey. "I don't think that's ... It's a personal ..."

"It's a workplace incident," Humphrey cut him off. "That means it's not just personal. The administration is looking into this, and it will be handled according to the Department's drug and alcohol policy. I've told Albert what happened."

"I'm glad you're OK," Fernandez nodded.

Donny ignored him. "Drug and alcohol policy? It was contamination!"

"Yes," Humphrey dismissed the objection. "But it's standard department procedure for any case involving opioids. The fire chief is not going to make a special exception for you. So you'll be subject to random testing for the next six months."

"I am not an addict!"

"I don't think you are. If anything, you're the type to go crazy while stark raving sober. And you've also got a positive genius for painting a bullseye on your own forehead."

Donny tried to keep his gaze steady. "I'm not sure what you ..."

"Like hell you're not," Humphrey scowled. "Neither you nor I are worried about you pissing in a cup for six months. At worst it's an inconvenience. Now, you can kick up a fuss and demand a formal hearing at HQ, but part of that also means a review of all recent events. That will include problems with a certain junior member of your crew," Humphrey raised an eyebrow, "*and* your delusional obsession with Constable Ericson. You really want that?"

Donny's jaw tightened; his knuckles whitened as he gripped the arms of the chair, but he said nothing.

"You want to get out of the hole? Stop digging." Humphrey pivoted in his chair to look out over the city skyline. "I am responsible for the safety and well-being of millions of citizens and hundreds of firefighters. A captain who's distracted and can't focus on the job at hand, that's a real problem. It's a danger to your crew and to the public you're there to serve."

Humphrey swung back to face Donny. "I don't want to lose you, but I will not place you or anyone before the good of the Department. And I cannot let you continue to damage the relationship between us and the police any further. Is that understood?"

Donny nodded.

"Good. Now, I have asked Albert here to explain a few things to you. I hope you'll listen to him."

Fernandez smoothed the crease in his trousers and turned to face Donny. "Do you have any idea how many people die in Toronto every day?" Fernandez paused, but Donny made no indication of responding. "No? Close to a hundred. Every day. About one every fifteen minutes. And not all of them from natural causes."

Fernandez smiled indulgently at Donny. It was more than a feeling now—Donny was sure he didn't like Albert Fernandez. He didn't like the condescension, and he liked it even less coming from a pretty boy in an expensive suit. "Yeah, but listen ..." he began.

"No, you listen. Normally I charge five hundred dollars an hour for this sort of advice. I'm doing this as a favour for a friend." Fernandez's smile warmed as he turned to Humphrey, but vanished as he looked back at Donny. "As a former prosecutor, I can tell you that the resources, both dollars and people, that the Crown and police have are limited. They need to use those resources wisely, not fritter them away. The notion that they would focus all those resources on the death of a drug dealer or a child molester, based solely on your gut feelings, is frankly ridiculous."

"You weren't there," Donny spluttered.

"Donny, please let the man talk." Humphrey's glare made it an order, not a request.

Fernandez took off his Armani glasses and folded them into his pocket, a gesture of intimate sympathy that Donny suspected had been performed in front of many juries. "It's not a perfect system, but it works. Most of the time. I know that better than anyone. And I also know Ari Greene, lead homicide detective for the Toronto Police. You bring him proof—hard evidence that a cop was involved in those deaths—and I promise you that Detective Greene will go after him hammer and tongs. But Ari's also been on the receiving end of a false murder charge. He will never go after someone based solely on innuendo."

Donny rose and stepped towards Fernandez. "I know what I saw. Am I just supposed to forget about that?"

"Sit down," Humphrey growled. Donny did as he was told.

"No, but it helps if you have a motive, means and opportunity before you start making accusations like this," Fernandez continued. "And a little bit of hard evidence would help, too. Or better yet, leave it to the professionals. I'm good at what I do—very good. But I don't try to fix teeth or design airplanes. I let people who know what they're doing look after those things. I suggest you do the same. Because otherwise the results can be disastrous."

Fernandez looked at his watch and stood. "Sorry, Tom. It's been good to see you, but I'm due in court."

"I understand."

"Maybe we can get together for a pint."

"That would be great. I'll give you a call." Humphrey came round the desk and retrieved Fernandez's coat from the rack. "Thanks for coming."

"My pleasure." The two men shook hands. "Captain Robertson." Fernandez nodded at Donny and left.

Humphrey closed the door and returned to his desk. "I hope you were listening to what he said. I did this as a personal favour. But that's it, because this is no longer a personal matter." Humphrey closed Donny's file. "For the next six months you will be under scrutiny. If I see anything that is interfering with your ability to do your job, I will not hesitate to fix that problem. Is that understood?"

"Yes, sir." Donny stood. "Is that all, sir?"

"Not quite." Humphrey pulled a resealable bag from his desk drawer. It contained a small sample jar. He set the bag down and sighed. "You know what I see when I look at you? I see me. Me, always needing to do more, always needing to be smarter, stronger, better; because if I could show people what a great firefighter I was, then maybe they wouldn't see what a failure I was as a person."

"You seem to have come through it OK, Chief." Donny regretted the pettiness of his comment as soon as the words left his lips.

Humphrey ignored it. "Focus and determination aren't always bad things. Depends on how you use them. When my daughter was murdered ..." He paused and swallowed.

Donny shifted uncomfortably.

"I used to hate it too, when people talked to me like this. Absolutely hated it." Humphrey picked up the bag and walked to the door. "I don't know what your demons are, Donny. I'm not a shrink, but I'll tell you this from experience: it's a losing battle to compare the way you feel on the inside with the way other people look on the outside."

Humphrey opened the office door. "You can return to duty tomorrow morning." He held the bag with the sample jar out to Donny "Leave it at the medical office on your way out."

CHAPTER 33

A SIMPLE FAVOUR

Amy Winehouse's voice rang out over the PA. "They Tried to Make Me Go to Rehab" flooded the apparatus floor. Donny, helmet in hand, bunker coat slung over his arm, turned from his stall in the racks of firefighting gear at the back of the station towards the floor watch room at the front. His shock was briefly replaced by anger before it resolved itself into a resigned smile.

Eddy was laughing so hard he could barely hold his phone in front of the PA microphone in the floor watch. Behind him, Scout grinned like a maniac, while Moose, snorting and cackling, leaned against the wall to keep from falling over.

Donny shook his head, grabbed the rest of his gear, and walked to the truck. Eddy shut off his phone. The three of them, still chuckling, came out to meet Donny.

"Welcome home," Eddy said.

"You're all assholes," Donny said, trying unsuccessfully to keep a straight face.

"And your point is?" Moose replied.

"I can't believe the three of you came in early just to set that up." Donny set his helmet on the dash, hung his coat from the side mirror, and placed his boots, with the pants rolled down over them, beside the front tire. "You know the guys up in the dorm are going to kill you for this."

"Totally worth it," Eddy shrugged. "You should have seen the look on your face."

Scout stood to one side, picking at a fingernail. "So you're OK?"

"That's what they told me. No lasting damage."

"That's good." Scout looked at Donny's gear carefully placed by the truck, then turned to the door that led to the hallway and the stairs to the living quarters on the second floor. "I'll go put on a pot of coffee."

"Strange kid," Donny said, watching Scout head up the stairs.

"There's a transfer sheet coming out next week." Eddy waved the matter away. "With any luck, by then he'll be someone else's problem."

"I'm going to go start breakfast," Moose announced. "And see if I can persuade the C shift guys not to kill Eddy."

"Hey, you were there too, buddy," Eddy objected.

"Yeah, but the guys on C shift like me." Moose winked and headed to the stairs.

"What a job, eh?" Eddy turned to Donny. "Risk your life for a total stranger, but throw your brother under the bus in a heartbeat."

"That's how you know they love you." Donny returned to the truck. There was one more task to complete. He took his face piece from its storage pouch and connected it to the regulator of the SCBA nestled in the back of his seat. He pulled the tank free of its bracket, checked the waist and shoulder straps, and turned on the air valve. A combination of lights, gauges and electronic beeps indicated that everything was functioning as it should. The last step was to don the face piece, turn off the tank, and breathe down the residual air in the system to verify the low-air-alarm. Donny brought the mask to his face and hesitated for a moment.

"You want me to check that for you?" Eddy asked from the back of the truck. He was going through the same procedure with his own mask.

Mountain climbers coil their own ropes. Skydivers pack their own parachutes. When your life depends on a piece of equipment ... Donny didn't even bother looking up. "You want me checking *your* mask for you?"

Eddy let him be. Donny put the mask to his face and breathed down the residual air. The low-air alarm sounded as it should. He tucked the SCBA back into its bracket and took one final look around the pumper's cab. Satisfied, he stepped down and walked to the stairs.

Eddy was waiting for him in the doorway to the supply room, at the bottom of the stairs. He held out a couple of small, oddly shaped pieces of white plastic. "Naloxone. In case it happens again. We talked it over and decided it would be a good idea if we each carried a couple in our pockets."

Donny wrinkled his brow. With their nasal applicators, finger flanges and plungers, the bottles looked like tiny plastic space ships.

"What happened to you could happen to any of us," Eddy continued. "That shit is everywhere now. What if there's no time to go grab the first aid kit?"

"I don't know." Donny turned away. "I'll think about it."

"How much other stuff do you carry in your pockets, huh? Stuff you've never used, but 'just in case.'"

Donny thought for a moment. Some things he used all the time: his folding knife, screwdriver set and a small pair of vise grips. But there were other things, like ten feet of nylon strapping that could be used for ... well, it had all kinds of uses, he'd just never needed it. And there were the side cutters he carried in case he became tangled in wires and cables in a building collapse. They had sat in the pocket of his bunker pants for almost thirty years without being used.

"C'mon, you know this stuff works. Christ, one second you were lying right there, barely breathing." Eddy pointed to the spot on the apparatus floor where Donny had collapsed. "Psshht, up the nose, and five seconds later you're sitting up, going 'where am I?'"

"All right, all right, if it makes you happy." Donny grabbed the two doses of naloxone and shoved them in his pants pocket. He would put them in his bunker coat later. Right now, the main thing he wanted was to sit in the kitchen, have a cup of coffee and forget that any of this had ever happened. "I'll tell you, that is one experience I do not plan on repeating."

"Ah, you never know. Friday night, nothing on TV ... maybe a little smack will liven things up."

"You want a little smack? I got one for you." Donny patted Eddy on the cheek. "Let's grab a coffee."

"Was it at least fun? You know, I've heard it's, like, the best feeling in the world," Eddy asked as they headed up the stairs to the kitchen.

Donny stopped on the landing, one hand on the railing. "I don't know. It was strange—not horrible, but it wasn't like a 'wahoo, let's party' kind of thing." Donny started up the stairs again. "Honestly, I'm not sure what the attraction is. Everything just kind of faded away."

"If your life's a steaming pile of crap, maybe that is the attraction," Eddy said. "Good thing you and I have our shit together, eh?"

"Yeah, that's always been my strong point. Do me a favour: just stop talking for a couple minutes, OK?"

"Just one more thing—that police lady called. Singh. She said she had some information you asked for. Something about forensics."

The day progressed with mundane regularity—the daily schedule of cleaning duties and equipment maintenance, a handful of routine calls, a refresher training session on relay pumping and aerial tower operations with the crews from Station Seven.

As afternoon faded into evening, Donny sat in his office wading through the stream of reports that fuelled the department's bureaucracy. He hoped the monotonous routine would drown out the tape of his meeting with Humphrey that kept playing over and over in his head. "You want to get out of the hole? Stop digging."

He paused for a moment and looked out the window. The pastel shades of evening softened the hard edges of glass and steel of the buildings that towered over the station. He took a deep breath. Yes, his life was a hot mess. And much of it was his own doing—all due to his bullheaded, obsessive refusal to accept common wisdom. "You want to get out of the hole? Stop digging."

And yet ... the image of Ericson standing over the dirty ex-cop Simpson and calmly pulling the trigger flashed into his mind. *And what about the eye bolt? The hardware store? And Daya's cryptic message about forensic evidence?* The little voice in the back of his mind wouldn't be quiet.

Not my circus, not my monkey, Donny told himself.

And isn't it convenient that you should have an "accidental" overdose just when it seemed like you were really onto something? the voice insisted.

NO!

From the kitchen came the aromas of sauteed onions and garlic, roasting meat, fresh bread, and pumpkin pie, along with the sound of clanging pots, Eddy's singing, and the occasional Portuguese curse. A deeper metallic thumping came from the gym, where Moose was lifting crushing stacks of weights. In all the world, there was truthfully no place he would rather be. This was home. This was where he belonged. Not on some wild goose chase.

Patrick Thompson sat in the padded swivel chair in the floor watch, feet up on the desk, scrolling through his phone. A fishing show played on TV, while the scanner spat out the chatter of the department's different radio channels. At first, floor watch had seemed like solitary confinement. He was beginning to see it now as his personal Fortress of Solitude.

His phone rang. Ericson. Shit. He stared, letting the phone buzz in his hand. He spun in his chair, reached out with his leg, kicked the door closed and swiped to answer. "What?"

"Nice talking to you too."

"He almost died! What the fuck were you thinking?"

"Dealing with a problem—yours and mine. Calm down," Ericson said. "Your captain is now officially on the record as a drug addict."

"No, that's just it! They don't believe Donny's a junkie." Pat peeked through the glass of the floor watch door, checking to see that the hallway and stairs were clear. "I mean, he has to do piss tests and stuff, but it's ... I don't know about the chiefs, but all the guys in the district are pretty sure it was an accident."

"Then we need to convince them otherwise and finish the job."

"'We?' No, I'm done. I'm transferring out of this station. I am done with this place, and you, and everything."

"You're not done with anything." Ericson's sneer came through the phone like a slap in the face. "You're in this balls deep, buddy. You ever hear of something called 'being an accessory?' That was your door pass I used to get into the station, just before Donny's little accident. There'll be an electronic record of that somewhere."

Pat collapsed back into the swivel chair as if all the calcium had been sucked out of his bones. "I ... I thought you were my friend. I was just trying to ..."

"I need you to do one thing. A simple favour. I'll look after everything else, OK?"

"Then we're done. Promise me that."

"Of course," Ericson soothed. "Now put on your big boy pants and listen."

"So what do you want to watch? *Trainspotting*? *Hillbilly Elegy*?"

"You are such an asshole, Eddy," Donny replied. "Remind me again why I put up with you?"

"Because otherwise you'd have to eat Moose's cooking." Eddy settled back in the recliner, reached for the remote, and began scrolling through Netflix. Moose and Donny sprawled on nearby couches.

The "living room," a small room off the kitchen, had once been the aerial officer's room, when Lombard had housed two trucks. The room had been converted into living space when the ladder truck was removed. At first it had housed a large console radio when shows like *Bing Crosby* and *Amos 'n' Andy* were popular. Now it was home to a state-of-the-art home entertainment system and a motley collection of furniture salvaged from various firefighters' basement rec rooms.

"What was it like?" Moose asked.

"Sorry, Moose, I'm just really tired of talking about it, OK?" Donny stretched out full length on his couch.

"Yeah, sorry. It's just we run these overdose calls all the time, right?" Moose continued. "And I always wonder, what's the attraction? I mean, I get the addiction part, but there's got to be more, at least in the beginning, to risk your life like that. Is it that good?"

"Like I told Eddy, I don't remember much. One moment I was checking my mask, then everything went soft. It was like I was falling through clouds. Then nothing."

"I've got it," Eddy declared, still scrolling through the list of movies. "The classic movie for junkies: *Panic in Needle Park*."

Donny shook his head and got up off the couch.

"Sit. I'll stop. I get it—too soon. Sit."

Donny eased himself back onto the couch and turned to Moose. "The thing I can't figure out is how Eddy's kids turned out so normal."

"Linda's a great mother. I think you really need only one sane, stable parent," Moose replied.

"OK, how about a nice rom-com?" Eddy pressed a button on the remote. The image of four desperate-looking young men appeared on the TV. "*Recovery Boys!*" Eddy collapsed back in his chair, giggling.

"You just can't help yourself, can you?" Donny sighed. "I'm going to go read. You guys watch whatever you want."

CHAPTER 34

LIKE HOUDINI

It was one of those rare quiet nights when the normal urban frenzy seemed to pass them by. Just a false alarm in one of the downtown bank towers shortly after eleven, and then nothing.

Donny lay in his bunk listening to the darkness. The pulse of the city filtered in from outside: the constant buzz of traffic, the occasional barking of dogs, the staccato laughter of late-night revellers, the distant sirens of someone else's calls.

Donny slept with the office door ajar, and from the dorm came the low rumble of Moose's snoring. It amazed Donny how easily and well the big man slept. He seemed never to have lost a child's ability simply to accept the world as it was, and sleep like a baby. Eddy had that ability too, to a lesser degree. Donny envied them that.

The station itself mumbled through the night. It was almost a hundred and fifty years old, and like most centenarians, had its own peculiar creaks and groans. Donny knew them all.

He was surprised to hear the sound of the door at the back of the apparatus floor opening and closing. It must be Scout going out to his car for something, Donny thought. Floor watch was supposed to remain at their post. Donny briefly considered getting up to address the situation, but he didn't have the stomach for another confrontation with Pat. He'd be transferring out soon enough. Let someone else deal with it.

Then the sound of quiet voices filtered up through the pole hole: Scout's and another male voice, lower and indistinct. Visitors after midnight? That was a definite no-no. Donny sat up and pulled on his pants. Like it or not, he would have to deal with it. He reached for his shoes.

He heard the unmistakable squeak of the second stair from the top. What the hell? Someone was coming upstairs. Donny stood and took a moment to collect himself. This was not going to be pleasant, but the kid was way over the line now.

The door swung open before Donny could get to it. The outline of a large man filled the frame, silhouetted by the nightlight in the hall. Donny could just make out the blond hair and square jaw. Even in the dim light, it was obviously Ericson, out of uniform, but Ericson nonetheless.

"What the fuck do you ..."

Ericson stepped forward. He held the gun out in his gloved hand so Donny could plainly see it. "Shhh," Ericson said softly. "Come quietly. If you make a fuss, it won't be just you that gets a bullet in the head." Ericson cocked his head towards the dorm. "Understand?"

Run? Fight? Call for help? There were no good options. Above all, Donny needed to protect his crew. Whatever madness was now unleashed in Ericson, the crew had no part in it.

"Yes," Donny said hoarsely. He stared at the gun. Fires, catastrophes, the random carnage of day-to-day life—those things he could handle. But this, the sheer malice—this froze his blood.

Ericson motioned towards the door with his gun. They made their way silently along the hall, past the kitchen and down the stairs.

Scout was standing in the door to the floor watch. "Oh my God! You're not going to shoot him, are you?"

"Not unless I have to. And keep your voice down," Ericson replied. "Take this and tie his hands behind his back." Ericson pulled a set of plastic zip tie handcuffs from his jacket and held them out to Pat.

Donny stared at Pat in disbelief. "You're part of this?"

"No, I just ..."

"Shut up. Both of you. Now take them," Ericson growled. The menace in his voice was unmistakable.

Pat took the handcuffs and zipped them around Donny's wrists. "I'm sorry," he whispered in Donny's ear.

"It's OK." It was too late for anger or recrimination.

Ignoring the exchange, Ericson turned to Scout. "If anyone asks, you were snoozing in that chair." He pointed to the recliner in the floor watch. "You heard the back door open. You saw Donny talking with a short, dark-haired man, about five-six, five-eight. Maybe Latino or Asian, it was hard to tell. You got that?"

"Dark hair, five-six, five-eight, Latino or Asian," Pat parroted. "I don't understand."

"You don't need to."

"But ... but what are you going to do?" Pat stammered.

"Solve the problem."

"This is crazy. I don't want to go to jail."

"You say what I told you and everything will be fine. If you don't, believe me, jail will be the least of your problems."

Donny felt the cold steel pressed against the base of his skull as Ericson prodded him towards the back door. Scout watched them leave. His mouth worked, but no words came out.

The call came in about fifteen minutes later—a minor medical, someone passed out on the Sherbourne bus. Moose, Eddy and Patrick stood by the truck, dressed and ready to go. Eddy looked at Donny's gear sitting empty by the truck, then at the pole, then back at the truck.

"I'll call him," Moose replied to Eddy's unasked question. He headed to the floor watch to use the PA.

"It's not like him to sleep through a call." Eddy sounded puzzled. "He's usually the first one down."

"He went out," Scout said.

"What?" Eddy took a step towards him. "What do you mean, 'went out?'"

"Out the back. I, uh, I was dozing in the floor watch chair and I saw him leave with some Mexican dude."

"You're just telling us this now?" Moose asked, returning to the truck.

"You saw him, or you were sleeping? Which is it?" Eddy asked.

Scout refused to meet Eddy's gaze. "I, well, I woke up just as he was leaving."

"He didn't say anything?"

"No."

"Why didn't you wake someone up? Tell us?" Moose asked.

"Donny hates me already. I didn't want to get in trouble." Scout turned towards the truck so he wouldn't have to face the other two.

"This is fucked up. Donny wouldn't just disappear like Houdini. Something's wrong." Eddy rolled his bunker pants back down and stepped out of his boots. "I'm going to call Ratzo."

Ericson stopped the car in front of the factory gate, got out, and opened the trunk.

Donny blinked up at him. Even though it was the middle of the night, inside the trunk it had been pitch black. The streetlight a dozen yards away was almost as blinding as the sun. "Where are we?"

"The end of the line." Ericson grabbed a pair of bolt cutters lying beside Donny's head and closed the trunk lid.

Donny was left in darkness again. It had been a short trip—five or ten minutes, maybe a few more. It seemed longer, but Donny knew that was only the stress of his captivity.

Ericson went to the gate, fit the bolt cutter's jaws over one of the links in the chain that secured the gate, and heaved. There was a metallic pop, and one end of the severed link skittered across the pavement. The chain hung limp, the lock still threaded through its ends. Ericson shook his head. People went to vast expense to buy big heavy locks and then used them with chains that weren't even half as strong.

Ericson dropped the bolt cutters on the passenger seat and drove slowly over to the factory's disused loading docks, where a blue mini-van was already parked. Ericson parked beside it, got out and walked to the door at the end of the line of truck bays. He rapped sharply on the door.

"Lowry, open up. It's me."

There was a pause, then the sound of a lock being turned, and the door opened a few inches. Lowry looked sideways out of the narrow opening. "Ericson? What are you doing here?"

"There's been a change of plan."

"No one told me about it. You sure? I'd better call." Lowry stepped back to reach for his phone.

Ericson pushed the door open. There was no resistance—Lowry was unlocking his phone. In one smooth motion, Ericson took the taser from his pocket and pressed it to Lowry's neck.

There was a brief buzzing, and Lowry collapsed to the floor like a marionette with its strings cut. Ericson pulled another set of plastic handcuffs from his jacket and secured Lowry's arms behind him. Patting Lowry down, he removed the 9mm from Lowry's shoulder holster and a set of keys from his pants pocket. Ericson stuck the gun in the back of his waistband with his own and sorted through the keys. One of them was marked with red tape. That had to be the master.

The interior of the loading dock was dark. The only light came through the window and open door of the shipping/receiving office. The loading dock was a spare, functional space, concrete and brick covered with coffee-toned, nondescript industrial paint, and high-lighted with diagonal yellow and black safety markings. There were a few empty cardboard boxes scattered around, a broken office chair and a couple of pieces of unidentifiable rusty metal leaned up against the far wall. Other than that, the space was empty. Anything of value had been salvaged and sold long ago.

The shipping office was set in the wall opposite the loading dock doors. It was mostly empty. A couple of bare shelves had been left attached to the wall, along with a whiteboard marked in a grid with labelled columns—date, time, loading dock number, and so on. A counter, where the receiver and truckers had signed each other's forms, extended from the wall beside the door. More recent additions included a lamp sitting on the counter, along with empty food wrappers and a coffee cup. There was a cooler on the floor beside a folding chaise. A paperback lay splayed on top of the cooler, where Lowry had left it when he had gotten up to answer the door.

Ericson grabbed Lowry under the arms and dragged him back to the office. Lowry groaned. Ericson sat him up and propped him against one of the legs of the counter. *The guy who invented the zip tie deserves a Nobel prize*, Ericson thought. He secured Lowry's bound wrists to the counter leg bolted to the floor.

Lowry started to come around. He tugged his arms and looked groggily at Ericson.

"Sorry, buddy," Ericson said. "I'll be back in while. I'll cut you loose when I'm done." He closed the office door.

He paused and took a deep breath. Now to deal with Robertson. It was not something he looked forward to, but Robertson had brought this on himself. The asshole refused to stay in his lane. And he was a threat not just to Ericson, but to the whole organization. Ericson told himself that he was the only one who saw clearly what needed to be done. The others would thank him in the end.

Or not. But in the final analysis, he really didn't give a damn. Shit needed to get done.

"His car's still here. We looked out back, and all around the station, inside and out. Nothing," Eddy reported. "It's like he just disappeared."

"Maybe we should call the cops," suggested Moose.

District Chief Joe Razzolini shook his head. "There are no amber alerts for firefighters who go walkabout. They won't even take a missing person report for the first twenty-four hours."

Ratzo sat in his department Tahoe with the window rolled down. Moose, Eddy and Scout stood beside the vehicle, in front of the station. A cold November wind swirled through the darkness between the buildings that towered over the station. Ratzo saw the three men hugging themselves against the chill. This situation was going to take some time. Ratzo turned off the engine and pocketed the keys. "Let's go inside."

They walked in through the apparatus bay doors. Moose pressed the button and the big doors slowly rolled down their guide rails to the ground. Ratzo turned to Scout. "Tell me exactly what you saw."

Patrick bit his bottom lip and stuffed his hands in his pockets. "Well," he began, "I was floor watch ... again." He glanced at Eddy and Moose on either side of him. "I guess I dozed off. Anyway, I heard the back door." Pat pointed to the door, as if anyone present was unfamiliar with its location. Eddy grunted.

"And?" Ratzo urged.

"I saw Donny, uh, Captain Robertson leaving."

"With another guy."

"Yes. Shorter, maybe five-six, five-eight. About your height. It was kind of hard to tell—I only saw them from behind."

"You said he was Mexican," Moose interjected. "How could you tell if you only saw them from behind?"

"Uh, well, he turned sideways, kind of profile, as they went out."

"So did you see his face or not?" Eddy asked.

"Only for a second. The door was closing. I mean, he could have been Asian. I don't know."

"So he was about my height. What else, Patrick?" Ratzo tried to take some of the tension out of the situation. "Anything you can tell us will help. Bald? Long hair? Fat or skinny?"

"Dark hair, sort of medium length, I guess. Not fat, maybe a little chubby," Pat riffed on what he had been told to say. "I don't know. It was quick, you know? Only a second or two."

"That's it?" There was more than a hint of anger in Eddy's voice.

Ratzo shut it down immediately. "Cool it, Eddy. We're all concerned, OK?" He turned to Scout. "You need to write this all down, Patrick. Get the Firefighter Observations form and fill it out. Ignore the fire-related stuff, but fill in the rest—time, date, anything you saw, heard or did, even if you don't think it's important. Put down everything."

Ratzo turned to Eddy and Moose. "I have to kick this upstairs. I need to call the platoon chief. I'm not trying to make trouble for Donny, but I got no choice—Humphrey needs to know about it. I'll be up in the captain's office." Ratzo headed towards the stairs. "You guys out of service for now," he called back over his shoulder.

Scout followed Ratzo to the stairs. "I'm going to go get one of those forms."

Eddy moved to stop him, but Moose put a meaty hand on his shoulder. "Let him go."

"Something's not right." Eddy watched Scout disappear up the stairs, then turned back to Moose. "So now what? We just stand around with our thumbs up our asses?"

"What do you suggest?" Moose asked. He took a seat on the truck's broad front bumper. "Look, I'm just as worried as you, but we don't even really know what's going on."

"If Wedge went missing at a fire there'd be Maydays, rapid intervention teams, a massive search." Eddy paced up and down in front of the apparatus doors. "But none of that is happening. Just Ratzo reporting him AWOL to the platoon."

"Yeah, but this isn't a building collapse or a flashover or anything. We don't even know where to start searching."

Eddy stopped in front of Moose. With the big man sitting, Eddy could look him straight in the eye. "This whole thing feels wrong, and you know it too. You got to admit, he's been acting weird lately."

"Yeah, but that's Donny. Normal is always a little weird with him."

"This is different. Call it Portuguese intuition."

Moose stood and stretched. "What? Scout said he just walked out."

"If he's telling the truth." Eddy resumed pacing. Like a shark, he needed to stay in motion. He couldn't think properly standing still.

"Hmm," Moose pondered. He was the sort of person who normally took whatever life presented at face value. "Too bad we don't have surveillance cameras around the station, like the cops do."

"Christ! I'm an idiot!" Eddy stopped and face-palmed himself. "My dashcam." Eddy started for the back door.

Moose followed. "But doesn't the car have to be running for that to work?"

"I've got it set to parking mode." Eddy opened the back door and headed to his car. He already had his phone out of his pocket and scrolling to the dashcam app. "Ever since that smash and grab last summer, I've set it to parking mode. It works like a motion detector. If whoever it was came anywhere near my car, they'll be on the camera."

CHAPTER 35

DASHCAM

Donny's whole body ached. The cramped space of the car's trunk forced him into an unnatural position. He thought back to how he and two or three of his buddies used to cram into the trunk of his friend's father's big old Buick to sneak into the drive-in theatre. But that had been for only a few minutes. And his young body was more forgiving of such treatment back then. And he had not had his arms tied behind his back. And the worst thing that would have happened back then was getting thrown out of the drive-in.

As comforting as it was to reminisce, he needed to focus on the situation at hand. Ericson wasn't going to listen to any plea Donny could imagine. The wheel had turned too far for that. Besides, Donny doubted that he could live up to any pledge he might make to forget and keep quiet, even if Ericson did listen.

There was nothing he could do right now. He had tried kicking, but the trunk lid was locked and the back seat was securely latched—there was no escape that way. He was left alone in the dark with his thoughts. They were not good company.

Time expanded.

Footsteps. Ericson returning. It could have been ten minutes; it could have been two hours. Donny wasn't sure. There was a short beep, and the trunk opened.

"Get out."

Donny pivoted awkwardly and hooked his legs over the lip of the trunk. "I'm not sure I can ..."

Ericson grabbed him roughly by one arm and pulled him up.

"Aowh!" Donny cried. The sudden pull sent a surge of pain through his already aching shoulder.

"What happened to the tough firefighter?" Ericson mocked. "Move!" He pushed Donny towards the personnel door of the loading dock. They entered and crossed the floor of the dock.

Rattling and a muffled voice came from behind the shipping office door. "Ericson! What the fuck?"

So Donny wasn't Ericson's only captive. That was interesting.

"Keep moving."

Donny felt the gun pressed between his shoulder blades. Ericson held his phone in his left hand, using it to light their way. They passed through another door, moving deeper into the building. Twenty paces down the corridor, right turn ...Donny created a mental map as they walked. It was second nature after so many years of crawling through unfamiliar places in smoke and darkness. Other corridors branched off the one they were in. He tried to keep track of them. Twelve more paces. They passed an alcove with a set of stairs leading up and down. Another turn, left this time. They crossed a large open area, at least two stories tall—perhaps warehouse space. There was a faint, soapy, floral smell. The old Lever Brothers factory at the foot of Broadview Avenue? It was possible.

They stopped in front of a steel door. Ericson fished a set of keys out of his pocket, opened it, and waved Donny through with the gun.

It was a large room, perhaps eight metres by ten. A double row of glass blocks served as a narrow window, set high in the wall to the left. There was an open doorway to the right. Through it Donny could just make out a row of sinks. Perhaps this had been an employee change room. That would fit with the rectangular discolourations on the terrazzo floor, where rows of lockers had once stood. Now the room was mostly empty.

Mostly. A man and a woman sat on cots set against the far wall. The only other furnishings were two folding tables set end to end, and three folding chairs. The tables held half a dozen or so glass beakers and flasks, as well as several large brown glass jars. It looked like a chemistry lab yard sale.

Ericson followed Donny into the room, picked up one of the chairs and placed it at the foot of the woman's bed.

"Sit."

Donny sat.

From inside his coat, Ericson produced two more from what seemed to be a limitless supply of zip ties. He tossed these to the woman, keeping his gun trained on the three of them. "Fasten his legs to the chair," he said to the woman.

She did as she was told without speaking, then returned to her cot.

"I'll be back shortly," Ericson said, and left the room, locking the door behind him.

Donny waited to ensure Ericson was indeed gone, then turned to his fellow prisoners. "I'm Donny Robertson. Toronto Fire Department. Do you have any idea where we are or what's going on?"

Eddy stood beside Ratzo, behind the desk in the captain's office. He pressed "Play," and the grainy video from his dashcam played back on his phone. He held it out and pointed to the lower left corner of the screen. "There. For sure, that's Donny, and I think that's that cop—Ellington or something."

"Ericson," Ratzo corrected. He put on his reading glasses. "Back it up a bit."

Eddy scrolled back and played the video again. It was hard to make out the details. The picture was dark, and the figures were some distance from the camera, but one of them was definitely Donny.

"And that sure ain't no short, dark-haired Mexican dude," Eddy continued. Donny was six foot two, and the person beside him in the video was at least as tall, with close-cropped blond hair. "Now watch this."

They both leaned in closer. A car's trunk popped open as the two figures approached. The blond figure pushed Donny towards the open trunk, and Donny stumbled forward. Eddy paused the video.

"See that? Donny's arms are behind his back. I can't tell, but I think they're tied. He doesn't even try to catch himself. And the blond guy, in his other hand—see? I think that's a gun."

"Could be," Ratzo nodded. "Is there any more?"

Eddy played the last few seconds. Donny was shoved into the trunk; the blond man closed the lid, got in the car, and drove away. "That story Scout told? Total shit, all lies."

Ratzo leaned back in the office chair. He thought he'd dealt with every conceivable sort of emergency, but a kidnapping? From a fire station? This was something completely new. "Where is he now? Patrick, I mean."

"In the kitchen. Moose is watching him. Just give me five minutes alone with him. I promise, I'll get the truth out of him," Eddy begged.

Ratzo could see the fury in Eddy's face. He felt it himself. Brotherhood was an essential, if intangible, part of the job. The enormity of this betrayal was staggering. The thought of putting Scout on the rack or something similar was appealing, but impractical. He took a deep breath. "I've known Donny longer than you have. We came on together. We need to focus on him, OK? This is a police matter now." Ratzo pointed towards the kitchen. "Much as I'd like to beat the crap out of that bastard, we can't. That would only screw things up. Let's show him the video, see what we can get out of him, and do what we can to help Donny."

Scout broke before the video was half over. He sat in the kitchen, Eddy's phone with its damning evidence on the table in front of him. Eddy, Moose and Ratzo stood looking over his shoulder.

"I didn't want to. He had a gun," Scout pleaded.

"Where'd he take Donny?" Ratzo asked.

"I don't know."

Eddy grabbed the front of Scout's shirt and spun him around. "I will rip your fucking balls off ..."

Ratzo laid his hand on Eddy's arm; Eddy let go and stepped back, muttering.

"Patrick, if what you say is true"—Ratzo struggled to keep his voice calm—"you need to help us. It's the only way to help yourself. Tell us anything Ericson said to you. What kind of car was he driving?"

"I don't know. Honest." Scout stared at the phone, unable to look any of them in the eye. "He just told me what to do. He didn't say if he had a plan or anything."

"Looks like a Camry," Moose said, leaning over the phone. "Late model. Silver or grey."

Ratzo headed back to the office. "I'm going to call the cops, then I need to talk to Humphrey again. Eddy, take floor watch. Let the cops in when they get here. Moose, you stay here with Patrick."

Eddy watched Ratzo leave. "You want to pray he's OK," he said to Scout. "Pray real hard." He considered describing in detail what he would do to Scout if anything happened to Donny, but decided that was better left to Scout's imagination. He turned and followed Ratzo out the door.

Moose took a seat directly across the table from Scout. "Don't worry about Eddy," he said.

"Thanks," Scout nodded.

"I'm the one you want to worry about."

"We need to activate 'Scorched Earth,'" the voice on the phone said. Collins checked his watch: 01:43.

"You think it's that bad?" Collins sat up in bed and turned on the light on his nightstand. His wife looked at him, then rolled over and listened without commenting. Middle-of-the-night calls were part of being married to a police superintendent.

Humphrey told Collins what he knew about Donny's abduction. Collins started to dress. "They have video, and it seems," Humphrey added, "Ericson has involved one of my other guys, too— Patrick Thompson. And he's talking."

"Shit," Collins muttered. "Have you called the police?"

"Razzolini is calling them, and if he hasn't already done that, I need to. It's an armed kidnapping in a fire station, for Christ's sake. With witnesses. I have no choice, Bob—I have to call it in. It's got to be 'Scorched Earth.'"

It was a contingency plan in the event the Committee were ever exposed or threatened. Cell phones would be destroyed, drives wiped clean, any printed records burned. They would try to isolate the damage, each of them accepting whatever happened in silence, without compromising the others.

"OK," Collins said, cradling the phone on his shoulder as he sat on the side of the bed, pulling on his socks. "What are you going to do?"

"I'm heading to the site. I think that's where he's taken Robertson. He's obsessed with Ramón and that's the only thing that makes sense. I'll try to talk to him."

Collins could hear traffic noise. "You're on your way now?"

"Yes."

"Are you armed?"

"No."

"Be careful. If he's gone this far ..." Collins didn't finish the sentence.

"I'll try. I knew his father." Humphrey wasn't sure that meant anything anymore. "Call the rest. Let them know it's 'Scorched Earth.' Then do whatever you can on your end to limit this thing."

They wished each other luck and said goodbye.

"I need to go," Collins said to his wife's back.

Grace rolled over to face him. She nodded silently.

"One of our people has ..." Collins wondered how much to say. He was aware that she knew more than she let on. "He's in trouble."

"Are you OK?"

Collins stood. She would have made a good detective, he thought. She could read the subtlest of his moods and expressions. He walked to the bedroom door and turned back. "I need you to do one thing. There's a box in the garage, a blue box, on the shelf over the snow tires. Light the woodstove and burn everything in that box. Then take the ashes and dump them in the pond. Now would be good."

"Now?" Grace asked, her eyes widening.

She would do what he asked, he was sure of that, but he owed her some kind of explanation. "I did some things. For Melissa. For our daughter." Collins felt the lump rising in his throat.

Grace nodded. "When will you be back?"

"I love you," Collins said, and headed to his car.

Collins made a mental list as he pulled out of the driveway. He needed to call the others on the Committee and let them know; then he needed to destroy his phone and get rid of it somewhere where no one would ever find it. But first he needed to try to get some control over the situation. He pulled out his department-issue phone and called the station.

"Fifty-one Division, Staff Sergeant Singh," the familiar voice answered.

"It's Collins."

"I was just going to call you, sir. There's been a ..."

"Robertson. I know. I understand there's a witness"—Collins searched his memory for the name—"Patrick something."

"Thompson." Daya wondered how the superintendent had heard about the witness when she had only just found out herself. She let it go. "I've sent an officer to bring him in and get a statement."

"No. I want you to go personally and sequester him," Collins instructed. "No one talks to him until I get there. Understood?" He knew that whatever Patrick knew would come out soon enough, but for now, putting him on ice would give Collins more time to think before he had to act.

"But sir, there's a time factor. We need to ..." Daya protested.

"There are bigger issues here, Staff Sergeant. Just do it." Collins' tone made it clear this was not a request.

CHAPTER 36

OLD SOAP

Ramón launched into a long, rambling explanation in answer to Donny's questions. Donny tried to get him to focus on their current situation.

"The blond man, Ericson—do you have any idea what he's planning?" Donny asked.

"No. I've only seen him once before. Mostly it was the others," Ramón answered.

Others? So Ericson wasn't acting alone. "What others?"

"I don't know," Ramón said. "They ask a lot of questions, about what happened, you know, with the cop ..." His voice trailed off.

"The two older ones seem to be in charge," Roxanne added. Ramón nodded.

Interesting, but none of that mattered if they couldn't get out of here. Donny noticed a nylon backpack on the floor beside Ramón's cot. "What's in that? Anything useful?"

"Not really. Just some clothes. New identity papers. We were going to start a new life. Leave all this behind." Ramón looked over at Roxanne. "I thought maybe I could even take you to Baja one day.

It's so beautiful ..." He shook his head. "There was some money, but they took most of it."

"Most of it?" Donny asked.

"I sewed a few thousand into the lining. You know, in case. They didn't find it."

"You're so clever," Roxanne smiled at Ramón.

"For you." Ramón smiled weakly and kicked the pack towards her.

"Nice," Donny agreed, "but money isn't going to help us." He surveyed the room. The steel door was right in front of him, but it was locked. He looked at the window to his right. It was high and narrow, and made of glass blocks. He'd need a sledgehammer to break them. The wall below was solid brick; the old paint was cracked and peeling in places. But he didn't have twenty years, and this wasn't *The Shawshank Redemption*.

The wall behind him was brick and concrete too, as was the one to his left. The doorway to his left led into a washroom/shower area. That was a dead end.

His eyes came back to the door in front of him. The wall on either side was smooth, the paint newer. Probably a partition that had been built later, after the original construction.

His thoughts were interrupted by the sound of a key in the lock.

Ratzo poked his head into the floor watch. Eddy was hanging up the phone. "Who are you calling?" the chief asked.

"The other stations in the district. I'm telling them to keep an eye out for the Camry or anyone that matches Ericson's description," Eddy explained.

Ratzo thought for a moment. "OK, good idea. I gotta go brief the fire chief and the deputy."

"OK."

"The cops are sending a car to pick up Patrick."

"Sure." Eddy lifted the phone to his ear again.

Ratzo could see the cords standing out on Eddy's neck. He stepped into the room and put his hand on Eddy's shoulder. "We all love Donny. Don't do anything stupid while I'm gone."

"That little shit is in this up to his neck!"

"Maybe, but he's a witness too. This is a police matter. He needs to be in one piece when they arrive."

Eddy nodded. Ratzo left, and Eddy watched him through the windows in the apparatus doors. A light snow had started. The flakes fell softly, drifting, twirling, sending rainbow flashes of colour when they caught the floodlights that illuminated the front of the station just right. Eddy pondered how something so delicate and beautiful could happen in the midst of something so terrible.

He looked away and punched the number for Station Five into his phone.

"Hey, Shelley, it's Eddy," he said to the woman who answered. "Donny's been kidnapped."

"What?! Are you high? Are you guys *all* on drugs over there?"

"Very funny." Eddy wasn't laughing. There were times that he regretted his reputation as a clown. "Listen, it's a long, story, but it's serious. This cop, he's off duty, but he looks like a cop. He took Donny at gunpoint."

"Holy shit, you're kidding!"

"No. Just listen. He's a big guy. Ericson's his name. Short blond hair. You've probably run a few calls with him."

A police car pulled up in front of the station. The door opened and Daya Singh stepped out. Eddy waved to her through the window. "You see a guy like that in a late-model Camry," he said into the phone, "just call me. I gotta go."

Eddy disconnected the call. There were several more stations to contact, but most of them were farther away. He walked down the hall and open the station's front door.

"Thanks." Daya Singh stepped through and brushed the snow off her jacket.

Eddy nodded. "Good to see you. Well, I mean ..."

"Yeah, I know. Where's the witness?"

"Scout? I mean Patrick? Upstairs, in the kitchen. Moose is watching him."

"You guys talk to him?" Daya asked.

"Of course," Eddy exclaimed. "How do you think we figured out what's going on?"

"OK. My orders are to bring him in. You guys need to write out statements—what you saw, what you did—you know the drill." Daya turned to head upstairs, then turned back. "Oh, and you have a video?"

"Yeah, from my dashcam."

"I'm going to need that. Who has copies?"

"Me, Ratzo—our DC, Chief Razzolini. Why?" Eddy asked.

"It's evidence. No more copies."

"What?" Eddy exclaimed. "You guys put that stuff out all the time—video from robberies, security cameras, all that shit. How is this different?"

Daya knew it was true. Normally they would use the media in a case like this, both to find the victim and to warn the public that there was an armed and possibly dangerous suspect on the loose. Her personal feelings aside, Collins' insistence on keeping a low profile on the case made her uneasy. But it wasn't her decision to make.

"This isn't a normal situation. A police officer has kidnapped a fire captain. We need to proceed carefully to avoid putting the whole city in an uproar." Daya tried to swallow her own explanation. It seemed like Donny's suspicions about Ericson were true. But there was more to it. There had to be.

"That's bullshit! Donny's taken at gunpoint, and you're worried about your department's reputation?"

"I got orders, Eddy. We don't always see the big picture." That was certainly true for Daya. And that's what nagged at her.

The phone rang as she headed upstairs. Eddy answered. "Lombard, Moleiro speaking ... Hi, Spike."

Daya listened as she climbed the stairs.

"Where? ... OK ... What? How would ... You're sure it was him? ... What exactly did you see?"

Daya paused on the landing.

"No, I got a cop right here with me. Good work."

Daya started back down.

Eddy met her at the foot of the stairs. "That was Spike—Pumper Seven. They were coming back from a call, driving by the old soap factory at the foot of Broadview. The gate's normally locked but it was swung open. They stopped to have a look. He said the chain had been cut, and there was a silver Camry parked there."

"Did they see anyone?" Daya asked.

"Um, not Ericson or Donny, but ..." Eddy looked back at the phone, his face pinched, trying to understand the incomprehensible.

"But what?"

Eddy looked back at Daya. "They kept going. They'd gone about a block, and the platoon chief, Tom Humphrey—remember him?"

Daya nodded.

"He drove past them, going the other way like a bat out of hell. At first Spike thought he was going to a call, but he had no lights or siren, and the radio was quiet. So Spike looked in the mirror and he saw the chief turn into the factory." Eddy shook his head.

"He's sure it was Humphrey?"

"Hard to mistake a big red car with 'Platoon Chief' written on the side. We gotta go check it out."

"I need to report this." Daya pulled out her phone and scrolled to Collins' name. She quickly relayed what Eddy had told her.

"Damn!" There was a moment of silence on Daya's phone as Collins thought. "All right. We need to get control of this situation. Inspector Marusic is the incident commander for now. You'll assist her in setting up a perimeter. No one goes in or out until I get there. But especially no one goes in. Got that?"

"But sir ..." Daya began.

"You have your orders, Staff Sergeant."

"For the record, sir, I want to register the strongest possible ..."

"When this is over, you can make whatever objections or protests you want." Collins ended the call.

Daya stared at her phone.

"What'd he say?" Eddy asked.

"My boss says to set up a perimeter and wait."

"WHAT?? And you're just going to do that?"

Daya pursed her lips. None of this made any sense. But sitting back and doing nothing? That made the least sense of all. She thought back to Collins' curious reaction to her looking into the Rothberg case, and the news about the fibres. "Maybe it's time for a new career anyway," she muttered to herself. Turning to Eddy, she asked, "The old soap factory, you said?"

Eddy followed her as she headed to the door. "I'm coming with you."

"No." Daya shook her head.

"Then you're going to have to shoot me," Eddy declared.

Daya had no doubt he meant it. "What about ..."

"He's with Moose. Don't worry, he ain't going anywhere."

Ericson shut the door behind him and put the gym bag he was carrying on one of the plastic tables. "Sorry," he said lightly, "I had to get some things from the car."

"Yeah, we missed you," Donny said grimly.

Ericson wheeled to face him. "This is on you, Robertson!" he yelled, overcome with sudden fury. "Him, he gets what he deserves. But you? You just couldn't mind your own damn business. This is your fault."

Good, Donny thought, make him mad. Maybe he'll make a mistake. Just not too mad. "What about her?" Donny turned to face Roxanne. "You just eliminate anyone who gets in your way? How many people are you going to murder?"

"It's not murder, it's justice. They killed Randy. She's part of it."

"Please ..." Roxanne's voice was thin and weak. "I didn't do anything."

"SHUT! UP!" Ericson pulled the gun from his waistband and pointed it at each of them in turn. "All of you, just shut the hell up." He waved the gun at them one more time. Satisfied with their silence, he turned back to the table, and started pulling items from the gym bag: a small vial of white powder, a few cotton balls, a bottle of water, a length of rubber tubing, a lighter, a metal spoon, and a syringe.

Donny's attention focused again on the wall with the door Ericson had come through. Smooth, and yes, the paint was definitely newer. It had to be a partition. If he could just ... He pulled against the cable ties that anchored him to the chair—no slack.

His attention shifted as Ericson tapped a little of the white powder into the spoon, added some water and started heating it with the lighter. Realization dawned, and with it the fear of death waned, replaced by a sickening wave of shame. If anyone remembered him it would be as a junkie, not as a firefighter.

"No, no, no. Not like that. Come on, please," Donny pleaded.

"Oh, but Donny, you've got a drug problem. It's already documented." Ericson shrugged. "Pressures of the job, PTSD, family issues—who knows? It's very sad, but it happens."

Ericson tore a piece off a cotton ball and used it as a filter as he filled the syringe. "There's going to be a little lab accident. You and your druggie friends just got careless while getting high." He pointed with the syringe to the gas cylinder at the end of the table. "Ammonia, the same way Randy died."

"No!" Donny wriggled, pulling at the cable ties that bound him to the chair. The chair's metal legs rattled against the floor.

"Don't worry, you won't feel a thing." Ericson looked at Ramón. "Randy wasn't that lucky, but it has to look right." He crossed over to Ramón's cot, the syringe in one hand, the gun in the other. He held the syringe out to Ramón: "For the girl."

Ramón stared at the needle, unable to tear his eyes away. "Señor, do what you want to me. I am sorry about your friend. For that and my many other sins, I ask God to forgive me. But she is innocent. Please let her go."

"Very touching," Ericson sneered. "God may forgive you, but I don't." He shoved the gun into Ramón's ribs. "Do it."

"She has done nothing."

"You want her to suffer?" Ericson asked.

Donny watched a remarkable transformation. The girl who had been trembling, barely able to speak, took a deep breath as the calm of inevitability washed over her.

"It's OK, baby," Roxanne said, looking into Ramón's eyes.

"I'm sorry, *mi amor.*" Ramón took the syringe. Ericson handed the rubber tubing to Roxanne, and she tied it around her arm. Ramón reached out for her hand, then whirled on Ericson, the syringe in a dagger grip.

Ericson stepped back and fired.

Roxanne screamed.

The syringe clattered to the floor and Ramón collapsed onto his cot. A red stain spread across his chest. He coughed, and scarlet foam sparkled on his lips. The smell of blood and gunpowder filled the air.

"Pick it up," Ericson instructed Roxanne, pointing to the syringe with the gun. "Pick it up and do it yourself, or you end up like him, drowning in your own blood."

Ramón rolled his head to face her, his eyes wide. He tried to speak, but managed only a gurgling moan.

Roxanne did as she was told, more to escape the horror in front of her eyes than out of fear. The needle slid into her vein, her eyes closed, and she slumped down onto the cot.

Ericson retrieved the needle and the rubber tubing. He dropped the tubing in Donny's lap and started refilling the syringe. "I hope you don't mind sharing."

Donny ignored Ericson's feeble attempt at a joke.

Ericson put down the syringe and pulled a pair of wire cutters out of his gym bag. For a moment Donny thought he was going to be tortured, but Ericson simply leaned over, cut the zip tie holding Donny's left wrist, and stepped back. "I'll cut the others when you're all in dreamland. It wouldn't do to have you found tied up." He pointed to the rubber tube on Donny's lap. "You know how it's done."

Donny used his left hand and teeth to tie the tubing around his right arm. "So who are you? Dirty Harry? Judge Dredd? The avenging angel?"

"Something like that. You got a problem with it?"

"I think most of the civilized world does."

"Well, you won't have to worry about that much longer." Ericson held the syringe out to Donny. "Take it."

Donny kept his hand in his lap. He stared at Ericson, his gaze unwavering.

"Really? You want to get all melodramatic?" Ericson asked.

Donny felt something under his hand. Something in his pocket. Yes, Donny remembered, the naloxone—the two little plastic rockets. If he could somehow ...

"I'm trying to give you a little dignity," Ericson snarled. "I could shoot you in the knee, or dozens of other unpleasant scenarios, but there's only one way this ends. What do you want to do?"

Donny reached out and took the syringe.

"Smart choice."

Donny picked a prominent vein and inserted the needle. The room was silent except for Ramón's wet, shallow breathing.

"Push it in," Ericson instructed.

Donny slowly pressed the plunger. He felt the warmth start to creep up his arm. "Hey, Ramón!" Donny called out. "How are you doing?"

There was a gurgling cry, followed by a crash.

Ericson looked over to see Ramón crumpled on the floor. He spasmed once, then lay still.

Donny pulled the needle from his arm and pressed the plunger to the bottom. The remainder of the syringe's contents dribbled onto his lap as the world faded away.

"What the hell?" Ericson looked back. Donny's head was slumped on his chest, his eyes closed. The syringe lay empty in his left hand,

and a spot of blood welled up on his right arm. Ericson prodded Donny with the gun. Donny's chest rose and fell, but there was no other response. Ericson untied the rubber tube and let it fall to the floor. He prodded Donny one more time, then reached back and slapped him full force across the face.

There was a crack like distant thunder, but it didn't bother Donny. He floated in a warm sea. Ribbons of rainbow colours swirled around him; fantastical creatures danced and twirled to music too beautiful to hear.

Ericson snipped the rest of the zip ties that held Donny to the chair. Donny fell sideways and sprawled face-down on the floor. Ericson put the remains of the ties in the gym bag with the cutters. The drug paraphernalia he left.

He took a cloth from the bag and carefully wiped down the gun. Using the cloth to hold the gun, he pressed Donny's hand around the pistol grip, then laid the gun on the floor. It would look like another drug deal gone bad. He hated to leave the gun behind, but he still had the one he had taken from Lowry.

Finally, he walked over to the ammonia cylinder, which was connected by a hose to the chemical apparatus on the table. He loosened the fitting by a quarter turn, then opened the cylinder valve. There was a barely audible hiss accompanied by the sharp smell of ammonia.

Ericson held his breath, grabbed his bag, and quickly left the room. He locked the door behind him—an overabundance of caution, perhaps, but he could return later and unlock it.

CHAPTER 37

UP AGAINST THE WALL

The gate to the old soap factory was open, just as Humphrey had expected to find it. The chain that had secured the entrance hung limply from the gatepost. It had obviously been cut. "Shit," Humphrey muttered to himself. He drove over to the loading dock.

Ericson's Camry was parked beside Lowry's blue minivan. Humphrey knew his Fire Department Tahoe would stand out like a sore thumb, and Aerial Seven had undoubtedly seen him roar past them. Who knows what they thought? But there was nothing he could do about that now. Ericson had already cast the die.

Humphrey got out and walked up the steps to the door. It wasn't locked.

"Hello?" His voice was almost lost in the cavernous space. He crossed to the shipping office and opened the door. Lowry blinked up at him.

"Tom! Thank God. I thought I heard someone out there." Lowry shifted to show Humphrey how his arms were bound to the counter. "Ericson jumped me."

"I figured as much." Humphrey pulled a small pocketknife from his jacket and cut Lowry free.

Lowry shook his arms and rubbed his shoulders, trying to get the circulation back. "I'm pretty sure there was another person with him. I heard him talking to someone."

"I know. It's blown. We're activating 'Scorched Earth.'"

"Christ!" Lowry exclaimed.

"You need to get out of here."

"Are you armed?" Lowry showed Humphrey his empty holster. "He took mine."

"No. If I need a gun, then ..." Humphrey shook his head. "Just go. Get out of here while you can."

Lowry ran across the loading dock and out the door. A few seconds later Humphrey heard the squeal of tires. He left the office and headed to the door that led into the old factory. He reached for his phone to light the way, then thought better of it. Better to remain in the shadows. It had been years since he had had to navigate blind through a darkened building. As platoon chief, he usually remained in the command post, at least until the fire was out, the smoke had cleared, and lights had been rigged. But the old skills never really disappeared. And he had been in this building several times before.

He reached out his right hand, brushing his fingers along the wall, silently placing one foot in front of the other as his eyes gradually adjusted to the gloom. The city was never completely dark at night, and enough light spilled in through the big old factory windows to make out the shape of things. He turned right, towards the room they had prepared for Ramón and Roxanne. With any luck, Donny would be there too.

He heard a door opening and closing up ahead, followed by the sound of footsteps. He stepped into the stairway alcove, completely hidden by shadow. He thought briefly of tackling Ericson as he walked by, grabbing the gun, and forcing Ericson to his will, but Humphrey knew he was no match for a man half his age.

Humphrey could see a glow on the floor as Ericson approached. He waited until Ericson had passed the alcove, then called softly, "Bill."

Ericson whirled, sweeping his phone and the gun in front of him, searching the shadows.

"Put it down." Humphrey squinted into the sudden light. "It's me. We need to talk."

Ericson lowered the gun. "OK," he said cautiously.

"Where's Donny?"

"With the others."

"Is he OK?"

Ericson didn't answer.

Humphrey stepped forward, but stopped when Ericson raised the gun again. "What have you done?"

"Finished what we started."

"You ..." Humphrey wanted to unleash a string of obscenities, but knew that would be pointless. He needed to regain control of the situation. "They have you on video."

"What?"

"The dashcam from one of the cars parked at the fire station caught you taking Donny at gunpoint."

"Oh." Ericson sagged. "The cops know?"

"Yes." Humphrey left out the fact that he had insisted on it.

"Do they know where we are?"

"I'm not sure. At this point we need to limit the damage. Is that your burner?" Humphrey pointed to the phone in Ericson's hand. "Give it to me."

Ericson handed over the phone without protest. He watched Humphrey remove the SIM card and drop it into a nearby floor drain.

A thumping, banging sound came from down the hallway, from the room Ericson had left.

"They're still alive!" Humphrey cried. He tucked the phone into his shirt pocket. He would deal with it later. "Let's go." Humphrey started down the hall towards Donny and the others.

"No. Stop." Ericson raised the gun again. It was probably Robertson pounding on the door. Maybe he hadn't given him enough dope. No matter; it would stop soon. "It's over. Get that through your thick head."

"Bill, I knew your father. Yes, he was a tough man, but this isn't what he ..."

"Leave my father out of this," Ericson hissed. "You know nothing. Nothing about him, about any of it."

"I know you think I don't understand, but I do," Humphrey said, trying to reason with him. "My daughter—my own flesh and blood, cut down. It's a pain that never goes away. But we have a real problem now. And more bodies are not the answer. They have video and witnesses. I'm probably burned too, but we'll get the best legal defence possible. Right now, we need to limit the damage. That means saving them if we can."

"No. I can't go to jail." Ericson put a hand to his head as if trying to hear the faint details of some complex plan. "They'll find your car here. Yes, you're the one. I have a family, but you're old, so it doesn't matter."

The distant banging stopped. The silence hung heavy.

"Bill, they have ..."

"They'll find your body here, one way or the other." Ericson pointed back up the way Humphrey had come. "Now move!"

Donny winced.

Smelling salts. He'd had them when he'd had his bell rung playing Junior B hockey. He took another breath, inhaled the sour acrid smell of ammonia and started to cough.

This wasn't the arena dressing room. But he was so tired. He could just lie here. Except for that terrible smell. Donny turned his head. A body swam into view, covered in blood. It was horrible. He had felt so light and wonderful. Now this.

The coughing gripped him. He rolled away from the body, and something sharp in his pocket dug into his leg. Memory floated just below the surface.

Donny reached into his pocket and pulled out a piece of white plastic. It looked so strange, and it was so hard to think. His eyes stung, his lungs burned, even his nose ... Yes, his nose. He inserted the rounded end of the white plastic into his nostril and pressed the plunger.

The naloxone hit him like a bucket of cold water. It all came back: Ericson, the ammonia, Ramón and Roxanne.

The wall beside the door!

To most people, a wall was just that—a solid barrier. To a fire-fighter, depending on how it was built, a wall could be an emergency escape. He had practised the technique many times over the years, in training. Now it was time to put it to the test.

The wall was only a couple of metres away. Donny crawled over, keeping his face close to the floor. Ammonia, he knew, was lighter than air, so the air was a little fresher at floor level. He tried to control his coughing, but it wracked him with every breath. He didn't have much time.

Stopping a few feet to the left of the door, he began rapping on the wall, moving his hand a few centimetres with each knock.

There! A good hollow sound. He punched the wall as hard as he could. The drywall flexed and dented, but didn't break. He rolled onto his back and kicked at the spot he had marked. There was a crack. He kicked again. The drywall broke, but his foot hit another layer, the outside skin.

His coughing was uncontrollable now. But he was so close. Donny closed his eyes, summoned the last of his strength, and kicked again and again.

His leg straightened. His foot was through!

Donny pulled his foot back, spun around, and put his face to the hole he had made. He lay there sucking greedily at the fresh air flowing through the opening. He was still coughing, but he no longer felt like he was going to suffocate.

Taking a deep breath, he spun around again and kicked at the wall, enlarging the hole. He tore away the broken pieces of drywall and tossed them aside. There was just enough space between the studs for him to lie on his side and wriggle through.

He was free, but now what? He wanted to just lie on the cool cement floor of the hallway and breathe fresh air, but there was no time. Ramón was dead or beyond hope, of that he was sure. But Roxanne? He had the second dose of naloxone in his pocket. He looked back through the hole and saw Roxanne lying on the bed, six, maybe seven metres away. He tried to calculate his chances of administering the naloxone and getting Roxanne out through the hole before he succumbed to the ammonia. The only thing he knew for certain was that the odds worsened with every passing second.

He had to try.

His cough had mostly subsided. Donny took three deep breaths, held the last one and dived back through the hole.

Getting to Roxanne was the easy part. He sprayed the naloxone up her nose, grabbed her under the arms, and pulled her off the bed. He started dragging her back towards the hole in the wall—pure deadweight.

"Aghhh!" As they reached the wall, Roxanne came around with a hoarse cry. "I can't ..." Her words faded into a fit of coughing.

The ammonia was getting thicker. Its caustic action burned Donny's eyes, his armpits, anywhere there was moisture. His breath gave out. He inhaled the foul air and started choking again. Trying to shove Roxanne through the opening would be like pushing a rope. And he needed fresh air himself or they would both perish.

Donny pulled himself through the hole, took a moment to fill his lungs with clean air, then reached back through. He grabbed Roxanne by the arms and pulled. Her head and torso came through. She gasped, unable to speak, but the fresh air seemed to partially revive her.

"Help me," Donny urged, pulling at her shoulders. Roxanne pawed at the floor and twisted her hips. Finally she was through—scraped, but through.

"Over here." Donny beckoned her farther down the hall. He spoke in short phrases between his coughs. "The air's better." They sat trying to catch their breath and gathering their thoughts.

"Ramón?" Roxanne asked, when she could finally speak.

Donny shook his head. "I'm sorry."

She nodded. There would be time for tears later. For now, it was simply survival. She needed to be gone from this place. Completely gone. Her street smarts took over. "The bag?"

"What bag?"

"Ramón's pack."

"Back there," Donny pointed to the room. "Forget it."

Roxanne stood. She was wobbly, but she stood. She pulled herself back along the wall and bent down to look through the hole. "I can see it."

"You can't go back in there."

She stood again. "I have to."

"The money's not worth it."

"It's not about the money." Roxanne cleared her throat. Her voice was still hoarse, but she could speak now without coughing between every two words. "It's the papers. Ramón sacrificed everything so we could have a fresh start." She wiped the corner of her eye. "I owe it to him not to give up."

"I'm not sure I have the strength to pull you out a second time."

"I know."

Donny saw that she was determined. "One breath. You need to be quick—in and out."

"I will." She took several deep breaths, then leaned down, put her arms into the hole and pulled herself through. Donny pushed on her feet. She crawled quickly across the room and grabbed the pack. She paused for a moment and reached out to touch Ramón.

"Come on," Donny urged.

She crawled back and tossed the pack through the hole in the wall ahead of her. Donny grabbed it and shoved it aside. Roxanne tried not to breath. She was so close, but her lungs were burning. She inhaled a chest-full of the foul air and started to cough uncontrolla-bly, curling into a ball.

Donny held his breath and stuck his head through the hole. He reached out, grabbed Roxanne by the arms and pulled. She was gasp-ing as her head emerged.

"That was foolish," Donny said when they were clear of the hole.

Roxanne nodded, once again unable to speak. They sat on the floor, their backs against the wall, Roxanne coughing, Donny think-ing. The ordeal had exhausted them both, but Donny knew they couldn't stay there. The ammonia was leaking out through the hole in the wall, contaminating the air in the hallway too. More import-ant, Ericson would be back at some point.

Roxanne's coughing eased. Another sound drifted down the hall-way: voices, faint but definitely voices, more than one, coming from where they had entered the building. Whether this was good news or bad, he wasn't sure.

"You hear that?" Donny asked.

Roxanne cocked an ear. "I'm getting out of here." She pulled her-self up the wall and grabbed the backpack.

"Right. Wait." Donny caught her elbow. He knew their chances were better if they split up, but she was also a witness. "How will I find you? I mean, if we make it, we'll need to talk to someone."

"Police? No, no, no. I've had my fill of cops." Roxanne pulled her arm free and started down the hall away from the voices. She stopped and turned back. "I'm sorry. It's my one chance."

He'd heard only part of her story, but it was enough. "Yes. Good luck."

"You too."

Donny watched her go. She kept to the shadows as she made her way down the corridor. She stopped; there was a soft click, and sud-denly she was silhouetted in pale moonlight. She had found a door. She waved and disappeared.

Donny waved back, then turned and started cautiously towards the voices.

CHAPTER 38

SHOTS FIRED!

"I 'm coming with you."

"No, Eddy." Daya parked the police cruiser in front of the loading dock, alongside a silver Camry and a fire department Tahoe with "Platoon Chief" written on its side.

"I need you here, with the radio." Daya rolled down the windows and turned off the car engine, leaving the radio on. It spat out brief messages: Lakeshore Boulevard shut down, Eastern Avenue secured ... There were still the railway yard to the south and other industrial properties to the east, but the perimeter around the old factory was tightening.

Eddy hunched his shoulders against the chilly night air that blew in through the car's open windows and wished he'd thought to bring a jacket. "But ..." he started to protest.

"What would you tell me if I wanted to run into a raging fire with you?"

Eddy had to admit she had a point.

"You see anyone come out of the building, anyone besides me, you get on the radio and you hit the siren—here." Daya pointed to the switch on the cruiser's console.

"I know how to use a siren," Eddy said.

"OK." Daya opened the door and stepped out. She pulled her Glock from its holster. Its weight briefly seemed more than she could carry. "The same, uh … the same if you hear shots—call it in."

"Good luck."

"Thanks." Daya smiled at Eddy and headed to the entrance, beside the loading dock.

She climbed the stairs and reached for the door handle. The door was unlocked, and opened with a soft click. She peered inside. Darkness. Silence. She stepped through and quietly closed the door behind her.

It was hard to make out anything other than vague shapes in the dim light. Daya pulled the flashlight from her belt but hesitated before turning it on. The light would give her away. She knew her eyes would adjust to some degree, but with no light she might also miss some important detail. She tightened the waist strap on her Kevlar vest and turned on the flashlight.

The loading dock was as she had expected: big and mostly empty. There were two doors in the back wall. The first led into a smaller room. Daya walked over and peered in. Everything was covered in dust except for a folding chair, a cooler, and some discarded food wrappers. Someone had used the room recently. A set of zip tie hand-cuffs lay on the floor. They had been cut.

Something more than just a kidnapping was going on—this scene, Humphrey's car here before she and Eddy arrived, Collins' strange orders. She would figure it out later. For now, her primary concern was finding Donny.

Donny. That was something else she needed to figure out later. There was so much to like about him; but there was also so much wrong.

Daya shook her head. Rule number one: never make it personal. The situation was dangerous enough as it was. Personal feelings would cloud her thinking and slow her down.

She turned to the other door, which led deeper into the building. She walked slowly and silently, and kept the flashlight low, pointed down. It illuminated the area around her clearly, but hopefully wouldn't attract attention.

The corridor was about two metres wide. There were footprints on the dusty floor—clearly, several people had been back and forth along here. A couple of doors opened off the corridor, but there were no footprints leading to them. Daya turned to the right, following the trail.

There were voices up ahead. She stopped and listened. Two voices. She couldn't quite make out what they were saying, but they were definitely men's voices.

"I am done talking!" That was Ericson, Daya was certain of that.

She switched off her light, and darkness swallowed her. The wall was within reach to her right. She trailed her fingers along it, inching her way forward. Her eyes would eventually adjust; in the meantime, she needed to find some cover.

"Bill, listen to me," said the other voice. It wasn't Donny's. Humphrey?

"And I'm done listening to you, too." Ericson again. They were getting closer, and they were clearly arguing about the situation. That might be something she could use.

The corridor branched. Daya could hear footsteps now, coming from straight ahead. Ducking around the corner to her right, she tried to formulate a plan, but she had too few pieces of the puzzle, and she still had no idea where Donny was or what had happened to him. There was no way to search the whole building, and no time. Talk was the only way.

"Ericson," she called out. "It's Singh."

The footsteps stopped, and there was a momentary silence.

"Staff Sergeant. This is a surprise. Have you become a one-woman SWAT team?"

Shit! Ericson was no fool. He knew that she would normally be in the command post. If she was here, he knew she was flying solo. She peeked around the corner. Her eyes had partially adjusted, and she could just make out two figures in the gloom. "Who's that with you?"

"A mutual friend," Ericson replied. "Tom Humphrey. You remember Chief Humphrey, don't you?"

"Sergeant Singh, I ..." Humphrey began.

"Shut up!" Ericson said, his voice full of menace.

"Bill, let's work this out." Daya tried to calm the situation. "I'm not going to lie to you ..."

"That's the first thing people say when they're lying to you."

"Fair enough," Daya admitted. "The fact is, there's a perimeter around the building."

"If there were a secure perimeter, there'd be a tactical team in here, not just you. Enough bullshit."

"OK, OK. You're right, it's still being set up." Daya peeked around the corner again, her vision a little clearer now. Ten metres or so down the hall, Ericson was holding Humphrey in front of him as a shield. "I actually disobeyed orders coming in here. I wanted talk to you before the cavalry gets here. It's not too late. We can all still walk out of here."

"You disobeyed orders? Well, that *is* something. I'm done talking, but I am getting out of here. Now step out where I can see you," Ericson instructed.

She needed to keep him talking. "Where's Robertson?" she asked.

"He's resting," Ericson replied.

"He's still alive?"

"Last time I saw him he was. Now step out, or the Chief's brains are going to be splattered all over the wall."

"Protect yourself, Sergeant." Humphrey's voice was remarkably calm.

"SHUT UP!" Ericson yelled.

"Bill, it doesn't have to be this way," Daya insisted.

"I'm not kidding. I'm in this deep. You think one more life matters to me at this point?"

She had known the risks as soon as she stepped out of the cruiser, but now that fate was staring her right in the face, things weren't as cut and dried.

"I'm not even going to bother counting to three. I'm just going to do it."

The only way to keep Ericson talking was to do what he asked. "OK, I'm coming out."

"Nice and slow," Ericson instructed. "No sudden moves."

"Whatever you say." Daya tried to keep her voice calm and soothing. She stepped out into the middle of the corridor. Her gun was trained on Ericson, but Humphrey was in front of him.

"Put the gun on the ground," Ericson told Daya.

"Let the Chief go."

"You're in no position to bargain. Put it down."

"When you let him go." She lowered the pistol to her side, so she was no longer an immediate threat.

Ericson shoved Humphrey against the wall. "Stay there!" he barked. He now had his sights trained on Daya. "Two fingers. Left hand. Put it on the ground, nice and slow."

Daya transferred the Glock to her left hand and bent down slowly. Out of the corner of her eye, she detected movement in the corridor across from where she had been hiding. Something or someone was moving towards her. She looked over and tried to make it out. Another person?

"Hey!" Ericson saw her looking away. "Don't even think about running."

Donny was back in the big open space, what had probably been a manufacturing area or warehouse space when the factory was operational. He could just make out two figures at the far end. One was obviously Ericson; the other he wasn't sure of. They turned and disappeared down the corridor through which Donny had been brought into the building. Part of him wanted to follow Ericson and his companion, to figure out what was going on. The more rational course was simply to get out of there.

There were a couple of other hallways leading out of the area. Donny crept across the open space, checking over his shoulder to make sure Ericson didn't return. Donny wasn't sure where he was going, but anything was better than being captured again.

The corridor he followed led to others. He tried to orient himself to the mental map he had made when Ericson had brought him into the building, but it was hard to keep his bearings. Donny knew the naloxone would lessen the effects of the heroin and whatever other opiates might have been in the syringe, but it wouldn't completely eliminate them.

The place was a labyrinth. Still, he figured he should be on a path roughly parallel to the route he had come in by. If he could get to an exterior wall, he might be able to find an exit, just as Roxanne had.

Voices somewhere to his left. And not just two.

"SHUT UP!" That was Ericson for sure.

Then another voice, higher—a woman's voice. Donny dropped to his knees and crawled towards the sound.

"OK, I'm coming out." He recognized Daya's voice, but he still couldn't see anyone.

Another corner. Donny looked to his left. There she was, in the half light at the intersection of two corridors, fifteen metres ahead of him. She was pointing her pistol at someone Donny couldn't see. Ericson. It had to be Ericson.

"Put the gun on the ground," Donny heard Ericson say. It was some sort of standoff. Fight or flight? Donny wondered, and quickly discarded the latter option. Daya had obviously come after him, and he wasn't going to run away now. He crept closer, making sure to keep out of Ericson's sightline.

"Two fingers. Left hand. Put it on the ground, nice and slow." Ericson again.

Daya bent down slowly and placed her gun on the floor. She turned her head towards Donny. There was an instant of recognition.

"Hey!" Ericson told her. "Don't even think about running."

Donny froze.

"OK," Daya said. She stood again slowly.

"Now kick it away from you."

Daya looked down. Using the side of her foot, she kicked the gun towards Donny.

"I meant towards me," Ericson growled. "Never mind. Turn around and walk backwards to me."

Daya turned slowly. For the briefest of moments, she faced Donny again. Their eyes locked. Then she stepped backwards out of his sight.

Donny picked up the Glock. He stood and advanced silently to the corner where Daya had disappeared. He dared to peek with one eye. Ericson's attention was focused on Daya. And the other man—my God! It was Platoon Chief Tom Humphrey! What the …? How …?

No—focus, Donny, focus!

"That's right, nice and slow," Ericson cooed. "You're going to be my ticket out of here."

Daya took another backwards step. She was halfway to Ericson now. She spotted Donny and gave him a barely perceptible nod. He had a clear view of Ericson now, but he had never fired a handgun before. What if he hit Daya or the Chief by mistake?

The urge to cough came over him again. It had largely subsided, but now it returned. He tried to suppress it, tried to ram it back down his throat.

It all happened in a fraction of a second, though at the time it seemed like everything was in slow motion.

"What?" Ericson's focus shifted to find the source of the coughing.

Humphrey leapt away from the wall, grabbed Ericson's gun hand, and pulled it towards himself. There was a flash and a sound like thunder. The cell phone in Humphrey's shirt pocket did little to slow the bullet. Pieces of the phone merely added to the carnage the bullet wreaked in Humphrey's rib cage. He fell, blood rising to his lips.

Daya dropped to the floor and rolled to the side. She reached for the taser on her belt, but before she could fire, more shots rang out.

It was pure instinct. Donny stepped out, raised the gun, and fired three times. Ericson staggered backwards and fell.

Donny's ears were filled with the sound of screaming—a dreadful, gut-wrenching wail. The gun clattered from his hand to the floor. It was then he realized that the terrible sound was coming from his own mouth. He was screaming and couldn't stop.

Daya put a hand on his shoulder. With her other hand, she turned Donny's head away from Ericson's body, to face her. "It's all right. You did good. It's all right, Donny."

He closed his mouth. There was a soft moaning in the silence that followed. A pool of blood spread on the floor where Tom Humphrey lay.

Bang!

Was that a shot? Eddy wondered.

Three more—Bang! Bang! Bang!

Eddy grabbed the cruiser's mic. "Shots fired! Shots fired!"

He wasn't exactly sure of correct police radio protocol, but he was pretty sure that would get someone's attention.

"Who is this?" the radio squawked back.

"Firefighter Eddy Moleiro. Sergeant Singh's inside with my captain. The old soap factory at the bottom of Broadview. And there's shooting. Send medics, send ... Send everything you got."

"How many shooters?" the radio demanded. But Eddy had dropped the mic and was rushing into the building.

He stopped inside the loading dock. There was screaming. Then it stopped. Eddy sprinted down the hall to where he thought the screaming had come from. He found Donny and Daya leaning over a man's body. Ericson lay a few metres away, staring blankly at the ceiling. "Donny, am I ever glad to ..."

"Shhh!!" Daya hushed him.

"It's OK, Chief." Donny was cradling the man's head. It was Tom Humphrey.

"No, it's my fault." Humphrey's voice was barely more than a whisper. "You were right about Ericson. I was helping. Thought I could control him. Stupid. Just me and him. Just me and him. I'm sorry, Donny. I'm sorry. I'm ..." Humphrey's head lolled to the side.

Donny felt for a pulse. Nothing. "I'm starting compressions. Breathe for him, Eddy." Donny stacked his hands on Humphrey's sternum and started pushing rhythmically.

"Donny, he's lost a lot of blood," Eddy said softly.

"Just breathe for him, goddammit!"

Eddy tilted Humphrey's head back, pinched his nose, wiped away as much of the blood as he could, and blew into the dead man's mouth.

"One, two, three, four ..." Donny counted a steady cadence as he pressed on Humphrey's blood-soaked chest.

They were still at it when the paramedics arrived.

CHAPTER 39

I ONLY WORRY WHEN HE'S NOT BROODING

The phone had rung just before three in the morning. "Laurie, it's Joe Razzolini. I didn't know whether I should call, but ..."

It seemed like ages ago.

Laurie glanced at the clock over Donny's hospital bed: seven thirty. She looked out the window. There wasn't much of a view, mostly just more buildings. The sounds of the city revving up for another day filtered in with the morning light.

They were keeping Donny in for observation, to ensure that the drugs had cleared his system and that there was no permanent damage to his lungs from the ammonia.

She was exhausted. And furious. And several other emotions she was too tired to identify. She looked back at the man lying in the hospital bed. He looked smaller, somehow; older, if that were possible. She felt sorry for him in a way, driven as he was by whatever inner demons compelled him. She saw them, but she doubted Donny ever would.

Yes, there was love too. Love and frustration, longing and anger. And fear. The image of Steve's flag-draped coffin flooded back. She couldn't go through that again. Wouldn't, she told herself.

"I can't keep doing this. I can't keep getting that phone call," Laurie told him.

"I'm sorry," Donny said. "For this, and all the other stuff too. I'm really sorry, if that still means anything."

"I don't know." Laurie crossed her arms. "I guess it depends. What's different this time?"

"Me." Donny's voice dropped. "I killed a man."

"Sounds like he wasn't a very nice man. Still, it's a terrible thing," Laurie admitted. "But what does that have to do with us?"

"It makes you think. About who you are." Donny paused, trying to find the words. "It's not exactly a straight line."

It never is with you, she thought, but she kept that observation to herself. Still, she would listen. She owed him that much.

"I don't know how to explain it," he began. "Something shifted. All my life I've never known what to do, what to say. I hid behind that big red truck and the adrenalin rush, playing the hero, trying to be enough. And I can't even tell you enough of what. But I want to change. All I want is to be enough for you and the boys."

He wanted her approval, she knew that; the magic wand of her acceptance that would make it all better. "Let me think about it," she said. "And speaking of the boys, I need to go. My mom's with them. We'll talk later."

"Sure."

Laurie picked her coat up off the back of the chair, walked out of the room and headed towards the exit. If she never visited a hospital again, it would be too soon—the antiseptic smell and décor to match, the ordered busyness of it all.

A tall, dark-haired East Asian woman in a police uniform approached her.

"Laurie? I'm Daya Singh."

Laurie stopped several feet away. "He's in five twenty-seven," she said stiffly.

"Actually, I'm here to see you," Daya said. "I asked Eddy how I could get in touch with you, and he said you were probably here."

"What can I do for you?" Laurie asked, her tone formal, perhaps a bit more severe than she wanted.

"A minute of your time, maybe two. If you don't mind." Daya gestured towards the visitors' lounge, which was empty at this hour of the morning.

Laurie stood rooted to the spot.

"Please?" Daya asked.

Laurie sighed and opened the door to the lounge. She tossed her coat across the arm of a chair by the window and sat. Daya took a seat kitty corner to her. The door closed with a soft click. Through the large windows, Laurie could see the doctors, nurses and orderlies trooping up and down the hallway, going about their duties. The lounge was quiet, an island of calm.

"I'm afraid I may have made your life difficult," Daya began. "I want to apologize for that."

Holy shit! Was everyone here looking for redemption? What did she look like, the hospital chaplain, wandering around handing out absolutions?

"When you're single, at my age, flirting becomes almost a hobby. The years click by, and somehow it's comforting that men still find you attractive. You know how men are. They're still boys inside, easily distracted."

Laurie nodded. She could sense the sincerity in what Daya said.

"Was I attracted to him? Yes. But nothing ever happened. I want you to know that," Daya assured her. "He talked a lot about you and the boys."

Laurie wasn't sure if Daya was telling the truth or simply trying to find a credible way to ease her own conscience.

"Thank you." Laurie stood up and grabbed her coat.

"He's a good man."

And complicated, Laurie was tempted to add. She opened the door to the lounge and made her way to the elevator.

Bill Ericson's funeral was a small affair, immediate family only. There were only half a dozen mourners, including his widow and three small, sad, confused-looking children.

Tom Humphrey's was better attended, though by no means a full department funeral. Still, the chapel was more than half full. Bob and Grace Collins sat with Tom's widow, Nancy.

Albert Fernandez, the lawyer Donny had met in Humphrey's office, sat in the back with a few other well-heeled people, judging by their clothes and the cars they drove.

Donny sat with Moose and Eddy, all in their dress uniforms. The three of them stood and saluted as Humphrey's coffin was wheeled out of the church. Ratzo and a smattering of other firefighters in attendance did the same. Patrick Thompson wasn't among them. He was out on bail, awaiting trial on charges of accessory to kidnapping and attempted murder.

"He loved you like a son," Nancy Humphrey told Donny when they were outside.

"And like most kids, sometimes I drove him crazy," Donny said, with a sad smile. "He was a firefighter's firefighter. One of the best."

"He was proud of it," Nancy agreed. The tears welled up in her eyes again. "But now everyone thinks he was some kind of monster."

"Not everyone," Donny said. "Not anyone who really knew him. He made a mistake—a big one, but he died trying to correct it. He'll always be someone I admire."

"Thank you for saying that."

Daya Singh gave statements to the SIU, the homicide detectives, and Internal Affairs. She stuck to the facts as best as she could, staying away from conjecture and supposition. The evidence pointed overwhelmingly to Ericson, from Donny's initial statements to her about Ericson's shooting of Darrel Simpson, to Leo Rothberg's supposed suicide, right up to the final night: Patrick Thompson's confession, the video from Eddy's dashcam, and Donny's account of what happened in the room where Ramón's body was found.

Humphrey's dying declaration and his actions—arriving at the factory before anyone else—showed that he was Ericson's accomplice. But it wasn't a complete picture.

Daya didn't minimize her own role in the matter. She had not only disobeyed a direct order, she had pretty much thrown the whole rule book in the garbage. She waited for the shit avalanche to start rolling her way, but it never did.

She was placed on administrative duty at headquarters while the investigation chugged along, but that was standard procedure. Six weeks later, she was back at her desk. The story had disappeared from the news long before. Collins had retired the week after the incident, and everyone seemed to be doing their best to forget about the whole thing.

Daya tried to focus on the emails, vacation requests, requisitions and duty rosters that needed her attention, but she couldn't concentrate.

"I'm taking an early lunch," she told the officer at the front desk.

Moose was bent over, wiping a haze of chrome polish off the bumper, when she walked in. The truck gleamed and sparkled in the sun that shone in through the windows of the apparatus bay doors.

"Is he in?"

Moose straightened and beamed a radiant smile at Daya. "Good to see you, Sarge. He's upstairs."

Daya climbed the stairs. The aroma of garlic and onions cooking slowly drew her upward. She poked her head in the kitchen door. Eddy was adding a handful of herbs to the pot he was stirring. "You staying for lunch?" he asked. "I always make extra—the Moose factor, you know."

"I can't. I just wanted to check in. How's he doing?"

"Meh," Eddy shrugged. "He's Donny. I only worry when he's not brooding about something."

Donny poked his head out from the open office door farther down the hall. "Thought I heard a familiar voice. Come in."

Donny indicated the spare chair, and Daya sat. He swung his desk chair to face her. "How are you doing?" he asked.

"Great," she replied. "I'm being considered for promotion to inspector."

"Wow! That's awesome. Congrats."

"Yeah, thanks." Daya picked at a fingernail. "Seems like everyone just wants to pretend the whole thing never happened."

"Hmmm."

"Doesn't it bug you?"

"What do you mean?" Donny asked.

"Come on, Donny. You were right about Ericson from the beginning. And you know there's more to it. There's got to be."

Daya laid out her case. Collins' strange orders when he learned Ericson had kidnapped Donny; Humphrey's dying declaration, his odd insistence, as he lay bleeding out, that it was only him and Ericson; the burner phone in Humphrey's pocket, which the bullet had smashed. There were other loose threads: Collins' sudden retirement, the food wrappers in the shipping office at the factory. Forensics had lifted a few partial prints from them, but they didn't match either Humphrey or Ericson. Or Collins, for that matter.

"You see?" Daya insisted. "There had to be more people involved."

Donny sighed. "I'm trying not to be that guy anymore."

"What about that girl you mentioned? The one who disappeared. What's her name?"

"Roxanne."

"Yes, Roxanne. She must have told you something."

"Not much, really." Donny waved it away.

"You expect me to believe that?"

Donny leaned back in his chair and looked at the ceiling. "She had some new ID."

"That wasn't in your statement," Daya declared.

"What are you doing reading my statement? It's not your case," Donny countered. "Anyway, she'd been through a lot. I figure she deserved a fresh start."

"That's not your call," Daya said.

"Proof." Donny tapped his index finger on the desk. "Isn't that what you kept telling me? Where's the evidence? You've got lots of suspicions. In a perfect world, I'd like things to be different too. Maybe you could make Collins' life miserable for a while, but is that a hill you're ready to die on? Anyway, he's gone, retired, right? Take the promotion. Do some good."

Daya pushed herself up out of the chair. "OK. See you around."

Donny caught up to her at the top of the stairs. "Hey, look, I don't want to be a shit stain in your life."

"You're not." She started down the stairs. "And for what it's worth, you're probably right."

"I owe you one," Donny called after her.

Daya paused on the landing. "For what?"

"What you said to Laurie. At the hospital that day. Thank you."

"Goodbye, Donny."

As afternoon turned to evening, a woman sat alone atop of the mountain, in San Pedro Mártir National Park. The air was cool and fresh at this altitude, scented with pine. It was a welcome relief from the sweltering heat below. The towering trees were widely spaced, allowing her to see the desert plains of Baja spread out on either side, to the Sea of Cortez to the east and the vast expanse of the Pacific to the west.

She sat with her back against one of the big pines and watched as the sun sank to the horizon, setting the ocean ablaze. The driver of the taxi waiting in the parking lot a few hundred metres back down the trail honked the horn. It would be dark by the time they got down the steep, winding mountain road and back to her hotel in Camalù. She reminded herself to tip the driver well.

Still she sat, watching until the last molten sliver slid beneath the waves.

AUTHOR'S NOTE

I dedicated this book to my sister Eva and my brother Rick. They are both incredible people in their own right: daring, creative and compassionate. We are different in many ways, but we are joined by a common love of family and a deep respect for each other.

We also had three other brothers who died in early childhood: Donny, Robert, and a third, unnamed infant. All three of them died before I was born, but I have always felt their ghostly presence—or more precisely, their absence, like missing pieces of a puzzle.

As any parent can imagine, burying your own child is an indescribable nightmare. How my parents survived that not once, but three times is beyond my comprehension. It is a testament to their character and their faith.

I named my protagonist Donny–Robert–son as a tribute, both to the late brothers I wish I had known, and to my parents, who despite the scars of grief went on to raise Eva, Rick and me as best they could. My parents both passed away before *The Spark*, the first Donny Robertson novel, was published, but I think they would have liked that tribute.

ACKNOWLEDGEMENTS

I'm not sure any writer can accomplish much without the assistance of a large and varied supporting cast. That is certainly true in my case. Several people who read the first Donny Robertson novel, *The Spark*, were eager for more. Thank you for the encouragement and gentle prodding. I apologize that it has taken me more than ten years to complete the second part of the story. I am an undisciplined writer, easily distracted by my many and varied interests.

As well as cheerleaders, you also need a team on the field. Chief among those is my friend and editor, Diana Tyndale, who delayed her retirement to whip my manuscript into shape. Editors are the unsung heroes of publishing. Their unseen work makes your experience as a reader so much smoother and more enjoyable. I am fortunate to have had Diana edit both this book and its predecessor, *The Spark*. I treasure her painstaking attention to detail.

The original cover concept was created by Annemarie Polis. Many thanks to Jennifer Stimson, of Jennifer Stimson Design for taking this concept and turning into beautiful reality. Jennifer also worked her magic on the interior design and formatting. Like editors, the work of book designers goes largely unappreciated by the average reader, but this is what turns a word processing file into a readable book. There's a lot more to it than you might think.

I am deeply grateful to my beta readers for their willingness to give their honest, critical assessment of this story. They are, in alphabetical order: Anne Bowden, Bridget Campion, Jeff Dovyak, Heather Ebbs, and Jane Gardner. Staff Sergeant John Drader of the Ottawa Police Service and Constable David Bird (retired) of the Ontario Provincial Police did their best to give me accurate information about police procedures. I confess that in the interests of my own narrative, I did not always follow their advice. Any errors in that regard are entirely my fault.

I want to express my sincere thanks to Robert Rotenberg, one of Canada's leading crime fiction authors and a practising criminal lawyer. Robert was my advisor/mentor in the Humber College creative writing program. His guidance and tough love have made me a much better storyteller. I asked to borrow two of his characters—Albert Fernandez and Ari Greene—for cameo appearances in this novel, as a tribute and thank you for his support. I hope I did not abuse that privilege.

Finally, to my biggest supporter, my wife, Liz Krivonosov: I could not have done this without your encouragement, patience and support. I love you.

ABOUT THE AUTHOR

John Kenny was born in Egypt in 1956, the youngest of six children. His father, Lorne, was a professor of Middle Eastern studies and his mother, Olive, was an English teacher. Though he grew up mostly in Toronto, the family traveled back and forth to Egypt several times and through other parts of the world.

John graduated from the University of Toronto with a B.Sc. in Biochemistry and Astronomy. He wrote and produced astronomy programs for the McLaughlin Planetarium for several years, before applying to the Toronto Fire Department, on a whim. It was perhaps karma, having accidently accidentally set fire to his parents' house when he was seventeen. (He has not tried to cook homemade french-fries since).

Most of his 33-year career with the TFD was served in the downtown core of the city, the area featured in his novels. In 1996, John was selected as the first Toronto firefighter to participate in the International Firefighter Exchange and served a year with the ACT Fire Brigade in Canberra, Australia.

John met his wife Liz while training to become a hazardous materials specialist. Liz, a chemical engineer herself, was one of the instructors on the course. They were married in 1999.

Several commendations were awarded to John during his career, including the Ontario Medal for Firefighter Bravery, the highest honor in the fire service. He retired in 2021 as a Captain. John and Liz now live near Carleton Place, Ontario.

Swift Justice is John's second novel, and the second book in the Donny Robertson series. He is also the author of the play *Smoke & Mirrors* and several non-fiction articles.

When he is not writing, John's other passion is adventure motor-cycle travel. He has ridden several hundred thousand kilometers on five continents, ranging from the shores of the Arctic Ocean to the bottom of South America.

www.ingramcontent.com/pod-product-compliance
Lightning Source LLC
Chambersburg PA
CBHW071105250626
47159CB00002B/606